KingMaker

Part II – Traitor

Michael Alexander McCarthy

D1706978

Rogue Maille Publishing

Also by Michael Alexander McCarthy

The First War of Scottish Independence Series

KingMaker – Army of God

Dedication

To Lorna – everything I do, I do it for you.

Traitor

Our hearts we make to harden,
For you there is no pardon,
For you the spike awaits,
Upon the traitor's gate,
And crows will eat your eyes.
Traitor, traitor!

Kilmister, Campbell, Burston & Taylor.

1

Ba sat high on the hill in the chill October
sunshine and watched as the great army marched
through the valley below. If he had possessed
the wit to do so, he would have assumed that the
three hundred and fifty horsemen, near six
thousand foot soldiers and the horde of camp
followers and heavy wagons formed the invading
army of the despicable traitor and outlaw
William Wallace. He might also have observed
that this army was smaller and less disciplined
than the English army he had watched march
northwards through the same valley several
months previously and larger and more orderly
than that same diminished force as it ran for the
south, defeated, disorderly, panicked and
divested of three hundred noble and richly
equipped knights, a thousand strong-armed
Welsh archers and five thousand men-at-arms
and lowly foot soldiers. He perhaps should have
also concluded that his best course of action
would have been, like his family and all the other
inhabitants of the village, to heft his meagre
possessions onto his back and walk purposefully
towards the south and away from the vicious and
ungodly Scots.

But none of these thoughts crossed Ba's mind and he instead continued to sit in plain sight, his eyes devoid of any recognition of the scene below him, his jaw slack, a line of drool at the corner of his mouth and his shoulders hunched forwards. Neither did he react to the cacophony of noise from below, the shouts of officers, the clatter of hoofbeats, the thunder of heavy wooden wagons or the crunch of boots on the stones of the valley road. The only indication that he had not frozen to death on the wind-lashed hillside was when his head tilted slightly to the left in response to the bleating of the herd of scrawny goats champing on the grasses of the slope above him.

Ba had been a summer baby and, at first, his parents had loved him and praised his sunny nature. His mother often boasted that he was the easiest of infants and that he, unlike any of his seven siblings, never cried and disturbed his parents' rest. But, as the seasons passed and spring once again turned to summer, Gilbert and Sibilla Douthwaite realised that there was something seriously wrong with their youngest son. Sibilla had long been concerned about the unnatural absence of crying, the reluctance to latch onto her nipples and the failure to react to any stimulus. Gilbert, who had less to do with the child and was invariably woozy with ale when at home, took longer to take note of anything amiss.

'Maybes he be blind.' Gilbert offered, as he slowly waved the tallow candle back and forth before the infant's eyes without so much as a blink in response.

'I thinks it be more than that Gilbert,' Sibilla replied. 'He don't even blink when the smoke goes in his eyes. Even a grown man's eyes will smart and tear up with tallow smoke. But there's nothing from him. Nothing at all.'

'Maybes he'll grow out of it.' Gilbert suggested, as he reached for his leather tankard in the hope that this irksome conversation could be brought to an end. He was to be frustrated in both of these wishes, as he found the tankard to be empty of ale and the expression on his wife's face told him that he would not be escaping into the familiar, warm embrace of drink.

'Look!' Sibilla insisted, as she bared the child's chubby, little thigh and pinched the soft skin of his inner thigh between her thumb and forefinger and twisted it viciously. This immediately produced a dark bruise, but not a sound of protest from the baby, who continued to stare vacantly off into space.

Though Gilbert had a deserved reputation as a lethargic and lazy man with too strong a fondness for the ale, he rose early the next morning and, with the baby wrapped up tight against the cold, begged a ride on a merchant's cart to the new mill and then walked the last mile to the Priory. At the gate, he handed his son over to a young novice and sat down with his back against the gate post to await the wisdom of the Sisters inside. His arse was numb from the cold ground by the time an older Sister hailed him from the gate and held the child out to him at arm's length.

'Was it a difficult birth?' She asked, her tone clipped and bereft of sympathy.

'Aye.' Gilbert stammered, unnerved to find himself in conversation with a nun. 'I am told it was a bloody labour which lasted a full day and a night. My wife was pale and weak for many days after and fairly struggled with her chores.'

The good Sister stared down at Gilbert along her sharp nose and nodded. 'So we thought. The boy is healthy enough in body, but damaged in his mind.'

'There is nothing you can do?' Gilbert pleaded, his heart sinking to have his worst fears confirmed by the Church itself.

'We will pray for him as we pray for all God's children,' she responded. 'You must nurture and cherish him as best you can.'

'Thank you, Sister.' Gilbert replied, but he spoke to her back, as she had already turned and was striding towards the Priory.

The road was empty as he tramped the five miles home and there was no passing cart to ease his journey. His heart and his footsteps grew heavier as he neared the village, the burden of an idiot child in a modest house with five daughters weighed down upon him. He knew well what needed to be done, but had no stomach for the task. Sibilla was distraught and urged him to do the hateful deed before winter set in. Many times he steeled himself to the task, but simply could not clamp his hand over the baby's face or smother it with a blanket. To his credit, he did

4

his level best to descend into a warm, alcoholic haze and escape his predicament, but the escape was sadly impermanent and the predicament remained when he surfaced heavy-headed and dry-mouthed. In truth, he secretly hoped that he would awaken to find that Sibilla had done the deed and saved him from the unpleasantness, but she stubbornly insisted and persisted that this horrible, sinful task was the responsibility of the man of the house. As often is the case with wives, the constancy of Sibilla's pleading and the obduracy of her attacks on his manhood eventually wore him down to the point where infanticide seemed preferable to the torment of her unceasing chiding.

As the winter snows and frosts took hold, he surrendered to her assault, but insisted, 'I will not, cannot do it with my own hands. I will place him in the goat pen on a night when the frost bites hard and let nature take its course. Let God take him back.'

Sibilla nodded with tears in her eyes, relieved that the decision had been made and that her stubbornly unimaginative husband had found a path which, at least in part, absolved them of guilt in this unsavoury, though necessary, enterprise.

The agony of waiting was drawn out for three more days, as the night skies were filled with fat clouds and the snow fell in great, lazy flakes, burying the village and the surrounding valley in a thick blanket of white. By the third night, the skies cleared, the temperature fell and the snow crackled under the hardest of frosts. Gilbert and

Sibilla exchanged not a single word or even a glance, as he lifted the baby into his arms and took him out into the night. His face tingled with the frost and he exhaled great clouds of frozen breath as he gently laid his child upon the straw and dung which covered the floor of the goat pen. The beasts were undisturbed by the presence of the man and the infant and continued to champ on their bedding as Gilbert gazed briefly at the heavens before hurrying inside to his fireside. However, his hearth gave him no comfort and his ale seemed to have lost its magic as he endured the longest, hardest night of his life. Only when the light of dawn finally began to seep through the cracks in the door did he start to feel any sense of relief. The winter looked set to be a hard enough one without having to bear the additional burden of a witless child. Gilbert nodded to his wife and signalled towards the door. The other children still slept in their beds, but, with daylight growing, it would not be long before they began to stir and their brother would need to be back in his crib before they did so.

The frozen crust of snow crackled and cracked as the Douthwaites gingerly approached the pen. The goats had huddled together for warmth against the night's chill and now lay in a circle against and around the infant's body. The boy lay still, his thin blanket coated with frost, his eyes wide and unmoving and a patch of dark, mottled skin around the tip of his nose. Panic rose in Gilbert's breast as he feared that the animals had begun to chew on the baby's nose, something that would be hard to explain to their neighbours. As he climbed into the pen he realised, with great relief, that the dark patch was due to frostbite and not to any gnawing goat. The goats began to bleat as he shooed them away and reached down to retrieve his son's corpse. Cradling him in the crook of his left arm, he climbed out of the pen and stood at his wife's side. Sibilla sighed as she gazed down at her youngest child and a tear formed in the corner of her eye at the shame and unfairness of it all. If the labour had been easier, he could have grown to be a lovely, strong boy. Such a shame. She reached out to gently close his eyelids, partly to give him some dignity in death, but mainly because his unwavering gaze unsettled her. She then jerked her hand back in fright, as the corpse of her dead son blinked.

'Did you see that?' Sibilla barked at her husband.

Gilbert paled and opened his mouth to respond, but he found that he could make no sound.

The baby opened his mouth and said, 'Ba!' In the pen behind them, his companions through the bitterly cold night responded in kind with their own bleats.

Gilbert jerked backwards, dropping the baby into the snow. 'Fuck!' He spat. 'Fuck!

The goats continued to bleat, but the bundle lying face down in the snow made no sound.

'He lives!' Sibilla exclaimed, her hands clasping her face in shock.

'Fuck!' Gilbert repeated, whilst gazing at the small, blanket-covered figure at his feet.

Sibilla reached down and snatched the baby up into her arms. 'It must have been the goats,' she stated. 'They must have kept him warm during the night. You saw how they were cosied into him. You should have just left him on the ground.'

'I need a drink!' Gilbert stated, as he turned and walked to the house, his wife trailing in his wake.

By the time two tankards had been drained of ale, the Douthwaite children had begun to rise and set to their chores. This precluded any further discussion of their predicament, but, despite studiously avoiding her frigid gaze, Gilbert knew that this morning's turn of events was far from being the end of the matter. He persisted in seeking solace in the contents of his tankard, but was disheartened by his lack of success, as the ale did no more than sour his guts. A hard rap on the door interrupted the business of pouring the contents of a fifth tankard down his throat. His eldest daughter opened the door a crack and turned to announce that it was Father Cuttinge who had come to call upon them. Though he sat hard at his hearth, Gilbert shivered with a chill which owed nothing to the glacial air which seeped in through the open door. Just the mention of the Priest's name was sufficient to send an involuntary spasm down his spine.

'Welcome Father! He sputtered as he forced himself unsteadily to his feet and gestured to the empty chair at the fireside. 'Would you like something to drink? We have ale or goat's milk if you would prefer.'

Father Cuttinge's nose seemed to wrinkle with disapproval as his eyes flicked around the sooty interior of the Douthwaite hovel and the dirty faces of its many inhabitants. He looked at the offered chair and shook his head with barely concealed disdain.

'This is not what I would describe as a social call, Douthwaite. I have come regarding your visit to the Priory. The Prior and the good Sisters were keen that I visit to assist you in your duty of Christian care for your,' he paused as he searched for the right word, before continuing, 'injured boy. A simpleton can often be seen as a burden for a family, especially for one which seems to multiply without even a modicum of restraint.'

Gilbert instinctively knew that Priest's words were dripping with disapproval of him and his family, but, as he was unable to discern to precise nature of the criticism, he merely nodded and allowed the Priest to continue, in the hope that he would conclude his sermon and take his leave with the minimum of delay.

'Such children are to be seen as a gift from God, as they, unlike the rest of us, remain pure and innocent, untainted by human weakness and frailty. They are to be cherished and loved and not considered to be burdensome or as a hardship to be borne.' Here the Priest paused and stroked his chin as he considered how to continue. 'A Godless and wicked couple might be tempted to spare themselves from the demands of caring for such a child.' His eyes flicked slowly between Gilbert and Sibilla, holding each of their gazes in

9

turn. 'I have heard of such children being smothered or being left out for wolves in the night. I know that I need not concern myself with the prospect of such a sinful act with good Christian folk like you.'

'Oh no, Father!' Sibilla exclaimed, her voice so many octaves higher and shriller than normal that the Priest would have instantly noticed if only he had bothered to speak with her before. 'We love our boy and will cherish him.'

'Good, good.' Father Cuttinge murmured as he looked at the infant in his mother's arms for the first time. 'It looks as if he has suffered some frostbite on his little nose, Mrs Douthwaite. Be sure to keep him wrapped up tight when you venture outdoors in this weather.' The Priest's eyes bore into Sibilla's before he turned for the door. 'Be sure that I will be taking a keen interest in how he fares. We do not want him to suffer any misfortunes, do we?'

Thus, the youngest Douthwaite child narrowly escaped an early death and, no small thanks to the continuing vigilance and oversight of Father Cuttinge, prospered and grew to adulthood. That is not to say that his life was free of misfortune. Though he grew tall and strong, the injury suffered at birth did not miraculously heal. At a distance, he could be mistaken for handsome, but, upon closer inspection, the rounding of his shoulders, the vacant eyes and the constant string of drool which flowed from the corner of his mouth betrayed his idiocy. For much of his life, he sat in cretinous silence, his knees pulled to his chest and his eyes wide and unfocused. He only became animated when he was with his beloved goats, his only speech the occasional imbecilic repetition of their baa-ing and bleating. From the time he could walk, he accompanied his father as he herded the family's goats onto the common pasture in the hills around the village. As he grew, he demonstrated an instinctive affinity with the animals and soon proved more proficient than his habitually inebriated father, with fewer kids being lost at birth and the herd gaining more weight over the abundant summer months. By Ba's tenth year, this freed Gilbert from the herding of the goats and enabled him to concentrate wholly on the brewing of ale, something he had always done, partly to trade for food for the family, but increasingly to feed his own insatiable thirst for the thick, brown brew.

Sadly, the ale was to be the main cause of Gilbert's demise, the manner of which could be considered to be somewhat ironic. It was just before Candlemas in Ba's twelfth year when Gilbert braved a bitterly cold February day to deliver skins of ale to the small hamlet which lay three long miles further up the valley. It was the miller who found him the next morning, sitting up against the trunk of a tree, frozen solid, with an empty skin of ale clasped still in his hand. When Sibilla wept and wailed that God had punished her husband for his wicked deeds and sinful thoughts, Father Cuttinge surmised that she was referring to his fondness for drink. In her grief, Sibilla came close to confessing what she and Gilbert had attempted on that winter's night long past, but was saved from the public exposure of their sin by the Priest's reluctance to converse directly with the grubbier, lowlier members of his flock.

A husband's death oftentimes signals the beginning of a family's rapid descent into dire, grinding poverty, but this was not to be the fate of the Douthwaites, at least not yet. With Ba's careful husbandry of the herd, the family could keep the wolves from their door by bartering the goat's milk, cheese and meat for grain and other essentials. Sibilla, already a proficient cheesemaker, turned her hand to the brewing of ale. Through years of observing her husband, she quickly grew in skill and was soon surpassing Gilbert's achievements. Lacking her late husband's prodigious thirst, she was able to let each batch ferment for longer and so produced a smooth, sweet ale with almost no sediment. Her ale was in such demand that it was promised and sold before it was even brewed. The quality was such that she could barter harder and even earn some small coin, which she squirrelled away against any hard times ahead.

The hard times came marching across the border in the form of a vengeful peasant army intent on pillage and destruction rather than battle and conquest. What they could not thieve and carry off, they put to the torch, leaving a pall of dark smoke hanging over the path they followed. Sibilla and her children packed up their belongings, dug out their hidden cache of coin and set off on the road south, away from the wild and heathen Scots. Away too from the mute and easily ignored Ba. Too late did they realise their mistake, as the village was already burning furiously and the traitor William Wallace and his malevolent horde already marched through the hills on which sweet Ba minded his flock.

Ba did not seem to notice when a group of four horsemen detached themselves from the winding column and stared up at him and his flock whilst deep in conversation. Neither did he react when they kicked their horses into a trot up the slope and quickly closed the distance between them. It was only when their shadows fell across him that he finally raised his eyes and a mildly concerned expression made its way slowly onto his face.

The mouthiest of the Gallovidians gazed down at the shepherd and spat lazily onto the grass between them. Like all the men of Galloway, he was hardened from years of raiding and reiving and was used to taking what he wanted at sword's point.

'We'll be taking they goats.' His words a statement and not an enquiry.

'Ba.' Said Ba.

Jack Jardine rolled back in his saddle, his eyes wide in surprise. He turned to his comrades, a smile spreading wide across his wind-lined face.

'Looks like we've got a half-wit watching the beasts here lads.' Despite the stiffness of his limbs from the day's long ride, Jack Jardine jumped down nimbly from his mount and leaned over to put his face close to the shepherd's. Being met with Ba's blank, unfocused gaze, he continued slowly, enunciating each word with

13

exaggerated care, more for his fellow's amusement than to ensure understanding. 'We're – going - tae – take – all – yer – goats – ye – fucking – daft – bastard. Are – ye – going – tae – dae - anything – aboot – it – ya – arse?'

He glanced over his shoulder to take in the amusement of his comrades before turning back to Ba. The absence of any reaction there caused a surge of anger to pulse through his body. The short punch was vicious and sent Ba sprawling on his back, his mouth smeared with his own blood. He lay there in dazed confusion as if stunned and unable to comprehend this sudden violence.

'Get the fucking goats!' Jardine snapped at his companions as he rose to his feet. Drawing his sword from its scabbard, he advanced towards the prone shepherd. He had only just begun to raise his blade when a voice to his rear stopped him in his tracks.

'Touch the boy and I'll drop you where you stand.'

The four Gallovidians turned immediately and, as they drew their swords, stepped towards the interloper. From his accent, they knew that he was Scots and that he was from further north than Galloway. He sat upon a massive black charger, a horse larger than any bred on the Scottish side of the border and therefore undoubtedly taken from an English knight at the battle at Stirling. Although shrouded in a heavy black cloak, they could see that he wore fine, English chain maille and boots reinforced with metal plate. They saw too that he carried two

14

swords, a finely wrought blade sheathed in a leather scabbard heavily finished in silver and a rougher, more primitive and well-used blade, which hung naked from his belt. Being faced by a soldier, maybe even an officer, from Wallace's army did not faze them at all. Several officers and soldiers, both English and Scots, had recently been parted from their goods and chattels and their lives snuffed out on the edges or at the points of their swords. Times of war made for rich pickings when it forced soldiers to make their way through the wilds of Galloway. What did make Jack Jardine pause was the man's face. He was young and lightly bearded, with black hair which had been roughly shorn from one side of his head around a recent injury. But it was the man's black eyes which caused an unfamiliar sense of fear and instinctive caution to creep into his mind. Deep-set and unblinking, the man's eyes appeared to be completely black and Jardine felt them bore into him. However, he could not lose face in front of his friends and so choked back his fear.

'You'll need to be going now!' He ordered confidently, deepening his voice to cover any quaver which might give away his disquiet. 'Ye may no' have noticed, but there are four of us and only one of you.'

'I'll kill you last if you don't take two goats and piss off now and leave the laddie alone.'

'Aye, aye, so you will.' Jardine laughed, though his voice did quiver perceptibly. 'Who the fuck do you think you are, ordering us about? We're Galloway men, here for the pillage. We

15

don't take orders from anyone, not Wallace and his lot and definitely no' from you. We're no' people you want as your enemies, that's for sure.'

'I am Alexander Edward. They call me Eck the Black and I have far worse enemies than you and these three wee fuckwits.' With these words, Eck continued to stare at Jack Jardine.

The sense of menace enveloping Jardine increased at these words. He had heard of Eck the Black and his exploits as the Scottish army had crossed the border and begun to render the north of England desolate.

'Let's go Jack!' Pleaded his young cousin, who was already at his horse with a small goat under his arm.

'Aye Tom, we need to be somewhere else the now anyway.' Jardine spat with annoyance. 'But you,' he said, pointing at Eck as he mounted his horse, 'you I will be seeing again. Count on it.'

'Aye, you can count on it. See if I come back this way and this wee halfwit's no' sitting here happily minding his goats, I will find you and I'll split ye from cock tae chin. Got it?'

'Aye, aye you've got me shaking in my boots the now.' Jardine retorted as he turned his horse down the hill. As he rode away, he was upset to note that he could not stop himself from actually trembling. Though he would never have admitted it aloud, he had decided that, if he could help it, he would never put himself under the gaze of Eck the Black again.

2

Rank struggled to raise his head and take in his surroundings. Dizzy and disorientated, he could make no sense of the scene before him, but he choked back his feelings of panic and forced himself to rise into a sitting position. He noted that he was not alone on the dark, muddy bank of the wide, slow-moving river. His companions gazed back at him with sightless eyes, their bodies bloated and swollen from the water and, in many cases, bearing the wounds of vicious and violent deaths. Breathing deeply to ward off waves of dizziness, it all started to come back to him. His separation from his 'master', Under-Sheriff Trasque, on the Bridge at Stirling, the heaving slaughter of the English army on the banks of the Forth and his plunge into the icy river to escape the vengeful Scots when discovered looting the dead on the battlefield. Like his blue-faced companions, the water had swept him away and dumped him on this bank on a curve in the river, unlike them, he had been deposited here still breathing.

Rank laughed to think that he had survived whilst all these others had died. He knew himself to be a cruel and ungodly man, a thief, a liar, a cheat, a rapist, a sodomite and an unrepentant murderer with a casual propensity for ferocious, unwarranted brutality. He knew too that he had lived while many pious, righteous men, such as his companions here, had perished and he threw his head back and roared his delight and his defiance to the heavens. This exertion caused waves of giddiness and nausea to wash over him and he spewed great spumes of dirty, muddy water from his guts. Suddenly aware of his vulnerability here, alone and lost in enemy territory, he pushed himself to his feet and took inventory. A jagged gash in his right thigh seemed to be his only injury, but, apart from the sodden clothes he stood up in, all of his possessions had been lost in the depths of the Forth. Both his sword and his dagger were gone, leaving him unarmed and defenceless, a perilous state to find oneself in when the Scots would be vigilant and searching for stragglers from the defeated English army. He was also missing one of his boots, not the most ideal of circumstances when a long march lay between him and the safety of the English border. Worst still, neither his purse of gold nor his bag of loot from the battlefield had made it to the riverbank with him.

He cursed his bad fortune, but, never one to wallow in self-pity, he immediately set about improving his lot. Having survived the great slaughter at the Bridge of Stirling, he was damned if he was going to succumb to Scots vigilantes. His injured leg made it hard work to advance through the mud of the river bank, so he gritted his teeth and ploughed on through the thick, cloying clay and the sewage which flowed down from the city upstream. With frequent stops to catch his breath and to prevent waves of light-headedness from overcoming him, he methodically searched each of the corpses in turn. His efforts were rewarded with a short but serviceable sword retrieved from the corpse of a man-at-arms whose face had been shattered by a blow from a blunt weapon. The wound had been washed pink by the frigid waters, but was no less grisly for the lack of blood. The scabbard was intact and the sword belt just long enough to fasten around Rank's waist. The second carcass was that of a hulking, great red-head, the remains of an arrow shaft protruding, splintered, from his chest. Rank assumed, on the basis of the available evidence, that he was a Scot and was accordingly brutal as he removed the man's boots and cloak. The boots were a little too big, but nothing that a few stuffed rags would not remedy. The remainder of the dead kindly furnished him with a few silver coins and two gold rings, surely enough to purchase sufficient bread and ale for the journey or, if necessary, to bribe his way to safety.

Once better-equipped, Rank struggled through the sucking, clinging mud and climbed the banking until he reached the forest above. Though he had moved not more than fifteen paces in all, the exertion forced him to his knees and the world swam before his eyes as he struggled to catch his breath. A lesser man might have capitulated and succumbed to the overwhelming desire to rest and fall into sleep, but Rank had suffered worse hardship in his miserable life and forced himself onwards with the river at his back. His progress was painfully slow, partly due to his feeble physical condition and partly due to his natural caution, as he was well aware that he would be easily overcome if he was discovered by even the weakest of Scots, all of whom would consider him to be their enemy.

When he spotted the hovel through the trees, he dropped to his knees and observed. The structure was familiar to him, as he had been born in a similar simple, one-room hut of rough-hewn wood, mud and straw, roofed with bundles of reeds. No smoke rose from the crude, blackened hole at the far end of the cottage roof, suggesting that it was unoccupied. Rank inched forward, but then halted, tilting his head to one side in an effort to catch a distant sound. He crouched silently and waited, the patience and clandestine skills learned from a lifetime of thievery, pilfering and ambush serving him well once more. Long minutes passed before his eyes caught small, slow movements through the thick foliage. An old woman approached the ramshackle hovel, her pace slow and her movements stiff with age. She must have been more than forty years old, as her hair was white, without a hint of the colour of her youth. Behind her followed an equally decrepit donkey weighed down with two sacks of provisions. Rank's stomach growled with hunger at the mere thought of what those sacks might contain.

He did not know how long it had been since his last meal in the English camp below the walls of Stirling Castle, but he knew that he needed to break his fast soon if he was to regain his strength. Deciding that necessity took precedence over discretion, Rank strode forward, stopping the old woman in her tracks.

'Archie? Is that you Archie?' She asked in a high, tremulous voice, straining her eyes to thin slits in a bid to focus.

Rank saw that a thick, milky film covered her pupils and knew that she was all but blind. He opened his mouth to speak, but was cut short by the crone throwing her arms around him.

'Oh Archie! I am so glad to have you home. I thought that you were lost to me. I prayed and prayed that you would come back.'

Rank knew that blind folk could sometimes recognise people by touching their faces, but none had had the audacity to put their hands on him. The old lady did so as she prattled on incessantly.

'Such a fine beard you have and you've grown so big and strong.' She gabbled. 'Such wide shoulders too. You must have been working hard. So strong. But here,' she exclaimed as her hand touched the top of Rank's right leg, 'you're hurt. What have you done to yourself? Let me get you into the house and get that seen to. Maybe you'd like some stew. I have a cut of venison here. You must be hungry after your journey.'

With that, she slowly unknotted the worn twine that secured the hovel door and ushered

Rank inside. Enticed by the prospect of a hot meal, he did as he was bidden. He did not speak and so reveal that Archie had not returned and the mad, old hag was oblivious in any case, as she chuntered on incessantly, heedless of his silence.

Rank sank into a creaking, wooden chair by the hearth as the old woman continued her deranged monologue and busied herself with setting and lighting a fire and preparing her venison stew. Overcome with weariness, his eyes began to close, only to snap open again a short time later as the wonderful aroma of cooked meat set his mouth to salivating and his guts to grumbling loudly. He emptied the proffered wooden platter in seconds and, without waiting for an invitation, refilled it twice and bolted down the greasy chunks of venison. With his stomach full to bursting and the fire hot at his side, he could no longer fight his exhaustion and slipped into a deep, untroubled slumber, barely conscious of the old wife's continuing chatter as he did so.

He awakened with a start and took several seconds to remember where he was and how had he got here.

'Ach, is that you awake at last, trachle bones?' The old woman asked, with laughter in her voice. 'I've never seen a boy who slept so much. A whole day and night ye've slept. If it was'nae for yer snorin', I'd have thought ye deid.'

He let her burble away and checked his surroundings. The hearth was heaped high with

22

ashes in testament to how long he had slumbered. The red-headed corpse's cloak was drying before the fire and his boots stood cleaned and polished beside the chair. He also saw that the wound on his leg had been cleaned and a poultice of moss and peppermint applied to it. The wooziness and nausea had gone and he could feel his strength returning.

'Are you hungry Archie?' The old woman asked, her milky eyes fixed on Rank's face.

He was ravenous and so risked a grunt in the affirmative. The old bitch chuckled and set to preparing a dish of eggs. Rank closed his eyes and basked in the heat of the fire, his enjoyment only partly spoiled by the sound of her voice as she gibbered away nonsensically with gossip about neighbours and relatives and people whose names she could not quite recall.

Rank could not remember being fussed over and looked after this well at any other time in his life, especially not by his own mother. He was sufficiently recovered to continue his journey after three days, but chose to stay another four just to enjoy the crone's hospitality as she tended to his every need. He was unconcerned by the growing tightness of his breeches at the waist, as he might well be glad of a little extra fat in the days and weeks to come. The preparations for his departure were all done. A sack full of the widow's provisions was packed, two plump chickens had been trussed for the journey, his sword sharpened and the old hag's coin and valuables, such as they were, added to his haul from the corpse-strewn riverbank. He tossed another log onto the fire and stretched far back in the chair to enjoy his last evening in the hovel. He raised his tankard in salute to the old woman and drank deeply of her ale. Though she sat in the chair opposite him before the fire, her witless jabbering did not irritate him this last evening as it had the previous seven. He had to admit that she was an excellent cook and that is why he had waited until he had enjoyed his last supper in her home before he snapped her neck. Her bones had been brittle with age and had crumbled with no more than one quick squeeze of his hand. He had been sorely tempted to do it earlier, but resisted the urge as he had no desire to cook for himself.

With the crone's mangy, little donkey, Mhorag, loaded with his supplies, the big Englishman set off on his arduous journey, his ultimate objective being the Trasque estates far, far to the south. Though the prospects of success were limited and the road ahead fraught with peril, his pock-marked face was set hard with the determination and pig-headedness which had served him well so far in a life afflicted by adversity. By keeping the smoky haze from Stirling's hearth fires to his right, Rank was able to navigate his way through the thick forest towards the main road south. The terrain made the going slow and hard and the further he walked, the more the wound on his leg began to re-open. By the time the southern road came into view in the valley below him, he was limping badly and the blood was seeping down the leg of his leather trews. A wiser and more tolerant man might have rested longer in the hovel and let his wound fully heal, but Rank had been unable to tolerate the old woman's demented monologue any longer. After only two days, she had already vocalised every one of her tales, her reminiscences, complaints, opinions, her many grievances and witless thoughts and observations at least once and had then proceeded to repeat them all again, over and over, time after time. If her repertoire had been wider and the frequency of repetition less, then perhaps he could have tolerated her long enough for his wound to mend fully.

The road itself provided another unwelcome obstacle. Freed from the presence of the patrols of their English overlords, the miserable Scots were now travelling freely and the road was busy with carts and men on foot and ahorse. As the afternoon wore on towards evening, he observed four bands of armed horsemen canter past. Two of these rode under noble banners, which Rank could not identify, and two had the appearance of lordless bandits. All of them were a threat to the English soldier and their presence on the road put paid to his intention to join the daily traffic and attempt to blend into the stream of travellers and merchants. Never mind his sword, his leather trews and jerkin alone would mark him out as a soldier rather than as a travelling trader, smith or artisan and would invite scrutiny and trouble. The only solution was to travel the road at night and risk the hazards of the rough, uneven and rutted surface in complete darkness. The first night brought little progress, as driving rain turned the track into a morass and Rank once again found himself struggling through squelching, sticky mud. Worse yet, whilst making his way into the forest to lay up during the hours of daylight, he tripped and ripped his wound open further. Hissing in pain and frustration, he tied Mhorag to a tree branch and dropped down onto the thick carpet of leaves with his back against the trunk. Sheltered from the worst of the rain by the thick canopy of leaves above him, he tied up his wound with a strip of cloth and devoured a miserable meal of hard biscuit. Mhorag brayed gently but insistently and nuzzled at the ground, turning over the leaf mould with her snout.

'Oh, no grass for you to munch little donkey?' Ranked enquired, as he stretched out his left leg and cracked her snout hard with the heel of his boot. 'Tough shit!'

His temper had improved little by the time nightfall came around again. He had slept only fitfully and was dreading the prospect of another night of scant progress. His leg worsened as the night went on and he took to supporting part of his weight by leaning one arm on Mhorag's back. The miles crawled by on that and several following night marches, with his pain and limp increasing imperceptibly with each movement. By the time he was, by his reckoning, in the vicinity of the border, every step was an agony and he would have made faster progress if he had dropped to the ground and crawled along the earthen road. In desperation, he climbed upon Mhorag's back alongside the now diminished sack of provisions. The small and ancient donkey teetered as Rank's great weight pressed down upon her creaking spine, but somehow managed to stay upright. With his boots trailing on the ground, Rank squeezed his thighs tightly to urge the pathetic beast onwards. Her faltering steps became steadier as she built momentum and, in spite of her ragged and laboured breathing, she slowly carried her heavy burden further into the hilly borderlands. Rank dozed as they made their way slowly past burnt and gently smouldering hamlets and small villages, only jolting awake when poor Mhorag stumbled on loose pebbles in the road. She was slowing now, but Rank encouraged her on with a heavy blow to the side of her head. When she again began to struggle, he struck her harder and she once more lowered her head and strove for greater exertion. By the time her breathing had deteriorated to desperate wheezing and gasping, poor Rank found that he could only keep her moving forward by continually rattling her skull with his fists, causing him no small pain. Always one to delight in the suffering of others, he was rather enjoying the feeble beast's pitiful response to his ferocious clouts. Its skull was undoubtedly as thick as stone, but the skin around its snout and head was burst and bleeding and tears streamed from both its swollen eyes.

'Don't cry little donkey. Papa's here.' He keened sadly, before swinging a punch so hard he nearly lost his seat.

Mhorag teetered sideways violently and it was all Rank could do to leap from her back before she crashed to the ground and rolled into a ditch with a pool of stagnant, murky water at its bottom. He stood over her and decided that there was no chance of getting her back to her feet. Her breath was fast and shallow, one eye was swollen shut and bloody foam bubbled at her nostrils. Rank felt a pang of regret at the pathetic sight before him. Perhaps he should have waited until he had secured an alternative mode of transport before he had indulged himself.

'If I had been slower, you would have broken my leg,' he admonished the animal, wagging his forefinger at her in disapproval. 'That would have been very bad, little donkey.' He then said his goodbyes, kicking her jaw so hard her teeth snapped together with a crack and her stomach so savagely that green bile poured from her mouth. Only the throbbing in his leg prevented him from finishing the job. He launched a great gobbet of phlegm at her head, before turning and limping on southwards.

Mhorag knew that she was dying. Her heart was beating far too fast and, as the last of her strength faded, her head sank into the water at the ditch bottom and she started to take water into her bruised, old lungs. Dark spots danced before her eyes and she teetered on the brink, resigned to her fate. Even on the very edge of death, the sound of approaching footsteps caused her eyes to widen in fright and her hooves to thrash weakly in a desperate, pathetic

28

parody of escape. As the dark figure climbed into the ditch, Mhorag steeled herself against the blows which the pock-marked and unwashed man would surely rain down upon her. She struggled feebly to pull away as the hands reached down to her poor, broken face. The figure bent, lifted her snout out of the ditch water and gently patted her thumping head.

'Ba!' Said the figure, as stroked her reassuringly.

3

Walter Langton, Lord High Treasurer and
Bishop of Coventry and Lichfield, sank into the
chair and leaned towards the steaming basin of
water the servant had placed before him. After
washing the dirt from the road off his face and
hands, he instructed the young man to wipe the
mud from his boots. From his time as the
Keeper of the Wardrobe, with responsibility for
the personal finances of the Royal household, he
knew that the lad, Allard, was Edward's bastard
boy to a servant girl unfortunate enough to have
momentarily caught the King's eye. It amused
him to have a son of the King grovelling at his
feet, but he was strangely discomfited to see
Edward's sharp, blue eyes staring back at him
from that youthful face.   It had been a long and
wearisome day and there was still the audience
with King Edward to come. The King was yet
ensconced in the castle's receiving room with
Roger Bigod, Earl of Norfolk and Magnate of
England and Humphrey de Bohun, Earl of
Hereford and Constable of England. Langton
resented being forced to skulk away and hide in
a back corridor, but he had no wish to encounter
those two powerful magnates this day. These

past days had been filled with whispers of their complaints and plots against his person. He was sore tempted to doze while he waited, but fought the inclination as we would need to be sharp when he came before the King. Edward's temper was unpredictable at the best of times and these days were very far from being the best.

The afternoon had turned to dusk before the mute servant motioned towards the open door. Langton marched inside, fully expecting to see Edward tired and drawn and in a foul temper after the endless days of meetings, negotiations and arguments.

'Ha!' King Edward of England called out, his eyes sparkling and a smile spreading across his face as he unfolded his long legs and rose to his feet. 'At last, a guest who has come to neither castrate nor pick the empty pockets of his King.' His tone changed to one of playful admonishment and he demanded, 'You've not come to cut off my balls, have you?'

Langton bowed his head and returned his King's smile. 'No, my Lord, I have not.'

'Come Walter. Come sit by me. It is good to see a friendly face. Since my sweet Eleanor died, God rest her, there is no one I can trust but you. It cheers me to see you here. I have much to share and I am eager to hear your news.'

'I have much to tell, but am keen to hear how you faired with the barons, my Lord.'

'Whining, bleating, ungrateful bastards one and all, Walter. These last days my ears have been filled with carping and grousing. I give

31

them lands and titles and strive to make their country stronger and they snivel like peasants and complain that they are taxed too much, that there is too much duty on wool and that they are in debt from providing their King with troops. That they only hold their lands in order to provide their King with soldiers is conveniently forgotten. And the Bishops,' Edward continued, his head shaking in disbelief, 'they sneak behind my back and go crawling to the Pope, begging him to issue a bull forbidding the clergy from paying taxes without the prior, explicit consent of the Pope. Snivelling wretches.'

'They have refused to support us in regard to the Scottish situation?' Langton enquired, in an attempt to divert Edward from embarking on one of his protracted diatribes against the nobles and the clergy. The night was growing dark outside and they had much ground to cover before he would see his bed.

'No. I will have a great army to lead against the Scots, to which all the barons will contribute. They will not emasculate me as they did when they refused to support my campaign in France.' Edward declared, smiling with pleasure at the surprise on Langton's face. 'But,' he continued, shaking his forefinger in the air, 'there were certain demands in return for this. Firstly, I am to sign the Confirmatio Cartarum,' he waved at a thick document laid before him on the table, 'confirming both the Magna Carta and the Charter of the Forest.'

'My Lord!' Langton exclaimed.

'I know Walter. These bastards think they have me by the balls and that I will voluntarily accept a reduction of my authority as King and let them plunder my income from the Royal Forests. Thieves one and all.'

'But you will sign?' Langton asked incredulously.

Edward smiled tightly and nodded conspiratorially. 'It is one thing to blackmail a King into signing a document, dear Walter, it is quite another to ensure his compliance. You know me very well. Can you see me bowing before Bohud and Bigod as they help themselves from my purse?'

'No, my Lord.'

'My fine Earls will live to regret their work this day and will learn that a cornered lion should be finished when you have the chance and not be loosed to take you unawares further down the track.'

'There were other conditions, my Lord?'

'Yes Walter, there was one more condition and it concerns you most directly.'

'I, my Lord?'

'The happy Earls have insisted that I remove you from my service and appoint a new Lord High Treasurer.'

'And their reason for this demand?'

'You know why Walter. They mean to isolate me and leave me surrounded by their placemen and spies. They did not say as much, but instead spoke of vague charges of witchcraft, adultery, murder and simony.'

33

Langton winced internally. The other charges were obviously figments of his enemies' imaginations, but the simony accusation could prove to be problematic as it was a matter of record that he had used his ecclesiastical influence to secure positions for friends and relatives and for others with sufficient gold to ease the transaction.

'Do not look so worried Walter.' King Edward purred. 'You will always have my protection. In any case, I gave no firm assurance on this particular matter. I merely said that you would not be Treasurer forever, which is true given that you are mortal. Now I would hear how you have fared in your undertakings. What say your priests in the North?'

Being indebted to the King was nothing new to Langton, but this clear reminder of how highly precarious his position would be if he fell from favour was somewhat sobering.

'The Scots army burns and pillages as it makes its way south through Northumbria, my Lord. Our nobles run before Wallace and leave him be to turn the North to ashes. Manors, churches, mills, villages, nothing is spared. Any stupid enough to stay are slaughtered and what cannot be carried off or consumed is destroyed.'

'Churches you say?' Edward enquired, deep in thought. 'I thought this Wallace was a godly man. I had heard that he had the ear of the Bishop of Glasgow.'

'Tis true my Lord, Wishart strongly supported his appointment as Guardian of

34

Scotland. So, I very much doubt that he has commanded his men to attack the Church. The ranks of his invading army have been greatly swollen by raiders and common folk intent on pillage after a poor harvest back in Scotland. These he has precious little control over and, unless he is in close proximity, they give in to their naturally savage instincts, thieving and murdering without restraint. I have heard that he issues proclamations and letters of protection to Churches, Priories and Monasteries, but that these are worthless unless he or his troops are physically there to enforce them and defend men of God from harm.'

'Good, good.' Edward murmured, absently stroking the point of his neat, white beard. 'This we can use against him. No matter that he does not give the command. If we make the sin his, then we can use it to discredit him. Even God-fearing Scots will turn from him if they believe he murders priests. And what of our strongholds in the North? Can they hold out while our nobles gather their forces?'

'The Scots show little interest in attacking your cities, my Lord. Lacking siege engines, they seem to prefer stealing crops and burning hovels to throwing their lives away against our city walls. But they lay waste to a great area of land. I am told that it will take many years to rebuild and recover.'

King Edward held his open palms before him, indicating the scattered parchments before him. 'This I already know, for our Northern Lords have not delayed in begging for reductions in their taxes. So quick to duck their liabilities, so tardy in settling their dues. How they would squeal if I were to do the same, cry poverty and refuse to supply their men once in the field. But I am King and will not shirk from my duty. I take it that we have the gold for the provisioning of our campaign.'

Langton steeled himself for the part of the conversation he had been dreading since he had ridden out of the city of Oxford that morning. His negotiations with both Simonetti of the Riccardi Bank of Lucca and Malachi Crawcour, the Jew, had been successful, but difficult and exorbitantly expensive. Simonetti was, superficially, the more pleasant of the two to deal with. Stylish, well-groomed and richly dressed, he was unfailingly polite and adhered meticulously to all aspects of social etiquette. He greeted Langton with a bow, addressed him as Lord Bishop and provided him with refreshment before listening politely as he detailed the King's pecuniary requirements in respect of the proposed Scottish campaign.

'My Lord Bishop,' Simonetti responded in perfect though heavily accented English, 'I am familiar with the proposal. It is the same case you put to me before the King's last conquest of Scotland, is it not?' This was delivered casually, but Langton did not miss the weight of insinuation it contained.

'It does have similarities.' Langton responded carefully to the Tuscan's query, well aware that the man's calm demeanour masked a sharp and calculating mind.

36

'On that occasion, not yet two years past, the Bank of Riccardi loaned the King,' Simonetti paused here, a small gesture of his well-manicured hand indicating the thick ledger open before him, 'a considerable sum for the self-same venture. I recall you assuring me that the Scots nobles were divided and too distracted with infighting to be capable of mounting any meaningful defence.' He smiled pleasantly though his eyes were cold like polished steel. 'Being so far away in Tuscany, it is difficult for me to stay informed of every happening and event. So, tell me, Lord Bishop, how did the King lose control of such a weak and disunited land?'

Langton, keen to avoid being drawn into a prolonged ritual intended to drive up the rate of interest attached to the loan, leaned forward and responded with directness. 'You do yourself a disservice sir. I have not the slightest doubt that you are as well-informed as any man about events beyond the border. King Edward recognizes that the level of risk to you is higher than before and this is accounted for in the proposal I have laid before you. He would grant you rich lands in Scotland. Lands which can generate a significant income for your bank in perpetuity.'

'The bank already has lands in Scotland, Lord Bishop. Those granted to us by King Edward following the decisive defeat of the Scots nobles at Dunbar in the spring of 1296. Do you know how much we have collected from those lands since they were granted to us?'

'Less than anticipated, I suspect.'

'Nothing, Lord Bishop. Not a single coin. The moment King Edward rode back across the border, chaos ruled in his place. The representatives we sent to Scotland returned empty-handed or not at all. We have no interest in holding more empty paper title to Scottish estates.'

'Lands in England then?' Langton countered, already having agreed with the King which of the vacant English estates could be placed upon the table if the negotiations required it.

Simonetti smiled and rubbed his fingertips together, a subconscious gesture which told Langton that they were about to arrive at the heart of the matter.

'The bank's interests lie in areas other than land, my Lord.' Langton nodded, encouraging the refined Tuscan to continue. 'It has come to our attention that the King intends to add to his coffers by way of a tax on foreign merchants. This we would be interested in administering on his behalf.'

Though momentarily taken aback by the Tuscan's knowledge of a scheme known to only the King and himself, he calmly enquired, 'With the bank retaining the revenue for how long?'

'For twenty years only. This is fair given the risk of this conquest going the same way as the last. These Scots are unpredictable, no?'

Edward groaned as Langton brought his account of the conference to a close. 'They'll have the kingdom hamstrung long after I have gone, Walter. They already have control of the duty on wool. God knows how I am meant to finance future wars. How went it with the Jew? After the pennies from my eyes, no doubt.'

Many Jews, persecuted and driven from their homes in Europe, had found safe haven in England and, during the reigns of Edward and his father, had prospered through lending money to both Kings and all of the noble families of England. The nobles, though happy to take the Jewish gold, resented having to pay it back and, as estates began to be forfeited for non-payment of the debts, the nobles lobbied against the Jews. In recent years, to gain their support for his campaigns in France and Scotland, Edward had conceded to their demands and taken measures against the Jews, forcing them to attend Christian sermons and outlawing usury, so preventing them from legally making loans. Despite these measures, Edward continued to be deeply indebted to them and relied upon them for the greater part of the funds he required to wage his various campaigns. All of this made encounters with Malachi Crawcour, the kingpin of illicit Jewish money lending, the most unpleasant and irksome of experiences for the Lord High Treasurer.

'My Lord, how good it is to see you again.' Malachi announced, rancour and bitterness evident in the mockery of a bow which brought his head almost level with his knees. 'I am humbled that you would honour me with such a visitation.'

Ignoring the feigned servility, Langton surveyed the room and noted that the Jew's reception chamber was furnished even more richly than his own, or even that of the King. 'I see that you prosper Malachi.' He stated in a counter to the old man's well-worn performance. 'Let us see if we can make you even richer.'

'If only, my Lord, if only. Now that we cannot ply our trade, times are hard for my associates and I. Our children must turn their hands to other trades and soon our skills will be lost.' Malachi complained in a Slavic accent barely softened by near forty years of residence in England.

'Did the money-lenders not survive and prosper after Jesus ejected them from the temple, Malachi? I think your craft will endure despite these current hardships.'

The big Jew smiled, the corkscrews of greying, once-brown hair at his temples bouncing as he nodded. 'Always to business my Lord, always to business.'

Their business was concluded, but the process was lengthy and painful, the price inflated by the risk of the enterprise and punitively increased by Malachi's resentment of the treatment of his people. His parting remark still stung in Langton's memory. 'Does your King realise that if he and his nobles were to default on their debts, half of his kingdom would be mine?'

'That insolent Jew needs to learn to hold his tongue!' Edward spat when Langton recounted the exchange to him. 'He and the Riccardi imagine that they have a tight hold on my leash, little do they know that there is yet enough slack to allow me to turn and bite them.' With the gold and soldiers necessary for the Scottish campaign secured, Edward's mood improved, despite the high cost in future revenue and power, and he called for the servant Allard to bring more wine. 'I know that you are weary after your good service, but your bed will wait a while. I have more work for you to do.'

4

John Edward stretched sleepily and peered into the dim light to ascertain what had disturbed him from a deep and satisfying slumber. An arm's length from him on the barn floor, his cousin Eck moaned and writhed in his sleep. He stretched his leg out and shoved hard against Eck's prone torso, causing him to stir and enter blinking into the new day.

'Whassit?' He enquired, rubbing the sleep from his eyes with the knuckles of his forefingers.

'You were doing it again.' John whispered, keen to avoid disturbing those of his men who continued to snore, snuffle and fart under the barn's great roof. A night under cover was becoming rarer as the invasion continued and, with November growing ever more frigid, he wanted his men to rest as well as they could. 'Was it the same dream?'

'Worse.' Eck mumbled, raising himself stiffly into a sitting position. 'Like before, I dreamed that I was falling, falling into blackness. Almost floating in total darkness, but always being drawn down and down, helpless to stop or slow my descent. But then I sensed that

42

something was reaching up for me, something scaly and unspeakable, stretching its claws. Then, just as its horny talon touches, just skiffs my back, I hear the witch's voice and I am pulled up out of the darkness at great speed.' Eck shivered at the thought and rubbed the sweat from his forehead.

John levered himself up stiffly and stretched, pushing his hands into the small of his back as he did so. Each day he thanked God for his cousin's recovery from the injury he had received after the battle at Stirling Bridge. With his head caved in, he had hovered between life and death for days with only the ministrations of Esmy, the Witch of the Glen, now John's mother-in-law, pulling him back from the brink. Though Eck had now recovered much of his strength, he yet retained something of the blackness into which he had descended. Gone were his jokes and good humour, replaced with an uncharacteristic moroseness and silence and gone too were his kindness and his joy in life, replaced with a reckless and insatiable hunger for fighting and killing. John did not like to admit it, but it was as if his cousin was only happy when he danced with death.

'It is the only time when I feel at peace.' Eck had told him. 'It is only with the clash of swords and the drawing of blood that I feel that those talons are not reaching out for me.'

John could only hope that, in time, Eck's soul would heal just as his body had. In the meantime, he had to concede that a skilled and homicidal swordsman was a valuable asset to have when waging war.

'C'mon Eck, let's see what these fuckers are doing the day.' John instructed, as he pulled on his boots and wrapped his cloak around him.

The small and ancient castle sat stubbornly atop the hillock above them. Though its walls were ill-kept and crumbling, they were sufficient to dissuade the Scots from attempting to breach them. The twenty men-at-arms and fifteen crossbowmen who lined the battlements had also proven to be an effective deterrent, as so they should, given the amounts of gold Sir Henry de Multon had been forced to part with to secure their service. His family had held these lands since the time of William the Conqueror and he was damned if he was going to abandon them and run from a band of Scots thieves. As Wallace had crossed the border, he had harangued De Warenne, the Earl of Surrey, and the Lords of both Northumbria and Cumbria, but could not persuade them to stand and could only watch in impotent rage as they marched their men away into the safety of the Castles at Newcastle and Carlisle whilst the Scots burned and raped and pillaged. He had heard that De Warenne, still stinging from the rout of his army at Stirling, had since left Newcastle and run still further south, such was his fear of Wallace and his rabble.

He watched as the leaders of the besieging force gathered at the bottom of the hill and knew that they could see him standing above the gate. 'Come on!' He seethed through his teeth.

44

Though the Scots far outnumbered him with two hundred and fifty men to his fifty, including his household staff, he knew that the crossbows would quickly winnow their ranks if they were to attack the gate. 'Come on!'

At the foot of the slope, the Scots leaders talked while their breakfast was prepared over the cook fires behind them. Scott Edward, brother to John and cousin to Eck, was arguing for bold action with a youthful lust for glory undimmed by the horror and slaughter he had seen in the last few months.

'Aye,' the Robertson agreed, his bald head reddening in the frosty morning air as he stroked his thick, grey beard thoughtfully. 'It would be a feather in our caps if we took the castle. No other keep has fallen since Wallace crossed the border. But there's good reason for that. The crossbows alone would take out half our men before they even reached the walls. It's no' worth the risk.'

John Edward nodded, he had fought under the Robertson in the months before the English defeat at Stirling and he respected him and trusted his wise counsel. 'You're right. We lost good men to arrows under the walls at Scone and those were neither as high or as thick as these. We should leave them to cower behind their walls and get on with laying waste to the North.'

'Let's no' be so hasty, John.' Strathbogie said slowly, his broad, scarred arms folded tight across his barrel-chest. 'We might be missing something here.'

John smiled and took the bait. 'Alright Strathbogie, out wi' it. I'm freezing here and I'm needin'my porridge.' Strathbogie had at one time, on account of his quick temper and clever, nasty tongue, been John's rival within the patriot camp. From fighting side by side, they had earned each other's respect and even a grudging modicum of friendship. Nevertheless, John knew of Strathbogie's tendency to over-milk any opportunity to be the centre of attention and was keen to hear his undoubtedly valuable thoughts with the minimum of delay.

'Alright John,' Strathbogie huffed in mock offence. 'This boy's the only one in the whole of Northumbria and Cumbria who has stayed to defend his manor. Everyone else packed up everything they could carry and scurried off to the south. You've got to ask yourself why he would do that. Either that wee castle is so full of gold he could not cart it way or he's a bad-tempered, stubborn, impetuous fucker. I'm thinking that if he had a cellar full of gold, he would'nae be living in a run-down dump like that.' Strathbogie jabbed his finger in the direction of the castle to punctuate his point. 'Afore we go running off, let's at least see if we can antagonize him first.'

Still standing erect on the wall above the gate, Sir Henry was an imposing figure. Tall and well-built, he was encased in maille, plate and helm, all of which bore the scars of battle and long months on campaign. He glared down at the horseman approaching him with a tree branch held aloft as a sign of his wish to parley. He raised his hand to stay the crossbowmen.

'I am John Edward! The horseman said, his voice loud, clear and confident.

'Your title?' Sir Henry demanded of the younger man, annoyed by the Scot's lack of basic courtesy. 'I would know with whom I speak.'

'I have no title, but am commander of the force which now besieges you. I come to parley.'

Sir Henry seethed. From the quality of the man's maille, sword and horse, he had understandably assumed that he was being addressed by a noble, albeit a Scottish one. To discover that he was threatened by a base commoner was tiresome and a little insulting. His estate teetered on the brink of ruin, his debts mounting fast as a result of the expenses he had incurred following his King into Scotland two years previously. The campaign had been a success, but precious little of the rewards had trickled down to him. Now his betters had abandoned him and left him to deal with the marauding rabble.

'A knight does not parley with a commoner. Be gone before I command my men to cut you down.'

Wary of the crossbows above, John turned his horse and started to pull away. Over his shoulder, he shouted up, 'I will go. But first we will burn your mill, your granary, yonder bridge, the hovels by the river and then your barn. We will burn it all.' He then kicked his horse into a canter back towards his comrades. This turned into a gallop at the 'thwack' of the first bolt being loosed from the castle wall. The bolt thumped into the ground behind him and was followed by a dozen more before Sir Henry raised his hand to stop his men as John went beyond their range.

John had composed himself by the time he dismounted at the foot of the hillock, but his heart still beat faster than he would have liked. 'Let's get burning.' He ordered, making sure that his voice was steady.

Sir Henry alternated between rage and despair as his already dwindling ability to generate income went up in smoke while he watched on impotently. The hovels scarcely bothered him, as they were mean and primitive structures and he cared not if his tenants had roofs over their heads. So long as they paid their dues and provided him with military service, they could sleep under the trees as far as he was concerned. The bridge bothered him greatly. His father had ordered it built when he returned from France heavy with loot. He had used his gold to buy dressed oak from the south. as local timber was too wind-bent and narrow to span the river. The finished structure had transformed their estate, as their lands on the far side of the river could be accessed without the need to trek three miles to the nearest ford.

That the granary had been emptied of grain was bad enough, but to see the Scots scurry into it with armfuls of straw and firewood was too much to bear. He had no gold to buy grain for the coming winter and did not doubt that the southern lords and merchants would already be raising their prices in anticipation of increased and desperate demand from the pillaged North. Rebuilding the granary was way beyond his means and its absence would sorely reduce his future ability to earn coin. As wisps of smoke escaped through the tiles on the granary roof, he cursed his ill fortune, he cursed his betters for their shameful treatment of him, he cursed the foul moneylenders and, most of all, he cursed the hated Scots. He blinked a tear from his eye as he realised with sudden, cold certainty that the departure of the Scots would be swiftly followed by the arrival of his creditors eager to lay their hands upon his estate. It cheered him not that they would take possession of charred and diminished lands. It shamed him that he had lost what his family had held for generations.

He was drawn from his self-pity by a dark figure pulling slowly away from the assembled Scots and advancing up the slope towards him. The man was tall, younger than him by about ten years, slim of build and dressed well in a black cloak, jerkin and trews with strapped boots which came to just below his knees. Lightly bearded, his hair fell to his shoulders, apart from on one side, which had been shorn much shorter than the other. The figure came to a halt in the midst of the crossbow bolts, which the garrison had left protruding diagonally from the ground. The man glared up at him, his eyes ringed with dark circles and his gaze unflinching.

'Impudent dog!' Sir Henry spat. 'Cut him down.'

The hired crossbowmen aimed carefully and sent their iron-tipped bolts flying towards the Scot, confident that one well-aimed shot would leave him disembowelled or his brains spattered across the cold earth. Most of the bolts fell short, as Eck the Black stood at the extremity of the crossbows' range, but a few struck the ground close to his feet. Eck did not so much as flinch, even when one thumped into the ground between his legs, a hair's breadth from crippling or emasculating him.

'He's out of range, Sire,' reported one of the mercenaries. 'Each bolt we loose is one less for the Scots should they decide to storm the walls.'

Sir Henry signalled for the men to halt. Staring directly into Eck's distant, dark eyes, a sickly smile found its way onto the knight's face. 'He mocks me. He mocks me for hiding away like a coward. I might well be a fool, but I'm no coward.' He spun on his heel and strode down the rough, stone steps, snapping out the order, 'Open the gate!'

'But Sire,' the crossbowman pleaded, 'the wisest course is to stay within your castle. They cannot take it and we can hold out for weeks, even months if need be.'

'It's not my castle,' Sir Henry retorted, as his servants unbarred the gate. 'He will pay you what you're owed,' he barked, his finger indicating a wide-eyed servant as he strode out onto the hillside.

When tales of mortal combat are shared around the fireside on cold, winter nights, the struggles are always epic, stretching on for hours as the hero battles through adversity and finally snatches unlikely victory from the shadow of certain death. In truth, a man can bring himself to exhaustion through mere minutes of swinging a sword, the thrusting and parrying consuming energy ravenously and leaving limbs heavy and leaden, the fighters staggering just to stay upright. Sir Henry, though a competent fighter, had never won a tournament. In his youth, he had acquitted himself honourably at one of King Edward's Arthurian tournaments, being amongst the last five men standing in the mêlée. His fellows would testify that he might well have won, if it had not been for a cowardly blow from behind, which jammed his helmet over his eyes and left him unable to fight on to claim his prize. Confident that he could easily slaughter a Scot's peasant in stolen maille, he flew at Eck with a flurry of scything swings, seeking the killer blow. The Scot evaded the sword's heavy blade with small, fluid movements and dainty steps more suited to a dancing ring than a field of combat. The Englishman paused, trying to catch his breath, his sword held high to ward off any attack.

Eck held both swords down at his sides and looked back at the Englishman serenely. A rare smile played on his lips as he recalled an annoyance practiced by Donald Murchie, the squat, wide-shouldered master who had taught him how to fight with sword in the patriot camp outside Perth. He echoed the taunt that Murchie aimed at him when he had vainly given everything he had to best his master, 'Are you ready to start yet?'

'I fought with my King at Dunbar,' Sir Henry puffed, blinking the sweat from his eyes and grimly absorbing this impudence. 'I saw your nobles imprisoned and the crown ripped from your King's head, the badges of office torn from his tabard. You will not prevail.'

'I fought with Wallace at Stirling.' Eck retorted calmly, his expression blank as though the struggle troubled him not. 'We slaughtered your nobles and stripped the skin from your Lord Treasurer's body while he lived. We may well lose, but the path there will be slick with English blood.'

'Not with mine!' Sir Henry countered and swung hard for Eck's head.

Leaning back just far enough to take his skull out of the arc of the stroke, a tight, shallow smile came to Eck's lips. 'The next time I go into battle to slaughter English knights, I will wear that helmet upon my head and think of the last English knight who perished at my hand.' He lied of course, the helmet being too plain and scuffed for his taste, but the lie had the desired effect and riled Sir Henry into imprudent action. He raised his great sword above his head and brought it down with all his might, every sinew strained to the point of agony. The blow would surely have split poor Eck from skull to gut if he had stayed rooted to the spot. By stepping nicely to the side, he let Sir Henry bury his blade into the ground and, as he strained to free it, chopped down hard at the back of his knee, separating the top of his leg from the bottom in a spray of crimson. The English knight crashed to the ground, roaring in pain as he stretched to stem the flow with his trembling hands. Eck kicked the prone knight's sword away and turned to the men atop the gate.

'If you come out now, you might still save your lord,' he shouted.

'He's not my lord,' the leader of the crossbowmen replied. 'We'll be staying safe behind these walls until you thieving Scots have gone.'

Behind him on the grassy slope, Sir Henry de Multon was busy dying. He grew weaker as the blood pulsed out between his fingers with each and every beat of his heart. As his life ebbed from him, he gave not a single thought to his young wife, who was safe within the walls of Newcastle in the house of her sister. Might he have spared her a thought if he knew that within her belly grew the embryo of his only son and heir? Might he have conducted himself more prudently, if only he had known the fate of that boy, damned to a life of bitterness and recrimination, weaned on tales of a birthright stolen and spared the truth of a noble inheritance squandered by a foolish, though well-intentioned, father? War is the mother of many tragedies and, though perhaps the least of these, a life wasted in the fruitless pursuit of an empty legacy is inarguably tragic.

John, the Robertson and Strathbogie joined Eck beneath the castle walls and continued shouted negotiations with the garrison. With their paymaster lying dead before them, they were keen to leave and seek gainful employment elsewhere, but were suspicious of the Scots and unpersuaded by John's guarantees of safe passage off the estate. They agreed only when John offered to place his men in plain sight on the opposite riverbank, the still burning bridge insurance that they could not suddenly fall upon the mercenaries as they retreated.

When his men were loaded and ready to depart, the mercenary leader turned to Sir Henry's servant and reminded him of the gold that was due to them.

'Of course,' the servant replied, hefting a bulging purse in his hand, 'let me count it out.'

'There's no need for that. We'll be taking it all.'

'You can't do that,' the minion responded, notes of both fear and annoyance colouring his tone. 'What is left is to go to his wife.'

The blade in the mercenary's hand was uncommonly slim, more like a needle than a dagger, but it pierced the retainer's throat and tore it open just as well.

'Open the gate lads,' he ordered, 'and keep sharp! These heathens can keep their word no better than they can stop themselves from thieving.'

The heathens watched from the far riverbank as the mercenaries trooped out of Mitford Castle and carried off the last of Sir Henry's borrowed gold. Once the last of the crossbowmen was out of sight, John Edward ordered his men to journey back to the castle walls, their intention being to destroy it and render it useless to the English when they returned. Though the castle walls were crumbling with age, they proved difficult to dismantle and the work progressed at an agonisingly slow pace.

Scott Edward wiped the sweat from his brow and whined to his brother, 'Can we no' just leave it? I'm bleeding here!' He held up his fingers to show that they were badly grazed from scrabbling at the rough-hewn stone blocks.

'Wheest laddie!' Strathbogie bawled cheerfully from atop the castle gate. Stripped to the waist and in possession of the only decent hammer in the patriot's armoury, he had succeeded in toppling one great block and was now attacking the stone arch itself. 'A wee bit o' hard labour will do you no harm. It might build up those scrawny wee arms of yours a bit.'

Scott cursed the older man in the way that only adolescents can, loud enough so that he knew that he was being cursed, but so quietly that he could not quite hear the precise nature of the insult.

This banter was interrupted by a rider galloping up the slope towards them. John Edward narrowed his eyes against the setting sun and saw that it was Al, the head of the band of scouts which served his troops. When John first met Al, he was a sorry creature. Bullied and ridiculed by his fellow rebels, he fairly crept around, skulking in the shadows to avoid attention and the unpleasantness it would bring. Now he was transformed, in his element scouting and tracking to ensure that his comrades were not taken unawares by their enemies. Though still slightly stooped, he stood much taller and basked shyly in the esteem his talents earned him amongst the Scottish ranks.

John reached out and grabbed the reins to steady his friend's mount. 'How goes it Al?' He asked, smiling to see him.

'Six horsemen coming. Scots. From Wallace.' Al announced, breathless from his ride.

Soon enough, the horsemen emerged from the trees and made their way up the incline, stopping before John, Al, Strathbogie and the Robertson at the castle gate.

'Which one of you is John Edward?' Demanded the lead horseman, his tone brusque with a hint of condescension, as if he spoke to beings far below his station.

'This is John Edward.' Strathbogie shot back aggressively. 'Who the fuck are you?'

The man reeled back as if he had been slapped across the face. 'I am Jack Short, retainer to the Guardian of Scotland, William Wallace and I will thank you to hold your impertinent tongue.'

John was known to be fair in his dealings with men and, by his nature, tended to give people the benefit of the doubt when forming his opinion of them. This man, however, he hated on sight. Tall and spindly, he was clearly no warrior, but nevertheless held himself upright and looked down at others along his sharp and pointed nose with unconcealed disdain and arrogance. When he smiled, the expression was both tight and false and more akin to a sneer which exposed his brown and mottled teeth. Strathbogie would later quip that he had the appearance of someone who had recently sucked upon a turd.

'How fares the Guardian?' John enquired, in an attempt at maintaining a level of civility.

'He commands that you attend him at the Priory at Lanercost immediately, without delay. He makes his way there as we speak. Break camp now and make haste.'

The retainer's blunt instruction caused John to rankle. 'I will break camp tomorrow. As you can plainly see, we have taken a castle here and will take the time to render it unusable for the English.'

Short's eyes flicked over the part-demolished walls. 'You must do as I command,' he insisted. 'In any case, it is not so much a castle as a fortified manor house and so scarcely worth the trouble. You will leave now.'

'You have delivered your message, so I will bid you good day.' John responded coldly.

Short laughed mirthlessly. 'The Guardian will hear of this insubordination, be sure of that. Things are different now. You are no longer a band of brigands who can wander where you please. Wallace was appointed Guardian by the nobles and has legitimate power over all Scots. You serve at his command and will regret this indiscipline. I am bound for Scotland now, but will be sure to report to the Guardian upon my return.'

'Travel safe,' growled the Robertson, as he stepped forward menacingly with the heavy hammer on his shoulder.

With a scornful glance at John, Jack Short kicked his horse and led his party away at a canter.

'Put your backs into it lads!' John shouted. 'No supper until this place is reduced to a pile of rubble. We break camp at dawn.'

5

The first fat flakes of snow began to fall lazily from the sky when John Edward's men of Perth were less than an hour's ride from the Priory at Lanercost. The heavy snowfall brought with it an eerie silence and the men rode on warily through the forest, the sound of their horses' hooves clattering on the road muffled by the thickening blanket of snow.

'I don't doubt that we'll be turning for home soon.' Strathbogie stated, confirming the thought that was on all of their minds.

'Aye,' the Robertson agreed, 'Winter is no' the best of times to be waging war.'

John nodded. 'As soon as we have seen Wallace, we should send the carts home to Scotstoun.' The rumbling carts at the centre of the column were heavy with grain, gold, silver and every moveable object of value the Scots had laid their eyes upon since crossing the border. 'If we wait much longer, the roads will become impassable and I'm loathe to leave any of it behind.' He broke off at the sight of a horse galloping towards them.

'It's Al!' Scott shouted from his rear.

Right enough, he recognised the figure of his friend through the thick curtain of snow and the sight of a black, wolf-like hound cantering behind him confirmed that it was he.

'What news Al?' He roared through cupped hands, apprehensive now, as the urgency with which he approached did not auger well.

'Trouble!' Al confirmed as he slewed his horse to a halt, great streams of frozen breath blowing from its nostrils. 'The Priory is being looted by a band of Scots. There's about twenty of them. They're carrying off the silver and look set to fire the place.'

Thinking it unlikely that Wallace would have ordered such an act against the Church, John ordered twenty men to him and set off after Al at the gallop. Within minutes, the Priory came into view and it was a wondrous sight. Three stories tall, held aloft with great pillars and a sweeping triple tier of arches, it was hard for John to believe that men could build such a thing. He scarce had time to drink it in before he caught sight of a brawl taking place upon the Priory steps. Two monks lay sprawled upon the ground, their habits stained bright with blood which was spattered across the virgin snow. The Prior was being restrained by two rogues who shook him hard to still his struggles, whilst their fellows roughly wrestled the Priory's silver and religious artefacts from the hands of tonsured monks.

John rode hard at them, leaping from his horse at the last moment and sending one of the rogues flying from the Prior's side with a foot planted squarely on his chest. Pulling his sword from its scabbard, he planted its point under the chin of the second rogue who immediately released his grip and took a pace backwards.

'They're Galloway men.' Eck shouted, a sword in either hand as he closed in on three of their number. He winked at Jack Jardine and he in turn blanched to find himself caught in the gaze of Eck the Black so soon after he had promised himself that he would never do so again.

The other Galloway men had stopped beating the monks and drew their swords, ready to defend themselves and their booty.

One of the older Gallovidians spat noisily on the ground before addressing the men of Perth. 'We got here first, so ye'll need to piss off and find yer own loot.'

John eyed him warily, keen to avoid further bloodshed. Not only did he have no appetite for taking the lives of fellow Scots, even those low enough to attack the Church, he was also heedful of the presence of the defenceless monks and the danger they were in amongst the fighting men.

'I think that you are the ones who should piss off. I have two hundred and fifty men who will be arriving here a few moments hence. If you are still here when they arrive, it will be the worse for you.'

The leader of the Galloway man spat once again and smiled at John, revealing the gap where his front teeth had once been. 'You bluff!'

'We shall see.' John retorted calmly, though every muscle in his body strained with tension as he awaited the Gallovidian's response.

'Pa!' Jack Jardine hissed, his eyes flitting nervously between Eck and his father. 'Horses!' He jerked his head towards the empty road.

The leader of the Galloway men, who Eck now noticed bore more than a passing resemblance to Jack, tilted his head slightly to the side as though listening. All there, Perth, Galloway and monks alike, strained their ears. It was the crashing and thundering of heavy, wooden wagon wheels which came faintly at first, before growing louder.

'Fucksake!' The older man spat furiously, as he slowly backed away from the Priory steps, his sword held high and his eyes sweeping backwards and forwards, alert to any emerging threat. 'Let's go lads. Leave they bastards to it.'

The Galloway men followed suit and backed towards their horses, swords at the ready lest they should be attacked. Only when they were mounted up and pointed in the opposite direction did they say their goodbyes.

'I'll remember yer face laddie!' The leader shouted at John. 'I'll still be wanting my silver. And if I can't have it, I'll be taking yer balls.' With these words, he spat thickly and put his heels to his horse.

Only with the departure of his tormentors did the Prior snap out of his terror induced daze. 'My God! Those heathens would have slaughtered us all if you had not arrived when

62

you did. Thank you! Thank you for delivering us from bloody murder.' He clasped John's hand as he spoke. 'Poor brothers Thomas and Bentley died defending our most sacred relics.' He fell to his knees beside the monks' corpses and sifted his fingers through the bloody snow until his hand closed around a small, wooden box. He rose to his feet and rubbed it clean with the cloth of his sleeve. Presenting it to John with great reverence, he whispered, 'Behold the finger-bone of St Mary Magdalene. It is our most holy relic. It was recovered from the Holy Land by the Crusaders nearly a century ago. The Priory was built to house and protect its healing powers. You may kiss it as a reward for your bravery and protection of the Church this day.'

With this, he held the little box up to John's face. His nostrils caught a faint, musty aroma as he bent his lips to what appeared to be an ancient chicken bone housed in a box lined with silk. He kissed it lightly, but felt no great power from it and noticed no improvement in the scrapes and grazes his hands had suffered during his recent, partially successful demolition work.

'Come Father,' he said soothingly, 'let us help you with your fallen brothers.'

Once the slain monks were tended to, the Prior invited John and his men to eat with him. John warmed to the man as he spoke and admired his dedication. He doubted if he would have been willing to accept such a post in this location, suffering as it did with periodic invasions and raids from across the border.

When he mentioned that the Guardian was due to arrive at any time, the Prior became quite agitated, convinced, as he was, that Wallace was a murderous monster who would burn the Priory, pillage its relics and butcher the few brothers who remained. John had to work quite hard to reassure him of Wallace's love of the Church and only partially convinced him that the Priory would have Wallace's protection, even from the more unruly and less devout Scots.

The work he had started was completed when Wallace himself arrived with a great host of troops, who made their encampment in the Priory grounds. Wallace assured the Prior that he had nothing to fear from him and shared with him a copy of the letter of protection he had written for the Abbot at Hexham just one day previously. He also promised that the Scots who attacked the Priory would be tracked down and hanged for their crimes at the Guardian's command. Somewhat comforted by this, the Prior eagerly agreed to celebrate mass when Wallace laid down his arms and asked that he do so. After the Host had been elevated, Wallace retired to a room provided by the Prior and asked John to accompany him.

'It is good to see you again John.' Wallace declared as he warmed himself at the chamber's roaring fire. 'The Prior tells me that Edward Plantagenet himself slept in this room on his way to invade us two years past.' The Guardian grinned as he inspected the chamber and its sparse, monastic furnishings. 'That'll explain the smell of shit then!' He roared with laughter at his own wit and clapped John hard upon the shoulder. 'If he was here now, he would have you executed for destroying his perfectly good bridge at Stirling.'

'If he was here now,' John responded, 'he would execute you for slaughtering his perfectly good army on the banks of the Forth.'

'True enough, true enough!' Wallace laughed, his blue-grey eyes sparkling with pleasure. 'I have heard that you have done your part in devastating Edward's northern lands. A little bird also tells me that you found time to besiege a castle and breach it, no less.'

'Aye, at Mitford. It was but a small keep. We left it ruined as much as we were able.'

'Ha!' Wallace replied in good humour. 'Then you have done better than I. All I could do was parade my army before the walls of Newcastle and Carlisle and invite them out to fight whilst they shouted insults at us and cowered behind their gates. It seems that, even in their own land, the English only like to fight when they far outnumber their enemies. Still, the job is all but done. Our mere presence here is an insult the English King cannot ignore. I am told that he already raises his army and will march it across the border early in the new year.'

As he spoke, three attendants entered the room and began to lay out a multitude of parchments and scrolls upon the large, plain table which dominated the chamber.

'Life is much changed John.' Wallace declared, indicating the document covered table with a shrug of his powerful, broad shoulders. 'Now that I am Guardian, I spend more time sat at table than I do in the saddle. The petitioners start to form a line at my door before I have left my bed and only disperse when I turn in for the night and there is no hope of an audience. I had thought to escape them by riding across the border, but they follow me and circle like carrion crows.'

John blew out his cheeks to reflect Wallace's exasperation, but in truth had little appreciation of the trials and tribulations which the bureaucracy of governing a kingdom involved.

'Look here,' the Guardian pronounced, plucking one parchment from the table. 'I am to decide who has the right to fish the river Ericht. And here, I am to write to the burghers of Lubeck and Hamburg to inform them that Berwick is once more open to trade. And here, I am expected to adjudicate in a dispute over land between a Bishop and an Earl. A dispute which has already run for three generations. It is enough to drive a man to drink.' He then signalled to an attendant who immediately filled two goblets with a dark, red wine and handed them to Wallace and John. 'Let's take advantage of the Prior's hospitality. Men of God make the best of wines.' He lifted his goblet and toasted John. 'To the hero of Stirling Bridge! If you had not smashed those timbers, I doubt if we would be standing here today. I doubt if we would be standing anywhere on God's good earth.'

John felt his face redden at such praise and drank deeply from his goblet before mumbling his thanks.

'I have work for you to do. Important work. Some good and some not so good. I ask you because I trust you and I value you. I know it will be done right. So,' he demanded, his expression serious, 'what do you want first? The good or the bad?'

'Give me the bad first William. It is the kind I am most used to.'

Wallace nodded. 'Our work in England is done. The land has been blackened and devastated, its buildings and bridges destroyed and its crops and livestock sent north across the border. When Langshanks marches north to take his revenge, he will see the wages of his many sins and, just as importantly, will be unable to strip the land to provision his army. Now we must do the same to the south of Scotland. His path there must be no easier and no less blackened than that which he finds here. The further he marches through empty, ravaged lands, the greater the strain on his resources and thus, the shorter the duration of his invasion. We might not be able to defeat him on the battlefield, but we can starve him and his greedy nobles right back across the border.' He fixed John with his steely gaze. 'It will be harder there than it has been here. To inflict such destruction and misery upon our own countrymen will not be pleasant. You will have to harden your heart. The desolation must be complete.' He waved John to the table and pointed to a map unrolled upon the table. 'This is the route you must take. Leave no building standing. Destroy anything the people cannot carry away north. Leave no shelter and no sustenance. No village is to be spared.'

John let out a long sigh. Though this was a task he did not relish, he nodded his agreement. He did not doubt that the peasants' suffering would be great, but believed that it would be worse for them should Langshanks succeed in fastening his grip upon the country. 'And the good?'

Wallace picked up a scroll and handed it to his younger companion. Unused to handling such things, John gingerly unrolled it, careful not to damage the heavy seal of red wax, and slowly read the Latin script. A smile crept onto his lips and grew wider as he realised its import.

Wallace grinned back at him, a slight blush upon his cheeks. 'I received this from Bishop Wishart not two days past.'

'You are to be knighted!' John stated unnecessarily, scarcely believing that such a thing could be true. It was unheard of for a commoner to be raised up in this manner.

'Aye!' Wallace replied. 'It seems that the nobles were struggling to accept the rule of a Guardian who was not one of their number. The Bishop of Glasgow has persuaded them that the solution is to make me a noble, rather than to replace me, which was likely their preference.'

'Congratulations Sir William!' John beamed.

'Ah, dinnae be starting with all that.' Wallace replied, his cheeks growing an even darker shade of red. 'I'm no' interested in all of that, but it will make life easier having that bit of extra clout. Anyway, I'll be needing witnesses at the ceremony. I wanted to ask if you would be willing to stand as one of my witnesses.'

'Aye!' John responded, his face flushing with pleasure. 'It would be a great honour.'

Wallace then did what all Scotsmen do when a conversation appears to be in danger of taking an emotional turn or when praise has been exchanged with another man. He changed the subject. 'There's more good news in the parchments,' he said as searched for a particular one amongst the great stack. 'If ye sift through all the shit and petty petitions long enough, there's the odd gem to be found.' He grunted as he located the right one and thrust it into John's grasp.

The Perth man spread the scroll out on the table and immediately recognised the Guardian's own hand. The document was a copy of a letter Wallace had sent a month past to the Chapter of St Andrews, urging them to elect William de Lamberton as Bishop to the Holy See of St Andrews.

Wallace spoke as John continued to read. 'As Guardian it seems that I have influence over the appointment of Bishops. Lamberton's installation has just been confirmed and so, a man loyal to our cause now controls the wealthiest and most powerful see in Scotland. He has already diverted silver to us, and with what Bishop Wishart already provides, we now have much of the funds required to maintain our army in the field. With what we have stripped from the North of England, we are in a strong position to withstand Edward's invasion when it comes. The Bishops' support greatly strengthens our hand.'

'Will there not be repercussions from what has happened here? The Bishops will not be happy to hear of monks murdered on Priory steps by Scottish troops.'

'There has been worse John, much worse. Churches burned, priests, monks and nuns murdered and relics stolen or destroyed. Our army grew as it crossed the English border, its ranks swollen with thieves, robbers, brigands and reivers eager to fill their purses. If we are to win freedom for our people, we must rely on men we find despicable. The Galloway men, such as those you encountered here, are wild and uncontrollable, but, without them, we could not have brought such desolation to all of Cumbria and Northumbria. If we are pernickety about who we march beside, we cannot prevail. I told the Prior that I would hunt down and hang his attackers, but I will not. Such an action would drive men from our cause, men whose swords and spears we will sorely need before this war is done. I cannot condone attacks upon the Church, but must accept such evils to win the greater prize. I will have to answer to God for these sins, and many others, of that I have no doubt.'

'As shall I.' John responded, his mind already on the gruesome task ahead of him on the other side of the border. He did not relish facing his countrymen when laying waste to the lives they had built for themselves through long struggle and hard toil.

'Go then John, go with my blessings and I shall see you at the Kirk o' the Forest.'

'Aye. Till then, Sir William.' His words were accompanied by the most dainty of bows.

'Get you gone!' Wallace retorted with mock severity, his forced frown quickly replaced with a beaming grin.

6

Tom Figgins awakened with a start, beads of sweat coating his wide forehead. He glanced quickly around to see if he had cried out in his sleep and disturbed any of the Perth men who dozed around him in the barn within the Priory grounds. Seeing that they all slept on, he heaved a great sigh of relief, blowing air through his yellow, slab-like teeth.

The dreams that disturbed his nightly rest were always the same. They began with agonisingly clear memories of his torture at the hands of Rank, his sometime subordinate in the English army based at Perth. The punches and kicks were recalled in a blur, but the hangings were always relived in great detail. He kicked and writhed uselessly against the noose until consciousness was lost, only to be revived and hoisted high once more. It would have been a mercy to leave him suspended until all life was extinguished, but Rank was cruel and knew no mercy, resuscitating him time and time again, before finally sending him to Stirling for execution.

It was whilst being transported to Stirling that he was captured by the Scots, the prison wagon seized and the escort slaughtered. Tom would have welcomed death at that point as he was battered and broken and sorely pained. The Scots mistook him for one of their own and carried him off and tended to his wounds. Such was his terror, he did not speak and the Scots assumed, on account of his noose-torn neck, that his injuries had rendered him mute. Like a drowning man to a floating timber, Tom grabbed onto their error and held on tight, playing the mute for month after month, whilst he awaited his chance to escape. The second part of his nightmare involved him crying out in his sleep, his English accent bringing his captors rushing to his bed, their faces twisted in hate and anger. This is when he awakened each and every night, fear coursing through him as his sleep addled mind fought to discern whether he had, in fact, shouted out or had merely dreamed it.

He had so nearly escaped from this purgatory when the patriot force camped across the Forth from Stirling. Just forty paces would have taken him across the bridge and into the safety of the English army. He had dropped his weapons and set one foot upon the planks when, in flickering torchlight, he espied Rank amongst the English guarding the other end. He could hardly comprehend how it was that, of all the thousands of English soldiers camped below the castle walls, it was Rank who was stationed there upon that particular night. He had returned dejected to his blanket, silently cursing that detestable, stinking bastard, whilst choking back his tears of frustration, anger and self-pity.

Instead of heading south to be re-united with his family, Tom Figgins had found himself fighting in the greatest and most terrifying battle he had ever seen. It made his previous experiences seem as mere skirmishes in comparison. He had not known which side he wanted to prevail. His sympathies lay, of course, with his countrymen, but he could see that his life would be in grave danger should they triumph. A routed Scottish army would be ridden down by the ranks of English knights, a fate he would most likely share given that he was amongst their numbers. In the end, he was relieved simply to have survived. The piled and torn corpses and the screaming of the wounded were worse than any vision of hell conjured up by the Priests. Enticed to head for Scotland by promises of great plunder, at the battle's end he would happily have returned home to live penniless and in poverty for the rest of his days.

With his eyes accustomed to the darkness of the barn, Tom pulled on his boots and cloak and carried his pack, bow and sword quietly to the door. He opened it just a crack and slipped out into the still-falling snow. The carpet of white reflected the moon so that it seemed as bright as day, even although dawn was at least an hour away. He wrapped his cloak around him against the chill and marched briskly to the road, taking care to check his bearings. He did not want to mistakenly head back to Scotland instead of setting course for home. He shivered at the thought.

He had scarcely set foot on the road when a voice called out, almost stopping his heart dead in his chest. 'Where the fuck are you going?'

Tom turned to see McCormack's cheery, ruddy face peering at him from beneath the tree which sheltered him from the worst of the snowfall as he stood sentry. He froze for just a moment, before returning the smile and pointing at the bow on his back with exaggerated gestures.

McCormack did what all the Scots did when they imagined themselves to be talking to a mute. He talked louder and more slowly as though the lack of speech would automatically be accompanied by deafness or a slowness of the mind.

'Make sure that you don't forget about me. I would love to break my fast with roasted pigeon or squirrel.' He hefted his great battleaxe and waved it in a good-humoured display of what would happen if the snow-flecked sentry did not share in the spoils of the morning's hunt.

Tom smiled and nodded and set off on his way.

For all of his first day on the road, he did not encounter another living soul. He did, at times, begin to wonder if he were the only man left alive in the world. The heavy snow and frosty mist gave the land a spectral aspect and the silence that often accompanies heavy falls of snow was increasingly eerie. His shelter that night was a fire-blackened hovel where the thatch had proven too damp to burn right through. Though open to the skies, there was sufficient cover to keep him free of snow and provide him with some shelter from the icy wind. He gnawed upon some goat's cheese purloined from a valley just across the border. It was sweet and creamy and filled his belly and soon carried him off to sleep.

It was the cold which brought him gradually back to consciousness and, as he rubbed his hands together to restore his circulation, he smiled as he realised that he had not been plagued by his nightmares. A breakfast of stale bread did not dampen his good humour and he hummed a tune as he set his feet upon the road.

As he put one foot in front of the other, he began to fantasise about his return home. His pack was full of silver and a small amount of gold, all looted from the North. He imagined his wife's eyes widening in delight as he poured his loot out on the table. In her joy, she would embrace him and his children would dance around in delight. His failure to provide for the family as a barrel-maker would be forgotten. So too would be the humiliation of being forced to ask his sister-in-law to take his family in, whilst he sought work as a roving labourer for scant coin to contribute towards their keep. Though he could scarce admit it to himself, he took the greatest pleasure from his daydreams of how his brother-in-law would react to his change in fortune. The man had always been haughty and superior and had looked down on Tom from the first time they had met. His disapproval of Tom's marriage had not been hidden and he seemed to go out of his way to make him feel uncomfortable. The lecture he had delivered when Tom lost his livelihood and the family home still burned hot in his memory. Just the thought of it made his cheeks redden and prickle with shame and anger both. He imagined himself casually tossing a handful of coins on the table and his brother-in-law's jaw gaping in shock as he led his family out of his cottage and onto a new life. His excitement grew as he left Northumbria behind and the roads gradually grew more busy with carters willing to exchange a seat for a penny.

He looked down upon the sleeping cottage and, relishing the prospect of his grand entrance, sat down to wait for dawn to break. He had spent the previous night at an inn just a few miles away. His excitement had kept him from sleep, so he had risen early, washed himself more thoroughly than he had in many a month, combed his unruly hair and set off on the last miles of his journey. The speech he would make had been rehearsed many times over, but still he let the words run through his head, drawing pleasure from his triumph before it had actually come to pass.

He dozed a little, as he was fair exhausted, and so did not see at first that the cottage had come to life. It was the reluctant scraping of the door being pulled open which brought him back to wakefulness. There was Brenna, not thirty paces from him, carrying a basket of ashes to the midden. She looked different to how he had remembered her. A little wider around the hips, a little greyer at her temples and a little kinder around the eyes. The frown that had never left her face during Tom's last months at home had disappeared, leaving her less lined and her countenance less severe. She looked, Tom thought, happy and not as someone miserable living on the sufferance and charity of family. The door creaked open once more and Haelan, his brother-in-law, stepped blinking into the brightening winter's morn. He pulled the door closed tight behind him and awaited Brenna on the stoop. Tom could not hear the words that they exchanged and could not unsee what they did. Brenna's smile was as wide and as bright as it had been when she had wed him as a young girl. Haelen's smile was just as broad before he leaned in to kiss her upon the lips and slip his arms around her. Tom's jaw dropped open as his brother-in-law patted his wife upon the rump and ushered her back inside through the door.

Tom struggled to comprehend what he had just witnessed and he paced furiously to and fro as he tried to make sense of it. He rubbed his eyes in disbelief, but could not wipe away the memory. He started down the hill to furiously confront the pair, only to pause to choke back sobs of angry despair. He was rooted in indecision as his emotions boiled from the fiercest rage to wretched anguish and then back again. Although he knew what he had seen, he still clung to a tiny grain of hope that he had been mistaken and so decided to skulk upon the hillside to see what transpired.

His mind still reeled when the creaking door was opened once again and his children spilled out into the snow, shrieking and chasing their cousins as snowballs filled the air. He marvelled at how much they had grown and at how healthy and happy they appeared. Bromwyn, his eldest, was now more a woman than the girl he had last seen. He smiled to see them contented, though tears streamed down his face. He watched on as Brenna emerged, lugging two great baskets, and shooed the children along the path to the village. As their happy shrieking and squealing fell to silence, Tom tramped down the hill with grim determination and murderous intent.

Haelen sat at the table, biting his lip in concentration as he shaped the fine leather with a razor sharp trenchet. He was oblivious as Tom applied careful pressure to the door to prevent it from noisily scraping against its frame where the wood had warped. He sat up in wide-eyed astonishment as the gold coin clattered onto the table-top.

'For your whore.' Tom growled, his face hard and stern.

Haelen leapt to his feet in fright and backed away. 'I have no coin here.' He stammered in fear, before narrowing his eyes to peer closer at his assailant. 'Tom? Is that you?' His eyes widened in panic as he realised that it was true.

'I left my family in your care and you take kisses from my wife in return for your charity.'

'Tom, no! It's not like that.' Haelen held his hands out as if to stop Tom from advancing. 'We thought that you were dead. We heard tell that you had gone north to Scotland with De

Warenne's army. When it was slaughtered by the Scots, we assumed that you had fallen.'

'And that gave you the right to hasten to her bed? What thinks your wife of her husband strumping her own sister? Or is she unaware that you steal to her in the night, eager for her tender attentions?'

Haelen pulled himself to his full height and looked down into Tom's twisted face. 'How dare you cast such hideous aspersions in my direction? My dearest Elfreda was carried off by fever no more than two months after you abandoned your own wife and children to this house. I was ever true and faithful to my wife. Near two year we waited for word of you with not a single coin sent to feed your children. Brenna and I worked hard to provide for all our children and made a new family. Twas only when the Priest declared you dead and Brenna widowed that we married.'

'And how much coin did the Priest require to make this proclamation?' Tom demanded bitterly. 'What was the price for speeding my demise and greasing your way to my wife's cunny? Not cheap I'd wager.'

Haelen snorted with derision. 'You have not changed, Tom Figgins. Your mind is still mired in the gutter. It was the baseness of your nature that Brenna could not stand. She was glad to see you go and gladder still that you did not return. She came willingly to my bed and has often spoken of her unsatisfactory times with you. Even your children never speak of you. They call me Pa and treat me with all affection. I have no doubt that they would curse the very thought of returning to the mean, uncertain poverty of life with you. Heavens know what sins and vile wrongdoings have filled your days, but your hands and face bear more scars than healthy flesh, no doubt testament to your villainy. They would be horrified by your rough and repugnant appearance. They have a good, respectable life in this community, something you cannot offer. You should go, their lives are immeasurably better without you around. Go back to whatever hole you have curled up in these long months and leave them to prosper.'

Tom nodded slowly. 'I can see that they are happy and I am glad of it. They deserve it after all that I have brought upon their sweet heads.'

'Brenna would not have you back. She has said as much many a time.'

'I don't doubt it. I always knew that she felt that she had married beneath her station. Her disapproval was both sharp and ever present. In any case, I am not certain that I would want her now that she has been spoiled by your eager pizzle. I would always know that she had lain with you and it would not be the same.' Tom's voice was filled with melancholy resignation and he stared at the floor as if in deep contemplation.

'Tis true Tom,' Haelen responded hopefully. 'It is better that you leave. You should be gone before they return. There is no sense in upsetting them.' He stepped towards the door, eager to see it close upon Tom's back.

'I fear that upset cannot be escaped. They will be distressed to find their new Pa murdered at his hearth.'

Haelen snorted incredulously, 'You do not mean to murder me here. You would not see your own children thrown out into the street with no one to support them with me gone. I do not believe that even as wretched a creature as you would visit that upon his children.'

'I doubt that they will starve!' Tom responded laconically as he kicked his pack onto its side, sending a river of silver flowing across the floor.

Haelen's eyes darted between his seated brother-in-law and the pile of coins, his confidence shaken, but not yet entirely diminished. 'But they will know that it was you. Brenna will tell them so. They will hunt you down and hang you.'

Tom stretched his head back so that the vivid, red gouges the ropes had left around his neck were clearly visible. 'The noose holds no fear for me.' He smiled at the shock in Haelen's darting eyes. 'In any case, I doubt that they would hunt for me seeing that they have already pronounced me dead. Hunting a man for execution would be a sorry waste of time if that man was already fallen.'

Haelen stepped back as Tom rose stiffly to his feet and drew his sword smoothly from its scabbard. His eyes never left the blade as he bargained for his life.

'And you would leave this fortune for Brenna after she has betrayed you so?'

'I may not want her now, but I cannot deny that our children love her. I want my children to be looked after well and that, if nothing else, I can trust her to do. Her penance will be her grief at losing the husband she always thought that she deserved.'

Haelen was sweating profusely now, though the cottage was not warm. Tom waved away his words dismissively as he pleaded tearfully for his life.

'Before you die I would have you know that, whilst I am killing you for lying with my wife, the suffering that will precede it is repayment for all those years when you looked down upon me with raw contempt. Each blow will be for a remembered insult or snide comment and, as my memory is not the best, I will add a few additional to ensure that restitution is absolute.'

A whimper escaped from Haelen's throat and he ran in terror for the back of the cottage. His attempt at evasion was in vain as the cottage had but one door and he had run away from it. Before the first blow landed, he had fallen to the floor and curled up tight to protect himself. Tom shook his head contemptuously at how such a pompous, superior and disdainful man could disgrace himself with such whimpering, craven cowardice. His disgust was such that he laid his sword aside, reasoning that a snivelling, cowering piece of shit did not deserve a warrior's death. He instead chose to kick and stamp down until his breath became ragged and laboured and his feet were bruised and painful. Coward he may be, but it could not be denied that Haelen had a strong grasp on life, for he breathed still, though his head was bloody, terrible swollen and horribly misshapen. Tom considered how to finish him as he rested and tried to catch his breath. The thought struck him like a thunderbolt. Dear Brenna neither knew nor cared that her first husband had been hanged, so it seemed somehow appropriate that she was left in no doubt that her second one had met this fate.

It took more effort to hang a man than Tom had appreciated. By the time he had Haelen secured and suspended from the rafters, the poor man had already kicked his last and stared blankly at Tom, his tongue split and swollen in his blackened face. Tom then drew his dagger and cut poor Haelen's trews and underclothes from his corpse, leaving his shrivelled cock on display on a bushy nest of wiry, black hairs. He wanted Brenna to see what she would be missing in the years ahead.

Satisfied with his work, he strode out of the cottage and off down the track. He did not look back and did not linger to catch a last, fleeting glimpse of his children. He felt safe leaving them in the care of his faithless, inconstant wife and the fortune he had provided.

Penniless and rootless once more, he turned his head to the north.

7

If his dear mother had lived, she would not have recognised Tarquil de Trasque and would have urged her carriage on to pass him in the road. His fine features, his rich clothes and beautifully curly, golden hair were still in place, but it was impossible to discern any of them through the dirt and grime which clung to every inch of him. If she had looked closely, she might have recognised the intricately carved pattern of the knee-length, leather boots she had gifted him on the occasion of his nineteenth birthday. She had designed the pattern herself and paid good silver for a leathersmith to spend near three months crafting the boots to the most exacting of standards. Though they were badly scuffed, water-marked and worn through to the soles, the pattern could still be discerned in places. Least of all would she recognise the ugly, jagged scar which now ran across her gentle son's forehead and she would be horrified to learn that this wound was caused by a Scottish arrow as her sensitive boy was about to march across the bridge at Stirling.

Tarquil had endured the most wretched time of his life in the aftermath of that great battle.

Shocked and dispirited by the enormity of the defeat, the English army had degenerated into an ill-disciplined rabble as it ran for the border. The English commanders, including de Warenne, had ridden so hard for Berwick that they had not stopped even to feed and water their horses, causing many of them to founder when they arrived there. Separated from his men and his possessions, Tarquil had been unable to secure a horse and walked south, sharing the road with the lowest and basest of the English infantrymen. Despite parting with the last of his silver to buy protection, he was robbed of everything except the clothes he stood in. His sustenance was limited to what he could scavenge from the forests and the little he could beg from the campfires of the few men-at-arms from the lower reaches of the nobility who found themselves in the same straits as he. By the time he reached Carlisle, he was foot-sore and gaunt of face, though somewhat reinvigorated and encouraged by the news that de Warenne had ensconced himself safely behind the walls of Newcastle.

Although weak and dizzy with hunger, he tramped on determinedly until he passed through the city gates. He was dismayed to find the place in a state of panicked disarray, with long lines of petitioners vainly clamouring for an audience with de Warenne or his commanders. With no better option before him, Tarquil had joined the lines and waited as the rain ran down his face and soaked his soiled clothes. If he had not been so weak and tired, he would have wept when word spread that de Warenne had already fled the city for the safety of the south. Gossip of the impending arrival of a Scottish army was the cause of great alarm and, swept along in the flow, Tarquil joined the chaotic exodus.

The discovery of a dead pigeon on the road gave him some relief. Its torn and bloody throat made him suppose that his approach had disturbed some fox as it began its feast. He would normally have turned his nose up at such a vile offering, but his hunger drove him to stride away from the road and other greedy mouths and spark a fire to life. His stomach cramped painfully and his mouth fair ran with saliva as the carcass slowly roasted. It was all that he could do to restrain himself from grabbing the bird from the flames and gobbling it down half raw. When he judged it fully cooked, he attacked it like a ravenous wolf, swallowing great greasy chunks even though they burned sorely as they went down. By the time he was finished, there was not a trace of flesh or grease left on the carcass. Never again in his life would he enjoy a feast so much. It left him very much revived and feeling human once again.

The road from here was less arduous, though not without its difficulties. The further south he went, the easier it was to scavenge for nuts, berries and roots. His belly was never full, but neither was it empty. His mood had brightened the closer he drew to home, but even as his family seat, Dragan Hall, came into view in the distance, his future was far from certain. The plan which had sustained him during the hardest of days was by no means foolproof and Tarquil could not deny that he had often proven to be a fool.

As the younger son of a nobleman, Tarquil had inherited nothing on the death of his father. Only the protection of his mother had kept him under the roof of Dragan Hall when his brother, Sir Bervil, returned from war to claim his birthright. His mother was scarcely cold in the ground when his brutish sibling ejected him unceremoniously from the family seat and abandoned the coddled and cultured Tarquil to make his own way in the world. By chance, both brothers became embroiled in the King's ill-fated and disastrous attempt to subjugate the stubborn Scots, but while Tarquil had escaped with his life, it was the warrior Sir Bervil who perished in that cold and wretched land. With his surly and hostile brother gone, Tarquil's hope was that he could ingratiate himself with his widow and resume his pampered life in Dragan Hall. The early signs were not at all promising.

The servants, recognising Tarquil, had afforded him the opportunity to wash and attend to his appearance before he was ushered into Lady Trasque's presence. Despite his greatest efforts, he was not an impressive sight. Although scoured of much of his grime and filth, there was no disguising the fact that he had lived roughly these past months. His sunken cheeks, scarred face and greasy, golden curls merely added to the downtrodden, vagrant air which surrounded him. In contrast, Lady Ingrede cut an imposing figure, thickset, big of bosom and with a face which radiated stern disapproval, even when she was most delighted. Her hair was tied up so tightly in a bun, her face seemed to be stretched by the severity of it.

'Ah, Tarquil,' she drawled as she looked him up and down, her expression showing that she saw little to her liking. 'I thought you dead. The last I heard, my husband had kicked you out onto the streets of Perth. But I see that you did not escape unscathed.'

'It is good to see you Lady Ingrede.' Tarquil responded, inclining his head to show his respect. 'Both you and my nephews have been much on my mind since I heard of my brother's sad demise. I have hastened here from Scotland with the greatest of concern for your welfare now that you are unprotected.'

'So, what has kept you so long? I have heard of other knights who returned home some weeks ago.'

Tarquil quailed at this admonishment and thought that this difficult woman had been the perfect match for his rough and boorish brother. 'Those knights who did not engage the Scots in battle were better able to make haste for the border.' At this, he ran his finger along his scar to emphasise its presence. 'Those of us caught in the rearguard made slower progress fighting as we went.'

'You are the most unlikely of warriors Tarquil, but as my husband said, a warrior without scars is one who has never fought. As for your protection, I am not sure that it is required.'

Tarquil nodded despondently It had never been likely that Ingrede would slip into the role of the weak and vulnerable widow. Indeed, in her presence, it was more likely that he would be the one in need of protection. He opened his mouth to ask for her hospitality, to save him from vagrancy whilst he sought out other, as yet unknown, opportunities.

Ingrede held up her hand to still him to silence. 'However, you may yet prove to be my salvation.'

Tarquil nodded enthusiastically in his astonishment.

'Though my husband's body is scarcely rotted in the earth, my father has already arranged a match for me. Some youthful cousin whose balls have barely dropped. By joining us in marriage, my father seeks to strengthen his grip upon this house and so control its income. I would not have it so. Dragan is my son's rightful inheritance and not my father's purse.'

'You want me to stand against your father?' Tarquil's face twisted in puzzlement as he tried to imagine how this might be done.

Lady Ingrede threw back her head and laughed, her expression lightening to one of mild annoyance. 'No, dear Tarquil, he would split you clean in half and wipe his sword off in your hair. My proposal is more subtle, but gives me what I crave.' She paused, awaiting the dawning of realisation, and then continued on seeing that Tarquil remained mired in bewilderment. 'If you and I were to marry, I would evade my father's grasp.'

Tarquil blinked in surprise. 'You want to marry me?'

Ingrede again guffawed, her laughter echoing around the hall. 'I would not choose you for myself, I like my men with meat. What I propose is a convenience from which we both will benefit. I protect my son's inheritance and you stay here as lord and master, though in name only, until he reaches his majority. What say you?'

Tarquil was dumbfounded and anxiously paced the floor. On the one hand, he had no desire to be joined to this fierce creature, but on the other, a comfortable life in Dragan Hall was sorely tempting and much preferable to the alternative of scavenging by the roadsides.

'Be quick Tarquil!' Ingrede chided shrilly. 'My father could arrive at any time and our plot will come to nothing. I had resigned myself to being under Father's control. I would not miss this unexpected opportunity to escape this fate.'

Still dazed from this turn of events, Tarquil nodded his agreement.

'T'would make a lady blush to see a man so eager to win her hand.' Ingrede responded with some gaiety, her natural frown still present, but softened by her smile.

Though a marriage of convenience, a noble union must nevertheless satisfy certain social niceties if it is to meet the scrutiny of irate relatives. If it is to survive challenges to its legality, it must appear both legitimate and credible, rather than the amenity that it is. Tarquil, Ingrede and their servants devoted the next week to making arrangements for the ceremony and the celebration feast. Invitations were extended to only the most local of nobles and those with any known connection to Ingrede's family were excluded. With only two days left until the ceremony, they were interrupted by a servant announcing a visitor who was most insistent on an immediate audience with Tarquil.

'This person claims to have fought with you in Scotland.' The servant's tone dripped heavily with distaste.

Tarquil and Ingrede exchanged glances, concerned that this visit might be in some way related to their wedding.

'Show him in. I would be most fascinated to meet one of your comrades-in-arms.'

Tarquil snorted in surprise as the unmistakable figure of Rank strode into the room, his heels clattering heavily across the floor. Though grubby and dishevelled, he had evidently fared better upon the road than Tarquil. Though not well-fed, his features were less skeletal and his pock-marked skin less pale.

'In God's name, I can scarce believe that you are here before me.' Tarquil beamed. 'How can this be when none escaped the slaughter?'

'But you escaped the slaughter Tarquil. It cannot be beyond belief that another did the same, especially one as big and strong as this.' Ingrede's eyes shone with gentle mockery.

Ever alert when his future was at stake, Rank immediately comprehended the lie that Tarquil had told. 'I fought my way out of the Scots' trap, just as you yourself did, sir. I struggled to once again regain your side, but I was wounded and could not.'

'Ha!' Laughed Tarquil, wincing slightly as Rank's familiar, foul odour assailed his nostrils. 'Both of us wounded by the treacherous Scots, but we live to tell the tale. What brings you to Dragan Hall?'

With the lie now shared between them, Rank reckoned that he should push his luck. 'I thought that I would take you up on your offer, sir.'

'My offer?' Tarquil said with some hesitation. The fellow was clearly after gold and he did not relish having to ask Lady Ingrede to furnish it.

'To be a retainer in your household, sir. On account of the good service I did provide to you.' Rank stared directly into Tarquil's eyes, silently emphasising their mutual reliance. 'You said that I would always have a place in your household, once the fighting was done.'

'Of course, I had not forgotten. We went through such hazard together. It is the least that I can do.'

'How could you promise a place in your household, when such you did not possess?' Ingrede enquired archly.

'It was meant in general terms.' Tarquil responded dismissively. Though taken by surprise, he was now warming to the idea.

93

Rank's presence would guarantee his own security. He would have paid dearly for such protection when alone and vulnerable on the road. The man's mere presence would be enough to deter Ingrede's family, or even the lady herself, from doing him any harm. 'Come, come,' he beckoned, 'let us find you suitable accommodations.'

Rank reckoned that he was going to like it here. With Tarquil stuffed quite firmly in his pocket, he could do pretty much as he pleased. He did, however, keep a wary eye out for the lady of the house. She was made of sterner stuff and he sensed that it would not be in his best interests to fall foul of her. He had guided Tarquil away from the servants' quarters and had been a given a room in the main house. It was small but well-appointed, the chamber dominated by a feather bed. Rank did not think that he had ever slept so well, though that may well have had just as much to do with his frequent visits to the kitchen to fill up on ale and meat. The new clothes made him itch, but he felt that they were more in keeping with his new position. His duties were that of bodyguard, but his time was mostly his own, as Tarquil seldom ventured from the house, spending his time engrossed in books or in making wedding arrangements. He closed his eyes and took a nap, hoping that he would awaken in time for supper.

The wedding day came around with great speed and seemed to pass by in a blur. With the Priest's words still ringing in his ears, Tarquil joined his guests and blushing bride in a great feast. He filled himself with wine and waved his hands in time to the minstrels' tunes. With his future secure and Rank there to fend off Ingrede's family, he was as satisfied as he could be. He drank a silent toast to his dear, departed mother, knowing that she would be smiling down upon him. His warm reverie was broken when the assembled guests began to rise from their seats and clap and stamp their feet.

Ingrede leaned down and whispered in his ear. 'It is time to consummate the marriage. You must take me upstairs and make me yours.'

Tarquil was quite taken aback. He had assumed that he would not have to do the deed, given that it was merely a marriage of convenience. He gaped at the sea of shiny, red faces as the realisation dawned. 'Ah! We must go through the motions if our ploy is to succeed.'

Waving to the swaying, clapping guests, he leaned down to lift his bride.

'Just walk me you fool!' Ingrede hissed, her spittle dampening his ear. 'There's no way you could bear my weight.'

To great cheers and whistles, Tarquil whisked his new wife to their chamber. Fastening the door behind them, he flopped woozily into a chair. 'Thank goodness that is over. I thought it would never end. I shall sleep well tonight.'

'There'll be no slumber yet.' Ingrede replied, as she eased her bodice off. 'First you must do your duty and truly make me your wife.'

It was with consternation that Tarquil took in Ingrede's ample but firm bosoms with their great, brown, stiffening nipples. 'I did not think this would be necessary,' he stammered, 'with this marriage merely a convenience.'

'Are you truly stupid Tarquil? If the marriage is not consummated then it can be annulled. Do you not think that it is the first avenue that my father will explore?'

'But how will anyone know? There's no way to tell what has gone on in this room. We can say that it was done.'

'Christ Tarquil. Are you really so naive? Do you not think that there will be servants listening at the door? That our sheets will not be inspected at the first opportunity?'

'But why would they check the sheets? It's not as if you are a virgin. They can expect no blood there.'

'Not I, you fool, you! Do you not think that my father will have his people sniffing at our sheets? If not soiled with your seed, that's grounds enough for doubt.' Ingrede now stood over Tarquil, her bushy, pungent quim only inches from his face. 'Now get you stripped and join me on the bed.'

Tarquil did as he was bade and went quickly to her side. She kissed him hard, her full lips enveloping his as her moist tongue darted in and out, eagerly exploring his. She slid her hand down his body and squeezed between his legs. She gently scolded as she caressed, 'Come dear husband, you must rise to the occasion if our intrigue is to play out.' She lifted her head and looked down at what lay between her warm fingers. 'I see that you are cold. Let us see what remedy I can provide.'

She slid down the bed and took Tarquil in her mouth. She had not suckled long before Tarquil began to moan, his eyes tight shut as he imagined himself with another.

Judging that he was now stiff enough, Ingrede rolled onto her back. 'Ride me hard and fill me with your seed,' she gasped, aroused by his hardness against her lips.

Tarquil did his level best to do as he was instructed, but, in truth, it was Ingrede who did the riding. It was all that he could do to stay inside as she bucked and writhed beneath him. The end came mercifully quickly and his nuptial obligations were thankfully satisfied.

Ingrede herself was not. 'So soon husband? Just a little longer please!' A glance confirmed that Tarquil's enthusiasm was already on the wane. 'It does not matter, for I know you have a clever tongue. Let's see how clever it can be.'

Tarquil knew what she wanted and he was not overly keen. The wine had soured his stomach and all of his exertions had caused his head to ache. All he wanted was a draught of water before he went to sleep. But Ingrede was quite insistent and pushed his head down between her legs. Her sex, upon close inspection, was most unappetising, gaping and soaked with fragrant juices. Unsure of the procedure, he reluctantly applied his tongue

'Harder Tarquil!' Ingrede moaned and pulled him harder onto her, her fingers tightly grasping his curly locks.

Tarquil struggled on manfully, though he was half suffocated. He soldiered on through the gagging, but had to admit defeat when a hair caught in his throat and caused him to retch violently. He was surprised by Ingrede's hostility as she banished him to his own chamber. He had expected her to be happy now that the deed was done, but he supposed that women were strange creatures, their moods a mystery.

Rank stirred as his chamber door creaked open, before closing gently once again. Lady Ingrede, wrapped in a blanket, stood before him and looked him directly in the eye.

'Pull down your breeches, I would see what you have there.'

Rank smiled and he did as he was commanded.

Her eyes examined him shamelessly as she licked her lips.

'You would not pierce me with your sword? Would you, sir?' She asked playfully, her eyes asparkle.

Rank did, and several times, to be sure to finish her off.

8

Few of his neighbours would have recognised Malachi Crawcour on this wet and wintry evening. The long, hooded cloak served to obscure both his features and his figure. His position, seated on the damp earth at the base of the well, would not be a place they would expect to find him. There would be no reason for him to rest there, just twenty paces from the door of his own fine residence. Those that scurried by, shoulders rounded against the rain, scarce glanced in his direction and those that did, assumed that he was an unwelcome beggar loitering on their street. Malachi hardly noticed as the cold and damp seeped through his clothes and began to chill his flesh. Though his head leaned forward, as if he was in a doze, his sharp eyes never left his own front door. He did not doubt the veracity of the intelligence his gold had purchased, but he needed to see it for himself. He was no stranger to vile treachery, but this instance had shaken him to his core.

He had always known King Edward to be a highly dangerous and unscrupulous man and he had been accordingly careful in their dealings. Though friendship with a Jew was never a possibility given its impropriety, his vanity had persuaded him that a mutual respect had grown up over the long years of their association. Without the gold of Malachi and his kin, Edward's reign would have been as unremarkable as his father's. Their loans had facilitated Edward's actions in France, the lasting conquest of Wales, his victory in Scotland and the building of his many great castles to solidify his gains. Admittedly, the returns had been great and Malachi's wealth and holdings had grown considerably, leaving nothing outwith his means. In truth, his anger was directed towards himself as much as it was towards the English King. He had allowed himself to trust the man and the betrayal cut him deep. Whenever the Church had moved against the Jews, Edward assured Malachi of his protection and fought to reduce the severity of the measures. The King had raged to him when the Church forced through the hated Statute of Jewry, which required each Jew of more than seven years to wear a badge of yellow felt to distinguish them from good Christian folk. This law had the effect of making all Jews easily and immediately identifiable and, in effect, legitimised their abuse. Malachi now realised that Edward's rage had been false, a deceit intended to ensure that gold would remain available to fund his dreams of avarice.

The sound of marching boots confirmed Edward's faithless duplicity and cruel ambition. Malachi watched on as the company of liveried pikemen halted outside his door. His heart sank as four of their number proceeded to kick at the portal until the wood splintered and the heavy metal lock crashed to the ground. The intricate lock had been crafted in Genoa to his own exacting specifications. It had taken six months to complete and spent two more in transport here to London. Now, parted from its key, it was nothing more than ornate scrap and the waste of gold and craftsmanship pained him. In spite of his fear of being captured, he could not yet flee and stayed rooted to the spot, his need for absolute confirmation not yet satisfied. He could not quite make out the features of the dark figure who stepped up to the gaping door, but his voice carried and identified him as Walter Langton, the King's Treasurer and confidante. In an instant, Malachi's mood transformed. He turned immediately and set out purposefully for the docks, without as much as one backwards glance at his now former life. Regrets and recriminations evaporated as he had much work to do. Avenging the treachery of a king would be both hard and perilous, but Malachi had much experience of toil, danger and adversity and was willing to suffer more.

Walter Langton ordered his men to guard the door and entered into the Jew's hallway. The house was lit but silent, the inhabitants no doubt cowering upstairs like rats. Jews were especially good at cowering and hiding themselves away, at least in Langton's experience. No matter, his men would winkle them out soon enough. He made his way into the Jew's den and found it unchanged from his last visit. The furnishings were of the finest continental craftsmanship and, Langton knew, ruinously expensive. The moment the King had laid out his plan, Langton had begun to picture several of these pieces in his own humble abodes. The reality was an improvement on his memories and he realised that he would have to order more wagons to carry it all away. However, the main prize lay at his feet. On one of his first visits to the Jew, when he had stubbornly and improperly insisted that Langton call on him rather than the other way around, he had noticed the slight indentations in the thick, Persian rug. He had immediately realised that the rug's purpose was less adornment than it was concealment. He pulled the rug back to reveal that, as anticipated, a large hatch had been expertly cut into the floor. Langton's palms grew moist with anticipation. Malachi was rich beyond imagining and he now stood upon the resting place of his ill-gotten gains. He slipped his fingers through the delicate iron ring and the hatch rose smoothly on its hinges. Langton grabbed a candle from the Jew's great desk and thrust it at the hole. The vault below was immense and lined with stone. It was also empty.

Aghast, Langton eased himself down into the vault, his eyes searching vainly for a door or a hidden panel. He bent down and rubbed his finger through the dust at its bottom. Even in the flickering light, its grainy texture told him that the dust was gold, evidence of the great fortune that had so recently resided there.

Langton cursed bitterly, 'Dirty, sneaky Jew!'

He pulled himself up out of the hole and marched into the hall. He threw open the first door that he came to and reeled to find it empty, save for two flickering candles, which had been melted to the floor. He found the same in every room he entered on this and the upper floor. Red-faced with fury, he stamped back to the Jew's den, searching the walls for a hidden panel or a secret door. It was then that he noticed the parchment upon the desk. He had missed it when first he entered the room, as he had been so intent on the rug and what lay beneath it. He snatched it up and read it with a curse.

'My dear, it would seem that I am not the only one to be betrayed. Be certain that I am far beyond your reach with my treasures safely secured. I would like you to have these few sticks of furniture, as I know that you have long coveted them. The desk is sadly infested with woodworm, which resist all attempts to shift them. However, I know that you have a liking for corrupted things, so have no doubt that it will serve you well.'

The letter was unsigned, but the hand was unmistakably that of Malachi. Langton had seen it often enough on the various deeds and promissory notes that had threatened to drain the treasury dry. He aimed a vicious kick at the desk and cursed the foul creature most vilely. The loss of his expected windfall stung him deeply and would smart for some time to come. The Jew's impudence cut much deeper. He mocked him by leaving fine furniture that he could not use as, even if it was treated, it was not worth running the risk of infesting the timbers of his own houses. The worst of it was the betrayal and he set his mind to identifying who had forewarned the Jew of his impending fate. Until today, only the King and himself had known precisely what was to transpire. The captains of his guard had only been informed of the details of their task earlier in the day and the Jew had obviously already made good his escape by then. He toyed briefly with the thought that Malachi might have somehow intuited their intention, but quickly dismissed the idea. The Jew was not one to jump at shadows and was well used to living under threat. Only solid intelligence would have led him to take such drastic action. Langton's machinations were interrupted by a messenger.

The soldier's nervous shuffling irritated Langton and he barked at him. 'What is it man? Spit it out!'

The messenger straightened his back and, staring off into space to avoid Langton's angry glare, dictated his message. Langton groaned and put his head in his hands, guessing what was to come. His despondency grew ever deeper as messenger after messenger arrived with the same report. Of the fifty most prominent Jews in the capital, only eighteen had been apprehended. The rest, like Malachi, had already disappeared, taking their gold with them. The eighteen who had been taken were found with remarkably little coin, suggesting that they had in fact been warned, and while they had not been sufficiently alarmed to take flight, they had taken the precaution of protecting their precious fortunes. It was some small comfort to find that, as the night passed into early morning, the great majority of the three hundred listed Jews had been put in chains. Langton decided that his report to the King would emphasise the overall numbers, rather than provide a detailed account of individual cases. He sat at the Jew's great desk and made a start on his report, as his men continued to vainly rip Malachi's home apart in the search for hidden gold.

Malachi stood upon the dock and embraced his wife. 'You should go now and get out of this cold rain before you catch your death. I want you well when I return to you.'

'I wish you did not have to go.' His wife responded as she stroked his cheek.

'I am sorely tempted to board the ship with you and leave this accursed place behind. But I have business I must attend to before I can have the joy of you once more.' He leaned down and kissed her soft, warm cheek and watched her cross the gangplank and disappear into the ship.

'Take care of her, brother, she is the most precious thing that I possess.' Malachi implored wistfully, his gaze still upon the creaking ship.

'I will.' Cael replied. 'You must do this? You cannot just walk away? I understand the desire, but it is too risky. I beg you to think again.'

Malachi grasped his brother's hand. 'You are right of course. You are always right. I should turn the other cheek, but there are times when a man must leave his cheek where it is. This man has wronged us so many times and we have just swallowed it down like hot soup. It is time that he had that bitter flavour on his own tongue.'

'He is a King, Malachi. I fear that you cannot beat him. It is much more likely that you'll end up dead. Then where would you be?'

'I do not need to beat him. I just need to hurt him. You doubt that I could do that?'

Cael laughed and squeezed his brother's hand. 'Even as a boy you were as stubborn as a mule. If you set your mind to something, you always succeed, which is good. If you set your mind to something, it is impossible to change your mind, which is bad. Stay safe. We will pray for your return.'

'And I will pray for you. I have put all that I possess into your safekeeping. Guard it well. I doubt that they will find you hidden away on our estates, but you must remain cautious and vigilant. The Plantagenet King never forgets a slight and his reach is long.'

Malachi watched sadly as his brother boarded the ship and the crew cast off. The sails flapped in the breeze and the merchant ship slowly edged out into the river. He watched still as it carried his family and his fortune away. Only when it had disappeared in the murky darkness did he turn and address his young companion.

'You have come for your gold Allard? I am happy to pay it.'

'Were you able to warn your friends?' The young servant enquired.

Malachi sighed. 'Some yes and some no. If I had told them all, then someone would have given us away, either by mistake or for some reward. Of those few I did tell, some have already fled, but others chose to stay. It weighs heavily on my conscience, but what can you do?'

'Some escaped. That is something is it not?'

'Yes, young Allard, it is something, which is better than nothing I suppose.' He drew a heavy purse from his cloak and held it out to the lad. 'You cannot go back to the palace now. It may take Langton a while, but he is a clever, tenacious man and will eventually work it out. He also has nearly as many eyes and ears on London's streets as I. You should leave this place and make a life elsewhere. This purse should set you up quite handsomely.'

Allard reached out and took the purse, secreting it about his person. 'I would rather come with you.'

'Malachi laughed. 'It is dangerous where I am headed. A wise man would stay clear.'

'I know not if I am wise, but I know that you have treated me with decency. No other dared to tell me how the King abused my mother. If not for you, I would have never learned the truth and would yet be tipping out his chamber pot, my mother turning in her grave.'

'Perhaps I was not so kind to tell you. There is comfort in ignorance.'

'I would rather live my life in truth than wallow in falsehood. I would like to serve you in your task.'

'Alright my boy, if that is what you desire. But the road ahead is steep and hard and I know not where it ends. But I know where it begins. To Scotland then!'

They did not tarry and set off that very night aboard a rough, ox-drawn cart. Swaddled in their long, thick cloaks, they attracted no attention. To the casual passerby, they warranted not a second look, appearing to be simple country folk going about their work. If they had paid closer heed, they might have remarked on how deeply the cart rutted the muddy road, as though it carried something much heavier than winter vegetables. By the time they approached the borderlands, the cart was visibly lighter, its load depleted as Malachi kindly dispensed his gold to every ship's captain he encountered.

9

Malachi's resolve had been sorely tested on the
journey north. It seemed that his very bones
ached from the violent rattling of the wagon as it
clattered and thumped its way along the muddy,
rock-strewn roads. He had taken to his feet on
several occasions to escape the jolting and the
juddering, only to be defeated as the glutinous
mud quickly sapped the energy from his legs
and his boots rubbed his feet raw, leaving them
covered with agonising blisters. He had thought
himself clever in using the ox-cart to ensure a
measure of anonymity, but now he wished that
he had taken the risk of choosing something
much less basic. He could not decide if his
suffering was due to his advancing years or
because the most physically demanding activity
he had engaged in for several decades was
lifting bags of gold and silver. Even this had
been limited, as he had young, strong servants to
hoist and carry the heavier bags. Allard, for his
part, was taking it all in his stride. He never
complained about anything, not discomfort,
fatigue, the constant rain or even of freezing
nights spent sheltering from the rain upon the
cold ground beneath the cart. Malachi

suspected, but would never admit, that he might have given up if not for his young companion.

The North of England had been a sorry sight to see. Malachi thought that it was like a vision of hell, though far worse than anything conjured up by holy men. The vast territory was completely devoid of people and livestock and the villages they passed through were burnt black. Every hamlet and lonely cottage was similarly destroyed, leaving no shelter for man or beast. The silence of the place was eerie and was made more so by the weather-blown corpses which lay rotting where they had fallen. Wolf packs howled mournfully in the night as though they too shared the sorrow of the land. Though they rode in forlorn silence, their minds reeled at the extent of the desolation. In one valley, where they stopped to set up camp, Malachi became quite disconsolate. With its lush, green slopes and gently winding river, it must have been a fine place to make a home. There was evidence of the generations of hard toil that had been invested to render it a safe and productive place. All of that now lay in ruins, a great barn, stout bridge and high granary now just crumbling, blackened skeletons, of no use to man or dog. The little castle, which had once offered protection to lord and serf alike, was now little more than a scattered pile of ancient stones. To Malachi's mind, it was a sad waste and he could not help but calculate the value of what had been thrown away. It would, he knew, take many years to bring the valley back to life.

When they left the city walls of Carlisle behind, they went days without encountering a single soul. It was just before the border that they finally clapped eyes upon another human being. They waved in greeting, glad to see another, but the lone goatherd gave no response and sat unmoving upon his hill, minding his scrawny goats and his little donkey.

'How long until we cross the border?' Allard enquired, as the cart shuddered its way slowly up a steep slope.

'We passed it a day or two ago methinks.' Malachi responded, without enthusiasm.

Allard glanced around in puzzlement. 'Are you sure? Every settlement we have passed this day has been razed to the ground. I don't understand.'

'The Scots have done it.'

'And why would they destroy their own country?' Allard retorted, his smug, incredulous grin betraying that he thought Malachi to be mistaken.

'They know that our good King Edward will soon march north at the head of a great army to punish them for slaughtering his other great army at Stirling. They mean to deny him sustenance by destroying anything in his path which could be of use or comfort to him. The further from England he marches, the harder it will be to maintain his lines of supply. An army would normally expect to strip at least half of what it requires from the land through which it advances. They mean to starve him into defeat. If his soldiers cannot eat, they will desert him in search of food and so his invasion will fail. It is a wise stratagem, though harsh for the people who lived here.'

Allard was silent as he contemplated this information. When he next spoke, he did so urgently. 'We are being watched.' He pointed to the brow of a hill where a horseman stood beside his mount, a large, black dog at his feet.

'He has been tracking us since yesterday.' Malachi replied nonchalantly. 'Let us pray that he is a Scots soldier and not a brigand. That way we will have at least a chance of escaping with our lives intact, if not our possessions.'

Allard's eyes widened in fear and he could not conceal his nervousness. Malachi felt his heart beat faster in his chest and, not for the first time, wished that he had better heeded his brother's counsel and left this business well alone. It was one thing to dismiss the perils of his chosen course when safely in the south. It was quite a different matter to experience them in much closer and less abstract proximity. He grimly gripped the ox's reins and prayed that he had not doomed Allard to an undeserved, early and grisly death. He steeled himself and summoned all of his courage to face whatever lay ahead.

As they rounded a long bend in the track, they found their way barred by a band of men who patiently awaited their arrival. The slow crawl of their cart had necessitated no pursuit. As the distance between them closed, Malachi studied them warily, searching for any indication of their purpose. If they were to

112

survive this encounter, he would need to have all of his wits about him.

'Leave the talking to me,' he instructed with whispered urgency.

'I'll say that you are holding me against my will.' Allard responded in a strangled attempted at replicating a rough, Scots burr.

'Feh! If you speak like that they'll kill us on the spot. Keep your mouth shut.' Malachi snapped humourlessly, though much later he would find it amusing.

Malachi's scrutiny of the Scots revealed little that was useful to him. All of them were heavily armed, but that would be true of both soldier and outlaw. There were about sixty men awaiting them, a large number for lawless raiders, but not so remarkable for a military force. The men were dirty, sooty and bedraggled, but that would not be unexpected if they had spent the last weeks burning, looting and murdering their way through the North of England, before continuing on to wreak havoc in the southern part of their own country. It was the manner of their dress which made Malachi conclude that they were soldiers rather than lawless rogues. Their tunics and trews were well-made, too well-made to have been procured honestly, as their cost was greater than the purses of ordinary fighting men could bear. The presence of so much maille and plate also led him to conclude that these items had not been purchased from armourers, but rather stripped from their rightful owners while their bodies were not yet cold.

Any small confidence gleaned from these machinations was soon lost as Malachi drew the cart to a halt. A glowering, dark figure stepped forward from the Scots ranks and morosely waved at them to step down. The Jew winced internally as he met this man's gaze. His pupils were as black as pitch and Malachi felt as if he stared into the abyss. With the utmost certainty, he knew that this man would not merely kill him at a stroke, but would also relish it.

'These are dangerous times to be on the road, old man.' Black Eck intoned icily. 'What business have you here?'

Malachi swallowed carefully, conscious that he teetered precariously on the precipice of death. His pulse quickened and his stomach cramped painfully, but he was astounded to note that he found the sensation strangely familiar. It took but a second for him to recall where and when he had experienced it before. Each time he had faced King Edward, his guts had clenched this self-same way, the knowledge that one slip or careless word could lead to execution, or worse, caused fear to pulse through his very core. A glimmer of a smile rested on his lips as he thought, 'I have been through worse than this and survived.' This reflection brought some small comfort and sparked his courage back to life.

'My business is with the magnates of Scotland.' Malachi announced loftily as he stepped towards the terrifying figure of Eck. He hesitated slightly as his eyes flicked over the side of the man's skull. Beneath the bristles of

his recently shorn hair, he caught sight of a
jagged wound and a ragged crater in the bone.
He shivered and could not comprehend how a
man could live after suffering such an injury.
He had seen corpses which had suffered less.

'What business do you have with the nobles?'
Another voice demanded.

'I come to support their cause.' Malachi
squinted so that he could focus on this second
man.

'How so?' John Edward enquired. 'You are
old and have no weapons. What support could
you provide?'

Sensing that this man was the leader of the
group, Malachi moved towards him, careful not
to brush past his intimidating compatriot. 'I
come from Europe,' he lied, 'the support will
come from there.' This second part was true. If
he was to provide gold to the Scottish cause, it
would, indeed, be shipped from his estate on the
Continent.

'France?' John demanded. 'There has long
been talk of support from the French.'

'Amongst other places.' Malachi responded
in vague, evasive confirmation.

'Then you shall have our protection until we
deliver you to them. You will not have long to
wait, we meet with some of their number in the
morn.'

'What luck!!' Malachi exclaimed as the cart
crawled along behind the body of horsemen.

'Luck?' Allard spat back in whispered
response. 'I preferred it when the land was
empty and the dead and the wolves were our

only companions. Do you see the way that they stare at us? Their eyes are hard and cruel as they wonder what lies within the wagon bed. I doubt that we will survive the night.'

'Shush Allard, all will be well. It is just as it is in England. They fear their nobles and will not trouble us lest they bring their superiors' displeasure down upon their heads. By morning we will be safely in the warm embrace of Scots nobility.'

They drew to a halt by a river just as the light began to fade. Men hurried to and fro, lighting fires and erecting a village of crude shelters and tents. Allard went off to collect firewood, but was careful to avoid the fighting men. He returned quickly and began to set the fire, while his travelling companion inspected their dwindling supplies. He sighed at the meagre fayre on offer and could not help but think about the delicacies he had enjoyed in his London home. With money no object, he could indulge his every whim and desire. The heavy paunch he had built up over the years was now all but gone. Twice on their journey north, he had been forced to gouge new holes in his belt to keep his trews from falling. He smiled at the thought of what delights the Scots aristocracy would be able to provide. It would be good to let his belt out a notch or two.

His reverie was interrupted by the leader of the Scots. 'Come join us while we sup.' John Edward said in invitation, as he pointed towards the largest of the fires. 'We have cattle to slaughter and you both look like you would benefit from a proper feed.'

Warmed by the flames and filled with hot, greasy beef, Malachi relaxed and found that he enjoyed the company of the Scots. Though undeniably rough and ready, they were not the heathen savages they were often described to be. Though he could not catch every word they said, he found himself becoming quickly attuned to their thick, harsh accents and so could follow most of their conversation. He picked up that there was to be an important event the next day involving their leader, William Wallace. They were obviously very excited by this and the fact that their own leader, John Edward, was to attend. They were scathing about their nobles and displayed, what Malachi considered to be, a healthy scepticism about the virtues of their betters. He especially enjoyed the accounts of their duplicity as they chopped and changed their allegiances depending upon which served their interests best. Their humour was dry and direct and no-one escaped unscathed. He had laughed loudly when one of their number, Strathbogie he thought him called, pinned two gnawed cow ribs to his temples in parody of his curly payots and did a passable impersonation of his own eastern accent.

The general good-humour abated only when they were briefly joined by a lanky, young man with teeth near as brown as his hair. The conversation died to silence when he appeared at the fireside.

'Jack Short.' John exclaimed in greeting. 'How did you find us here?'

'T'was not difficult,' Short replied condescendingly, 'I merely had to follow the trail of burnt-out hovels to find you at its end. I come with news of Wallace's ennoblement. The ceremony will commence mid-morning at the Kirk o' the Forest,' he informed the assembled company. 'Only the Edward boy is to attend. The rest of you must remain here, out of the sight of the nobles. They will not want such an occasion to be marred by a rabble.'

John did invite him to join the company, but did so without the slightest trace of enthusiasm and the messenger, in any case, declined.

'I have matters of import to attend to!' He had announced with haughty self-importance, before making his departure.

The curses aimed at his receding back would have made an old whore blush. Some of these old Malachi understood and some were new to his ears. What was clear was that the young man was universally disliked and the older man could not help but feel some small sympathy for him.

The mood was not subdued for long and rose to new heights as more and more of the bitter, Scottish ale was consumed. Malachi belched loudly and basked in its inner warmth. He was returned to immediate sobriety when John Edward addressed his young companion.

'And what brings you here?'

Allard seemed to freeze, his goblet half way to his mouth.

'He is not from these parts and has not yet learned the tongue.' Malachi interjected, employing a ruse he had devised when clattering along in the Scots' wake.

'France?' John persisted, before asking a series of questions in perfect French.

Malachi would have been impressed if he had not been so anxious. 'He is from further east than that and knows no French.'

'Interesting.' John responded, his eyes never leaving those of Allard. 'He seemed to follow the discussion fine. A neat trick for one without knowledge of the tongue.'

John then left them mercifully alone and, as the first of the Scots began to drift off to their tents, Malachi and Allard quietly slipped away and made their beds beneath the cart. He had been asleep not more than two hours, when he was awakened by a scraping on the boards above his head and an urgent, whispered admonishment. He froze, his ears alert for any sound.

'They're robbing the cart.' Allard whispered from the darkness.

'Thieves!' Malachi roared in order to raise the alarm. He opened his mouth to shout again, but shut it with a snap as an armed snaked around his neck and a knife point jabbed roughly into the underside of his jaw.

He felt warm lips and spittle in his ear as a voice hissed, 'D'ya want yer throat slit?'

Conscious of the blade at his throat, Malachi shook his head almost imperceptibly.

'Clever boy.' The voiced cooed gently. 'This'll no' take long.'

Malachi closed his eyes tight shut and prayed. He was in such a state of terror, he was hardly aware of the scraping and bumping in the cart above him. Although most of the original load had already been distributed, there remained a not inconsiderable amount. He cared for this not at all. He would happily have them take all the gold, so long as they left him fully intact. He prayed harder than he had ever done before, because he did not believe that this would actually occur.

He jumped involuntarily at the sound of a great meaty crack to his side in the darkness. The arm around his neck immediately relaxed and the knife fell away to the ground. He scrambled desperately away from his attacker and crawled out and up from under the cart. He stepped back from the men with drawn swords and raised his hands in surrender. It took but an instant for him to realise that the swords were not pointed in his direction, but at a prone figure on the ground, two men in the bed of the cart and one man at its rear who stood over a stack of wooden boxes. As his eyes adjusted to the darkness, he saw that John Edward, his brother Scott, Strathbogie and the frightening Eck the Black were the men with their swords drawn.

'Thieving bastard!' Eck the Black growled at the man who lay groaning upon the ground. Blood oozed from the wound suffered when Eck had cracked his head with the flat of his blade.

'Put it back!' John ordered the others. 'These men are under my protection. That includes their possessions.' He turned to Malachi. 'Make sure that it's all there. I'll hang them all if any is missing.'

Malachi tried to calm his nerves as he squinted in the murky gloom and counted the boxes. He nodded with relief that all twenty-four were safely back in the cart. It would be several weeks before he discovered that two had been emptied, their contents replaced with Scottish stones.

'Thank you!' He stammered as the dazed and bloody thief was carried off by his fellows. 'You saved my life.'

'It was not as bad as that.' John Edward replied. 'But I apologize. I meant to provide you with better hospitality. I should have posted a guard to discourage the more curious of my men.' His next words were undoubtedly well-intentioned, but they guaranteed that Malachi would not sleep a wink. 'Eck! Stand guard till morning. Make sure our guests are not disturbed again.'

10

John Edward revelled in sleep's warm embrace, his cloak insulating him from the frigid air and the damp, cold ground beneath his wind-stirred canopy. In his dreams he was back in Scotstoun, buried under his sheepskins, his limbs intertwined with those of his Lorna, her body soft and warm against his. He murmured softly as he dreamed that he nuzzled into the soft skin at the side of her neck. She nuzzled him back, her nose cold and wet, her long tongue licking wetly at his face with a foul, cloying stink of fresh-licked arse and raw meat. Her insistent tongue jolted John back into sudden consciousness, only to be instantly and closely confronted by the Black Dog's gaping jaws, his tongue lolling wetly between his long white fangs.

'Fucksake!' John cursed, wiping the sickeningly aromatic drool from his face, the hound meeting his scowl with a wide and toothy grin, his tail thumping the ground in pleasure at a job well done.

'Dougal! Here!' A voice commanded sharply from the darkness.

'Al! What the hell? I was sound asleep there!' John snapped in a biting tone. He counted Al as one of his closest friends and valued him as the eyes and ears of his force of men, but he could not hide his foul temper at being so rudely ripped from such sweet reverie.

'You need to get going John. The nobles gather already at the Kirk.'

John laid back and closed his eyes. 'The accolade is not until mid-morning. I have an hour yet.'

'I think not.' Al responded persistently. 'The Kirk is lit and they start to file in. You must go now.'

'Shit!' John cursed. 'You must be mistaken. Jack Short clearly said that it was to be mid-morning. Why would they do it at dawn? The magnates would not travel in the dark.'

'They arrived in Selkirk late last night. Tis only a short ride away. Rouse yourself John, or you will miss it and another will take your place.'

'Jack Short!' He exclaimed ill-temperedly. 'It would be he who took my place. He has misdirected me.' He rose to his feet and struggled to pull on his boots as he cursed the Wallace's deceitful retainer most foully. 'Get the Robertson! He is to be there too.'

'I am already here young Edward.' The Robertson announced cheerily as he ambled to their side. 'My old bones protest when I lay them on hard ground and so I seldom sleep. I am up and dressed and have already had my oats. Let's mount up quick and ride for the

Kirk. I never thought that I would see this day and I'll be damned if I will miss it.'

They rode hard along the track, even although only the weakest of dawns lit their path. By the time they tied their horses hastily to the gate, the Kirk was near full, but its doors were mercifully still wide open and they strode quickly inside. The pews were packed with sma' folk from the town and worthies crowded before the alter. Unsure of their place, they had hesitated nervously for only a few seconds before a tall figure broke away from the throng and advanced towards them.

'Laird Robertson! John! By God it is good to see you.' Malcolm Simpson's grin lit up his face as he embraced them each in turn. 'Come, come! Your places are down here at the front. You have arrived just in time.' Malcolm then guided them to their places on the second pew from the front.

'And where is the bold Wallace himself?' The Robertson enquired, his head flitting from side to side as he searched for the figure of his old friend.

'He is in the chancel with the magnates and the Bishops. They take him through the order of the ceremony. It would not do for him to disgrace himself upon an occasion such as this.' Malcolm wrung his hands with nervous excitement. 'Can you believe that he is to be raised up?'

John's stomach lurched at the prospect of being part of such a momentous day. To be present to witness it was wondrous in itself, to be a participant was beyond his wildest imaginings. He could not wait to regale his family with this tale and imagined their wide-eyed astonishment when he related it all to them.

The chatter in the Kirk suddenly dropped to a hush as the chancel door was opened and Wallace emerged, followed by half a dozen other men. Of these, John recognised only Edward de Bruce, the man who had first introduced Scott, Eck and himself to the Robertson and his patriot fighters.

'Who are they?' He asked Malcolm in a whisper.

'That,' he replied, leaning in close to John's ear and jabbing his thumb in the direction of the man directly behind Wallace, 'is Robert de Bruce, Earl of Carrick.' John had to admit that the man looked every inch the nobleman. Taller than all but Wallace, his black, lustrous hair fell straight to his shoulders and framed a pale face bearing the neatest and most well-trimmed beard John had ever seen. His eyes were dark and brooding, as if troubles weighed heavily upon his mind. His surcoat and trews were of black damask and his tunic fashioned from red velvet trimmed in black. A heavy chain of gold links hung regally from his neck. His boots of soft black leather were spotless and polished to a shine so high, the candles of the Kirk were reflected in their surface. John glanced down at his own worn, mud-spattered boots and groaned inwardly. His own clothes, which had seemed so fine when he had first looted them, now seemed dirty and shabby in comparison. He lifted his hand self-consciously to his tangled, unkempt hair and tried to surreptitiously comb it with his fingers.

'That,' Malcolm Simpson whispered, with another jerk of his thumb, 'is the Red Comyn, Lord of Badenoch.' Although unmistakably noble, this man was neither as handsome nor as richly dressed as Robert de Bruce. His greying hair was close cropped and his bearing and attire were those of a military man.

'They are the competitors for the crown, with King John in Edward's tower. But that man there, he is the real power in Scotland now. Lamberton, Bishop of Saint Andrews.' Malcolm nodded towards the taller of the two churchmen. Like Wallace and Bruce, Lamberton was young to hold such high position, with none of them being yet thirty years old. As his appointment had not been consecrated by the Pope himself, Lamberton was dressed in the plain black robes of a common priest and only the tall, tapered mitre upon his head and the heavy, gold, ecclesiastical ring worn over his white glove indicated his recent elevation. 'While the Bruce and Comyn bicker and manoeuvre over the throne, the Bishop courts anyone who might frustrate Edward's desire to rule here. He means to keep his Church independent of that in England and supports any who can further that aim.' Malcolm looked about him as he spoke, to ensure that he was not overheard.

Their conversation was cut short as the ceremony began. John could not remember the last time he had paid such close attention to a religious sermon, but he followed this one avidly and gave silent thanks to Father MacGregor in Scotstoun for his tenacity in drumming Latin into his reluctant, boyish head. When the Bruce stepped forward and performed the adoubement, dubbing the kneeling Wallace on each shoulder with the flat of his sword blade, John had to stifle his urge to cheer. At his side, Malcolm threw him a glance and blew hard as if to expel his pent-up excitement.

The Bruce then kissed William upon each cheek and turned to present him to the congregation. 'Sir William Wallace!' The Kirk then erupted in most unseemly cheering, causing Bishop Lamberton to look momentarily stern, before a smile stole onto his face.

With the accolade awarded, only the formalities remained. The Red Comyn was the first to be called forward to make his signature to attest to his presence at the ceremony. He was followed by some more minor nobles, who bent their heads and scratched their names onto the parchment with quill and ink. John dried his sweaty palms on his cloak and tried to still his quickening breath. He would rather have faced snarling English knights than the scrutiny of these gathered worthies. When his name was called, it seemed suddenly surreal and he hesitated before forcing his reluctant, trembling legs to propel him from his pew to the table before the alter. He felt that all eyes were on him and fat beads of sweat formed instantly on his forehead and upper lip, though the Kirk was icy cold. The priest who had assisted Lamberton in the ceremony looked him up and down and evidently found him wanting.

'No matter that you cannot read it,' he intoned disapprovingly, 'just make your mark here.'

'If I am to put my name to it, I'll read the script before I sign.' John took great satisfaction at the arching of the priest's eyebrows in his surprise. His chest puffed out with pride to see his own name already printed neatly at the foot of the document. 'John Edward of Scotstoun, Man-at-Arms.' He signed his name above it with a flourish, keen that his signature bore favourable comparison with the noble ones already there. He fair floated back to his place and watched with great satisfaction as the Robertson and Malcolm took their turns.

The Earl of Carrick and Sir William then led the congregation out of the Kirk pew by pew and into the morning mist to a celebratory breakfast in the grounds. The most enticing of aromas filled the
air as breads and meats were cooked over three great fires and skins of ale were poured into wooden goblets. John ate, drank, exchanged news and gossiped with Malcolm and the Robertson. Though enjoying each other's company, their eyes were irresistibly drawn to the circle which had formed around Wallace. After all, it was not every day that they were in the company of nobles and the opportunity to gawp was far too good to miss. John's memory was filled to bursting and he looked forward to

sharing his tales with friends and family, knowing that they all would be amazed. A Scotstoun boy in such exalted company would seem beyond belief.

A hand clamped down hard upon his shoulder, as a familiar voice loudly declared, 'John, so good of you to have made the effort to dress up for the proceedings!' John turned to see the handsome, grinning face of Edward de Bruce.

John did feel ill-at-ease, as his hurried, dawn departure had robbed him of the chance to tidy himself and scrape the mud from his boots. Nevertheless, he was glad to see Edward and smiled back at him. 'That's the trouble with invading England. It does not leave much time for fussing with one's tailoring. If, like you, I had been loitering in my castles, I would have instructed my servants to trim my beard and see to my attire.'

Bruce, for his part, laughed loudly, his eyes glimmering with mischief, as they always did. 'Tis true. This loitering is such hard work. But, let me look at you. Is this the same young boy I found hiding in the woods those short months ago? I would have thought you dead by now. Laird Robertson, it seems that you have made a man of him. When I delivered him to your camp, I thought that you could have him scrub your pots.'

The Robertson joined the laughter. 'And scrub he did, his brother and cousin too. So bad a job they did, I put them to swords instead.'

'I can see that he's a stranger to the scrubbing brush.' The younger Bruce replied. 'His hair is full of soot, from burning English manors no doubt.'

Still smiling, but with a redness to his cheeks, John came to his own defence. 'I was told that the ceremony would be mid-morn. I scarcely made it here and had no time to bathe. Why is should be held so early is a mystery to me?'

'Ah! That would be my brother.' Edward declared with a rueful look. 'With the ceremony at dawn, he has time to get elsewhere, with witnesses that he was at that location and not here upon this day. That way he can plausibly deny his involvement, if circumstance so requires it.'

'Aye, still playing both sides against the middle.' The Robertson made the accusation with a shrug of his shoulders. 'He's as slippery as an eel.'

'True, my friend. I cannot deny it, though he be my brother. It is not called blind ambition for nothing. He is blind to anything that stands betwixt him and his crown. Like my father and grandfather before him, he was weaned on tales of the legitimacy of his claim. I oft think that, if he had died in infancy, it would be I who was inculcated with such ambition. All I can say is that his heart is good and I do not doubt that he will do the right thing by his countrymen. What exactly the right thing may be, is yet debatable.'

'The right thing is to join with Wallace,' the Robertson insisted. 'King Edward will soon be on the march and we must all be ready to repel him.'

'Wallace has done well, no one would deny it.' Edward Bruce waved his hand in the direction of the Kirk o' the Forest in reference to Wallace's ennoblement. 'But the straight path he has taken has no guarantees. King Edward could yet triumph. I admire the man for his achievements, but he is all virtue and that may seal his fate. Our Lord Jesus was all virtue and they nailed him to a cross. Long after he was dead, Pilate continued to rule as Prefect of Judaea and Tiberius as Emperor of Rome. Robert has no intention of being so martyred and will follow a crooked path if that is what leads him to his throne. He will have his reward in this life and not in the one that follows. For Wallace it is victory or death, a very dangerous wager when playing with Edward Plantagenet. My brother prefers to stack the odds. Only time will tell who has chosen the best road.'

'I detest all of this politics.' John interjected. 'Why can't they just get on with it? Edward comes, we defeat his army and he scurries off back to England. Simple!'

The Robertson laughed and took a long draft from his goblet. 'You don't like politics, John? It's all politics when you decide to involve yourself in the affairs of kings. It was you who chose to leave a happy hearth and home to avenge a loved one slain. All that you do now is politics, whether you live or die, prosper or perish. You might not like the politics, but you have no other choice than to embrace them.'

'Tis sadly true.' Edward admitted before emptying his goblet. 'Ah, look! I think we are being summoned.'

John looked up to see Wallace waving them to come to him.

'These are the men I was telling you about.' Wallace was saying as they joined him. 'This is Laird Robertson.'

'Ah!' Robert de Bruce said, as the Robertson bowed his head to him. 'Was it not you who was responsible for harassing the Sheriff of Perth so much that he rode for the border as though the devil himself was on his heels?'

'It was m'Lord.'

'And this,' Wallace continued, 'is John Edward of Scotstoun, the breaker of the bridge over the Forth at Stirling.'

Robert nodded his approval. 'I very much enjoyed that tale. The castle garrison fell trees to strengthen their defences and you then use them as floating battering rams to destroy the bridge. That was most clever. You are indeed fortunate to have such men under your command, Sir William.'

In spite of his feelings about de Bruce's refusal to fully commit himself to the war, John felt himself glowing from the Earl's praise. He could see why men might want to fight for him.

'Sir William, I must take my leave as I should be elsewhere. Congratulations once again. Very well deserved.' Robert then bowed and took his leave.

Edward de Bruce raised his eyebrows in a 'I-told-you-so' gesture and followed in his brother's wake.

'Laird Robertson, let me introduce you to the Bishop of Saint Andrews. A very good and generous friend of ours.' Wallace held out his hand to indicate the Bishop, although the mitre made it impossible to mistake him for anyone else. The Robertson bowed and kissed the proffered ring.

John did the same and stood as Lamberton looked him up and down.

'Am I right in assuming that you are engaged in the scourging of the south?'

'Yes, Lord Bishop.' John replied, feeling himself perspire under the Bishop's unwavering gaze.

'Then you must burn faster. Leave nothing for the English when they come. The further they march without finding sustenance, the faster Edward's coffers will empty. War is fuelled by gold as much as it is by blood.'

'Yes, m'Lord.' John continued, a little hesitantly lest he should speak out of turn. 'Talking of gold, I have a man in my camp who I should introduce to you. He is a foreign money-lender by the name of Malachi Crawcour. He says he would do business with those opposed to the English King.'

The Bishop's eyes widened in surprise. 'Malachi Crawcour? Banker to the English crown? Are you sure?'

'I have no reason to doubt him.' John replied as he exchanged glances with Wallace.

133

'Bring him to me in Selkirk this evening.' Lamberton ordered. 'This may be very good for us if it is true. Very good indeed. Bless you my son. Bless you.'

The Bishop turned back to Wallace. 'You see William, the pieces fall into place if we have patience. For your part, you must take friends where you can find them. The Bruce and Comyn will undoubtedly bend the knee to King Edward if it keeps their hopes of the throne alive. Nevertheless, we must strive to stay in their good graces. It is a victory for us if they merely stay upon the sidelines for now. They will, I am certain, come to our side once they accept that Edward will never release his grip on the Scottish crown and that he is determined to outdo his weakling father by winning two crowns instead of losing one. Only when that realisation dawns upon them, will they plunge in with us to snatch it from Edward by force. Then we will have to find a way of deciding which of their noble arses will perch upon the throne. That day will surely come and all we can do is wait for events to so unfold.'

'You know me well, Lord Bishop. I will leave the politics and scheming to you and our friend Wishart. I will do what I do best and fight on, fight on.'

Lamberton laughed mirthlessly. 'That you must William, for Edward marches already and means to have your head.'

11

Edward Plantagenet could seldom be accused of wallowing in self-pity, but few would have condemned him for descending into that state as he sat shivering in his pavilion. The fabric walls snapped and shuddered as they were buffeted by the bitingly cold and violent gusts of wind which blew off the churning, grey North Sea. Though his accommodations offered greater comfort than the simple structures suffered by his troops, they did not escape the punishments meted out by the accursed Scottish climate. The sodden material sagged as it grew heavy from the incessant rain and water dripped ceaselessly, leaving puddles on the earthen floor. The constant dampness caused great, spreading patches of mildew, which gave off a stench of corruption and decay. The King pulled his furs around him and struggled to stop his shivering. He closed his eyes as he reflected on what had brought him to this miserable place.

The march on Scotland had begun so positively. Much better, in fact, than he had expected. He had arrived at the parliament in York fully expecting to face strong opposition from the magnates and demands for further concessions in return for their men and arms. He and Langton had already discussed what further compromise could be offered if it was needed and he was both surprised and delighted to find that none was required. This was, in part, a happy consequence of the previous year's debacle at Stirling. The scale of the slaughter there had left few noble families who had not lost one or more of their kin dead upon that bloody field. Set on vengeance, many of the great families had thrown in their lot with him most enthusiastically. The loss of a few hundred noble knights seemed, to him at least, a small price to pay. For those who had not suffered personal loss, there was yet a keenness to put the rebellious Scots in their place and renew English pride once more. Such faithfulness to the Great Cause was further inflamed courtesy of the Scots nobles themselves. By failing to appear at the parliament as commanded, Edward had been able to declare them traitors and disinherit them one and all. It was this, and the resulting prospect of winning vacant Scottish lands and titles, that most motivated the aristocracy to rally to his standard.

In spite of his miserable condition at the Kirkliston camp, Edward laughed dryly. 'Greed will always prevail.'

This thought prompted him to think of the visit he had received on the eve of the York parliament and, despite his current lamentable circumstances, it did not fail to bring a smile to his lips. He had been told that Robert de Bruce had arrived at the gates of York incognito, riding without his standards and his men without livery. As the Bruce was ushered into his presence, he knew that the Scottish magnate had not come to pledge his fealty and commit men to the campaign ahead. If this had been his intention, he would have ridden through the gates with all fanfare and not slithered in, his face hidden by his cloak.

'De Bruce,' he greeted him coldly, 'it is good to see you here. Your men will be a welcome addition to my force.'

The Scots noble had knelt to kiss his hand, but then, as anticipated, had begun his usual dance, squirming like a snake in danger of tying itself in knots. The weasel words had flowed from him like the squirting piss from a drunkard's pizzle. Bereft of originality, the self-seeking proposal was the same as it always was. In return for some half-starved infantry and a score of broken horse, all the bold Bruce wanted was a crown upon his head. When, at last, he had spilled his guts and stilled his forked tongue, the King had made him wait in silence for his response. Only when the space between them weighed agonizingly heavily, had the King deigned to speak.

'Do you think we have nothing better to do, than to win kingdoms for you?'

Edward had delighted in the Bruce's reaction. He had jerked back as if the words had stung him physically, his deep brown eyes wide with shock and hurt. His mouth had opened and closed as if in search of words that stayed beyond his grasp. To the King, it called to mind a guppy gasping on a riverbank. The King had struggled to maintain his composure then and keep his face set straight. Only when the deflated claimant had left his presence did he allow himself to vent. He had laughed and laughed until he was overtaken by a fit of coughing, which almost made him vomit. He did not know what had given him more satisfaction, delivering these words to Robert within the walls of York or speaking the self-same words to his father, the elder Bruce, several years before. The father had withered so much beneath their weight, he had retired immediately to his Essex estates and had not set foot in Scotland since. With luck, the rebuke would serve to similarly emasculate the son. In any case, the loss of the support of the Scots nobles mattered not.

He smiled wryly at the memory of the great army that had gathered beneath the walls of York. The rows of tents had stretched out far into the distance, their population exceeding that of the city itself. The smoke from the hundreds of fires had shrouded the surrounding land in grey clouds for miles around. The force itself surpassed any that he had ever commanded, their numbers exceeding those of the crusading army he had led to the Holy Land, that which had conquered the rebellious Welsh and the force which had defeated the Scots at Dunbar less than two years ago. The pay ledgers stored in the chests at his feet recorded twenty-six thousand infantry and a mightily impressive three thousand cavalry. There was not a king or prince in Europe who could boast such martial might. When the colossal column had begun to wind its way onto the northern road, there was no one present who doubted that the treacherous Scots would be crushed and their lands conquered within a few short weeks. The crash of so many boots and horses' hooves shook the very ground as they thundered on the road and their echo had rumbled around the hills announcing their advance. Edward's stoop had disappeared and he rode proud and upright at the head of this invincible horde.

The difficulties had begun within a few short days of their departure. Their progress through Northern England and the south of Scotland was much slower than they had hoped. The hundreds of wagons transporting the supplies necessary for the campaign moved at a crawl, the horses and marching men ahead having churned the roads to mud. The toil and drudgery alone would have been enough to sap the early eagerness and enthusiasm of the campaign, but the bleak and empty land they passed through served to blunt the zeal of even the most fervent of participants. Not a single structure stood intact to offer shelter from the perpetually pissing rain. Villages once teeming with life, were now blackened, empty shells. The marching men had soon lost count of the many tattered skeletons which lay abandoned and mouldering at the roadside. No man's soul could be shielded from this devastation and ruin. Edward himself had to concede that he had not expected the Scots to be so brutal, especially in their own land. Though their savage thoroughness caused him suffering, he could not but admire their ruthlessness. He would have demanded no less himself. He had pushed on regardless, certain that such desperate action would only serve to delay the inevitable, final conquest.

The first slivers of doubt and fear had only begun to creep into his mind when they were a few days south of Edinburgh. The expected confrontation with Wallace's forces had not occurred. Worse than that, his scouts and spies had been unable to so much as locate the Scottish forces. Edward knew all too well that it could prove disastrous if the Scots continued to evade him. His supplies were dwindling and the English nobles had already started with their complaints. Having reached parts of Scotland which had not been burned, he vigorously set about provoking the Scots to action. Towns and villages were put to the torch and their people subjected to vicious torture. Burning, raping, flogging, hanging and stoning were employed wherever his men could reach. The old, young, men, women, boys and girls, few were spared and then, only those who were to carry word of these outrages to the ears of the Scottish leadership. Near two weeks of this barbarous desecration yielded no response or retaliation and the Scots stayed hidden beyond the reach of Edward's great but impotent force.

It was the parlous state of Edward's supplies which had forced him to move further north and pitch camp at Kirkliston to await the expected arrival of ships from the south. After five days of fruitlessly staring out at a grim and swelling sea, which remained stubbornly empty of ships, had he retired to his pavilion and shut himself away. A further three days had passed before he was roused by shouts and cheers from the encampment below. In his haste and excitement, he had burst from his tent without his cloak and immediately caught sight of sails on the far horizon. The damned, never-ending wind had then, at last, done service by bringing the merchantman quickly to the dock.

'At last!' Edward had hissed, his fist clenched in triumph. Now that the ships had begun to arrive, he could wait the bastards out. He knew that to have been starved into defeat and hurried retreat would have sounded the death knell for his ambitions for Scotland. He stayed in the biting wind until the unloading had begun and then returned, shivering but reinvigorated, to the shelter of his pavilion. He had barely rested his arse upon the seat when cheering broke out anew. He stiffly regained his feet and stepped quickly to the flap. He squinted and scanned the empty sea until he spotted a second set of sails, white against the dark, foreboding sea. Satisfied, he returned to warm himself afore the fire.

He was still rubbing his fingers above the flames when a servant announced the arrival of a noble delegation. This was one encounter with the magnates that he was certain he would enjoy. He had suffered enough of their niggling complaints and veiled criticism these last weeks

141

and meant to savour this opportunity to remind them of his superiority and experience when it came to martial campaigns. He warmed himself a little more, judging that it would be of benefit to his nobles to remember that he, as King, did not jump at their every beck and call. Ever vigilante for any advantage he could gain over these ungrateful lords, he let them chill awhile, until his fingertips were no longer white with cold.

With his back to the brazier, he pulled himself to his full, impressive height and fixed a smile upon his lips as the magnates filed in.

'By God, it is good to see you!' He boomed cheerfully, as Roger Bigod, Earl of Norfolk, Humphrey de Bohun, Earl of Hereford, Henry de Lacey, Earl of Lincoln and Anthony Bek, Bishop of Durham filed into the pavilion and bowed before him. These self-same men had sought to neuter him and reduce both his powers and income in return for supporting this campaign. Now that the supply crisis had passed, he had no intention of sparing them from his censure of their fainthearted conduct and near panic of recent days. Several times he had been forced to have his servants send them and their emissaries away, to spare his ears from their persistent whining and wailing. His eyes sparkled as he prepared to flay them with blistering reprimands, several of which he had been refining and turning over in his mind. 'I hear that the supply ships have arrived, just as I said they would.'

The four men dropped their heads in unison, as though afraid to meet their King's piercing gaze.

'Did I not tell you so? How could you doubt your King?'

'My Lord.' Bohun began hesitantly.

'My Lord indeed.' Edward retorted, fixing him with a glare.

'No, My Lord.' Bohun insisted, with an edge to his voice which Edward did not miss. 'Two merchantmen have docked and unload upon the quay. Our men have crowded there in hope of bread and ale.'

'Well, break it out man and let them eat their fill! There will be plenty more where that came from. You do not need me to do your work.' Edward snapped back, irked by his insolent tone.

'My Lord, there is no bread, no barley nor dried fish.' The Bishop interjected softly, his eyes still set upon the ground. 'There is only wine.'

The King reeled at this news, his stomach lurching painfully. 'Wine? What? Both ships?'

'Yes, my Lord. Not a peck of barley, just barrels of French wine.'

Edward fell into his chair as if dizzied by this unwelcome revelation. 'Jesus! It cannot be. I have laid out enough gold to have every ship from here to London anchored in this bay. I have emptied every granary in the south to fill the bellies here. What treachery is this? There is not a storm big enough to have sunk every single ship.'

The magnates fidgeted uncomfortably as their King both riled and raged and flecks of foam gathered at the corners of his mouth.

When the King's fury had died to silence, Norfolk dared enquire, 'And what of the men, my Lord? They have eaten nought these last few days and will make havoc if there is none to have.'

'Then let them drink wine, they will like it well enough. It was intended for you noble lords to drink to our victory.' Edward did not raise his head from his hands as he issued this instruction.

'Is that wise?' Norfolk challenged, though without great conviction.

'You would be wise,' Edward drawled, fixing Norfolk with an icy stare, 'to do as you are bid.'

Once the magnates had made their exit, Edward retired to his bed. He had thought to doze, but was prevented from doing so by a sharp pain that shot through his head as if a spike had been driven into his very skull. The pain was not helped by a growing hubbub at the quayside, which the gusts of wind brought intermittently to his ears. It seemed that there was dancing, as he sometimes caught the tootling of a pipe and, later, the banging of a drum. If he could have risen from his bed, he would have ordered them to silence, but every movement caused more shooting pains, so he chose to remain still instead. It was mid-afternoon before he finally and mercifully drifted off to sleep and so gained some small respite.

He had been asleep for what seemed like minutes, when a cold, gloved hand shook him roughly awake.

'My Lord King, you must awake!'

'My Lord Surrey!' The King exclaimed sleepily, his eyes blinking in the light. 'You disturb my rest.'

'You must come now my Lord. Our army fights itself!'

The sight that greeted Edward when he emerged onto the hill, was one that he would never forget. The slope, which only hours earlier had been lined with neat lines of tents, was now the site of a pitched battle. The brawling men covered all of the ground from the quayside up to the cavalry pens. Bonfires fuelled by the staves of broken barrels burned brightly in the dusk, their flames spreading to the tents in several places.

'Christ! Edward spat, aghast at the hellish scene before him. 'What in God's name is happening?'

'The Welsh and English infantry fight over the last of the wine.' Warenne, Earl of Surrey informed him. 'Some fool ordered it distributed to men with empty stomachs. If we do not put a stop to this, all is lost.'

'To see the death of an army is a terrible thing. It can disintegrate before your very eyes.' Edward appeared dazed, almost in a trance.

The Earl grasped the King's shoulder and shook it hard. 'Edward, you must act now!'

Edward snapped out of his shocked state and instructed Surrey to rouse his knights. 'No time

145

for saddle or armour. Order them to ride with lances into their midst and scatter them about. No matter if they break some heads.'

Surrey hurried off as fast as he could and shouted breathless orders as he went. Only minutes passed before the cavalry thundered down the slope. Even men high on drink will shy away from heavy horse and the men parted hurriedly at their approach. A few still rolled and wrestled on the ground, but the majority separated and backed away, ready to take to their heels. The King watched impassively as one knight broke ranks and spurred his horse to where he and Surrey stood.

'Lord King, the Welsh are most aggrieved and threaten to switch sides to fight with the Scots. The situation is quite tense and I am unsure as to how I should proceed.'

Edward met the knight's gaze, a thin smile upon his face. 'Tell them that I care not if they join our enemies. We shall beat them both in a day.'

A puzzled look spread across the young knight's face and he turned quizzically to Surrey.

'Turn your men and have them ride down the Welsh.' The Earl commanded. 'That should set them to fleeing and bring their English fellows to their senses.'

He looked to the King, who nodded his agreement. He did as he was commanded and the Welsh were soon dispersed with only eighty fatalities. Among their number were three clerics who had been caught up in the melee when trying to separate the two warring sides. It was a pity, but no great matter now that discipline was restored.

His duty done, the young knight tramped wearily to his tent. He paused as he caught sight of something on the ridge beyond the camp. The fading light caused him to strain his eyes before he brought the figure into focus. There, beyond the sentry posts, sat a lone horseman, a black dog at his side.

12

Walter Langton, Lord High Treasurer and
Bishop of Coventry and Lichfield was not a
happy man. The ride from Newcastle had been
the worst he had ever suffered. There had been
not a day's respite from the damp and the
pouring rain. Even a whole night suspended
over a roaring fire would not dry his sodden
cloak. His thighs were rubbed raw from where
his soggy trews had scoured his flesh as they
scraped against the swollen leather of his saddle.
His boots, so recently purchased, were already
mouldered white. His informants had advised
him of the destruction of the North, but their
intelligence had not prepared him for its reality.
The devastation had made him melancholy and
he found that he could not shake it off. His
mood had not improved when he had received
the news that Edward was still encamped to the
west of Edinburgh. He had expected that he
would reach the King only after the battle was
won. Each day without a victory meant that
gold flowed out of the Treasury, while nothing
flowed back in. The Riccardi and Crawcour
gold was already spent and that lately squeezed

from the persecuted Jews was paid out as quickly as it was received.

The sight of the encampment before him only served to dampen his spirits further. The rows of tents were not crisp and neat, as they had been before the walls of York. Their fabric sagged under the weight of water and was smeared with dirt and soot, giving the site an air of bedraggled indiscipline. Gone too was the excited and enthusiastic hustle and bustle of York, replaced instead with subdued and lethargic indolence amongst the men, most of whom were huddled atent as though they lacked the energy or the will to venture out. Worse still was the far side of the camp, down towards the quay. The remains of large fires scarred the grass and blackened tent frames lay upon the ground. The earth was churned to mud as if by a hundred charging horse. Even the smell of shit, a feature of any place where large numbers of men gathered, was sour and foul as though infected with disease. The portents were not good as Langton rode towards the sentry post.

'What men are these?' The Bishop asked, indicating a large group of men digging in the muddy earth outside the limits of the camp.

'Bastard Welsh!' The grizzled sentry replied. 'Them's a punishment company sent to bury their own dead.' He pointed beyond the diggers, further down the slope, at rows of corpses laid shroudless upon the ground. 'If it were up to me, they'd join their fellows in the ground.'

'Was there an engagement? I thought the Scots evaded us.' Langton enquired, hoping that the savages were finally being drawn out of their holes.

The sentry leaned hard on his spear and spat a gobbet of phlegm in the general direction of the punishment company. 'There was a fight, that much is true, but not with the Scots. Those theivin' whores thought to mess with Lincoln men and came off the worse for it. If the nobs had not ridden them down, we'd have killed the lot of them.'

Langton sighed and rolled his eyes. The situation was more dire than he had feared.

'M'Lord,' the sentry pleaded, 'would you have a crust to spare. I've not had a bite for days. They say the ships is coming, but they deliver only wine. My belly won't stop grumblin' and aches from being empty.'

The Bishop turned to scan the white-capped sea and cursed silently to find it empty apart from one small merchant ship tied up at the quay. There should have been sails as far as the eye could see. Waving his servant forward, he ordered him to give the man a loaf. He rode into the camp to the sound of the man warning off his fellows as they crowded round to share his prize.

Langton had never thought to see his King in such a diminished condition. He did not rise to greet him, but stayed huddled by the fire, holding his furs tight around himself. His flesh was an unhealthy shade of grey, his shoulders were slouched and his left eyelid, which had always drooped slightly, hung half-closed, giving him the appearance of a man deep in his cups. Though he was near sixty, Langton had never seen him as an old man, not until now at least. The Bishop's heart sank to see his King so reduced. Unpopular with the magnates and despised by Edward's son, Langton knew that his fortunes were inextricably linked with those of Edward. Without the King's protection, he doubted that he would last a month. He set about coaxing his patron back to life.

Edward glanced at Langton and gave voice to his misery. 'Curse this wretched country. Everything thing that touches it turns instantly to shit. A pox on its miserable, treacherous nobles, who know no constancy. Like leeches they suck the very blood from me, but will give nothing in return. Not one of those penny-pinching, grasping bastards has lifted so much as one finger to aid me. Selfish and ungrateful, they look only to themselves. To think of what I have done for them without the slightest recompense. They would happily leave their King to starve, marooned in this Godforsaken place. Not one word of Wallace do they bring to me. It is as if they wish him to prevail.'

If Langton possessed one singular talent, it was his ability to draw Edward from his rages and back to sanity. Few others shared this capacity and either sat in silence till his spleen was vented or interjected and risked the fury being turned on them. Intervention was a perilous gamble and he had seen earls, lords and bishops showered in bile and spittle and thrown out in disgrace for a few ill-judged words. He

151

could not articulate his method, as he acted only as his instincts guided him.

'Of course, they wish Wallace to prevail, my Lord. You have called them traitor and disinherited them. Their lands and titles will be forever lost if you are victorious.'

Edward turned his head as if he had forgotten that Langton stood at his side. He locked the Bishop in his terrible, intimidating glare. Langton forced himself to hold the gaze, even although the cruelty and hatred in those eyes caused his pulse to quicken.

Forcing a smile to his unwilling lips, he continued. 'Which is just as well, we shall destroy all of our enemies at one sweep and clear the shit away.'

Edward's stare wavered almost imperceptibly and Langton silently breathed a sigh of relief. He knew that he had him on the hook. Now to see if he could keep him there.

'Tis true Langton. I should be done with them all at once. Clear the shit away.' The King rose slowly to his feet and began to pace, something which helped him think. 'But what about the supplies Langton? Where are all my ships? How are we to prevail if my men and horses starve?'

'We must have the courage to wait it out. How many times did defeat and failure seem inevitable when you were conquering the rebellious Welsh? Their lands were impenetrable, their towns impossible to hold. Now your great castles hold the whole country in your peace. All of that was achieved through your great courage, your ability to remain steadfast when lesser men cried defeat.'

'You speak true, Lord Bishop, as you always do. A thousand times the nobles begged me to retreat. With each and every setback they implored me to back down, to treat with the Welsh nobility and give away my claim. Who now is the Prince of Wales? Not Llywelyn ap Gruffudd or his issue, but my own son. I had Llywelyn crowned with ivy to mock his claim to kingship and his head still sits upon a spike in the Tower.'

'Aye, my Lord, without you he would yet be Prince of Wales. Hold fast here and we will yet see the head of Wallace skewered on its own spike alongside that false prince.'

'If I had yielded to the snivelling nobles then, I would not have won that prize. I must close my ears to them and be true to my conviction. There is a kingdom to be won, but only if I stiffen their spines.'

With Edward back in the saddle, Langton allowed himself a smile. 'Leave the ships to me, my Lord, I will not have your army starve. But first let me cheer you with a happy account of my business with the Jews.

'I would hear that account, Lord Bishop, I need something to lift my spirits.'

Langton's account of the treatment of the Jews was essentially factual, as he was too careful to put himself in a position where he could be later caught out in a lie. But in the telling of the tale, there was both light and shade and he used both skilfully. The aspects which would gratify the King were laid out in the light, whilst those which might displease him were carefully hid from sight. The Bishop was careful to omit mentioning the many individuals who had escaped the net. He was greatly relieved that the King did not enquire about the fate of Crawcour, as that was far from a happy tale. There had been no firm sight or sound of him, leaving Langton clinging to a rumour that he had loaded his family and riches onto a ship and sailed for lands unknown. He also failed to mention just how much he had gained personally from the exercise. To have doubled his own fortune might, at first glance, appear to have been excessive, but that did not take into account just how hard he had worked to extract it.

The King took great pleasure from hearing about the vast amounts of gold that the Jews had contributed to the Treasury. Langton did not see any reason to burden the King with the knowledge that these amounts would keep his army in the field for a week at most. Edward had never appreciated just how quickly his schemes emptied the Treasury and Langton had been forced to become very adept at keeping financial crises at bay and very creative at identifying and exploiting new sources of income. The truth was that the Treasury was just days from collapse and the Bishop was relying heavily on providence to stave disaster off. If nothing came up, he might have to resort to prayer, but that desperate stage had not yet been reached.

The greater part of his account, that which was intended to most distract the King, was that concerning the methods employed to persuade the Jews to give up the locations of their hidden riches. One tale made him laugh so much that he almost seemed restored. Although the particular Jew's name escaped him, Langton regaled Edward with a description of how much torture he had endured before he finally broke and spilled his guts. With every finger snapped and his knuckles reduced to mush, the stubborn man had refused to betray his gold. Hours upon the rack had separated all his limbs, but still he would not talk. The hot iron was not enough to persuade him, though it left barely an inch of flesh that had not sizzled and had cooked his plums right through. The great spiked shaft had left his arse in ruins, but, though he screamed most horribly, he would give nothing away. It was only when they drowned him, that he begged to be released. They had let him thrash a while longer, before letting him confess. Almost as soon as the details had been taken down, his heart stopped in his chest and he slumped down dead, his body still in the ducking tub. Though Edward had much enjoyed this report, it was the punchline that caused him so much merriment that Langton feared that he too would fall down dead. The idiot Jew had endured such punishment for a meagre bag of coin, the contents of which were scarcely enough to buy a decent horse.

'But why in God's name did he not just say?' Edward guffawed, tears streaming from his eyes.

'Tis no wonder they are rich, if they defend each penny with their lives.'

With the King back in good spirits, Langton rose to take his leave. 'I am eager to engage my informants, my Lord. I have outlaws and ships to find, if our enterprise is to succeed.'

Edward rose to his feet, his face still flushed with hilarity. 'I will need you here tomorrow evening. I want you to be a witness when the magnates line up to kiss my arse. All of their estates are deep in hock to the Jews. Now that I have freed them from their debts, I expect that they will be more faithful and obedient.'

'That,' Langton replied, 'I would like to see.'

Edward reached out and clasped the Bishop's upper arm tightly in his grasp. 'It is good to have you here Walter. You must stay by my side until this business is done.'

The frigid, Scottish air refreshed Langton as he stepped out from the pavilion. Satisfied that the immediate crisis had been averted, he set immediately to work on avoiding the next.

Pointing to the merchantman still moored at the quayside, he growled at his retainer. 'Seize the captain of that ship and find me a place where we can do our work. It will be a long night.'

The captain of his guard led him a mile along the coast to a small, poorly built church. His men had already started to clear the pews when a small, balding priest appeared at his side. Short, nervous and timid, Langton guessed that he was the younger son of some miserable, impoverished, Scottish noble. His robes were worn shiny with use and had faded to a patchy, dark grey. Irritated by the constant, nervous hand-wringing, Langton snapped at him.

'What is it?'

'I am the priest here.' Though he spoke most quietly, his rough, Scots accent vexed Langton intensely.

'Why have you not run off with the others? You know that a vast army sits just along the coast. I can scarce believe that you have not been strung up from a tree already.'

'I am the priest here.' He repeated timidly. 'I stayed to protect the kirk.'

Langton looked the priest up and down and concluded that a stiff gust of wind would be enough to knock him over. 'How? I doubt that a cripple would be much discouraged by your presence. And why bother? I have sties more impressive than this. My pigs would turn up their snouts if I were to house them in a pile of stones such as this. If you must protect it, do it from over there. We just need its use this one night.'

Langton turned at the sound of the kirk door crashing open and watched as two of his men dragged a body up the aisle.

'Any trouble?'

'None, my Lord,' the captain of his guard replied. 'He came without a fuss. Be careful though, he did piss himself as we dragged him here.'

Langton wrinkled his nose as the tang of hot urine reached his nostrils.

'We found this in his cabin,' the captain said, as he held out a rich leather purse, heavy with gold.

'Well, well.' Langton purred. 'How did a humble sailor come by so much gold?'

The ship's captain was wide-eyed with fear and shivered as he lay upon the cold, stone floor. He shuddered violently, partly due to having been dragged out into the night in only a thin tunic and partly because he was terrified. He stammered and stuttered through his chattering teeth, but was silenced by the Bishop.

'Hush! Hush now. Say not a single word. Anything that comes out of your mouth now, I shall surely treat as lies. I find that a little suffering does wonders for a man's tongue. It does seem to grease the truth, so it easily slips out.' He turned now to his captain. 'I am afraid that I have been remiss. I have come out this evening without my implements. We shall have to improvise.'

The captain pulled a thin-bladed dagger from his belt and offered it to the Bishop, his eyebrow arched as if questioning its suitability.

'An excellent choice Browby. Now strip him and pin him to the floor.'

It was now that the timorous priest found his voice. 'Stop! You must stop now. This is sacrilege. You cannot harm this man on consecrated ground.'

'It is not sacrilege if we do God's work. This man has sinned against his King and must do penance for this sin. Now stand back and let us do our work.'

158

'Who are you to say that it is God's work, when you do evil in this place?'

'I am the Bishop of Coventry and Lichfield and outrank a common priest. You must do as you are commanded and leave us to our business.'

If the man had not been so irritating, Langton might have admired him for this pathetic display of courage. He was clearly terrified and intimidated by the appearance of armed men in his church, yet he steeled himself to do what he thought was right. Tired of his whining, Langton punched him viciously on the nose, shattering the bone with a crunch and sending him sprawling to the floor in a spray of bright, red blood.

'If he speaks again, cut his scrawny throat!' He ordered the largest of his men.

'Here? In the church?' The guard asked, his voice betraying his reluctance to obey the command.

'Christ!' Langton snapped. 'Take him outside and introduce him to your boots. Just make sure he cannot crawl back in. I would see this business done without these tiresome interruptions.'

The captain of the merchantman screamed and squirmed as the fingernails of his right hand were prised off with the skinny dagger. Although small and wiry, it had taken four of Langton's men to hold him still whilst the procedure was completed.

Langton crouched down and held the purse out towards the sailor's wide, swivelling eyes.

'This is an awful lot of gold for a man like you to have. How long would it take you to earn this amount honestly? A year?'

'Near two year,' their captive groaned, 'maybe more.'

Langton bounced the purse in his hand causing the coins to chink together. 'Two years? That long? This would not keep me in cheese for a single year.'

Langton's captain looked at him quizzically. 'Really?'

Realizing that he had said too much, Langton lied. 'I exaggerate of course.' It would take more than a year for the captain of his guard to receive a similar purse from the Bishop's coffers.

Turning back to the prone sailor, he gently probed for information on the source of the purse of gold. In truth, the man could not unburden himself quickly enough and the story soon became most clear. By the time a further three fingernails had been removed from the man's left hand, Langton was satisfied that he had it all. His mind whirred away at several trains of thought, all at the same time.

'Right,' he said, addressing his captain, 'that filthy Jew has spent his gold bribing captains to delay their arrival here. The longer they tarry, the more gold they will receive. At this very moment, near twenty ships are at anchor off Berwick. We must get them here quickly. Take twenty men and this man's ship and speed their journey here. Take him with you, so that they can see what they will suffer if they continue to defy their King.'

'My Lord?' Browby intoned, glancing towards their prisoner, the question clear from his expression.

'Quite right Browby. A few ragged fingers may not be sufficient for our purpose. Take an eye and an arm. Their absence will have greater impact.'

The sailor's eye was popped easily and the clear jelly ran down his cheek. The arm was another matter, as he struggled and writhed so much, it was impossible to remove it cleanly. After much hacking and sawing, it was removed, but it was a sorry, ragged mess. Even searing it in the fire did not improve it much.

The Bishop watched his men ride off and sighed with satisfaction at a good day's work. With the King revived and the supply problem near solved, his spirits had improved quite markedly. Sometimes he did marvel at his own handiwork, but he never paused to gloat for long. As he kicked his horse towards the camp, his mind was already focused on how to winkle the sly and cowardly Scots out from wherever they skulked.

13

The return to Scotstoun had been just the tonic
the lads required. Weeks of burning and
despoiling the countryside had left them
exhausted and dirty with soot. They had cheered
when Wallace had given them the permission to
take a short leave to transport their hard-won
spoils home. They had left the patriot army
encamped by the Allan Water, in deep forest at
the foot of the Ochil Hills. The position had
been carefully chosen to allow them to pour over
the Forth in pursuit of the English baggage train
if Edward's army retreated and provided them
with easy escape if the English were to advance.

As the Edward boys travelled towards Perth,
they anticipated a warm welcome home, as two
of their three heavy wagons were laden with
grain and corn. What they had stripped from
northern England would more than replace what
the village had lost in the year's poor harvest.
The contents of the third wagon would, they
were certain, be the cause of even more
excitement. Its heavy wheels fair thundered
under the weight of every item of value they had
been able to plunder from English lands. Though
the bulk of gold and silver was carried on their

162

saddles, the wagon still rattled with valuable things. Goblets and plates of silver, good oak tables and chairs, swords, axes, forks, hoes and bejewelled daggers had all been thrown in together. There was even a great anvil and a wooden plough bound with iron. Each item had a story to tell and the Edward boys looked forward to relating each one.

Their reception had exceeded even their fevered imaginings and a feast of celebration and homecoming was held in the square. Cattle, goats and sheep were slaughtered and slowly roasted over the fire pits. Casks of ale were broken open and the lads' goblets were never allowed to empty as they held court. As the air was filled with the tantalising aroma of animal fat spitting in the flames, the cover was pulled from the wagon and the spoils of pillage shared with the villagers. Not a single family was left without a gift. John's father, Andrew, now more interested in agriculture than adventure, marvelled at his plough. Its construction was so sturdy he doubted that it would ever break, even on the stony ground down by the loch. It was all that his wife, Isobelle, could do to stop him from trying it out, there upon the square. John's Uncle Angus, father of Eck, fair whooped with delight to see the great anvil, which was much larger and more finely wrought than his own. If he could have induced anyone to help him, he would have had it carried and immediately installed in the smithy. Father MacGregor's eyes glinted as he received silver goblets for the kirk and they glinted even more brightly when presented with a fine English cavalry sword. The enthusiastic priest near took off a parishioner's head when he swished it about to test its balance and weight. The widow Cumming had blushed when a fine, silver comb was pushed into her hands. Her cheeks burned even brighter when the village women suggested that she use it to smooth her locks to attract the attentions of a new man.

John Edward saw little of these smiling faces, as he had eyes for only one. He had seen his Lorna's slim figure the second she had stepped onto the square and his eyes never left her as he squeezed his way through the throng. His heart thumped as if he had run a mile, though he had moved only twenty short paces. He drank in her pale, white skin and silken hair as dark as night. Tears of joy hung heavy in his eyes as he wrapped his wife in his tight embrace. He kissed her soft lips and breathed her fragrance in. Her slender, little fingers hotly grasped his cheek and her delicate white teeth nibbled at his tongue. When he finally surfaced, he felt as though he was in a dream.

'Did you miss me then?' She teased, the rasp in her voice sending shivers up his spine.

'Only in the morning, the afternoon and the night.' He replied, his smile stretched taught from ear to ear. 'Did you miss me too?'

'Only when there was work to do.' The single tear sparkling on her left cheek gave away her lie.

'I have something for you.' John said, still drinking in her beauty and unwilling to release her from his arms.

'I know, I can feel it.' She whispered back mischievously.

'Not that!' He laughed. 'Something better.'

'So I would hope.'

Their reunion was interrupted by Scott clapping John hard upon the shoulder. 'Put him down Lorna. We need to go home and get ourselves ready for the feast. This one is in sore need of a dip in the loch, if he is to be fit for civilised company.'

But there was work to do before they could see to their appearance. In the houses of both Andrew and Angus Edward, their sons set to digging up the floors.

'There's precious little space for any more loot.' Andrew declared. 'We dug up half the house to bury what you took at Stirling Bridge.' This time they had to dig far deeper, for they had much coin to hide.

Once the job was done, John, Scott and Eck strode down to the loch and stripped out of their clothes. As they soaked in the still, frigid waters, Isobel came and collected up their crumpled and soiled garb.

'Goodness!' She exclaimed in her French accent tinged heavily with Scots. 'These will take some washing. I will need to let them steep. I will find something else for you to wear tonight.'

By the time they made their way into the square, the sky had darkened and the fire-pits

165

were sending showers of sparks into the night air. The whole village was gathered and they chattered excitedly as dripping meat was cut from the spits and distributed to one and all. The din died down when the Edwards took their place and the townsfolk crowded round, demanding to hear their tales. A smiling John took centre stage, with Scott chipping in with missed details or to correct him when he was mistaken. Eck, for his part, was content to lean back in the shadows and drink his fill of ale.

John started by describing the great Scots army that had crossed the border into England and the destruction they had wrought. The village folk lapped it up delightedly, having themselves suffered horribly at the hands of the detested English. They were rapt to hear how the loot, which had been so recently distributed, had been won and from where it had been seized. John told how the silver comb, now in the possession of Mrs Cumming, had been found outside a manor house not three miles from Carlisle. He surmised that the lady of that manor must have dropped it in her haste, as she scurried off to evade the advancing soldiers. He also told how his father's plough had been found abandoned in that same manor's barn. To the delight of his uncle, he told how it had taken eight strong men to lift his new anvil from a blacksmith's shop near Newcastle. Each tale of theft in England brought murmurs from the crowd, as though learning of their provenance served to enhance the value of their gifts.

166

As John had scarce touched his beef or taken even a sip of ale, Scott jumped in to tell of their castle siege. The picture he painted had them squirming in their seats. They cheered when told of Eck's bravery as crossbow bolts thumped into the ground around him. They cheered louder still to hear of his battle with an English knight and of how he had insulted him before he killed the man. The villagers cooed most excitedly to hear that their Edward boys had captured and destroyed an enemy castle. It would be fair to say that Scott stuck mainly to the truth, his only deviations being intended to entertain his kin. In this he did good work.

With his belly full and thirst well slaked, John leapt back into the fray. The villagers listened wide-eyed as he told the tale of the knighting of Sir William Wallace. John could tell that they were most impressed by his involvement in the proceedings. For one of their own to have participated in such a historic event was an honour for them all. Such things always happened at a great distance from them and seemed to occur in a completely different world. To hear of wee John Edward signing an official document was something that would be spoken of for years. If that alone was not enough, he had dined with the nobles. Robert de Bruce, the Red Comyn and a Bishop, no less. Though they themselves had done no more than tend their land, they felt their chests puff out with pride at their association.

When the tales were told and carcasses stripped, Scotstoun set about the serious work of emptying every cask of ale. Before too long, a chanter began its skirl and the square was full of dancing feet and swaying bodies.

With his arm around her waist, John leaned into Lorna and watched her gnaw delicately on a rib of beef.

'You'd better no' have too much of that. I don't want you running to fat.'

She leaned away from him and glared with her eyes held wide. 'You saying that I'm fat?'

John made a show of looking her over before he responded. 'Well, maybe a wee bit, just around the belly.'

She squeezed his hand tightly and asked, 'And what do think might have caused it to swell?'

John moved his eyes between her face and her stomach. 'No' the beef then?'

'No. It's no' the beef.'

'You mean?'

'Aye! I mean that.'

Tears jumped into John's eyes and he furiously batted them away. 'Well, how did that happen?'

Lorna shook her head. 'If you don't know that, then I'll be needin' a new husband.'

John laughed with joy and threw his arms around her. 'I'm going to have a son.'

'Or a daughter.' Lorna replied as she squeezed him tightly.

'If she was to be anything like you, then that would be even better.'

They slipped away from the feast as soon as they were able and walked arm in arm to the

168

lochside. It was a short walk, but it took them some time as they stopped every few paces to kiss and embrace and chatter in their excitement.

'If it's a boy, what would you call him?' Lorna asked as they lay down on John's cloak at the water's edge. 'Andrew I'd bet, after your father.'

Nah!' John responded, leaning back on his arms. 'My family's not really one for using the same name for every new generation. Neither Scott nor I were called Andrew.'

'William then, after your great hero.'

'I don't know. I might call him after Al. He's grown to be such a good friend. Can you imagine how proud our Al would be? He'd probably burst.'

'You'll be burst if you call him after Al. Are you remembering what his full name is?'

John exploded with laughter. 'Alphonse! I had forgotten. Maybe not then.'

'What if it's a wee girl?'

'Christ! I don't even want to think about that. Can you imagine our mothers fighting over that? Esmy or Isobelle? Choose one and have the other as an enemy for all eternity.'

'At least my mother wouldn't actually kill us.'

'Aye,' John retorted, waggling his fingers in front of his face, 'She'd just put a spell on us and turn us into frogs.'

Lorna responded by making a most unseemly gesture with her fingers. 'Did you see my mother tonight?'

'Aye,' said John, 'though only very briefly. I was surprised to see that she still has that knight from Stirling Bridge in her captivity. I thought she would have ransomed him long since.'

'I don't think that she's going to ransom him and I don't think he's being held against his will.' Lorna gave John a knowing look.

'No! You mean?'

'I think so. I'm not at her place as much since I moved in with your parents, but when I do go, he's never far from her side. She calls him Nigel.'

'Christ! She's far too old for him. Why doesn't he just walk off? It's hardly as if she could stop him.'

'Maybe it's the fact that a great, big army lies between him and home, but I think it has more to do with my mother's charms. I think he does her good. She looks better every time I see her.'

John shuddered at the thought. 'Let's not speak of them. Did I say that I had something for you?'

'You did indeed.' Lorna replied and squeezed him through his breeches.

Her searching fingers made him quite forget the gold necklace he had brought for her. He kissed her hard and cupped her breast in his hand. 'Will it be alright, you know, with the baby. I wouldn't want to harm it.'

'Unless you have been growing it while you have been away, I'm certain it will be just fine.'

It was just fine. Several times and long into the night.

While Scott and Eck were keen to take to the road and rejoin their comrades, John found the prospect of departure too painful to endure. The lure of his beloved was far more powerful than even the prospect of the great riches to be taken from the English baggage, when their starving army inevitably broke and took to flight. He somehow managed to persuade his brother and his cousin to stay for two more days, but these passed most rapidly and the day of leaving came around much too fast. Once again, the villagers gathered to see their heroes off, filling their ears with good wishes and blessings and thumping their shoulders and backs until they were bruised.

'Looks like you'll no' be leaving empty-handed.' Andrew Edward announced, a grin spread across his face.

John turned in the direction his father had indicated and groaned at the sight of three village boys with packs strapped to their backs.

'You're too young!' He barked. 'Maybe next year. When you're a wee bit bigger.'

The tallest of the three jutted his chin out in defiance and retorted, 'I'm near the same age as your brother. Why shouldn't I come? Are ye wanting to keep all the spoils for yourselves?'

John sighed and looked him up and down. He knew the McAlpine boy and had shared lessons with him when they had learned their letters. He was around fifteen years of age, reasonably tall, stick thin and sported a thin covering of downy hair on his upper lip and chin. There were many boys of his age in the patriot army's ranks, but

John hesitated to pull a Scotstoun lad into a life that was both harsh and dangerous. Neither did he relish the thought of having to return here and tell his mother that her little boy had perished. Mrs McAlpine stood behind her son, her chin set hard in support of her offspring's plea. John knew that, whilst she might be keen to see him set off to seek his fortune, in her grief it was towards him that she would vent her fury.

Before he could respond, the second of the trio stepped forward, his face set in similar, surly defiance. 'It's no' up to you anyway. If you'll no' let us come with you, we'll just follow you anyway. Ye cannae stop us.'

John shook his head and groaned. The Cumming boy looked even younger than the first. He was short, fat and had not a wisp of beard on his face. His mother had cropped his hair to his scalp in a bid to rid him of flechs and, as a consequence, he looked daft as well as young.

The third boy, McAllister the carter's son, said not a word, but stood with a stern and determined expression on his hairless face and with his arms folded tightly across his chest.

'For fuck's sake!' John cursed under his breath. He could see that all three had their parents' support, all of them keen to have one less mouth to feed and further encouraged by dreams of what riches their progeny could win.

Andrew Edward roared with laughter at his son's discomfort. 'How does it feel son? Not so good, eh?'

172

His brother Angus joined in with the laughter. 'Do ye mind us having this self-same conversation with you when you three marched out o' here? It's good to see ye feeling a bit of what we felt then.'

John cursed, but silently this time, as he knew that his father's one good arm could still deliver a good, hard skelp.

'Alright! I cannae stop you from coming, but you'll have to keep up.'

He and Lorna had said their goodbyes in the wee small hours of the morning, but he still embraced her long and hard before taking to his horse.

'Let's go!' He instructed Scott and Eck. 'If we gallop ahead, they'll soon lose heart and turn their heads for home.'

14

By the time the Edward boys stopped to make their camp, the new recruits had long disappeared from sight. In fact, the youths were all but forgotten as the fire was lit and beef skewered for the roasting. The cousins rested their weary bones and stretched out upon the ground, their conversation focused on the journey ahead and what might await them at its end. Eck, as now was his habit, busied himself sharpening his swords, the light scraping of the whetstone honing the blades to razor sharpness. They had scarcely begun to bite into their feast when Eck nodded towards the road.

'Looks like you were wrong, John. They're more stubborn and persistent than you thought.'

John sighed with exasperation. 'Then we had better ride even harder the morn.'

The three Scotstoun lads lumbered into camp, their faces red and coated in sweat and grime from the road. Throwing himself to the ground by the fire, McAlpine groaned.

'I'm bloody dying here. We've run for most of the day. What's for our supper?'

With that, he rolled onto his side and stretched out a dirty hand towards the dripping chunks of meat. He withdrew it quickly, but not fast enough to avoid the flat of Eck's blade rapping him across the knuckles.

'That's the first rule.' Scott said, fixing the boys with a disapproving glare. 'Ye get your own food. If you can't manage that, then you're no use to anybody and you might as well go home to your mammies now.'

'We're no' going anywhere!' McAlpine retorted. 'Nice try though.'

He then dug into his pack until, after much rooting around, he found what he was looking for and produced a package wrapped in a worn and stained cloth. With some gusto, he unfolded the cloth to reveal a stack of thick oatcakes. He passed one to each of his fellow recruits and balanced another on his skinny thigh while he closed the package up and returned it to his pack. Minutes passed in which the only sound was that of teeth crunching into biscuit. Most men will take their time with such hard tack, but the boys were so hungry they rushed their meal, heedless of the very real risk of breaking their teeth. As soon as the last crumbs had disappeared into their mouths, their eyes, almost in unison, turned back to the roasting meat, their yearning writ large on their faces.

The Cumming boy turned his dirty, round face to them and narrowed his eyes as if he was about to make a pronouncement of some import. 'How about this? If I give you a song, you give us a piece of that beef.' He subconsciously rubbed his belly as he made his tentative offer.

'It would have to be one hell of a good song for that much beef.' Scott laughed as he spoke and his brother grinned at Cumming's cheek. 'Let's hear your song and then we will judge what it's worth.'

The young lad cleared his throat with such an expression of seriousness on his face, that John and Scott could not help but laugh. With his close chopped hair and rosy cheeks, he cut a ridiculous figure and they awaited his tuneless screeching with glee. Such entertainment at camp was rare indeed and they settled back to enjoy the coming spectacle. When the Cumming boy opened his mouth, the sound he made was as sweet as any they had heard. Each note was hit perfectly, the melody without a single fault. The song was one which they all knew well, but had never heard performed quite so exquisitely. The ballad told of a poor, young girl, the most beautiful in the land, she fell in love with a farmer boy, who asked her for her hand. Before they could elope to exchange their vows, her furious father killed the lad, and soon she followed him to heaven, as she could not stand to be so sad. As the refrain filled the air around him, John found that his heart was aching and his eyes filled with tears and he was only able to blink them away with some difficulty. When the Cumming boy brought his song to its sad, sad end, he dared not speak lest his voice gave away how deeply it had affected him.

'Good.' Scott declared, nodding his head in appreciation. 'But maybe no' quite good enough for so much beef.'

176

'Come on!' Cumming protested. 'Yer brother was near greetin' at that one.'

John shook his head in denial. 'I got something in my eye. What else can you do?'

The McAllister boy, who had not yet spoken in the Edwards' presence, then piped up and offered to tell a joke. He started shyly, stammering and stumbling over his words, before growing in confidence as he told his tale of the fat farmer, his beautiful, young wife and the handsome goatherd's son. The punchline was so filthy and was delivered with such aplomb, John and Scott rolled around in laughter and even Eck the Black did grin. Scott wiped the tears from his eyes and thrust the skewer of beef into the hands of the young recruits. The Scotstoun boys did not have to walk the next day, but shared their kinsmen's mounts.

The day was winding towards evening when they caught sight of Dunblane Cathedral's great bell-tower through the trees. To see that they were close to their destination gave them renewed energy after a hard day in the saddle. By the time they could clearly make out the wooden framing erected by the masons around the tower, they realised that they had company.

'You see them?' John asked, keeping his head pointed to the front so that the horsemen tracking them would not know that they were observed.

'Aye.' Eck replied. 'Four in the trees on either side. Cavalry, judging by their tunics, though I cannot make out their colours.'

The Scotstoun party continued on regardless, though they were tensed and ready to react if it was needed. Then, as they traversed the long, slow curve in the track leading down into Dunblane, they saw the dozen horsemen who blocked their way.

'Horsemen on the road behind us too.' Eck hissed. 'Let's hope the fuckers are friendly.'

John brought them to a halt three lengths from the horsemen barring their way.

One of their number spurred his horse forward until its muzzle almost touched that of John's mount. The beast snorted aggressively and was only reined-in by its rider hauling sharply on its reins. The rider was dressed in an almost identical fashion to his fellows, with a cylindrical helmet, maille tunic, maille gloves and heavy boots adorned with strips of iron. A heavy sword hung from his side and a battle-axe was strapped to his saddle. The tabard worn over his maille caught John's attention, as it was of rough, unfinished cloth, rather than the more common dyed material which indicated which noble house a soldier belonged to. John reckoned the man to be only a few years older than himself. The many small scars on his face suggested that he was someone who was used to both fighting and training hard. His gaze was direct, unflinching and full of challenge and John returned it in kind.

'Who the fuck are you?' The horseman demanded menacingly.

'I'm John Edward, one of Sir William Wallace's captains. I am on my way to rejoin his force.' John delivered his reply in an even, confident tone, reluctant to give way to this man, even although they were badly outnumbered and would have no choice but surrender their arms if it was so demanded. 'Who the fuck are you?'

The horseman's face lit up in delight and he twisted his head back to share his amusement with his comrades. 'I heard that Wallace is desperate to increase his numbers, but I did not know that he was asking his men to bring their wives.' He leaned to the side to give himself a clearer view of young McAlpine as he sat at John's back. 'She's no' even pretty, I just hope that she can fight.'

John gave out a wry laugh. 'Very good, but if you're done playing the fool, we need to get on.'

'Never heard of a John Edwards, not in Wallace's camp. Who are these other turds?'

'That's my brother, Scott and that is my cousin, Eck.' John responded, ill-temperedly jabbing his thumb in the direction of his companions. 'These three behind are new recruits.'

'Wait a minute now. Eck Edward? I have heard that name before.' He frowned as if he tried to recall some elusive memory and then his eyes widened when he had succeeded. 'Not Eck the Black?'

'Some call me that.' Eck responded. 'But you are the first of John Comyn's men to call me such.'

The man recoiled at Eck's words and he frowned fiercely in denial. 'Who says that we are Comyn's men? I have said no such thing.'

Eck snorted with amusement. 'You may wear your surcoats inside out, but the wind does betray your true colours with every little gust. If you wish to remain incognito, you'd do well to leave them in your camp.'

'Alright. You've got me there right enough. But don't be saying that I told you. The Comyn doesn't want it known that he has thrown his lot in with Wallace.'

'Aye.' John laughed ruefully. 'As usual with your nobles, John Comyn will likely want to keep his options open. If Wallace triumphs, he'll take his share, but if Edward comes out ahead, he'll deny he was ever here.'

The big horseman's cheeks reddened, although whether it was with shame or anger, it was impossible to tell. 'Anyway, you should cry him the Red Comyn, that's what he demands.'

'Why the Red Comyn?' Eck enquired, his eyebrows raised.

'Well, I suppose it sounds better, you know. Red, like blood, more warlike than John I suppose. More scary.'

Eck shook with laughter in his saddle. 'I've heard it all now.'

'Like you can speak, Black Eck. You're just as bad.'

'No, I'm no'. I don't ask anyone to call me that. It's different if the name is given. If you have to tell folk to call you it, the name has not been earned.'

'Can we be on our way now?' John interrupted. 'I'd like to make camp before it's fully dark.'

'Fair enough.' Comyn's man replied. 'And thanks for telling us about the surcoats. We'll be leaving them off from now on, just as you suggested.' His smile was a grudging one, but John took it to be genuine.

Aye,' John replied, 'and it's good to have you wi' us. Wallace always says that in this struggle we must take friends wherever we can find them. We're sore in need of cavalry and so you and your men are very welcome.' John too gave a grudging smile as he reluctantly admitted, 'The jibe about the wives, that was actually quite funny.'

'Hey, no it wisnae!' Young McAlpine protested from behind. 'It wisnae fucking funny at all.'

Comyn's man laughed good-naturedly. 'I'd shut your mouth if I was you, my girl. I've got hard biscuit here that has seen more years than you and if your lips flap again, I'll knock every tooth out of your tiny head.'

'I doubt that it would stop him talking.' John shot back with a wide grin.

'It was good to meet you, John Edward. I will look for you when we pursue the baggage carts of the English King. I have no doubt that you will be following in our stead. We will be sure to leave you some small crumbs. My name, should you want it, is Peter Davidson. You can mention it to Wallace, if it pleases you.'

John had warmed to the man and took his teasing in good part. 'I will indeed mention you to Sir William and would ask that you, in turn, remember me to your lord. I last dined with him in Selkirk when Wallace was raised up. Please send him my best wishes and say that I hope to see him again soon.' John took a second to enjoy the perplexed expression on Peter's face, before he kicked his horse on down the road.

They smelled the camp long before they reached it and long before any sentry challenged their approach. The stench of stale pish and rotting shit over-powered even the smoke, which rose from a hundred cook-fires and hung in a cloud amongst the treetops. This foul odour was common to any place where large numbers of men took up temporary residence.

'If we'd got lost, we'd only need to follow our noses to find our way back.' Scott stated with distaste, his nose wrinkling in disgust.

'Aye, it's ripe right enough.' John replied. 'It's time that we moved the camp. I'll mention it to Wallace when I see him, but let's have our supper first.'

John had scarcely dismounted when he was informed that Wallace had commanded that he attend him the moment he returned. Already two days late, John decided to forgo his meal and make immediately for Wallace's tent. An awning of oiled cloth had been erected to provide shelter for the parchment-strewn table where the Wallace held his court. As he approached, he saw Sir William sat behind the desk with a group of petitioners before him. He smiled at the memory of Wallace complaining about the weight of bureaucracy which came with the position of Guardian. It was only when he was just a few short paces from the group that

182

he realised that this gathering had nothing to do with petty claims or the settling of ancient disputes. The first man he recognised was John Comyn, Lord of Badenoch and the second was Malcolm Simpson, the Guardian's most trusted aide. The presence of these men and the animation of their discussion told John that something was afoot. He also caught a glimpse of Jack Short, lurking around the meeting's edge. He reminded himself that he had not yet pulled the weasel up about that nonsense with the timings at the Kirk o' the Forest. This thought evaporated when he arrived at the table and caught sight of his old friend, Al, standing hunched at the other side.

Wallace briefly nodded his acknowledgement to John, before turning back to Al. 'Tell his Lordship exactly what you observed at Edward's camp.'

Al, always ill-at-ease in company, was almost crippled with shyness when in such an exalted circle. John willed him on with all his might as he stuttered and stammered and studiously avoided eye contact with anyone at the table. He had only recounted how he had made his way to Kirkliston when he realised that John had arrived at the gathering. His friend's presence seemed to reassure him and, looking directly at John, he delivered his report adequately. His audience drank in every word, consuming his intelligence the way a starving man would devour honey and bread. He was constantly interrupted with questions, but was able to answer each and every one to their satisfaction.

John took great pride in his friend's performance and winked at him in appreciation when his account was done.

'So,' Wallace announced, scarcely able to hide his delight, 'the Bastard King's army is on the point of disintegration. Supplied only with wine, they kill each other and do our work for us. The good Lord hears our prayers.'

'Aye,' John Comyn replied, 'it's near time for us to sally across the Forth and position ourselves for the pursuit. It would be a pity if we were to miss the retreat and see him make the border with his baggage train intact.'

Wallace pushed himself to his feet. 'Tis true, my Lord, we would not want that prize to slip from our grasp. But we must take care not to act too precipitously. I would rather lose that fortune than risk the lives of all those here. Let us send out more scouts and spies and move only when Langshanks breaks his camp.'

Comyn shook his head. 'By the time news reached our camp, he would have stolen two days march on us. Even with poor roads to slow them, we would struggle to catch his carts. You heard this man's report, they teeter precariously on the brink of collapse. Let us seize the day and be bold in our actions, ready to pounce when disaster overtakes him.'

'As always, my Lord, your case is most convincing, but yet I do hesitate. The beast is wounded, but not yet dead and outnumbers us by five to one in infantry and three to one in cavalry. If we were to encounter them head-on, I would not wager on our chances.'

Comyn squinted at Wallace and took some seconds to consider his arguments before replying. 'There are risks, that I will not deny. However, these are risks that can be mitigated without us being held hostage to caution. Let us move across the Forth and position ourselves where we are better able to spring, but are still not too far from the Forth. Then, in the unlikely event of an English advance, we can yet retreat and stay beyond their reach.'

Wallace nodded and reached his hand out to the Lord of Badenoch to seal their agreement. 'But let's double our scouts so that we are not caught unawares.'

When the Red Comyn and his men had departed, Wallace called for ale and sat with his captains.

'I am not over keen on crossing the Forth. It feels that we are tempting fate. I would much rather let Edward's army collapse on its own, but I must keep the Comyn on our side. I can delay our departure, but only for a few days and I pray that it will be enough. In the meantime, we must double our scouts and drill our men hard so that they are ready if we meet Edward face-to-face. I pray that this does not happen, but let's be ready should the worst come.'

Wallace was able to postpone the advance across the Forth, but his excuses soon tested John Comyn's patience and four days grace was all that he could buy. Those four days were hard indeed for the Scottish infantry, as they ran their schiltrom drills under Wallace's watchful eyes. There were two men to each long, sharpened stake, their combined strength required to manoeuvre it into position and brace it on the earth to repel the charge of heavy, armoured horse. At first the formations were most clumsy, but with the perseverance of their captains, could soon slowly traverse from left to right as well as advance and retreat. John Edward commanded the schiltrom made up of Perth and Stirling men. By way of a system of simple commands and a drum to sound each step, he succeeded in drilling his men to a high level of competence. This earned him the praise of Wallace, who commanded him to so teach the other captains.

'Watch John Edward and how he makes his hedgehog dance,' he ordered, 'and make your schiltroms caper just the same.'

Of the three other schiltrom captains, Malcolm Simpson was the most keen to learn and had John put his bordermen through their paces.

'If we had another week,' Malcolm announced to John, 'we could have them dance a jig.'

Alas, there was no more time and the following morning the men of Scotland broke camp and hauled their great spears on across the Forth.

15

Walter Langton, Lord High Treasurer and
Bishop of Coventry and Lichfield shivered in his
tent. Even the blanket pulled tight around his
shoulders was heavy with damp. When he
leaned close in to the fire, he could see steam
rising from its surface. Even as the flames
warmed his front to the point of burning his
flesh, his back was chilled and stiff from the
cold. He cursed this wretched, rain-soaked
country and wished that he was back in his
London house, dry, warm and in the lap of
civilisation. Even a campaign in France, with its
arrogant people and terrible food, would have
been preferable to this current misery.

What ailed him more than the miserable
climate, was the lack of progress he had
achieved in the days since his arrival on this
sodden hillside. He had, it was true, succeeded
in rousing King Edward from his torpor. The
King now spent less time staring into space, but
could not be said to be back at his best. More
achievement on Langton's part would be
required if Edward's revival was to be
maintained. The dire state of the army's supplies
had scarcely improved. One small merchant ship

had made it into port, its hold heaped high with barley. What should have lasted a week, was consumed in a little more than two days, as starving soldiers had gorged themselves while they could. This sudden and isolated feast had caused many to sicken and the camp was shrouded in the foul stink of the watery shit which erupted from their bowels. Langton already knew that the Jew had plotted to disrupt the army's lines of supply, but he had still tortured this ship's captain just to have his suspicions confirmed. The sailor's anguished confirmation had done not a bit of good. Knowing the author of his misfortune did nothing to speed its resolution. His other problem, and arguably the most pressing, was his lack of information on the location of William Wallace and his outlaw army. There was no prospect of victory if the Scots could not be brought to battle. If this could be brought about, all other concerns would pale into insignificance.

His thoughts were interrupted by the arrival of the captain of his guard at the entrance to the tent.

'What is it Browby?' He demanded, his ill-temper barely concealed.

'One of your informants has arrived, my Lord. He would speak with you.' Browby replied, rainwater dripping from his sodden cloak.

'Bid him enter then!' Langton ordered tersely.

'Ah, My Lord, but he will not enter the camp. He would see you at the gate.'

Langton clenched his fists tightly and tried to control the fury and frustration which threatened to overcome him. He prided himself on his ability to keep his temper in check and maintain a calm, disciplined façade at all times. This damned campaign was sorely testing him.

'Tell him that he must come here, that he will come to no harm as he is under my, and therefore the King's, protection. He does not have to force me back out into the rain when I have scarcely dried my clothes.'

Browby briefly considered a biting response concerning how fortunate his master was to have spent much of the day under cover. Instead, mindful of Langton's evident irritation, he confined himself to shaking his cloak to release a shower of droplets onto the earthen floor at Langton's feet.

'He is afeart my Lord and will not come. He resists all inducements and threats.'

Langton leapt to his feet and hissed with repressed anger, 'All right! Let the High Treasurer and Lord Bishop pander to the disloyal servant. If he will not wait on me, then let me attend to him.'

Browby was careful to hide his grin as he trailed after Langton, who strode quickly ahead like a spoiled child in a foul, infantile strop.

The bedraggled servant cowered at the Bishop's aggressive advance. Langton recognised him as a serving boy in the service of Robert de Bruce. He had purchased the boy's eyes and ears from his father, who sold his son for mere pennies.

'What news boy? Tell me all that you have heard. What whispers have reached your young ears as you prowl de Bruce's halls?'

The boy talked for some minutes, but had nothing of import to impart. Gossip about the Earl's crops, hunting parties, relatives, nocturnal habits and social life was of little interest to Langton.

'I care not which wretched serving girl the Earl chooses to tup. What have you heard about Wallace and where he hides his army away?'

'Nothing m'Lord!'

'Nothing?'

'Nothing. I have heard nothing of this.' The boy was wide-eyed with fear and leaned back as the Bishop put his face only inches from his.

'So, not one soul in the Bruce household is even a little bit curious about where Wallace and his peasants skulk?' He turned to Browby with a puzzled expression. 'It seems odd, does it not, that not a single member of Bruce's house has the slightest interest in the whereabouts of a man who could snatch away their Lordship's crown? Not one question? No idle speculation as to where the outlaw might have secreted himself? I find that hard to believe. In my experience, people live for their gossip and like nothing better than chattering away about things they have no business chattering about. But you,' he said, prodding his index finger hard into the boy's chest, 'would have me believe that the subject has never once come up in the Bruce household. The subject that has the whole country babbling is a matter of indifference to the whole Bruce clan.'

The boy opened his mouth to answer, but was hushed by the Lord High Treasurer.

'Don't say a word. Think carefully before you answer. If you once again tell me that you have heard not a whisper, then I will know that you are lying to me. If I know that you have lied, I will have to find out why and that, I guarantee, will not go well for you.'

Browby almost fell sorry for the boy, as he was shivering with fear.

'So, what's your answer boy?' Langton demanded, as he flicked the rain from his face. 'Choose carefully and tell me now.'

The answer had scarcely passed the boy's lips when Langton's fist crashed into his jaw with splintering force. The boy's teeth smacked together with the loudest of cracks and he flew backwards, landing dazed on his back. Langton dropped to his knees and carried out a meticulous search. Finding nothing in his clothing, he pulled the boy's boots off and gave a grunt of triumph as a small leather purse fell to the ground. He loosened the drawstring and poured its chinking contents into the palm of his hand. He held it out to Browby and asked him what he saw.

'Six gold coins, my Lord. French if I am not mistaken.'

'That's right Browby. Now how would a common serving boy come to be in the possession of such coin? I have heard that the

Bruce is most generous, but I doubt that he dispenses such things to low-borns such as this. If you'll kindly lend me that thin boning knife, I am certain we'll arrive at the truth.'

It took but a few moments for the boy to sob out his story and confirm what Langton had already guessed. It pained the Bishop to see a child endure such suffering, so he brought it quickly to an end. The blade's edge was keen and opened up his throat with just the one smooth slice.

'The filthy Jew has been busy, my dear Browby.' Langton said as he wiped the blade on the boy's wet cloak. 'Now that I know that my informants' ignorance has been purchased with his gold, I can act accordingly. I will kill each one when they bring their empty, treacherous reports to me. The Jew will soon get the message that he has wasted his gold on corpses.'

'My Lord, would that be wise?' Browby enquired cautiously, fearful of arousing his master's spite once again.

'Come Browby, you have known me long enough. Out with it, I would know your thoughts.'

'Well my Lord, once you have slaughtered all your spies, then you shall have no information at all. We will be completely blind.'

'That's right Browby.' Langton replied, staring into space as his mind raced. 'That's exactly what Crawcour would have me do. That old snake knows me too well. He almost reads my thoughts and manipulates them at will.' Langton clenched his fists, partly in anger and partly in admiration of the old man's skill. 'He nearly had me there. Let us not do his work, but instead play him at his own game. As each informant comes in, we shall confront them with the truth, though they might need a little tickle to help them find their way to the light. Once all is in the open, we pay double what he has offered and untangle his duplicitous web.'

'Very good, my Lord.' Browby agreed.

'It is well that my mind is so quick. A lesser man would have fallen for his tricks.' Langton turned back to the gate and set off for his mildewed tent.

'Yes, my Lord, it is well that your mind is so quick.' Browby responded with heavy irony, his words aimed at Langton's retreating back. 'How would we manage without you?'

Although not a warrior or a man skilled in the sword, Langton was, amongst other things, primarily a man of action. Consequently, his current position, marooned in a freezing, dripping tent atop a muddy slope, did not suit him well. He could patiently wait for his plots and schemes to unfold, but struggled with complete inactivity when bereft of opportunity to poke and prod his conspiracies along. As he awaited developments with both ships and spies, he busied himself by attending closely to the King. He buoyed him up with salacious tales of the nobles' goings-on. The King was unfailingly delighted with details of their perversions, as he was with news of any misfortunes that they had suffered. Though he did enjoy these afternoons with Edward, he was all too aware that he was merely marking time and diverting the King from his melancholy. Without substantial news to report, he feared that he could keep Edward from despair for only a few days to come. If the King lost his nerve, the game was up and the campaign would end in disgrace. He did not think that Edward would cope well with such a failure and there was the risk that he would quickly fade.

With so many nobles set against him, Langton had no doubt that Edward's death would end with his neck in a noose, or, if the whispered charges of witchcraft against him were to be pursued, with him roasted on a pyre. Neither possibility held much appeal for him and he had recently found that the lack of progress had led him to resort to prayer. He did not, of course, fall to his knees on the damp earth, but, when lying abed in the dark of night, he often found himself silently entreating God above to intervene on his behalf. He did not for one second believe that the good Lord would strike down the rebellious Scots, but he found that it was of comfort, given that no other course was open to him.

In spite of the Bishop's lack of faith, his prayers were soon answered. In the darkest hour of a wild and windy night, his sleep was disturbed by Browby roughly shaking him back to life.

'Christ Browby! What's so important it could not wait until morning?'

'It's an informant, my Lord. This one you will want to see immediately.'

Browby's expression was one of real excitement and this was enough to arouse the Bishop's curiosity and rouse him hastily from his bed.

'Show him in then, show him in.' Langton ordered, as he ran his fingers through his hair in an effort to smooth its greasy tangles.

Browby held the tent flaps open and ushered a hooded figure inside. The man was sopping wet and rivulets of water streamed from him, quickly forming a puddle around his feet. His face was shrouded by his hood and his sodden cloak clung to his tall and spindly figure. The leather satchel on his shoulder was soaked and heavy with water.

'It's you!' Langton declared in surprise, a rare smile of genuine pleasure spreading across his face. 'It's been so long since I heard from you, I had presumed you discovered and dead.'

'No, my Lord. I yet live, though not for much longer if I do not get some heat into my bones.' The man returned Langton's smile with a grin full of brown teeth.

'Come, come!' Langton entreated, ushering his guest to the fire and prodding it back into life with an iron poker. 'Browby, go and rouse the cooks to make hot broth for our guest. We must warm him before he expires.'

'Thank you, my Lord. This terrible weather is both a blessing and a curse. The lashing rain and howling wind made my journey here most perilous, but it was only under its cover that I was able to slip away without being observed.'

'Warm yourself and tell me all, I would not miss a word. Quickly now, we must not tarry if you are to be back before you are missed.'

Within the hour, Langton was striding towards the King's pavilion, oblivious of the sheets of rain which soaked him to the skin. Never before had he given an informant so much gold, but he knew that it was worth every single penny. The sentry at the pavilion's entrance was surprised to see the Treasurer at such an ungodly hour, but what more discomfited him was the cheerful greeting and the great smile upon his face.

The interior of the pavilion was in darkness, save for the glowing embers in the brazier. The King's manservant lay snoring on his roll and was jerked into wakefulness by the toe of Langton's boot.

'Rouse the King, I would speak with him.'

The servant sat up and tried to rub the sleep from his eyes. 'His Majesty sleeps and cannot be disturbed. You should come back in the morning after he has broken his fast. He will see no-one before that, not even you m'Lord.'

'Get off your arse and see to the fire, I will raise the King myself.'

Langton ignored the servant's feeble protest and strode to the curtain which kept the King's bedchamber hidden from prying eyes. He pulled it back and had to strain his eyes in the darkness. The room was more cramped than he had expected. A dozen wooden trunks lined its edges and a great wooden bed dominated its centre. The King lay, gently snoring, on a huge feather mattress which almost seemed to envelop him. As his eyes adjusted to the dim interior, he stepped closer to the bed. Stripped of all his finery, Edward looked vulnerable, almost frail. His breathing was slightly laboured, as one would expect from a man of his great age. Langton hesitated before reaching out to shake the King's arm. The limb his fingers closed around was colder and thinner than he had expected and he shook it gently.

'My Lord,' he called softly, 'you must awaken. I have news that you would hear.'

The King stirred and moaned and tried to turn away deeper into his blankets. Langton shook him slightly harder and kept hold of his arm to prevent him from rolling over.

'What?' The King asked sleepily, reluctantly blinking his eyes open. 'Is it time for my eggs already? I feel as though I have barely slept.'

'It is I, my Lord. I have important intelligence to share.'

Edward peered at Langton in the gloom, his eyes widening in the darkness. 'Is it you Walter? Why have you disturbed my rest? I dreamed that I was in London with not a drop of rain.'

'We have him, my Lord. I know where Wallace lurks. If we move quickly we may bring an end to him and secure the Crown of Scotland upon your head.'

The change was sudden and wonderful to behold. One moment Langton disturbed the sleep of a tired, old man, the next his fingers grasped the arm of a warrior king. The Bishop would never forget the instant the spark appeared in Edward's eyes like a fire ignited into flame. Edward now gripped Langton's arm firmly, his fingers squeezing tight.

'We have him?' Edward demanded, holding Langton in his terrible glare.

'Yes, my King, we have him. You must up, we need you now.'

The magnates grumbled about being awoken so early and shot Langton glances full of suspicion and naked hatred. He, in turn, paced slowly around the pavilion with the pretence of being oblivious to their enmity. Not being a stupid man, he was absolutely aware of their dislike for him and did not miss a single hostile gesture or whispered word of disapproval. No sane man would willingly choose to have any of those present as an enemy. Though they bore the title of Earl or Lord, they were kings in all but name and commanded great armies and their word was law in the lands which they controlled. Of the near one hundred noble families that made up Edward's army, only the ten most senior had been rudely shaken from their sleep and summoned to this Council of War. Foremost amongst these were Roger Bigod, Earl of Norfolk and Magnate of England, Humphrey de Bohun, Earl of Hereford and Constable of England, Henry de Lacy, Earl of Lincoln and Anthony Bek, Bishop of Durham.

The drone of their whispered complaints died when the pavilion curtains were drawn back with a flourish and Edward the First of England strode into their presence. The King's appearance drew gasps from even the most hard-bitten, self-serving cynics amongst the nobles. Edward towered above them all, resplendent in a purple tabard adorned with lions embroidered in gold, an ermine cloak which reached down almost to his feet and boots of polished black leather reinforced with iron strips, which came to his knees. The golden Crown of England sat upon his head and his great battle-sword hung from a silver belt at his waist. For Langton, as much as for the others, what shined most brightly was not the gold or silver or the sheen upon his boots, but his piercing eyes, which blazed with hot fury and flaming ambition. The Lord High Treasurer noted with satisfaction that, in the face of such imposing majesty, the magnates bowed more deeply than they had for many a year.

The King was brief to the point of brusqueness in updating the magnates on the location of the traitor's army and his plan to march west immediately to confront and defeat it. When he was finished, he glared at them and waited for their inevitable objections. It was not a surprise when the Earls of Norfolk, Hereford and Lincoln joined forces to voice their concerns and put forward their alternative, more cautious proposals. They were unnerved by Edward's silence, as he did not once argue back, instead he remained impassive and waited until their arguments had petered out.

'So, my Lords, your suggestion is that we stay on this dung heap and await more favourable developments. That is what we have done these past weeks and it has brought us not the slightest benefit. Perhaps you imagine that this Wallace will come crawling to our gate and beg us to give him pardon.'

'No, my Lord,' the Earl of Norfolk responded tersely. 'That is not what we mean at all. It is just that such a march in this inclement weather is most inadvisable.'

Edward laughed without a trace of humour. 'You are worried that our men will get wet? You think it better that they continue to rot upon this hill?' He waved down Norfolk's attempt at a riposte. 'I know well, my Lord, that your men are not what gives concern. Rather you are driven by your need to spay me and curb my royal powers. Alas for you, on this occasion, methinks the spaying shears are in my grasp and your fingers close on empty air. Be sure that while I hold the shears I will use them as mercilessly as you.' Edward ignored the nobles' bewildered indignation and turned to Langton. 'Lord High Treasurer, tell me this, if it was by my decree that all the Jews were expelled from all of England, then to whom would ownership of all their debts fall? Would they drop into abeyance and become null and void or would there be some legitimate claim to be made?'

Langton bowed to his King and answered the question he had suggested to him no more than an hour ago. 'There is indeed precedent for this, my Lord. In cases of banishment, it is common for ownership of vacant estates to pass immediately to the crown. Of course, any credible and legitimate claims would be heard and judgement made upon them.'

'And who,' the King enquired in feigned curiosity, 'would be called upon to make such judgements?'

'That would be yourself, my Lord. The monarch would be the final arbiter in the event of a disputed claim.'

Edward turned to the four Earls with a thin smile upon his lips. 'Do you, my Lords, not owe significant debts to the Jews? Debts incurred against your estates? It would seem that, from what the Lord High Treasurer has advised, I am now your creditor.'

'That man can twist and turn the law until he proves a circle square. We'd all be damned if his kind was to thrive and leave no peace for decent men.' The Earl of Lincoln shook with repressed rage, his eyes shooting daggers in Langton's direction.

'Excellent! Excellent!' Edward crowed. 'So, we march at once. I am glad it is all agreed. We will march and deploy in three battles. The Bishop of Durham and I will command one apiece and Lincoln, Hereford and Norfolk can share command of the remainder.'

With that, the magnates were dismissed and hurried off to brave the pouring rain and order their men to break camp.

16

Al stopped stock-still and listened. No matter how much he strained his ears, all sound was drowned out by the torrential rain battering into the earth and the wind gusting violently through the trees. The elusive sound might well have been a figment of his imagination, but Al had long ago learned to trust his instincts. The faint clank of metal on metal was not a sound that occurred in nature and that, he believed, was why his ears had detected it.

The other scouts had laughed when he set off into the downpour.

'No one would be mad enough to travel in this foul weather.' They had jeered. 'Even Wallace has hunkered down until the storm passes.'

Their words had come back to him several times as his cloak had grown ever heavier and water filled his boots. By the time he reached the shore of Linlithgow Loch, he could not stop himself from shivering and he reluctantly turned his horse back towards Falkirk, where he could find a fire to huddle by.

His retreat had been prematurely halted by the phantom sound. Unable to leave the potential threat unchecked, he slid from his horse's back and tied it to a tree. The Black Dog looked at him quizzically, as if questioning his decision to tarry on such a filthy night.

'It's alright Dougal, I just need to take a quick look.' The dog's ears pricked up at his master's whispered voice and he leaned into his hand so he could give him a good clap. 'Quiet now, there's a good boy.'

Stealthily, he advanced through the darkened forest, stopping, as was his habit, to make his mark on every third tree. Many a time the rudimentary carvings in the shape of an eye had proven invaluable in helping him to retrace his steps when reconnoitering unfamiliar territory. His technique was painstaking, but had served him well throughout the struggle against the English. The Black Dog needed no such device and disappeared into the gloom. Al had counted out fifteen trees when another alien noise caused his ears to twitch and rooted him to the spot. This time he knew that there was no mistake. The voice had come from only twenty paces to his front.

With stealth a necessity at such close proximity, Al set about divesting himself of anything which could make a noise and give away his presence. He pushed his sodden cloak and squelching boots under a bush, before reluctantly unfastening his belt buckle and abandoning his sword there as well. With his dagger clenched between his teeth, he moved tentatively forward at a crouch. He was a little surprised to note that the absence of his cloak did not cause him to shiver more. He supposed that it must have been so soaked through that it gave him little warmth.

When he thought that he neared the location of the voice, he eased onto his stomach and snaked along the ground, taking care to use what little cover the forest provided. It was while he was paused, listening beneath a bush, that the voice came again. Though he could not yet see him, Al knew that a man stood no more than ten paces from where he lay. He also knew that the man was English and that his accent was from the North. He inched slowly forward until he could make out the dark figure of a man leaning against a tree. The spear shaft in his hand suggested that he was standing sentry. Al cast his eyes around in a bid to locate whoever the sentry had been addressing when he had spoken before. Long minutes passed before Al concluded that the sentry was, in fact, alone. The tree gave little protection from the elements and the miserable conditions caused him to moan and complain to himself periodically.

'Every fucking night!' The sentry lamented bitterly to himself. 'Why has it always got to be me? I've got a good mind to piss off and leave them to it.'

Al smiled grimly to himself. Their own sentries always had similar grievances and were not averse to murmuring their displeasure to themselves as they whiled away the long hours of inactivity, discomfort and boredom. Al's anaemic smile melted away as the grave implications of the presence of an English sentry washed over him. No scout stood vigil with spear in hand and, if there was a sentry, then there needed to be something here worth guarding. His heart thumped loudly in his chest as he decided what he should do. His first inclination was to crawl back out of there and gallop the two miles to Wallace's camp and raise the alarm. His reluctance to return with such incomplete intelligence persuaded him to take another course.

He spent long minutes squelching and crawling his way twenty paces back. He then hopped up into a crouch and circled around the unhappy Englishman. He found the next sentry fifty paces from the first and in much the same condition. More crawling forward led to the discovery of a second line of guards. Though this in itself could be taken as proof of the presence of a considerable force, Al's inbuilt curiosity and courage forced him on to see what actually lay beyond. He realised that the top of an incline lay just ahead, when he saw the Black Dog's silhouette disappear over its lip.

He slithered the last few paces flat on his belly and raised his head to peer down the slope. Even in the black of night he could see that a moor stretched out before him. He was relieved that he did not see the light of the fires that would mark out an enemy encampment. His relief was brought to an end, not by his eyes or his ears, but by his sense of smell. A gust of wind driven across the moor delivered an unmistakable odour to his nostrils. There was no doubt about it, he had smelled horse shit where no horses should be. The next thundering gust brought confirmation in the form of the neigh of an unsettled steed. Al squeezed his eyes into slits and stared, unblinking at the moor. Slowly but surely, shadows and shapes began to reveal themselves in the murk. His eyes widened in horror and his heart seemed to jump into his throat. Tents. Row upon row of tents stretching far into the distance. The shadows seemed to dance and flicker as the canvas structures were buffeted by the wind. To his right, the shadows were both larger and had more substance to them. From the corner of his eye he could detect movement, but the shapes did not flutter as though blown by the gale. The scout's stomach turned to liquid as his brain caught up with his eyes. These were not shadows, but great horses moving languidly at their tethers in search of another mouthful of moor grass. The realisation that the whole of the English army was camped not two miles from that of Wallace and Comyn caused Al to gasp. He took a moment to still his breathing before he began the long crawl back through the sentry lines.

As Al inched his way across the puddled forest floor, King Edward's valet stood in the valley below wallowing in the misery of his long night's watch. After weeks of mouldering in the Kirkliston camp, he had been excited to see the King so restored and welcomed the burst of activity as the English army broke camp and set out in hasty pursuit of the elusive enemy. His initial enthusiasm had been dampened, though not extinguished, by the rigours of the long forced march. By the time the advance was halted and the weary soldiers hastily pitched their tents, he was footsore and exhausted and yearned only to drop down onto his bed-roll in the shelter of the pavilion. These hopes were dashed by the King himself when he announced that he would show solidarity with his knights and forgo his royal comforts by sleeping in his armour with his horse tied up at his side.

'It will inspire them for the morrow, to see their King endure the same hardships that they themselves do face.' Edward had announced with enthusiasm. 'Bring me a simple waxed cover, it will be enough to defeat the rain.'

The valet did as he was commanded, but hid his surly face. He doubted that a single knight would notice, as it was already dark and they all huddled from the rain. It irked him further that the King, despite his bold proclamations, did not entirely deny himself the privileges of his rank. While his army collapsed upon the ground with their bellies sore and empty, Edward kept his valet busy fetching wine, nuts, fruit and cold roast foul to satisfy his newly reinvigorated appetite. With his stomach full and tired from his long day in the saddle, Edward soon fell asleep whilst his valet stood guard with only the pattering of the rain and Edward's light snoring to keep him company.

His eyes did not register the dog's approach, as its black coat merged into the shadows. He only caught brief sight of its shape when it lunged and snatched up the bones from Edward's discarded meal. The beast's sudden appearance caused the King's horse to neigh and rear up in fright. The valet looked on in horror as its great hoof crashed down upon the sleeping form of the King. Edward's roar of agony sent the poor valet running to bring others to his aid.

By the time Langton arrived at the pavilion, Edward had been put to bed, where he writhed and groaned in horrible discomfort. The Bishop cursed inwardly at this reverse. Within the space of a single day, he had seen Edward restored to his best, only for him to be once again reduced to a pitiful state. He had to keep his voice low, so as not to disturb the King, but he had nevertheless shown no mercy when lashing the hapless valet with his tongue. The man had been weeping and shivering by the time he ordered him from his sight. In truth, it was Edward, and not his servant, who was to blame, but Langton had sorely needed an outlet for his frustration. There was also a hint of guilt at his failure to keep Edward within his sight at such a critical juncture in this accursed campaign. That was not a mistake that he would allow to happen again.

His train of thought was interrupted when he detected a presence at his side. He turned his head to see the Prince of Wales taking in his father's state of health. He had seen little of the Prince since arriving in Scotland, though he had heard that he spent his days engaged in drinking and horseplay with a group of young, noble knights.

'He doesn't look at all well Langton.' The Prince drawled, his breath thick with wine. 'If we are to take to the field on the morrow, I

208

doubt that he will be capable of leading us there.'

Langton realised that he was grinding his teeth as he returned the Prince's gaze. The young man was tall like his father, but with the fine features that had marked his mother out as a great beauty in her youth. He could be described as handsome, but not in a manly way. Langton detested him and knew that the feeling was returned in kind. He had his father's cruel eyes and the Bishop knew that he would find no mercy there when he succeeded his father on the throne.

'We'll have to see about that, my Lord. Now if I may be excused, I have matters to attend to on behalf of the King.'

The Prince laughed and mocked Langton with a false grin. 'By all means, my Lord Bishop, run along, though I doubt that even your scheming can do much for him now.'

Langton gave a curt bow and made his way out of the tent. He had, he was aware, reached the stage where he was clutching at straws. There was nothing he could do to repair the injuries King Edward had suffered. The dark bruising covered almost the whole of his torso and the left side of his ribcage was horribly caved in. Still, it was not in his nature to accept defeat until the last horn had been sounded. It took him some time to find what he was looking for, as the camp was a temporary, makeshift arrangement and had been thrown up with no regard to the usual military protocols. It was almost by chance that he happened upon the tent of the young Henri Le Gray. If the youthful baron had not been careless and left his shield out in the rain, Langton would have missed the blue and white stripes of his coat of arms and continued on stumbling fruitlessly through the darkness.

Le Gray was well known for only two things, his skill at arms, for which he was lauded, and his raging hypochondria, for which he was ridiculed. It was impossible to have a single conversation with the man where he did not complain about a long list of ailments and speculate anxiously about which one would likely end his life. To his credit, once roused from his sleep, he proved himself most eager to help and provided the Bishop with what he required. Conversely, the baron's apothecary was only reluctantly teased from his bed and bemoaned the uninvited intrusion all the way back to the King's tent.

Langton ushered the old man inside and pulled the flaps closed behind him. The curtain before the King's bedchamber was still tied back and, in the half-darkness, Langton could make out a figure standing over the King. He quickly padded over to the opening to see the Prince, with a pillow in his hands, staring intently down at Edward's face. The younger man's eyes momentarily widened as he sensed Langton's quiet approach. He jerked back from the bed in fright, before quickly recovering himself and making a show of re-arranging his father's pillows.

Langton glowered at the Prince and flexed his fists at his sides. 'I doubt that the King will die this night, my Lord Prince. You may have a while to wait for your throne.'

The younger Edward feigned astonishment at Langton's words, but this was quickly replaced with a sneer. 'I don't know Langton, dawn is yet a few hours away.'

As Prince Edward took his leave, the Lord High Treasurer waved the apothecary into the bedchamber and ordered him to examine the King. He watched the old man methodically poke and prod his sovereign. He muttered as he worked and emitted periodic sighs and expulsions of breath. His appearance put Langton in mind of the wizard from the old tales of King Arthur. His bald head was crowned with the same wispy white hair as his beard and the robes he wore, though ragged and threadbare, would not have looked out of place on a monk. Langton just prayed that there was some magic in those long, thin fingers.

'Well, can you do anything for him?' Langton barked when the apothecary finally turned to him.

'He has, as far as I can tell, three broken ribs. Whether they have caused damage to his innards, I will only be able to tell if there is blood in his dirt or his piss. I can make him more comfortable, but the doing of it will cause him much pain. I will give him something to soften the agony before I begin.'

'Can you get him mounted on his horse by dawn?'

The old man laughed and shook his head. 'There's little chance of that, my Lord, I am not a worker of miracles.'

'If you get that man into his saddle by dawn tomorrow, I'll shower you with more gold than you can carry.'

The apothecary licked his lips. 'Well, there is one plant, but…'

'Out with it man!'

'I have seen this plant used to most wondrous effect. Men at death's door have made the most astounding recoveries, but others have dropped dead as soon as it passed their lips. I fear it would be too dangerous to try upon the King.'

Langton took only seconds to decide. 'Let us try it. He is finished if he stays abed. Where can we find this plant? Please tell me it grows even in these climes.'

'I have some in my baggage. I am almost certain it will still be good.'

'Come then! I will walk you to your tent. If this night's work does go well, I'll make you a wealthy man.'

As Langton and the apothecary made their way through the camp, Al had crawled through the sentry lines and recovered his cloak, boots and sword. He now desperately cast around in the dark for his horse. He was certain he had reached the right tree, but there was no sign of his mount. The remains of muddy hoofprints told him that he was indeed in the correct place. With no time to fret about the horse's fate, he set off for the Scottish camp at the run. The wind, rain, darkness and terrain conspired to slow his progress, but Al ran as fast as he dared.

17

The grizzled sentry rubbed his hands in a vain attempt to make them warm. The night had been long and had frozen him to his bones. He would have happily exchanged his boots for just one goblet of grog, even though it was his love of it which had put him here. His captain was a sour, joyless man who punished those who had the cheek to take pleasure in their cups with long nights of sentry duty. He had filled his night with imaginings of what punishment he would inflict on him, if ever the tables were turned. He was pulled rudely from his grim reverie by something rustling in the grass. His fellow, who had the enviable ability to doze whilst leaning on his spear, was jerked into wakefulness by a hard poke in the ribs.

He peered intently into the darkness and then sighed dismissively. 'It's just a fuckin' dog Boab. No need to shit your breeks. I was near asleep there.'

'Wheesht!' Boab hissed. 'Something's coming.'

The very edge of the horizon was barely touched with dawn, leaving the land still shrouded in darkness and a thin, persistent mist.

They heard him long before they saw him, his breath coming in great grasps, his bare feet thudding into the sodden, hard-packed earth and his legs swishing through the wet, knee-length grass. The sight that greeted them was indeed a sorry one. The runner's face was an alarming shade of red, his clothes were filthy and caked with mud and blood flowed from the scratches which covered him from head to toe. It was little wonder that the sentries did not recognise him and readied themselves to halt his charge. He was only three spear lengths from them when Boab lowered the point of his pike.

'It's him!' He exclaimed in alarmed recognition. 'It's that Perth boy fae last night.'

They both moved forward to catch Al before he hit the ground. At first, they could make out not a single word he said, but once his panting was diminished sufficiently for them to grasp his meaning, they immediately lifted him and dragged him to the Wallace's tent.

Wallace sat astride his horse and gazed out across the valley. Immediately before him on the downward slope, his men still struggled to manoeuvre their long, sharp poles and get their schiltroms into position. In contrast, the army on the opposing slope was already arrayed in disciplined formations. The four Scottish schiltroms and their small force of cavalry were dwarfed by the scale of the English army. Even one of their four battalions alone outnumbered the Scots.

'Jesus!' Wallace exclaimed. He had known the numbers of men Edward had led across the border, but that intelligence had done little to prepare him for having the enormous reality of it spread out before him.

'I know.' John Comyn replied. 'But at least it has stopped raining at last.'

'That,' Wallace replied, 'is likely to be the only good thing to come out of this day.'

Comyn nodded slowly as he too took in the intimidating sight before them. 'So, Sir William, what is it to be? Do we fight or take flight?'

Wallace turned in his saddle and surveyed the landscape to their rear. 'We are two miles from the shelter of the Torwood. Our horsemen could easily find safety there, but all of our foot would be ridden down before they were halfway there. It would be a slaughter.'

Comyn nodded grimly. 'Aye, and my cavalry is so outnumbered, we could do little more than delay them. My men would be lost and still the foot would be destroyed. Is seems that we have no choice but to stand and let the pieces fall where they may.'

Wallace then turned to John Comyn. 'Right enough, that is true for us, but you could still ride across this field and swear fealty to King Edward. It is not as if you have shown your colours on the field. I do not doubt that he would accept you into his peace.'

A thin smile touched Comyn's lips. 'I cannot deny that the thought has crossed my mind, William. Unfortunately for me, I am a Comyn and not a Bruce. I have given my word and am

216

therefore bound to keep it. For good or for ill, we are bound in this together and will see how the good Lord favours us.'

'If God had heard my prayers at all, Edward would already be back in London licking his wounds.'

Comyn sighed deeply before responding. 'We are in no position to attack that great host, so I suppose we must simply await their first move. I will keep my cavalry poised should they try to advance their archers into position. If we can drive them off, that should even the odds a little.'

'I have ordered Sir John Stewart of Bonkill to position our archers between the schiltroms. If Edward sends his heavy horse to crush us, they will find their reception quite hot.'

'I doubt that he would be so rash, but we can only hope and pray. I will see you on the other side.'

'Aye.' Wallace replied. 'Whether that is to be the other side of the veil or the other side of the glen, only time will tell.'

At the top of the opposite slope, the English magnates inspected the battlefield from their saddles.

The Earl of Norfolk was in fine spirits, despite an uncomfortable and sleepless night. 'It seems that we have taken our Scottish friends by surprise. See how they scurry hither and thither and hurry to straighten their ragged lines. I have half a mind to charge straight in and catch then before their breeches are fully up.'

'Only a man with half a mind would order the charge before the King has taken to the field.' Anthony Bek, the Bishop of Durham had tried to keep his tone light, but Norfolk did not miss his disapproval.

'Where is the King?' Norfolk enquired with feigned innocence. 'Surely not still snug and warm in his feather bed? It would be such a shame for us to have marched all this way, only to let the Scots melt away while the King takes his rest.'

'He'll be here soon enough.' Bek replied sourly. 'If it were not for him, you would still have us idling by the coast. It is the King's insistence which has led us to this place and therefore it is for him to decide the order of battle.'

'They have precious few horse.' The Earl of Lincoln observed. 'We could drive them from the field in a trice.'

'And look at their infantry formations.' The Earl of Hereford added. 'I can see few men-at-arms in their number. Their great circles would seem to be made up of peasants armed with sharpened poles.'

'They are most curious,' commented Lincoln, 'almost like great hedgehogs. Heavy horse would just sweep them away.'

'In my experience,' opined Hereford, 'a hedgehog will be squashed underfoot in spite of his pretty spikes.'

'Perhaps so,' Bek responded, 'but in my experience, a prick can be a very dangerous thing.'

'So, my Lord Bishop, can I assume that you have much experience with pricks?' The Earl of Lincoln, to his credit, managed to stifle his laughter, though his own wit tickled him so.

'More experience with each passing minute.' Bek retorted, as he leaned round in his saddle in the hope of seeing the King approach.

'We have waited long enough.' Norfolk snapped. 'The Scots have had time to neaten their formations, I mean to deny them the opportunity to prepare any further. In the King's name, I order the charge.'

The Bishop of Durham did protest and ordered the Earls to wait, but as soon as the command was given, the battalions of heavy horse began to move forward.

'The King will have your guts for garters if our men do not prevail.'

'Don't fret so Bek,' Norfolk retorted, 'how could we possibly fail?'

Despite his misgivings, the Bishop could not conceal his awe as the mass of heavy horse began to canter down the slope. Even before they hit the gallop, the din was thunderous as the beasts' great hooves hammered into the ground, throwing up great clods of earth and churning the ground instantly to mud. Added to this cacophony, were the sounds of clanking armour and the battle-cries of the young knights as they screamed their exhilaration to be part of such an invincible and unstoppable force. The Bishop, more man of war than man of God, had seen his fair share of such charges, but few compared to this. He could scarce believe that he was seeing near three thousand knights at the charge and he could not contemplate how terrifying it would be to be on the receiving end. If the peasants with their poles had not been Scots, he might have said a quiet prayer for their souls.

Wallace watched with growing horror as the body of English knights moved off en masse. The scale of the attack was so huge, he could scarcely believe it was real. The thundering rhythm of the advance seemed to hold him in a trance and it was only with a great effort that he was able to tear his eyes away.

He looked around at his captains and ordered them quickly to their schiltroms. 'May God forgive me, for I have brought you to the ring, now let's see if you can dance.'

The Bishop of Durham watched with a mixture of wonder and horror. The charging horsemen were now at full gallop and closing fast on the circled Scottish ranks. It seemed that their weight and momentum alone would simply sweep the Scots aside and leave them trampled underfoot. It was true that the enemy formations sat a little way up the far slope, but the incline was not steep enough to much slow the English charge. His heart beat fast as he awaited the inevitable clash, the grasping, glory-seeking Earls at his side all but forgotten.

The Earls themselves were still cheering when the Bishop sensed an almost imperceptible change in the lines of the attacking formation. The centre seemed to be slowing, while the wings charged on at speed. For a few seconds, it seemed to correct itself, but then, rather than a straight, unflinching line, it transformed into a ragged horseshoe shape, the centre near stopped and the wings thundering on unawares. The Bishop felt the blood drain from his face and his stomach turn to acid.

John Edward stood outside the ring of the schiltrom he commanded, transfixed by the heavy horses' advance. He could not tell if the ground shook, or if it was his legs trembling at the horrific sight. When the enemy had been at a distance, the formations behind him had appeared solid and threateningly impenetrable. With the English now close enough for him to make out individual snarling faces, their defences looked puny, makeshift and inadequate. It seemed to him that the English would simply wipe them from the earth with this one charge. With certain death mere seconds away, he offered up a prayer and asked God to save him from his fate.

The whispered words were hardly formed, when the English charge fell into sudden disarray. The heavy rains of the past few days had caused water to gather at the bottom of the valley floor, turning it to marsh. The first lines of the English centre hit at full pelt and their horses sank and foundered in the mud. The following knights were carried on by their momentum and crashed into the backs of those ahead. From being an impenetrable wall of horseflesh, lance and armour, the army's centre fell into a chaotic mess of thrashing and riderless horses and injured knights, who had been thrown from their seats.

The wings charged on and angled in to hit the schiltroms at full speed. The Scottish archers positioned between the schiltroms were able to slightly thin the English ranks, their arrows snatching knights from their saddles and inflicting grievous injuries on several heavy horse. They bravely stood and shot their bows until, alas, they all were ridden down and perished beneath the horses' hooves. The knights who struck the archers fared better than their fellows, for all their weight and all their plate counted for little when they crashed into the schiltroms' spikes.

The world around John Edward seemed to explode in a shower of earth and blood as the English knights crashed in. Horses screamed as they impaled themselves on well-aimed pikes and dropped thrashing to the ground. To his left, a riderless mount had made it through the wall of spears and, as it was trained to do, it bit and kicked viciously and was hacked to the ground only after it had inflicted serious injuries on a dozen men, whose screams were now added to the din. To his front, a knight still sat upon his dying, staggering horse and split every skull within reach of his battleaxe. He continued to fight bravely, even when his mount collapsed and pinned him helplessly to the ground. From this prone position, he still swung his mighty axe and reduced at least three shins to splinters, before a dozen blades and stamping feet brought his battle to an end. To his right, a dying horse thrashed in his death throes, his flying hooves destroying everything within their reach. The legs of two more horses were so destroyed and at least ten Scots patriots were killed or horribly crippled.

John hesitated for a moment, as he could not quite believe that the schiltrom had held and that the English charge had been repulsed. He turned to his drummer and, with a calmness which surprised him, ordered him to sound the advance. The fast double-beat instantly restored order, all spaces in the line were filled with men and pikes and they marched forward all in time. As the spearmen advanced, they pushed back the Englishmen who had kept their saddles and the schiltrom marched over those who had fallen and struggled to regain their feet when weighed down with heavy armour. Though some of these men fought until their very last breath, others had their souls ripped from their bodies even as they begged for mercy and offered themselves for ransom. Such pleas might have found influence with noble men-at-arms, but a peasant army knows no such niceties and noble throats were slit with rough daggers, even as their corpses were stripped of anything of use or value.

The immobile English knights were held at length by the points of Scottish spears and they shouted at the cowards to come out and fight them like men. John looked along the line to ensure that each man was in his place behind the wall of spears. The men stood poised in their

223

teams of six, two axe-men to chop each horse down and four swordsmen to kill each knight. He raised his arm above his head and looked to see that every eye was on him. He then swept it down towards the ground and sent the Scotsmen surging forward between the pikes. Though the English knights still jeered and shouted, they seemed astonished that their wish had indeed been granted. Before they could react, their mounts were being cut from beneath them and swords were being savagely stabbed down upon them before they hit the ground.

John had followed his men out onto the field and could hardly believe his eyes. Everywhere around him lay dead and dying horses and men. The unstoppable English force had been reduced to ragged chaos in a matter of moments. He ran forward to join his men in the slaughter. Strathbogie roared as he reduced another horse's leg to splintered ruins and stood back to let Eck and Scott stab down at its rider. An English knight in a crimson tabard spurred his horse on and swept his blade down at John's head. John ducked down and stepped back, before swinging at the man's leg, his blade slicing deeply into the back of his unprotected knee. Strathbogie came in from the side, his great axe smashing into the small of the knight's back, sending his horse galloping off with his crippled master clinging to its back. As John watched him go, he caught sight of activity at the foot of the valley. The English centre had freed itself from the marshy ground and looked to be ordering themselves for a charge. John shouted for his drummer and commanded him to sound the recall. The Scots disengaged as quickly as they could and ran for the protection of the schiltrom's spikes.

18

The Bishop of Coventry and Lichfield's
queasiness had nothing to do with the suffering
of his countrymen on the field at Falkirk, as he
was not yet aware of that unfolding disaster. It
was the failure of the apothecary's attempts to
rouse the King that was causing his stomach to
churn and hot bile to burn at the back of his
throat.

'Give him more!' Langton snapped, his voice
betraying a little of his rising panic. 'I can hear
that the battle has started, though the King has
not taken the field.'

'I dare not give him any more, my Lord. I
fear that it will surely kill him. I have seen men
die from less than that which I have already
poured into him.'

'Give him the rest!' Langton growled.
'Unless you want me to remove that old head
from your shoulders right here in the
bedchamber of the King.'

The old man held Langton's gaze long
enough to see that his threat was not an empty
one. He reached his long fingers into the small,
wooden bowl and scooped up the last of the
light green mush that it contained. He then

gently prised open the King's lips and smeared the paste on his tongue. Edward continued to breath raggedly and remained stubbornly unconscious. The apothecary reached for a goblet, held it to the King's mouth and tipped it so a trickle of wine washed over his tongue and down his throat. The effect was instantaneous and the apothecary jerked back, the goblet dropping from his hand and staining the blankets with wine, as Edward sat up with a roar.

'What is this? Do you poison your King?' The King of England spat and dribbled, soiling his own bedclothes.

Langton dismissed the apothecary with a jerk of his thumb and called for the King's valet. The man fair skulked into the chamber and began dressing the King as Langton succinctly laid out the events of the night and early morning. The King was indeed revived and his eyes burned brighter with malice the longer the Bishop spoke. The valet still struggled to secure the King's armour as his master strode out to his horse.

Anthony Bek had watched in horror as the premature cavalry charge had unravelled and then descended into catastrophe.

'Sound the recall!' He snapped, in irritation. 'Sound it before you lose them all.'

The Earl of Norfolk had turned paler and paler as the force of knights was whittled down, but his reluctance to admit to his mistake caused him to lay one bad decision upon another. 'But the centre readies itself for another attack. The

227

heavy horse will yet prove their worth and destroy the rebellious Scots.'

Bek's response was cut short by cries from the infantry and the approach of galloping horses. The Bishop turned to see King Edward, resplendent in his crown and his armour, approaching fast on his great charger, with Langton and his colour-bearer following in his wake.

'You'll answer for your folly now!' Bek spat at his fellow nobles, taking no small pleasure in the discomfited expressions on the faces of the hapless Earls of Norfolk, Lincoln and Hereford.

Edward reigned his horse in and ignored his nobles as he assessed the situation in the valley below.

'Sound the recall!' He ordered tersely.

'But, my Lord,' Norfolk pleaded, 'the centre have regrouped for the attack. We can finish the Scots, of that I am certain.'

Edward turned the full, terrible force of his glare onto Norfolk, bringing him, stuttering to silence. 'Should I take my lessons from one who is as inconstant as you? Seek counsel from one who has led my army to the brink of defeat in his impatience to snatch glory from his King? I think not, my Lord. I think not. Rather, it should be I who teaches the lesson and you who should watch how a King wins victory in battle, despite treachery in his own ranks. Stand down my Lords and observe, you will learn something this day, even if it is not humility.'

Wallace watched from the other side of the valley as the remains of the heavy horse responded to the horn and retreated to rejoin the main army. Great cheers broke out from the schiltroms and a torrent of jeers and insults were thrown at the backs of the English knights.

'Heavens William!' John Comyn exclaimed. 'I did not expect that the schiltroms would be able to stand! All of that expensive horseflesh forced back by our peasants with big sticks. I can scarce believe my eyes.'

'I did doubt it myself, my Lord, but I fear that it is only a temporary reprieve.' Wallace pointed at the opposite slope before continuing. 'Look there and tell me what you see.'

Comyn reduced his eyes to slits and peered across the glen. 'Ah! I see it now. It is the battle flag of the Plantagenet King. I did not spot it before.'

'That is because he has only just ridden onto the field. I doubted that he would order such a foolish attack and he certainly will not do so again. Now that he is at their head, our struggles may only have just begun.'

John Edward had watched the English horse make their slow retreat up the opposite slope and then he ordered the water bearers to allow the men to slake their thirst. He bid them to lay down their poles to give their arms some rest and many took the opportunity to leave their places and empty their bladders and bowels at a short distance away. He also gave permission for a small number of men to start the business of stripping the dead, although this was on the condition that any loot was to be shared with the rest. Before long, it seemed as though half of his men were dressed in English armour or carrying their weapons and shields. A group were even amusing themselves with a captive, taking turns to torment him as he flailed blindly and tried in vain to remove the helmet which had been crushed tight onto his head. Although he did not begrudge his men this respite from the battle, his eyes never left the English army. His gaze flicked back and forth constantly, hungry for any slight sign of movement.

At first, he thought that the cavalry had been ordered to repeat their charge, but quickly observed that only the two wings were made up of heavy horse and that they trotted forward only to protect the great numbers of archers who made their way down the slope at their centre. He cursed at the realisation that the placement of the English troops was very wise indeed. The archers would be protected from the small force of Scottish cavalry by the horsemen to their sides and by the marshy ground at their front. He had experienced coming under attack from archers once before and he did not relish going through such terror again. He rushed to organise his men to defend themselves as best they could. He ordered the pikemen to raise their poles above their heads. By crowding them together, they were able to form a loose, raft-like structure, which would provide some protection for them and for as many men as could huddle down amongst their feet. In this manner, John guessed that around one third of his schiltrom was under some kind of cover. About a third of the remainder had looted English shields to share and the rest were on their own.

John's stomach turned to water as a command sounded clearly across the glen. 'Nock!' There was the slightest of pauses before the same voice ordered, 'Draw!' A slightly longer pause followed before the dreaded, 'Loose!' A single arrow makes relatively little noise in flight, but when a thousand shafts are released at the same time, the 'whooshing' is quite distinct as the air rushes past the fletching and the shaft. When cowering beneath flimsy cover, this sound is so terrifying it can reduce a strong man to a quivering, sobbing wreck. But even this is nothing when compared to the din and carnage as the arrows arch down and hit their mark with devastating force. Hundreds of arrows crashed down into the thick, wooden poles above John Edward's head, their force enough to drive some men to their knees, with some pushing their way between the poles, sinking their metal bodkins into the ground or clean through flesh and bone. Even through the cacophony of the screaming of the injured, John heard the commands given again. By the fourth time the orders were shouted, men from the unprotected rear of the schiltrom began to break. John did not even call to them to hold, as he could hardly blame them for running. Without anything to shield them, their part of the field was already strewn with jerking corpses and men screaming their agonies to the sky.

231

With each new flight of arrows, more men were cut down and the once stout poles were reduced to splinters. All John could do was cower low and pray that the English would soon exhaust their supplies. This hope was cruelly dashed as he watched carts heaped with hundreds of bundles of arrows trundle down the slope and a crowd of boys rush to unload them and distribute them quickly to the archers. He cursed violently at the inevitability of defeat. When the archers' arms grew weak, as they surely would, the English horse would simply charge in and slaughter what little of the schiltroms remained.

It was then that Eck appeared at his side and slapped him on the back. 'We need to run John. We're all dead if we stay here.'

'We can't!' John protested dejectedly. 'The English horse would ride us down long before we reached the Torwood. We're done whatever we do.'

'Then, let's at least give these men half a chance. The Wallace said that you could get your schiltrom to dance, then why not dance it back from here? The knights will not attack while you are still in formation. You could buy a few hundred paces.' Eck gave his cousin a sickly smile. 'I will distract the English for a while. Make the best of it.'

With those words, Eck marched out of the meagre protection of the schiltrom and down the slope until he had covered a third of the distance between the Scots and English lines. He then stopped, drew both of his swords and held them out at arm's length, inviting the enemy to him.

'Jesus Eck!' John spat, not wanting to see his cousin cut down, but still unable to avert his gaze.

The change happened quite slowly, but John detected that the tattoo of bodkin strikes above his head had lessened, as many of the Welsh archers were tempted to test their skills on a smaller target than that offered by the schiltroms themselves. As the earth around Eck started to fill with shafts, John was determined that his cousin's inevitable sacrifice would not be made in vain. He called to his drummer to sound the reverse, only to find the boy with his skull split in two and his brains spread across the grass. He snatched up the drum himself and sounded it as loud as he could. Still in shock from the onslaught from above, it took the men several beats to respond, but then they moved as they had been trained and the schiltrom began to inch slowly back. To his side, he caught sight of Wallace riding urgently to the other battalions and, by gesturing in his direction, he urged them to follow his lead. The deadly shafts still crashed down and thinned their ranks as they moved. John was struck hard in the thigh and sent crashing backwards onto the ground. Strathbogie pulled him up before he was trampled and the blood-spattered Robertson took his place on the drum. The bodkin had pierced deep into his bone and neither he nor Strathbogie could shift it. As they continued to pace backwards, John sawed at the shaft with his dagger, his teeth clenched tight against the pain and still the deadly arrows arched up into the sky.

King Edward looked on with satisfaction as his archers achieved what his nobles' knights had failed to do.

'I paid a pretty penny to have all those arrows made, Langton. It must do you good to see that it was gold well spent.'

Langton grinned in spite of himself. The King had indeed spent a fortune on the manufacture of armaments over the years, but it was he who had been forced to scrabble around to ensure that all of the financial commitments were met. Though he had cursed the man at the time, he could not at this moment begrudge him anything, for, although he was tardy, he had done his part and won the day. Victory in Scotland would strengthen his position with the nobles and so make Langton's own life much less arduous.

'Look at that impudent dog there!' Edward exclaimed. 'He mocks us all. Bek, tell the archers to hit him. I would like to see him fall.'

'They are trying, my Lord. See the arrows spring up around him like wheat. It is hard at this distance to hit a target so small.' Bek shrugged his shoulders in resignation. 'We should send a knight to cut him down. That's a sight which would raise a cheer from our men.'

A voice came from their rear, 'I would gladly have that honour, my Lord.'

Langton waved the man forward so he could directly address his King. The knight was no more than twenty years old, he was handsome and wore the most shiny and immaculate armour the Bishop had ever seen. He carried a fine shield of white with red markings, which Langton thought was a work of art in itself.

King Edward stared hard at the young nobleman for a few seconds before turning to Anthony Bek. 'Command the archers to hold while this,' he paused slightly before continuing, 'young man puts an end to our friend on the field.'

The young man thanked the King most prettily, dropped his visor and kicked on down the slope.

Edward turned to Langton, his expression uncommonly grim, even for him. 'Let's hope he can see to this knave as enthusiastically as I am told he sees to my gentle son. I doubt that his proclivities will prevent him from putting a man to the sword.'

Langton kept his face impassive and his eyes to the front. King Edward had never spoken of the Prince in this way before and Langton's instincts told him that entering into such a conversation would be fraught with peril.

The earth around Eck Edward fair bristled with a thousand arrow shafts. They formed a wide circle around him that was thicker at the centre and thinned out towards its edges. No man who possessed his sanity would stand under such a ferocious shower of arrows, but Black Eck stood there defiant, unruffled and serene. At a distance, it appeared that not one Welsh archer had succeeded in hitting him with a single shaft. A closer inspection would reveal that his cloak was in tatters, ripped through by more than a dozen sharp bodkin points. Blood flowed from his shoulder, where only a slight, involuntary, reflex shrug had spared him from more serious injury. His right boot had not escaped unscathed, a shaft having pierced it at the toes and skewered it to the ground. Eck was glad that he had taken the boots from a man with bigger feet than he.

He watched impassively as the knight cantered down the slope and moved only when he kicked his horse into the gallop and lowered his lance ready for the strike. Eck casually swept his sword from one side to the other to clear a space for himself among the arrows. From atop the slope, it appeared that the dark figure scythed at a deadly summer's crop. Young Huntercombe was already daydreaming about the praise the King would surely heap upon him once he had reduced the insolent peasant to broken bones, torn flesh and rags. The Prince had forbidden him from participating in the charge, but would concede that he could scarcely disobey what had effectively been his King's royal command. With his target only two strides away, he had his lance aimed true and straight at his heart. The dog was only inches away when he suddenly disappeared from view. Eck had dropped one sword and, with the remaining one gripped tight in both his hands, he ducked below the lance's tip and swung at the charger's legs with all the force he could muster. The impact had jarred him hard and almost ripped his arms from his shoulders. The steed went down in a shower of earth and threw his rider to the ground with a sickening crunch. Young Huntercombe was badly dazed and found that he could not move his legs. He did try to crawl away, but Eck kicked him hard and pushed him onto his back. With that self-same foot, he forced the knight's visor up to reveal a face bloody from where it had struck the ground. To the cheers of his retreating comrades, Eck made it bloodier still. He placed his sword's point on Huntercombe's ruined nose and leaned full on the blade until his skull cracked and his helmet filled with blood. Without a backwards glance at Edward's mighty army, he strolled back up the hill to join his fellows in their retreat.

Few songs are sung in celebration when an army is heavily defeated, but from Falkirk there came one which was sung for many a year to come. In the darkest days of the war against the English, men sang it around campfires to stay their courage and reassure themselves that victory could be won.

Upon the field of battle,
Eck, with swagger, stands,
Defying the bastard Edward,
A sword in baith his hands.

The Welsh archers did their work,
They filled the sky wi' shafts,
Every arrow aimed at Black Eck,

And he just stands and laughs.

The arrows flew and flew again,
And came crashing to the ground,
And in the middle stood Black Eck,
Unmoving, wi' arrows all around.

Kind Edward was most furious,
His face knotted in a frown,
He told a brave, young knight,
To quickly ride Black Eck down.

Upon his great black charger,
He thundered down the hill,
His lance pointed at Black Eck,
As he closed to make his kill.

Eck did watch him coming,
He did not move a pace,
First he killed the charger,
Then stabbed the poor knight's face.

King Edward in his fury,
Sent his army down the hill,
But even ten thousand Englishmen,
Could not Eck the Black kill.

Black Eck, Black Eck,
A sword in baith his hands,
Black Eck, Black Eck,
Edward trembles where he stands.

Black Eck, Black Eck,
They couldn't cut him down,

Black Eck, Black Eck,
With arrows all around.

19

Even as young Huntercombe spurred his horse into the fray, King Edward had noted that the Scottish formations were gradually backing away. Eager to ensure that no man was to escape his wrath, he ordered the whole army to advance and cut down every last one of them. The knights whooped their excitement and whipped their heavy horses into the gallop. He watched impassively as the small Scottish cavalry force came to meet them.

'Why sacrifice the few cavalry they have when the battle is already lost?' Langton enquired, as the distance between the two forces closed.

Edward roared with laughter, 'This is why I command armies and you count coins Langton. The Scots do not mean to engage in battle. They will swerve away at the last moment and hope that our knights will be foolish enough to pursue their faster, more nimble horses. That way, they hope to give their foot soldiers the chance to reach yonder forest and escape the slaughter.'

Even as he spoke, the Scottish horsemen broke to the left and accelerated away. Then, to his horror, the greater part of his force of knights spurred their horses into the pursuit.

'Jesus Christ!' Edward cursed furiously, sending specks of white spittle flying into the air. 'The fools will never catch them and they leave the Scots foot to escape.'

Langton fought to repress the wry grin which threatened to steal onto his face. The stupidity and greed of the nobles did not surprise him at all. Each and every one of them would choose to pursue the Scottish horse in the hope of taking a noble prisoner for ransom or of garnering their knightly reputation by putting him to the sword. By comparison, riding down dirty peasants would hold little appeal for them, even if to do so would bring the Scots' stubborn resistance to an end. He opened his mouth to make some placatory remark, but was stopped by a strange noise coming from the King.

Though he remained upright in his saddle, the King's head was arched backwards and his eyes were rolled so far back in his head that only their whites were visible. White foam bubbled at the corners of his mouth and hot pish ran down his legs, causing his trews to lightly steam. Langton glanced anxiously at the other nobles and saw that their attention was concentrated fully on the field of battle, the Scottish formations having broken down into a desperate, disordered retreat. He reached for the reigns of the King's horse and quietly led him off and away from curious, critical eyes.

The English knights chased Wallace and Comyn's horsemen for almost two full miles,

241

the Scottish leaders taking care to moderate their speed enough to persuade their pursuers that they would soon catch them up. All too soon, the English realised that their heavy chargers could never run down the smaller, faster beasts and they turned to join their infantry in hunting down the remnants of the schiltroms that had so recently taken the lives of their fellow knights. The Scots then turned their horses and harassed the English rear, but being so heavily outnumbered, they suffered heavy losses and did not delay them long.

John Edward, aided by Strathbogie and the Robertson, had covered almost three-quarters of the distance to the safety of the Torwood before the thunder of cavalry sounded to their rear. In panic, they quickened their pace and cast hurried glances over their shoulders to see the noble knights scything down the stragglers and the wounded who hobbled behind. The trail of dead lay scattered all the way back to the great heaps of corpses which lay, full of arrows, where the mighty schiltroms so recently stood.

'You should leave me!' John gasped as he limped on, his leg leaden and numb.

'Save your breath laddie!' Strathbogie snapped. 'We've lost more than enough men today. I'll no' leave another behind.'

They ran on, ignoring the sounds of slaughter behind them, their eyes fixed on the thick forest ahead. They had almost begun to think that they would reach the trees, when heavy hooves thundered down upon them. The Robertson threw John to the ground as he spun on his heels and raised his great axe high above his head. The horse collapsed, screaming, to the ground, its skull shattered by the Robertson's vicious swing. The knight was nimble enough to pull his feet from his stirrups and keep his balance as he stepped to the ground. The Robertson was still in the act of freeing his weapon from where it was embedded in equine bone and the knight cut him down with a sharp thrust to the old man's broad chest. That thrust was the knight's last act on this earth, as Strathbogie's blade landed with enough force to break his neck in spite of the armour he wore.

'Run for it lads!' The Robertson moaned, his torso soaked in his own blood. 'He has finished me.'

Strathbogie looked long at the pulsing hole in the Robertson's chest. He then fell to his knees and kissed his old comrade on the forehead. 'We will remember you Laird, and will never forget all that you have done.'

'It is my time to go,' he replied wearily. 'I should have died at Stirling with the sweet taste of victory on my lips. Instead I will meet my maker choked with the bitterness of defeat. Go now and ease my passage, I will die happier if I know that you live. Get the Edward boy away, I know that he has much more to give.'

Strathbogie nodded and rose to his feet, pulling John up with him. With a final salute, they left the Robertson dying on the field and continued their flight. The din of fighting and dying increased at their backs just as they entered the forest. They turned to see a scene of such slaughter that their hearts seemed to seize in their chests. The scale of it did not match the butchery they had witnessed at Stirling, but the victims of that bloodbath were English and here it was good Scotsmen who were slain. The knights, having driven off the last of the Scottish horse, rode around and cleaved down to break any skulls that they could reach. The English men-at-arms and infantry had now caught up with the retreat and they set themselves to the slaughter with the most terrible efficiency. They speared and stabbed at any Scot they could find, be he living or wounded or dead. Those who could find no target for their murderous intent upon the field, set their eyes upon the forest and advanced in search of wretched Scots to kill.

'Go John! Lose yourself in the forest!' Strathbogie drew his sword as he issued this command. 'I will hold these bastards here a while, so you can make good your escape.'

A glance along the tree-line told John that others followed Strathbogie's example and stood to buy their wounded comrades at least a little time. The English spotted them lurking in the shadows and hesitated, reluctant to rush in while unsure as to what they faced.

'Now John, go! You're no use to us here. I promised the Robertson that I would see you safely away. I would not have you make a liar out of me.' Strathbogie then turned his back on his young friend and peered through the foliage at the gathering English.

John limped away using his father's sword as a crutch to speed his progress deeper into the trees. Though his breath was ragged, he could still hear the terrible sounds from the field. Men screamed and moaned and begged futilely for mercy which would not be granted. He had not travelled far when the air was filled with aggressive cries and the clash of blade on blade. He quickened his pace knowing that the English foot had overcome their fears and plunged into the forest. They would soon learn that the line that faced them was thin indeed and would not hold them for long. John pushed on far into the evening and, though he saw not a single soul, the sounds of pursuit, capture and retribution were all around him. The length and pitch of many screams told him that his countrymen did not die well, but that they were tortured horribly before their throats were slit. As darkness fell, John began to hope that he could actually evade the enemy and get himself away. Though his leg throbbed horribly and sweat fairly soaked his shirt, he did not slacken off and concentrated on making just the next two steps, not thinking of the long struggle ahead. He did pause briefly to listen for a sound which came from far away. Though soft and distant, it chilled him to the bone. It seemed that darkness would not deflect the English from their hunt and they sought to defeat the night by bringing in dogs to track their prey.

Closer and closer their barking came, until John knew he would not out-run them. Despite the numbness of his leg, he pulled himself up into the branches of a tree and perched there listening as the hunters and their hounds passed him by. For a moment he was sure that he had been discovered, as the dogs' barking erupted into a loud frenzy, but they moved steadily past him until their din faded away. He waited a while longer, not least because he needed rest, and then, slowly and silently, he slipped back down to the ground. With his back against the tree, he closed his eyes and listened, alert for any sound. He breathed a quiet sigh of relief when he heard nothing but the breeze rustling in the leaves. He was about to make a move when a voice from the darkness froze him where he stood.

'I told thee there was one slinking hereabouts. The hounds are never wrong, they smelt him hiding in the tree.'

'Tis true Barret, I'd wager my life on their snouts. That's three already they've winkled out, but this one looks the best. Judging by his cloth, he'll have silver somewhere about himself, plenty enough for the three of us.'

'Charlie will take his boots, that's for sure, his are so full of holes. You can have his jerkin, if I can have his sword. It's so much finer than my old thing and would look perfect hanging at my side.'

'Look! This one is young and is handsome to boot. We won't get another that's so pretty, we should keep this tyke whole so we can bugger him.'

'Oh 'eck Curtis!' Barret complained. 'Can't you rut him once he's dead? It always takes much longer if we have to disarm them first.'

'Look at what happened with the last one. Shat himself he did. I wasn't touching that dirty bastard. I'm not a fucking pig.'

John could make out the shapes of the two men in the darkness, but did not know the position of the third man of whom they had spoken. He had drawn his sword to defend himself, but now braced it against the earth to steady himself against a wave of dizziness.'

'Look!' Curtis exclaimed. 'He's near to dropping. We can just wait the bastard out.'

'Jesus!' Barret cursed. 'It's always the same with you. We'll give it a while, but I'm having the sword. If he's not dropped by the time I've eaten this cheese, I'll cut him down myself and you can do what you like.'

'Fair enough!' Curtis responded, nodding his agreement. 'Ah look! Here's Charlie now!'

John listened in horror as the pair related the situation to their comrade. His wooziness had worsened and the forest swam before his eyes, though he was alert enough to gather that Charlie agreed with his fellows' plan and was indeed keen to take his boots.

'Not long now!' Curtis announced cheerfully. 'That arrow hole must have been leaking for hours now. He can have scarcely a drop of blood left in him.'

In spite of his poor state and the predicament he found himself in, John found his stomach grumbling painfully as the Englishmen ate. If he had possessed sufficient energy to raise his sword, he would have fought them for just one mouthful of their bread and cheese. He detected movement at the edge of his vision. but dismissed it as a trick of the light. The Englishmen saw it just as John did, but were already too late to react. Barret's cry of alarm was cut off as his head was severed from his neck. His eyes were still wide with astonishment when his head rolled to a stop at John's feet. Charlie had immediately reached for his sword, but was unable to grasp its hilt as his arm had already been severed at the elbow. His bleeding stump had given him little protection as a sword point punctured his throat, sending him crashing to the ground in a crimson spray. Curtis had proven himself to the most sensible of the three by immediately turning to run. If he had moved a little more quickly, he might have avoided having his skull split in two.

John could barely keep his eyes open as the dark figure sheathed his swords and stepped towards him. Black Eck bent down and gently lifted John onto his shoulder. John mumbled his thanks as Eck marched on into the forest.

'Wheesht John!' Eck whispered back. 'The woods are filled with the English. We must pick our way through their lines. If we're no' out of here before morning, there's no doubt we'll die at their hands.'

When John next regained consciousness, nearly another full day had passed. He was wrapped up tightly in Eck's cloak and, though sweat poured from his face, he shivered uncontrollably with cold. At first, he had thought that he was in a cave, but then realised that he lay in an eroded cavity, high on a riverbank.

'Where are we?' He asked weakly, barely able to lift his head enough to meet his cousin's eyes.

'Just outside Stirling. It was far as I could get. I walked all night and collapsed here just as the sun was rising. I have slept all day and, as soon as darkness falls, I'll set out to run some errands. Once they are done, I'll get us back on our way.'

Though Eck was in far better shape than he, John could see that the last few days had taken a toll on him. Dark rings surrounded his eyes, giving him the appearance of a man on the brink of exhaustion. He was covered in crusted blood, some of which came from his shoulder wound, some from carrying John and some from the English knights he had slaughtered upon the field. John closed his eyes for just a moment and, when he opened them again, the world was dark and his cousin gone.

Eck's priorities were food and a horse, but providence had delivered him a chance to right a wrong. A wiser man might have limited himself to his stealing, but Eck did not think that justice would take him long. Pure chance had led him to seek shelter on that bank on a bend in the Forth, but he saw the hand of a higher power in placing him not half a mile from old Saint Ninian's Kirk.

The hinges of the Kirk's door screeched loudly as Eck pushed it open. The priest turned his head at the sound and looked Eck up and down. This was not the first fugitive Father Campbell had seen today and he would likely not be the last to be sent away empty-handed, save for a hurried blessing.

'We have no food here, my son.' Father Campbell announced, in a tone which was bereft of any real regret.

Eck stared back at the priest and took in his tonsured head, flabby cheeks and great protruding stomach. There was no doubt, this was the man Al had pointed out to him on the field before Stirling Bridge.

'I'm no' here for food. I'm here for a friend.'

Eck then spoke the full name of his friend and watched the holy man's face drain of all colour. He then advanced towards him down the aisle and told him that he knew all about his vile, nocturnal habits and his perverted liking for little, orphan boys. The priest raised his hands to protect himself and rambling excuses stuttered from his mouth. When his denials did nothing to slow Eck's advance, he then tried vainly to lay the blame upon the boy and his inherent sinfulness. Eck's fist stilled his mouth and sent him crashing to the Kirk's stone floor. He sat there stunned and bleeding, his teeth around him on the slabs. A single kick to his left temple was enough to knock him senseless and let Eck get to his grim work. He lifted his robe, removed his stained underclothes and gelded him with a single, practised stroke. He then wiped his knife and strode back out into the darkness, his mind already on the thievery that he must complete that night.

The widow watched the dark soldier stride off into the gloom and, with her grown-up daughter close by her side, crept cautiously to the Kirk's door. She peaked inside and saw Father Campbell spread-eagled on the floor. She took her time to gaze around and ensure that he was alone. Once confident that no-one lurked behind the pews, she took her daughter's hand and made her way to where her priest lay bleeding. Her daughter put her hand to her mouth in shock, but the widow shook her head.

'It was always going to happen. It was only a matter of time. The dirty, fat bastard couldn't keep his fingers to himself. At least he'll no' be botherin' any more bairns now.'

The daughter was still in shock and stared down at the spreading mess. 'Oh my God! Look at his thing. It's so small and shrivelled there. It looks nothing like my Donald's.'

The widow stifled a laugh. 'Maybe that's how your Donald's would be if you sliced away his plums. Now run along and fetch some cloths, or Father Campbell will bleed himself to death. Who knows, there may be some pennies when he knows we saved his life. There'll certainly be silver if he wants us to keep this quiet.'

20

The English trackers were tired after their long day's hunt. Their Lord had promised them silver for every outlaw they caught and killed and would exchange one coin for every left ear they brought to him as proof. Their sack had grown heavy as the day progressed and, with their fortune assured, they at last sat down to rest. In any case, they had come so far, the pickings had grown quite thin. With driftwood from the river, they soon had a fire lit and a thick stew bubbling in their pot. They stretched out on the grass and relaxed their weary legs. The conversation was a happy one, as they looked forward to their feast. The loaf of bread was hard and stale, but would do just fine if it was toasted in the flames. One man had a skin of wine and, in his good humour, offered to share it with his fellows.

The pleasant atmosphere was destroyed by a demon leaping suddenly into their midst. Silent, dark and furious, he whipped at them with his swords, ripping them to ribbons before they could raise themselves. Whilst two of them still lay groaning, their lifeblood squirting into the grass, the demon helped himself to their horse, their steaming stew and their dry, old loaf.

The Robertson blinked his eyes and stared up at the sky above. There was not a single cloud and a host of stars twinkled in the black. The moon was full and shone brighter than any the old man could recall. He had momentarily believed that he had reached the afterlife, but his aching bladder soon convinced him that he was still rooted to the earth. He doubted that one would have the need to pish once inside the heavenly gates. Though he breathed, it could scarcely be said that he remained among the living, for the field was strewn with corpses. Most had been stripped of their clothing, the moonlight reflecting off pale white skin and revealing the terrible, gaping injuries which had snatched their souls away.

He ran his trembling fingers over himself to check that he was whole. His arms and legs remained intact and he seemed unscathed, apart from the crusted wound at his breast. He gingerly raised himself up, groaning at the pain caused by the wound's scab stretching as he moved. He sat there for a moment, still astonished that he had not died, then cursed when he realised that he was dressed in only his gore-soaked simmit. His boots, trews, tunic and cloak had been stripped from him and he had been left all but naked on the field. The thief, whether an Englishman or godless local, must have thought him dead. His axe, dagger and purse had also disappeared. He had a faint memory of lying bleeding in the grass as the English foot advanced. He had steeled himself as he heard them put other wounded men, screaming, to the sword and as their footsteps grew closer, he had made his whispering peace with God. After that he could recall nothing and assumed that he had fallen into unconsciousness. With death having rejected him once again, he struggled to his feet and went in search of some torn and bloody rags to cover his modesty.

In that same moonlight, John and Eck struggled up the steep slopes of the Ochil hills. The going was slow, tough and dangerous, but the pair had little choice, for the roads around Stirling were already busy with English soldiers, now that the vanguard of their army had arrived there. The horse Eck had stolen was old but sure-footed and proved its worth as it carried John on through the night. Once they reached the summit, the brightness of the moon enabled them to move much more quickly and Eck led the horse downwards at a run. They risked the road to Perth and followed it until they sighted the walls of the moated castle above Auchterarder. Being unsure as to who now held the castle, its previous lord having sworn fealty to the English King, they left the road and turned overland and struck out in the direction of Crieff. With dawn now lighting the horizon, Eck searched for a place to see out the day.

They stumbled upon the stone circle as they pushed through a ring of small trees in the midst of an overgrown meadow. The four stones stood about as high as a man and, along with the trees and grasses, provided some shelter from the wind and sufficient cover to shield them from the view of any villagers going about their business.

Eck helped John down from the saddle and settled him with his back against one of the stones. He then thrust his hand into his pack and withdrew the cloth which contained the remaining chunks of meat from the previous night's stew. He chewed away ravenously and encouraged his shivering, sweating cousin to do the same.

Once they had eaten, they both soon fell asleep. John twisted and jerked on the ground as he suffered fevered dreams of a hail of arrows falling on the earth like winter's rain. He moaned and whimpered as, in his delirium, he saw all of those he loved struck down by the great shafts. When he awakened, it took a few seconds for him to realise that he had dreamed it all and that his friends and family were not dead, apart, that was, from those comrades who now lay rotting on the field at Falkirk. He glanced over to see his cousin sound asleep, seemingly untroubled by the visions of hell which had plagued his every dream ever since his dance with death following the battle at Stirling Bridge. He let his cousin slumber on and shivered and sweated alone as the afternoon dragged on interminably.

The sun was still high when Eck arose, yawning, from his grassy bed.

'By Christ,' he said through a yawn, 'that is the best rest I've had in an age. It must be the magic in these stones that has banished my nightmares. Father told me that they were erected by the ancients who sacrificed women here to give power to their spells. It certainly worked well for me.' He turned to examine the tallest of the stones and ran his fingers across its rough surface. 'Look here! You can still make out where they carved their signs. This one's a hand with the thumb pointed down. Maybe it shows where their treasure was buried.'

Eck's enthusiasm died as his cousin's quavering voice interrupted him in mid-flow.

'You must leave me here Eck. I am starting to die. You must go and save yourself.'

'No!' Eck replied simply. 'That's no' happening.'

'Eck!' John implored. 'My fever grows hotter and my leg festers, don't tell me you have not noticed the stench. We have both seen this before and there is no doubt where it will end. I would not weigh you down with my corpse.'

'Answer me one question first and you must speak the truth. When I was cut down at Stirling and you carried me home, did anyone tell you that it was hopeless and that you should lay me down to die?'

John nodded. Many of their comrades had looked at Eck as if he was already a corpse. It was only he, his brother Scott and Al who had refused to prepare him for his shroud.

'And yet you carried me home. That is my answer to you. I would not leave you to die, not while there is still blood running in my veins. If you ask me again my answer will be just the same. Now rest while I fetch water to drink.'

John opened his weary mouth to pursue his argument, but Eck had already slipped away through the stones.

Billy Bardine had the rabbit fixed in his sight. He moved slowly and silently to load a stone into his slingshot, taking the greatest of care not to scare the wee beastie away. In his mind, he already saw the smile on his mother's stern face when he strode in with something for the pot. He ducked down fast when he heard footsteps swishing through the long grasses to his right and cursed as the rabbit twitched its ears and shot off into the undergrowth. The loss of his prey, though sore, was of less concern to him than the danger of being caught poaching on castle lands. He had seen lads much younger than him swing from a rope for just that crime. He crouched unmoving and waited, his eyes fixed on the source of the sound. The figure that emerged from the bank of the stream filled young Billy with both relief and excitement. He was relieved that he was a stranger and therefore unlikely to be on the hunt for miscreants such as he. His excitement came from the prospect of silver, as the castle would surely reward him if he told them where outlaws were to be found.

While Billy could hunt and run as fast as a deer, not even his mother would claim that he was the brightest of boys. In his eagerness for silver, he ran for the castle without thinking of how he would explain his unlawful presence on castle land. Once he had breathlessly relayed his tale, he found himself not showered with silver,

257

but subjected to a terse interrogation and assailed with accusations of stealing the Laird's game. He ran from the castle empty-handed, with the captain's boot speeding his arse's way over the moat.

The Scotstoun men sat quietly as the afternoon slowly meandered its way towards dusk. Though still tired and sore from their hurried flight, they were impatient with waiting and eager to get on the road. The English would not tarry long in Stirling and they could not risk being overtaken when that great army lumbered its way north. The sound was slight and distant, but Eck's ears were sharp and he caught it on the breeze. He leapt to his feet in one fluid movement and crept to the edge of the trees. At the far side of the moor, on the outskirts of the village, a line of men advanced towards the stones. With around twenty paces between them, they formed a curve which suggested that they approached them on all sides.

Eck stepped back into the stone circle and bent down to hoist his cousin onto his shoulder, a hissed whisper warning him of the coming threat.

'Leave me Eck! I will only slow you down.' John's face was dreadfully pale and his voice weak, shaky and easy to ignore.

With John held over his left shoulder and a sword already drawn in his right hand, Eck took five long strides and splashed down into the bed of the stream. Though it was shallow, the stream's banks were overhung with bushes, long

258

grasses and the small trees that thrive in marshy ground. This provided almost complete cover as Eck sprinted swiftly along the stony bed. The sound of voices brought him to a sudden halt and he crouched down as low as he could go and fought to still his laboured breath. Between the leaves and stems, he saw a maille-clad spearman searching from left to right, thrashing his weapon through the undergrowth as if he hoped to spur his prey to flight. Eck's heart near stopped when the spearman seemed to momentarily lock eyes with him, but he must have been mistaken, as the man did not hesitate and continued on in his hunt. The same thrashing was being carried out on the other bank, but that man also failed to spy the Edward men and he too passed them by.

Eck let the soldiers march on ten paces before he rose and stepped forward, his strides slow and deliberate so his feet splashed as quietly as he could manage. As the distance opened up between them, he lengthened his stride and increased his pace, with less concern for the noise he made. A great shout went up from behind them and told them that the trap had been sprung at the standing stones and that their hiding place had been found to be empty. However, the hunters would have found sufficient evidence of their recent presence, in the form of the old English steed and Eck's meagre pack, to convince them to stiffen their pursuit. As Eck advanced, the vegetation thinned and they found themselves traversing open moorland and it was not long before the shout went up and the soldiers appeared in a group at the top of the slope. Eck ignored the shouts and running feet and fixed his eyes on the village in the distance. He knew that he would never reach Crieff, but would not stop until he had no other choice before him. It was the sound of distant, thundering hooves which brought him to a halt. He lay his cousin down upon the ground as gently as he could. He smiled at him and stroked his face and told him that he had taken him as far as he was able. A single tear formed in his eye and he apologised for not being able to get him home.

John grasped his hand and squeezed it. 'Now you must run! You have done all you can for me.'

Eck broke away and rose to his feet, drawing both his swords as he stood. 'I told you that I would stay with you while there was blood still running in my veins. My words were true, but I fear that it will not now run there for long. Still, my promise will be kept and I will die the happier for that.'

Eck turned and cast his eyes up the long and gentle slope. Though the setting sun blazed on the horizon, he could see that the garrison soldiers were marching determinedly down towards him. Though he could see only their silhouettes, he estimated that there was at least thirty of them, most armed with heavy spears. The force of horsemen, just cresting the hill, was fewer in number, but approached at greater speed. Eck guessed that they would pass the men on foot and reach him a few paces before their fellows. He allowed himself a smile as he realised that it mattered not. The outcome was not in doubt and did not hang on the order of their arrival. He steeled himself and prepared to die, but was determined that he would not be the first to depart this life this day.

It was as he squinted into the dying sun that the foot soldiers began to shout out in alarm. Although the horsemen could not be unsighted, as the sun was at their backs, they drove on straight and did not deviate from their course. The spearmen tried to scatter, but were ridden down without a trace of mercy. The riders swung their long cavalry swords and cut down those few men who were still left standing. Eck overcame his puzzlement and despatched two who had fled in terror and had stumbled in his direction. Still unsure as to what had just occurred, Eck kept his sword held high as the shadowed horsemen came near. It was only when they were close enough to touch that Eck's face broke into a grin.

'Could you no' have arrived a wee bit earlier? I thought I was going to have to kill them all myself.'

'Next time I'll just leave you to it.' Edward de Bruce laughed as he dismounted and embraced Eck. 'Now be a good lad and sheath your swords. We wouldn't want you taking someone's eye out, would we?'

'I thought we were done for there. What the hell are you doing here anyway?'

'My elder brother has me tracking the progress of the English King. He is, as we speak, riding into yonder castle with his whole army at his back. You should see it Eck. It stretches back near as far as Stirling.'

'I have seen it.' Eck replied. 'And I'd wager that it was at closer quarters than you.'

'Ah, of course. You were at Falkirk with Wallace. Was it as bad as they say it was?'

'Worse. The army was destroyed. Their archers cut down men by the thousand and their knights rode down the rest. John himself took an arrow and I am trying to get him home.'

De Bruce looked down at the prone form Eck had indicated. 'Christ! John? Is that you?' John's eyes flickered open but he made no sound in response. 'He looks bad Eck. I don't know if he'll make it, but I will help you all I can. I would not risk the road to Perth, though the English are yet to reach that far. The defeat at Falkirk has the nobles all astir and they will be eager to show their loyalty before Edward reaches their doors. There is no better way to do this than by capturing any who fought with Wallace and throwing them at the tyrant's feet. Come, we meant to make camp at Perth tonight, so we can accompany you for most of the way.'

Langton rode at King Edward's side as he led his army along Auchterarder's single, muddy street. The local folk lined its edges and tossed flowers beneath the hooves of the King's horse.

'See how they toss petals at my feet whilst glaring at me with their sullen, bitter eyes. Methinks it would be better if I was to scour every last miserable Scot from this land. I win them victory after victory and still they give their loyalty only grudgingly and will switch it the moment I depart. The Scots are such a stubborn, graceless race, I cannot see what benefit they bring.' Edward shook his head in disbelief at the people's lack of gratitude.

'But, my Lord,' Langton replied, 'who would work the fields if they were all put to slaughter?'

'Ah, Langton, why must you always think of coin?' The King again shook his head, though this time it was at his Treasurer's obsessive fixation with the lowly matter of money.

'I suppose that it is well that one of us thinks of coin.' Langton replied archly.

Edward laughed uproariously and threw his head back. 'Very amusing Langton. You grow wittier as your beard grows whiter.'

Langton was tempted to tell Edward that his expenditure was no laughing matter, but decided that it would be foolish to test his temper. He instead excused himself and fell back down the column until he rode at the side of the apothecary.

'As soon as we get to the castle, I want you out finding the plant for the King's tonic. He'll need his energy for the days ahead.'

The old man kept his eyes to the front and studiously avoided the Treasurer's gaze. Langton was long enough in the tooth to know that he was about to be played with.

'That might be difficult, my Lord. I have other commitments to keep and am too old to be traipsing about in the woods and hunting through hedgerows. It might be best if you found another who is better able to minister to the needs of the King'

'As you well know, sir,' Langton replied sourly, 'I am stuck in the wilds of this godforsaken country and have no other options to choose from. Let us cut this dance short and reach an agreement that works for us both. I will double your price and provide a serving girl to pick your plants for you. What say you?'

The apothecary risked a quick glance at Langton before replying. 'I would need at least three girls to ensure a sufficient supply for the King's needs. The plant is not easy to unearth.'

'Done!' Langton snapped. 'I shall have five Scots whores sent to do your bidding. If they do not fill their baskets, I will slice away their teats and leave their filthy fathers with naught to suckle on long winter nights.'

'And would I be able to, you know?' The old man raised his eyebrows and waggled his tongue obscenely between his lips.

Langton grimaced at the thought of the old fool hoisting his skeletal frame onto some slip of a girl. 'As long as they fill their baskets with your weeds, you can fill them with whatever you choose, it is of no matter to me.'

The apothecary nodded with satisfaction before a frown brought a mass of wrinkles to his forehead. 'But what of my other benefactors? I bring comfort and relief to many of the great nobles who are here with us. It will be hard to see to them with so much needed by the King.'

'They are no longer your concern. In any case, it will please the King to know that they suffer with their ailments with naught to ease their pain.'

21

With Edward de Bruce's men escorting them, Eck and John made good progress, despite the darkness of the night. News of the English victory had travelled more quickly than they had and every village they passed was closed up tight, their inhabitants huddled behind their doors praying that the clumping horses' hooves would pass quickly by and leave them unmolested. Crieff itself had been in darkness and they saw not a crack of light from the cottages that lined its muddy street.

They had been in the saddle for several hours when they reached the south bank of the Tay at Dunkeld. Across the dark, slow-flowing depths of the river, they could see the old monastery and, beyond it, the wooden scaffolding surrounding the half-built cathedral. There was, however, no sight of the monks who manned the ferry point. The ferry itself was just visible in the gloom, tied up safely on the far bank. De Bruce's cries failed to rouse the brothers and he ordered his men to test their arms, with a gold coin for the first to strike the monks' hut with a stone. The first attempts were met with derisive laughter, as the rocks plopped into the water and

266

fell far short of the bank. Then the largest man in the party threw with all his might, sending a fist-sized stone arcing over the river and crashing down upon the slates with a splintering crack. There were a few seconds of silence before a door could be heard slowly creaking open.

'Who's there?' A timorous voice enquired.

'It's alright, we're no' the English!' Bruce boomed across the water. 'Now punt your ferry over here and transport us to your side. We have a wounded man with us and do not wish to tarry here.'

'It is too dark for us to venture out. You should come back in the morning.'

'I have gold enough to light your way, it should see you through the darkness. Now raise your brothers and set to work, I'll pay a coin apiece, but only if you hurry.' Edward shook his purse so that the chinking of the gold would reach the brothers' ears.

'These are the darkest of days, my son, how would I know that your words are true?'

'Let my name be your guarantee, I am Edward Bruce, brother to the Earl of Carrick. He is as good a friend to the church as any and will be generous to any that aid his kin.'

The owner of the nervous voice did not respond, but there was enough whispering and scraping within the hut to suggest that the proposal was being debated. After a few short minutes, torches were sparked into flame and dark, robed figures could be seen fussing around their craft. It seemed to take an age for the ferry to cross, as the brothers pulled on their ropes and inched it from bank to bank. The Bruce ordered his men to lend a hand and the first four of his horsemen traversed the Tay at speed. Eck was among them and he lay his cousin down upon the ground before the monks' dilapidated cabin.

'I fear that your companion does not have long to live.' The small, nervous monk looked down at John with wide, sad eyes. 'He should give his last confession so that he can repent of all his sins and speed his soul to Heaven.'

'It's not prayers he's needing.' Eck responded firmly. 'He needs to get home so that his wounds can be treated.'

'Then I hope that you are now close to home. I doubt that he will last over long.'

'With luck, we'll reach there before the dawn.'

The monk nodded. 'It would be good for him to reach his home, then his own priest can attend to him. I am sure that would give him great comfort. Let me see what I can do to stop the rot's advance.'

The little man scurried off into the darkness and returned moments later with a cloth bag over his shoulder. He kneeled at John's side and gently uncovered his wound. Eck gagged and involuntarily stepped back a pace as the stench of putrefaction hit his nostrils. John's face was deathly white, apart from the thick, dark rings surrounding his eyes, and sweat ran from him like water. He did not stir, even when the monk's fingers explored the blackened flesh around the embedded bodkin point. The monk expertly applied a thick ointment to the oozing hole and then wrapped it with a strip of cloth.

'That might keep him going for a while, but I have something which will help him even more.' The monk's eyes shone as he spoke these words and his eagerness gave Eck fresh hope.

The monk dug into his bag and pulled out a box of dark wood which had been polished to a deep sheen and decorated with silver and gemstones. He mouthed a silent prayer over the box and kissed it, before laying it gently on John's chest and opening its lid. He then took the utmost care in lifting out a small, mouldy stick, which he also kissed, before placing it on John's lips and then touching it on the flesh around the wound. His lips moved silently throughout the ritual. When he had finished and placed the closed box back inside his bag, he turned to Eck with a smile of great satisfaction.

'It is said that Saint Columba performed great acts of healing. His finger-bones no doubt retain some vestiges of that power and will help your friend this night. Blessings on both he and thee and may God speed your journey home.'

Eck normally placed little store in such relics, but now he invested what little remained of his faith fully in those mouldy bones. Once he had taken his leave of Edward de Bruce and his men, he prayed soundlessly like the little monk all the way back to Scotstoun.

His heart leapt in his chest when he recognised the path which wound down towards the village he had been born in. He was sorely tempted to follow it down, as he knew that within minutes he would reach his father's door and have others to share his burden. But so poor was John's condition, he believed that he had not a moment to waste and he rode on in search of the cottage of the Lady of the Glen. It was she who had saved him after Stirling, when all said that he was lost, and he prayed that she could do the same for his cousin. Several times he was near overcome with panic, when his probing fingers could detect no pulse in his cousin's breast. It was only with brutal perseverance that he was able to detect weak movement there.

He could have wept with relief when, as the cottage came into sight, he saw the Lady standing by her door, as if she had been waiting for him to arrive.

'Carry him inside and lay him upon the table. I have already cleared it for him.' Esmy ordered tersely. 'This one will need more than magic finger bones, if he is to make it through to dawn.'

Eck jerked back in surprise at her words, but Esmy was already striding purposefully through her door.

'Nigel!' She hissed. 'Put the knives in the fire. I will have much cutting to do.'

Eck placed John's ice-cold body onto the table and stepped back to give Esmy room to do her work. The woman had always unsettled him, but he trusted her with John's life. If she could not save him, then he knew there was no other who could.

Eck jerked as a hand was placed softly on his shoulder. 'Come sit Eck.' Sir Nigel Thwaite

270

implored. 'It's best to leave her to her work. She'll certainly shout if there is anything she requires. You look like you could do with some ale.'

Sir Nigel had changed markedly since Eck had last seen him. At the time of his capture in the aftermath of Stirling Bridge, he had been as fat as any man Eck had ever encountered and his leg had been badly broken. Now, not only was he walking without even the slightest trace of a limp, he was slim, toned and in the rudest of health.

Without averting his eyes from the table, Eck shot a question at Sir Nigel. 'What are you still doing here? I thought that she was going to ransom you as payment for bringing me back from the dead.'

The English knight laughed cheerfully. 'I know that was her intention, but I think that she soon realised that I was of more value to her here. I think she had missed having a man to tend to her needs.' Nigel raised his eyebrows in a conspiratorial expression.

'You mean?' Eck asked, his disbelief preventing him from finishing the question.

Sir Nigel again raised his eyebrows, before winking lewdly in confirmation.

'But she's…'

'I know.' Sir Nigel replied. 'She's a little older than me, but, like a fine wine, some things improve as they age.'

Eck stared at Esmy in amazement. He had remembered her as a witch, wizened, wrinkled and cronish, but had to admit that her looks had much improved. Her long, grey hair was no longer wild and untamed and she did not look as ancient as he had remembered her. Her teeth were still more brown than white, but that could be said of anyone above their twenty-fifth year. Nevertheless, he shivered involuntarily in revulsion at the thought of the young knight coupling with her. She must have bewitched him, that was the only explanation he could believe.

Sir Nigel poured two tumblers of ale and talked as they watched Esmy attempt to snatch John back from the jaws of death. He explained that when he had decided to stay with Esmy, he had written to his family and told them that he had won lands in Scotland. Both his father and his mother had been delighted to hear of his achievement, as they had feared that gluttony and gambling were to be his only passions in life. The state of lawlessness on this side of the border had thankfully kept them away, but they had instead sent messengers with money, so allowing the couple to live most comfortably. He told Eck how he had never been so happy, spending his days working the land and his nights cosied up by the fire. Eck could do nothing but drink his ale, shake his head and keep his eyes on poor John's prone form.

Sir Nigel was an amiable fellow and chattered away quite cheerfully. Eck, for his part, caught only parts of his monologue, as he was more concerned with what was happening on the other side of the cottage. Esmy seemed to be butchering John's thigh, her red-hot knives hissing as she cut away his flesh. The pile of scorched meat at her feet had grown alarmingly high. Eck's concern had reached the point where he was about to intervene, when Esmy dropped her knife onto the table and let out a great sigh.

'I think that's enough of the chopping. I've cut him down to the bone. There's just the head of the arrow to prise out and then we can close him and see what the fates have in store.'

She then lifted a bowl full of a thick green paste and began to apply it to the gaping wound. Its smell was so strong that it caused Eck's eyes to water, even although he sat at the far side of the room.

'She's been collecting that stuff for four days now.' Nigel announced cheerfully. 'She said that John would have need of it.'

'How could she have known that John would have need of it? He would not even have been wounded then.'

Nigel winked and nudged Eck with his elbow. 'Come now Eck, you've known her longer than I. She just knows. There's nothing more to be said.'

Esmy then turned from John and fixed Eck in her gaze. Even in the dim interior of the cottage and at its full width away, Eck could not disengage from her wide, hazel eyes.

'So, Eck the Black, you have tasted bitter defeat. Not so sweet as victory, is it?'

'Will he live?' Eck asked, his cousin's fate now his only concern.

'The world is not done with John Edward yet, it would have him suffer more. He will yet be a father to the babe that grows in my daughter's womb. Now go and fetch my Lorna and bring his parents too. They will want to tend to him during his long recovery.'

Esmy wisely excused herself from John's care and thus saved herself from involvement as Lorna and Isobelle battled to nurse him back to health. John could not have asked for more, as his brow was never unmopped, his mess never lay uncleared for long and a spoon of broth was never further than six inches from his lips. Eck visited each and every day, but never stayed for long, as just watching the competition between wife and mother left him feeling tired and worn. He often joked with his Uncle Andrew that John would heal fast, just so he could get to his feet and hobble off to find some peace.

Though John's survival was wondrous, Eck found that he was in no mood for celebration. The defeat at Falkirk had been a disaster both personally and for the sake of their cause. The Scottish army had been destroyed and its remnants scattered across the land. King Edward now marched with impunity, with no credible force to prevent his advance. The fate of friends and comrades was unknown, although it was most likely that they had perished upon the field or had been viciously murdered as they fled. This was a morose time for Scotstoun as they hunkered down and awaited news.

Eck was walking back into the village from visiting his cousin, when he heard a hubbub in the square. He unsheathed his sword and ran straight in to be confronted by a sight which

274

gladdened his heart. Dirty, ragged and dishevelled, three men most dear to him stood where he had never thought to see them again. He dropped his father's sword in the dirt and threw his arms around Al. He held his dusty face tight in his hands and stared as if he needed to make sure he was real.

'I thought you dead!' He cried, with fat tears running into his beard.

'So did I.' Al replied, as they broke out into happy laughter.

Next, he threw his arms around Strathbogie's great shoulders and clapped his back both hard and long. Once they had been uneasy comrades, but now they were forever joined in blood. Strathbogie's face was gaunt and thin and his shirt crusted with blood. It was evident that he had fought his way to safety and had been harried all the way.

'You've no' been eating your porridge, have ye?' Eck teased his older, bigger comrade.

'That is true, young Eck, but now I'm here, I'll be taking yours.' Strathbogie shot back, returning his grin.

Lastly, he turned to Malcolm Simpson, Wallace's most trusted aide. Of the three, he was in the poorest condition, with wounds on his arms, left leg and torso bound tight in dirty cloth, torn ragged from his shirt. This man he embraced more gently, as it was plain that his wounds still pained him greatly.

Eck quickly escorted them to his father's house and saw to it that they were fed and watered and that their wounds were attended to.

Clean clothes were found for them and water buckets brought so that they could rinse off the filth gathered in their flight. Then, and only then, did they sit to share their tales.

Strathbogie told them of the retreat to the Torwood and, without the slightest shame, shed fat tears as he described the fall of the Robertson. Everyone agreed that the man's last words were true to his character and lamented that he had died in defeat. Not one person present speculated about his ultimate fate, as no-one wanted to think of how he must have felt to lie helpless as the murderous English foot approached. Eck silently prayed that his great heart had given out before the bastards reached him with their blades. Strathbogie then described how he and a handful of patriot fighters had turned at the Torwood's edge and fought to delay the English, so that their comrades might get away. The English had, at first at least, entered the forest most timidly and were cut down quickly and with ferocity. They had then attacked in greater numbers and Strathbogie had swung his axe until his arms ached and the dead piled at his feet.

Soon he found that he fought on alone and it was then that he turned and hacked his way through the English line, swinging until he found open forest before him. With all strength in his arms used up, he took himself to running. He ran and ran long into the night, the din of pursuit at his heels. He thought that he had gained some respite, until he heard dogs in the distance. This set him to running again until he reached the banks of the Forth. With the dogs much closer now, he had just waded straight in. The current caught him and swept him along until he thought he could no longer keep himself afloat. Then, just as he had given up and let his head slide beneath the surface, his feet touched the river's bed and he dug in hard and kicked his feet and had soon reached the shallows.

Though he was near dropping with exhaustion, he forced himself to walk on well into the forenoon and only collapsed to the ground when he had crested the Ochil Hills. He had slept where he dropped and only awakened when dusk began to fall. A full night's walk had taken him into the Forest of Perth and, with the ground familiar to him from his days of raiding, he had taken the time to rest and fill his belly with berries and nuts. Unable to tell if the soldiers at Perth were friend or foe, he had moved west of the city and, from there, swum to safety across the Tay.

Malcolm Simpson told his tale succinctly, as was his habit. He had been with Comyn and Wallace's horse as they tried to lead the English knights away from the field. When they had relinquished the chase and turned to slaughter the Scots foot, Wallace and Comyn had ordered their men to harass the English cavalry's rear. Though heavily outnumbered, the brave Scots horse had desperately attacked again and again, until their numbers were dreadfully thinned. It was only then, when exhausted and injured, that their leaders had led them from the field. Malcolm's wounds had all been inflicted in this struggle with the English knights. Unbeknownst to him, they had also mortally wounded his mount. Within a mile of the field, it had slowed and then collapsed, dying to the ground. Left alone and unhorsed, Malcolm was forced to evade the advancing English and so was pushed towards Stirling and then on along the road to Perth. Unable to find his way back to his native Borderlands and remembering Scotstoun from his previous visits, he had set his course here and came seeking sanctuary.

Al too had a story to tell, but, in one respect at least, it differed from all the others. While John, Eck, Strathbogie and Malcolm had all run for their lives after the battle was lost, Al had stayed and risked his life to spy on the enemy camp. He had watched while Edward's encampment emptied and every English soul rushed to run down the retreating Scots, to slaughter them and fill their pockets with their silver. He had still watched as they slowly began to return, tired, bloody and weary from the hunt. He had tracked them as they moved onto Stirling and then followed them along the Perth road. It was here that disaster befell him.

He had not long crossed the Black Ford over the Allan Water, when he came upon a group of English soldiers who had left the road to hunt. There were archers amongst their number and they loosed shafts at his retreating back. One of the arrows had struck his horse in the flank and caused the poor creature to throw him and run away in fright. The English soldiers then chased him and he ran for his life for miles through the hills. He was on the very point of exhaustion when he came to the Kirk of St Margaret. It was then that he saw Father Seivewright and the priest waved him urgently inside. When the English barged through the door, the good Father sent them away swiftly with the sharp edge of his tongue. After a meal and a good night's sleep, the priest had blessed him and sent him on his way. After three more days of walking, he had encountered Malcolm and Strathbogie and together they took the sloping track down to Scotstoun's square.

That night there was much celebration and they toasted the resurrection of friends they had thought to be lost. But, as they drank on into the small hours of the morning, their thoughts were with the many who had joined the ranks of the dead.

22

The King's stay at Auchterarder Castle had done
him much good. After weeks of mouldering in a
damp and mildewed pavilion, he had luxuriated
in the warmth of his chamber and had spent
much of the first day dozing in front of the
roaring fire. He had surprised Langton by
refusing all of his host's invitations to join the
hunt and had instead devoted himself to resting
and keeping his belly full. He had also wisely
chosen to ignore the nobles and refuse their
many insistent requests for a conference. The
victory at Falkirk had swung the balance of
power decisively in Edward's favour and he was
consequently in a position where he did not have
to suffer their vexations. Though not yet back at
his best, Langton thought that his condition was
much improved and so was unconcerned when
he announced his intention to move his court to
Perth.

'If the disloyal Scots nobles are too stubborn
to surrender themselves to me and seek my
pardon, I will mock them by occupying the
ancient crowning place of their kings. From
there, I will gift their lands to loyal English
lords, appoint English sheriffs to govern their

towns and send out troops to recapture and garrison their castles. I am content to see them skulk in the mountains whilst their people yield to my subjugation. With no army to defy me with, they must stand, impotent, with their manhoods in their hands and see my rule stiffened with each day that passes.' Edward made this proclamation with calm and confident authority. His determination was expressed without a trace of the rage which often accompanied such pronouncements when his position was weak and his mind racked with frustration.

The Lord High Treasurer looked on with growing satisfaction as the King's plans were executed with ruthless efficiency. Lands were parcelled out to deserving and reliable friends, appointments made to ensure proper governance and the most strategic strongholds laid to siege. It could not be denied that the Scots garrisons were obdurate and tenacious in their resistance, but, by means both fair and foul, they were worn down until all but a few keeps were in English hands. It seemed that the conquest of Scotland was all but complete and, with their army routed, there was nothing the Scots could do to loosen this choking stranglehold.

When Edward's face was set hard in anger or even mere disapproval, its fierceness was enough to loosen the bowels of even the bravest and most high-born of men. On the rare occasions when his expression was one of joy, his smile could illuminate a room and brighten the souls of all it touched. It was the latter which

281

Langton experienced when summoned to the King's chambers within the walls of Perth.

'Walter! See what is in my hand!' Edward beamed with happiness and waved a parchment back and forth in his left fist. 'It is here reported that the traitor Wallace has been ended. I am certain that the intelligence is good. Come, we must have a drink in celebration.'

'The outlaw is dead?' Langton asked, scarcely able to believe the news.

'Not dead, Langton, better than that. He has resigned the Guardianship in shame at the extent of his defeat. No-one will follow a man who has been so disgraced. Remember how they all abandoned old King John Balliol when I ripped the royal badges from his tabard? He's finished. I have taken a Scots hero and reduced him to a figure of pity and scorn. They have no-one left who is worth following. My victory is almost complete.'

Langton smiled and accepted a full goblet from the King's own hand.

'The Scots nobles apparently accepted his offer of resignation before it was out of his mouth. His power came from the debacle at Stirling and, with the slaughter at Falkirk, they dispensed with him with undue haste. They have entrusted the future of their resistance to no others than Comyn and Bruce. They have made them joint Guardians of Scotland. I could not have asked for more.'

Langton's brow furrowed at this revelation. 'But they still stand against us. I do not see how that is good. I would rather have them swear fealty and come over to our side.'

Edward laughed and shook his head as though he despaired of a child who is slow at his learning. 'Think Walter. Those two pretenders to my crown must work together if they are to defy me. What chance is there of that? Both are so blinded by naked ambition they will be too busy squabbling with one another to bring any trouble to me. While they bicker and fight, they will scarce notice as I steal away with their throne.'

Langton took a long sip of his wine and pondered the King's argument. There was, he had to concede, some merit to the situation. Comyn and Bruce were capable men, but their families had been at loggerheads for generations and neither would risk helping the other, lest they inadvertently strengthened their claim to the crown.

'So, my Lord, the situation with the Scots nobles would seem to be settled. Is it time to make amends with our own?' Langton had no great love for the English Earls, but had raised the issue as he knew that they chattered and raged behind the King's back and, whilst they were a loathsome, self-serving bunch, it was not wise to push them too far.

'Ha!' Edward spat. 'So they still complain, despite the reverse they suffered on the field. You'd think that their shame would have stilled their tongues. I will hear them if I must, but tell them that they should approach on their knees and be prepared to kiss my ring.'

The Earls, when they came, were in no mood to either kneel or kiss, as they had been nursing their grievances and feeding them each time Edward had refused to see them. By the time they came before him, their tempers bubbled furiously just below the surface.

'My Lords Hereford and Norfolk.' Edward addressed them coldly. 'The Lord Bishop tells me that you are eager to seek my forgiveness for your conduct upon the field of battle. I was not minded to do so, but he has persevered and persuaded me that I should hear your excuses.'

Langton cringed inwardly, though his face did not betray his emotions. He had said no such thing of the Earls and did not deserve the hatred and hostility which burned in both of their eyes. He silently cursed Edward. It was all very well for him to toy with the magnates, as he was unlikely to suffer at their hands. He, on the other hand, would be at their mercy once the King was no longer there to protect him.

'His Lordship is mistaken.' Norfolk hissed, with a sideways glance in Langton's direction. 'As he is very much aware, we were keen to speak with you, my Lord, to settle your obligations to Hereford and myself.'

''Tis true, my Lord. We have spent heavily to support you in this campaign. All we ask is for that promised to us. No more and no less.' Hereford's jaw was set firm with determination and he returned the King's gaze unflinchingly.

Langton was praying that the King would keep his temper and that his previous calmness would not desert him. It could not be denied that the nobles were irksome, but it was also true that the campaign was not yet over and their support would be required to see it through. Langton's heart sank as he saw Edward's eyes begin to blaze with fury. The magnates seemed to be oblivious to the gathering storm and pushed on with their claims.

'You did, my Lord, promise me the lands of the Earl of Carrick when I agreed to march with you. With the Bruce outlawed and hiding in the hills, I would like to secure my new possessions, but, though I have waited patiently for weeks, they have yet to be granted to me. No man would blame me for fearing that you are about to repeat the injustice you inflicted upon us after the conquest of Wales. Though we supported you then with men and materiel, you granted us not one patch of land, whilst the Earls of Surrey and Lincoln were given huge estates. It would be both unwise and unjust to repeat that folly. I would not suffer it lightly a second time.' The Earl of Norfolk had begun quietly, but his pitch and volume had increased as he went along and the last of his words were shouted at the King.

Langton watched as the King sat with his eyes wide and his body trembling. For a few seconds, he feared that Edward was in the midst of a seizure, but then he erupted to his feet and towered over the two Earls.

'You think that you can threaten your King?' Edward screeched, his fists clenched hard at his sides as though he struggled to hold himself back from beating the two men into a bloody pulp. 'You ungrateful, inconstant dogs. I have filled your pockets for years and still you assail my ears with your constant begging and complaining. Should I entrust either of you with estates after you near lost me my army at Falkirk in your haste for glory? If I had not arrived when I did, you would have damned us to defeat and now all of our corpses would be rotting in some Scottish grave. If you ever dare to threaten me again, I'll have your heads mounted on spikes and damn the consequences!'

The Earls were so sorely aggrieved they did not quail before Edward's wrath, but instead stood their ground and pushed him to make good on what he had promised.

'Tis too late.' Edward retorted. 'I have already granted those lands to others more deserving of the reward. Others who did not disgrace themselves and neither tried to upstage their King nor made threats in his presence. You shall have what you deserve from this campaign and what you deserve is naught.'

Hereford leaned back in astonishment. 'Who? To whom did you grant my lands?'

'They were not your lands, but were mine to give and have been granted to those who did me good service. Just this morning, I awarded the Isle of Arran to the good Sir Hugh Bissett.'

'That Irish adventurer!' Norfolk spat in disgust. 'I have more men in my kitchen than that man provided to the cause. This is intolerable! I will not suffer here a moment longer.'

'Then go!' Edward replied tartly. 'I did not want you here at all. Take yourselves from my sight before I do something I will regret.'

Though he could not deny that he had enjoyed the magnates' discomfort and revelled in their unhappiness, Langton feared that Edward's temper had led him to make a mistake which could yet negate all the benefits accrued as a result of the battle at Falkirk.

His worst fears were realised two days later when Browby, his loyal captain, roused him from his bed and ushered him to the city walls. The English army had been encamped on the area of moorland outside the city known locally as the North Inch. Just the previous day, it had been filled with row upon row of tents and pavilions, hastily built enclosures for both war and cart horses and had been studded with campfires which raised a cloud of smoke which drifted far over the city and the surrounding countryside. The camp's population had exceeded that of the city itself and had covered an area of roughly four times its size. To Langton's eye, it looked as if nearly half of the expanse had been vacated and the dust kicked up by the departing column could be seen for miles along the track to Stirling. It seemed that the magnates must have persuaded quite a number of more minor nobles to join with their exodus. The Lord High Treasurer and Bishop of Coventry and Lichfield mumbled furiously to himself and used language not befitting a master of coin, let alone a man of the cloth. His stomach already clenched at the prospect of his next audience with the King, as he knew from bitter experience that this setback would somehow be attributable to him, rather than to the King's intemperate nature.

As the trees took on their autumn colours, stragglers from the defeated Scottish army limped their way into Scotstoun on an almost daily basis. Many were familiar faces from the days of raiding and ambushing, some were remembered from the desperate struggle at Stirling and a few had only recently been encountered within the schiltroms at Falkirk. Some brought their families along and not one of them was turned away. The supplies of grain and barley plundered from farms in the North of England had been stored away for the winter and, although belts would need to be tightened a few notches through the months of cold, it was reckoned that there would be enough to ensure that starvation was kept at bay. Scott Edward supervised their accommodation and a camp was thrown up in the forest on the far side of the loch. The wilderness there would provide both shelter and fuel and was far from any road or track and prying eyes. With Edward's army camped less than a day's ride away, it would not do to attract any unwanted attention.

The defeat at Falkirk and the subsequent slaughter had the effect of lowering folk's spirits and ushering in a collective feeling of hopelessness and depression. The melancholy atmosphere had been further exacerbated by the news of the English King's proximity and of

288

Wallace's resignation of the Guardianship. When Wallace had been raised up, his followers had taken great pride in his remarkable achievement and had rightly felt that they had played their part in bringing it about. The loss of the office had been a heavy blow to bear and was borne almost as if it was a personal failure. It was also hard to live with the feeling of impotence brought on by the English occupation and the constant reports of Englishmen being appointed as overlords to rule the Scots. The prospect of a hard winter, on top of all else, served to squeeze the last vestiges of joy from life.

However, the autumn winds did blow in some causes for celebration along with the leaves. It would not be an exaggeration to say that one chill September morning caused the whole of Scotstoun to rejoice. There had been neither sight nor sound of the three since the collapse of John Edward's schiltrom and all had assumed them to be lost. Words had been said for them in the Kirk and their families had donned black in their grief. Scott Edward was out with the first birdsong and on his way to help out at the camp, when he spotted the three slight figures, slowly making their way down through the trees. He rubbed at his eyes as if to chase away apparitions, but when he looked back, he could see it was true. He rushed to bang on their families' doors and urged them to come out and see.

The figures were thin and ragged and filthy, but were instantly recognisable as the boys

McAlpine, Cumming and McAllister. Though embarrassed by all the fuss, they grinned as they were enveloped and welcomed home like prodigal sons. On hearing the news, even John Edward rose from his bed and limped to the square on a crutch. He had been so guilty at their loss, he had been unable to so much as meet their mothers' eyes. He said that his tears were caused by the pain in his leg, but his brother and cousin knew well that he lied. The responsibility for each man that had been lost was something which John took heavily to heart, but the loss of the boys from Scotstoun was the one which had caused him to lose the most sleep. His Lorna smiled and shed grateful tears, as she had not seen her husband so happy since she had found him butchered on her mother's table. The months of loss had been hard on the village, but that night they all felt that they had won something back.

Not one week later, there was another, less significant, but still happy, return. As Eck stood sentry at the side of the road to Perth, he spotted a figure quietly stalking through the trees. He had crept to intercept him with his sword in his hand and then smiled as he recognised the battered face. Tom Figgins looked like he had been on the road for a month and he smelled like he'd been there a year. Still, Eck embraced him and walked him to be presented in the square. Though it was early in the day, a cask was broken open in his honour.

'You know,' Scott said in between gulps of ale, 'I cannae mind seeing the boy at Falkirk. Do you think he stood with the archers?'

Eck scratched at his beard and stared off into space. 'You know, I don't remember seeing him since the night we spent at the abbey wi' Wallace. I suppose he must have been there or thereabouts.'

'It's no' as if we can ask him.' Scott replied. 'It must be hellish frustrating, no' being able to talk and that.'

Tom Figgins drank his ale and smiled and nodded at his old comrades. The road north had been long and hard. What little had escaped the Scots' destructive invasion had been stripped away by the advancing English army. He had been forced to leave the road and walk deep into the countryside to find any game worth hunting. He had learned to avoid the villages and hamlets, as the North of England had fallen into a state of complete lawlessness with the noble authorities choosing to remain safe on their estates to the south. The roads on both sides of the border had been too dangerous to use, due to the bands of desperate robbers who lay in wait for any travellers they could rob. Several times he had run for his life and, more than once, only his skill with the bow had saved him from their clubs and their knives.

He had, by his reckoning, now killed more Englishmen than Scots. His long walk north had seen him kill an English scout who had stumbled upon him as he roamed far ahead of the English army. Tom had taken him down with a single shaft to prevent him from alerting others to his location. He was dismayed when the unfortunate man's mount had galloped off into the distance, but delighted when he discovered that his boots were a near perfect fit. His journey onwards had been much more comfortable, now that he walked on soles that were not worn through.

Knowing that he could not stay ahead of the advancing English, he had taken to the hills and hidden himself to let them pass. The great column rolled by slowly and it was three full days before the last of the wagons had rumbled into the distance. By this time, he had made his camp quite agreeable and, with decent amounts of rabbits and birds to hunt, he had stayed on for more than a month. The solitude gave him time to think and to ponder upon the options which were open to him. With his family and livelihood irretrievably lost, the military life represented his only opportunity to rebuild his fortune. Ideally, he would have rejoined the English army and fought alongside his countrymen, but he had enemies there and would not take the risk of being tortured and condemned a second time. That left him with the prospect of rejoining the ranks of the Scots under John Edward. They had accepted him as a fellow patriot who had been left mute after torture and hanging at the hands of their enemy. The fear of being unmasked had never left him, but he had a place there and was made welcome by his fellows.

Tom nodded his thanks as Eck Edward refilled his goblet with ale. He could still clearly recall the first time he had stood on this square. He had been collecting the King's taxes, when the vile Rank had sliced open a villager's belly and left him to die in the mud. He still remembered the anger in the villagers' faces and how he and his men had been forced to make a hurried retreat. As he sipped his bitter ale, he scanned the faces around him and marvelled that not one of them recognised him. For the first time in an age, Tom Figgins felt safe and at home.

23

The winds of October stripped the trees to their branches and brought a taste of winter's chill to Scotstoun. The encampment on the far side of the loch had the effect of more than doubling the village's population and the place was busy with preparations for the cold, hard months ahead. The presence of so many able men meant that stocks of firewood were high enough to heat every house through at least two long winters. There were also enough skilled men to ensure that every house and shelter was repaired sufficiently to provide protection from the coming frosts, blizzards and gales. The food stores were not neglected, with many hands attending to the slaughtering of animals, the salting of meat, the collection of autumn nuts, the hanging of root vegetables, the drying of fish, the smoking of meat and the pickling of fruit and vegetables. All of these activities were supervised by Scott Edward, who had shown an unexpected talent for the work.

'Are we set fair for the winter?' Andrew Edward asked his younger son.

'Aye.' Scott replied, wrinkling his brow as he surveyed all of the activity around him. 'We'll need to take a cart into Blairgowrie and see if we can buy more ale and a barrel of fat if we can get it.'

'Maybe we'd be better taking two carts. All these men will get through a powerful amount of ale in the course of a winter.'

'True enough.' Scott replied, mentally adding it to his list.

'Ah, look!' Andrew announced, pointing across the square.

'Not another one.' Scott responded with a scowl. 'That's the third auld mannie in a week.'

The ongoing English occupation was causing a massive displacement of people as estates were seized by the English and unwanted tenants evicted from the land. As always, it was the old who suffered most, as the English nobles, unswayed by past service and loyalty, replaced unproductive tenants with those better able to earn them coin. The roads were filled with vagrants in search of shelter and charity.

Scott shook his head as the bedraggled old man limped towards them. 'We have enough mouths to feed and cannot take another not fit to make a contribution.'

'Scott, give him a wee coin and send him on his way. It would be a shame if he were to have nothing.' Andrew Edward patted his son on the shoulder and implored him to be less harsh.

'I cannot Faither.' Scott responded. 'If I give him silver, he will tell the next ten tramps he meets and afore long we'll have them lining up in the square. I must be cruel to him to ensure we can take care of our own.'

Scott gave his father a rueful look and strode towards the elderly vagrant. 'Keep walking! There's nothing for you here.' He was about to grab him by the arm when a voice stopped him in his tracks.

'If you put your hand on me, Scott Edward, I'll rip it from your wrist and then shove it up your skinny, wee arse.'

Scott stared open-mouthed at the old man. He would swear that he had never clapped eyes on him before, but the voice was strongly familiar to him. The man's face was haggard and thin and was smeared with grime. His clothes were little more than rags and hung limply from his skeletal frame. His wispy hair might have once been white, but was now dark with dirt and leaves. His father's voice broke the spell.

'Laird Robertson? Is that you? We were told that you were dead.'

'Do I look fucking dead to you?' The Robertson retorted.

'Aye!' Andrew Edward replied, a laugh rising in his throat. 'You look as close to it as any man I have seen.'

The Robertson looked down at himself before breaking into laughter. 'I suppose I must look bad, I can scarce remember the last time my bed was not laid in a ditch.'

'Christ!' Scott cursed. 'I did not recognise you. You have grown so thin and frail.'

'Aye laddie, the starvation will do that to a man. That and the fever that a wound can bring. I've said my last prayers a hundred times since I last set eyes on you. Now, if you're not still set on chasing me off, could you spare me a bite to eat? I'll be chewing off my ain fingers, if I don't get something in my belly soon.'

Andrew Edward hurried the Robertson to his house and went to fetch his friends while Isobelle warmed him by the fire and fetched him meat, bread and ale. Strathbogie was the first to arrive, his face white with shock.

'I thought you were dead, Laird Robertson, otherwise I would never have left you on the field. I have mourned you hard these last few months and still cannot believe that you are here.'

The Robertson waved his apologies away. 'I told you to go and have not a single regret. If you had stayed, then we would have both been slaughtered. I would say that things turned out for the best.'

The Edward house was soon filled with old friends and comrades who rushed in to see the miracle for themselves. They all gave thanks and embraced the old man, though none for too long, as he was terrible ripe from the road. The last to arrive was the limping John Edward, tears already formed in his blue eyes. He fells to his knees at the Robertson's feet and begged him for his forgiveness. The Robertson rejected his pleas and told him to stand and stop his nonsense. He looked him over and said that he was glad that he had got away, even although he had not escaped entirely unscathed.

'I think that my fighting days are over and, if you'd have me, I would like to end my days here.' The Robertson's voice was firm and unwavering, but there was an underlying infirmity to it, which had never been evident before.

There was not one man there who would refuse him and the very next day the villagers made a start on building him a house with a fine view right down to the loch.

The walls of the Robertson's house were only half up when fifty horsemen arrived in the village with Wallace at their head. John had worried that he would find Wallace diminished by his defeat and by his loss of office. Instead, the man who greeted him when he arrived at the Kirk was as vital and energetic as he had always been.

'Edward still sits behind the walls of Perth and we keep our eyes on his men from a distance.' Wallace reported to a jam-packed church. 'Any messengers or scouts who are unwise enough to venture out, find themselves ambushed and killed on the roads.'

'So, we are back to the days of raiding and ambushing, making the English afeart to leave their strongholds.' The Robertson stated with a nod of his head.

'Aye Laird.' Wallace replied. 'It is back to those days indeed. The English King must be realising that one victory in battle does not a conquest make. He has beaten us and destroyed our army, that I cannot deny, but what use is a country to a king if he cannot rule it? That is our role now. If the English cannot control the land and its people and extract taxes from them, then they must cut their losses and go home. We must help them on their way.'

The congregation applauded their leader's words, but their enthusiasm was muted, not least by the presence of the English army less than a day's ride from the doors of the Kirk.

Wallace did not miss this and addressed it directly. 'Edward cannot keep his army here for long. Half of his men have already left and crossed the border back into England. I know this, for we harassed them all the way there. What is left at Perth is still a considerable force, but he will not be able to keep it there throughout the winter. The Scottish nobles have, for the most part, refused to come to his aid and he already struggles to keep his remaining troops supplied. Soon he will follow his nobles back to England and leave his sheriffs to rule from behind their castle walls. I am sure that you will help us to keep them there and spare our people from their brutality.'

'Aye, Sir William.' John Edward replied. 'We will, of course, join with you. The tactics are familiar to all men here and we will return to them keenly enough. You have our support.'

'I never doubted it.' Wallace replied. 'There is not one amongst us who would miss the opportunity to take revenge for the slaughter at Falkirk. Let's drive the bastards out and let the sweetness of Edward's victory turn to foul decay before his very eyes.'

Though it had been good to see Wallace in such fine spirits, John had felt relieved when he left with his men the following morning. The village's food stores would have dwindled dangerously with another fifty mouths to feed. It was also true that his adherence to the cause was not universally shared by all of the inhabitants of Scotstoun. Many were tired of war and the loss and suffering it brought and still more were apprehensive about taking any action which might bring the wrath of the garrison at Perth upon them. John's boyish fantasies of winning his country's freedom through one great, decisive battle had long since vanished and he was resigned to the struggle being a long war of attrition. The victorious side would be that which could take the most pain without yielding. His aim was to play a part in the struggle without exposing the village to grave levels of risk.

After long days and nights of discussion, a plan was agreed. Those men who wished to fight would take themselves away and build a base in the Forest of Perth on the far side of the Tay. From there, they would harass the English, ambushing supply carts and killing messengers and scouts and anyone else who left the city walls without sufficient men to protect them. Eck and Strathbogie would lead the men until John had healed enough to allow him to ride again. They left on a drizzly and misty morning with sixty men following behind.

Langton sent the girl away and instead paced the floor of his frigid, drafty chamber. He had found no fault with the girl and she had attended to his needs with practised efficiency, but he had found that he could not keep his mind on the task in hand, so to speak. The chill in the air found its match in his mood. Just a few short months ago, he had steered events away from certain disaster and towards glorious victory. Now he was surrounded by gloom and despondency once more. He unrolled the parchment and leaned in close to a smoking candle and read it once again. The flickering light did not improve the words and again he threw it down in frustration. Simonetti of the Riccardi Bank had written to politely remind the Lord High Treasurer of the terms of the loan which had financed this latest Scottish campaign. It was evident that the Tuscan's spies were keeping him well informed of the difficulties now being experienced by the King. Langton's agitation was caused by his inability to find a solution to the problem of the outstanding repayments. Every ready source of income had been mined to the point of exhaustion. Any creative routes which Langton could conjure up were blocked by the unhappy magnates, who were in no mood to support any action which could further their King's ambitions.

To make matters worse, the campaign itself was becoming more bogged down by the day. A guard of at least twenty men was required for every cart or messenger who left the castle. On every occasion a smaller escort had been employed, the emissary and the escort had simply disappeared, never to be seen or heard from again. The Scots seemed to prowl every

301

road and lowly track and lay in wait, ready to ambush every English official. This was putting an intolerable strain on resources and significantly impacted their ability to exercise anything more than the lowest level of authority over the country. With winter fast approaching, the question of supplies was still a highly problematic one. Few ships made it up the Scottish coast and, for the inadequate number that did, transporting their cargo to Perth was a massive undertaking and was often impeded by Scots engaging in ambush and sabotage. Langton suspected that the current scarcity of ships was as much attributable to the sulking English magnates as it was to the vile, scheming Jew. To a large extent, the cause was immaterial, the effect, on the other hand, was considerable. If the slowly starving army was not adequately fed, then it was inevitable that men would start to desert in greater numbers. It was obvious to the Treasurer that the only sensible course was to pack up and march back to England before winter closed in. Unfortunately, this was not as plainly apparent to the King and he stubbornly refused to contemplate such a retreat and instead clung on desperately and deludedly to the decisive victory he had believed to be won on the field at Falkirk.

Langton had colluded with the apothecary and denied the King his usual tonic in the hope that he would fall into a torpor and thus become easier to manipulate. The ruse had failed miserably and the King retained his energy and doggedly refused to listen to any reason. Langton had been on the verge of giving up when the King himself unwittingly provided the lever which could free them from their deteriorating situation.

'The siege of the castle at Saint Andrews does not go well, my Lord.' Edward waved a parchment at Langton as he spoke. 'The Bishop Lamberton has ordered the garrison to hold out at all costs.'

Langton immediately sniffed out a golden opportunity to profit from the King's temper. 'Would that be the Bishop Lamberton appointed by the traitor Wallace?'

Edward obliged him and swallowed the bait whole. 'You know full well that it is. I wrote to Pope Boniface and urged him to annul the appointment, but, in his great wisdom, he decided to ignore my words and consecrated him instead. Now I have yet another Bishop who conspires to be a constant thorn in my side.'

Langton ignored the barb and pushed on. 'Perhaps we could give the impudent Bishop a slap and finish this year's campaigning with a message to all of our enemies.'

Edward narrowed his eyes with suspicion and urged his Treasurer on. 'Let's hear it, my Lord Bishop, but your scheme must be an improvement on your most recent efforts. I have made it clear that the King will not leave Scotland with his tail between his legs. I mean to overwinter here and mock my enemies with my presence.'

Langton licked his lips and leaned in conspiratorially. 'What if we were to break the Bishop's castle, empty his vast coffers and put Saint Andrews to the flame? Would that not put the impudent dog in his place and show the Bruces and the Comyns that no man is beyond your reach?'

A smile stole onto Edward's face. 'The Pope would be outraged!'

'And would realise his mistake in deciding to trifle with the King of England.'

'And you, Langton, would have all the coin you could want.'

'Enough to pay for this campaign and to fund the next, when we return to finish the job.'

'But, would it be enough to convince the rebellious Scots nobles that it is time to bend the knee?'

'Perhaps if we burned more of their cities, they would see the futility of their continued disobedience.' Langton returned the King's grin, delighted to see his scheme succeed.

'I will give the orders to prepare for our departure. Lamberton's castle will fall quickly if my whole army is camped at its door.'

Sir Kenneth Lamond stood rigid as his squire strapped him into the last of his armour. His face was grim and his stomach churned at the thought of riding his horse through the castle gates. For two long weeks, his tiny garrison of thirty men had defied the thousands of English soldiers who surrounded them on all sides. Three full frontal assaults had been repelled by the shower of arrows and rocks his men had rained down upon them, leaving a tide mark of rotting corpses beneath the castle walls. With a grain store full to bursting and a fresh water well within their walls, he had been confident that they could hold out for a year or more, if the English were unable to transport their siege engines in by sea. He had been optimistic that the siege would not last that long. From the high castle walls, he and his captains had observed the poor state of the English soldiers and how their ranks thinned with each passing day. If they continued to desert in the same numbers, he doubted that there would be an army there by the turn of the year.

What the English could not achieve with their great numbers, the sickness had done in mere days. The first man to break out in boils had been quickly banished to the dungeons, to prevent his corruption from afflicting his fellows. By early the next morning, the poor man was deep in his delirium and fever and three others had scabs on their faces. After only four days, they had dumped five corpses over the walls and less than ten men had yet to succumb to the plague. With the situation so hopeless, Sir Kenneth had decided that he must surrender the castle before the pestilence took off all of his men. It pained him to give up the castle, but he knew that if he waited, the garrison would perish and the stronghold would fall to the English in spite of his refusal to yield.

As he clattered over the drawbridge, he saw that the English knights already gathered to meet him. He was surprised to see the English King at their centre, recognisable from his great height and the golden crown upon his head.

'My Lord, I come to treat with you.' Lamond had promised himself that he would not bow to the English King, but his nerves had betrayed him. The lives of his men depended upon him and how well he begged for mercy.

Edward's expression was impassive. 'I would wager that you have come to beg for mercy, knowing that you could not long resist my great army. Get on with it. Let me hear your pleas and I will take your surrender.'

Edward's dismissive tone irked Lamond and his face flushed red with anger. 'I come, my Lord, to treat with you, not because I fear your ragged army, but because the castle is infested with disease. My men are afflicted with a plague of boils and I fear that all will die if they do not escape the keep. If you will let us pass and guarantee our safety, I will leave the castle open for your men to take possession.'

'What say you Langton?' The King enquired. 'Do we let them go or leave them to die and then scale the walls unopposed? It matters not to me. Can you wait a while or must you raid the Bishop's exchequer without delay?'

Langton stared at Lamond in disgust. 'I would rather not enter the castle while it is so contaminated, as I have no desire for boils. Let this man lead his diseased garrison out, but only once they have emptied the treasury outside the castle walls.'

'Very well.' Edward responded. 'You have heard my Treasurer's response. Lay your gold out for his inspection and your men may pass us peacefully. Do it quickly mind, I do not mean to wait here long.'

Lamond had the sense to bite his tongue, but resentment burned in his eyes. 'Yes, my Lord. I will command my men to hurry.'

Edward and Langton watched as Sir Kenneth rode his horse back through the castle gates. 'I was sorely tempted to refuse the impudent dog, just to see the look upon his face.' Edward laughed grimly, before continuing. 'Did you hear him? He does not fear my ragged army. His insolence is beyond belief. If I was not so keen to leave this miserable, wind-lashed place, I would have told him to stay inside his walls and grow boils with all the rest. Once you have your coin, my Lord, leave not one of them alive. I will not have him insult the King and then suffer him to live.'

Langton nodded his agreement and watched the King trot back towards the camp. 'You heard the King, Browby. Once the gold is outside the walls, see to it that all the Scots are killed. Then search their corpses. I have no doubt that they would be impudent enough to take my gold for themselves.'

Browby now nodded his agreement and watched the Bishop follow in his King's wake. He turned in his saddle and gave orders to his men. 'Go and round up some of the infantry, I'll not have one of you touch a single unwholesome, infected Scot. Tell them that there's silver to be had for no more than a few moments work.'

With the great wooden chests stacked against the castle wall, Sir Kenneth rode out with his few remaining men marching at his back. Being a man of his word, he believed that the English King would keep to their agreement and was aghast when the English spearmen rushed in to slaughter his men. He had scarcely drawn his sword when three archers hit him with their shafts. He was dead before he hit the ground and lay jerking on the wet earth.

As he rode south, Langton thought that his mood was better than it had been for many a month. The retreat from Scotland had not been depressing, as he had feared, but had proven to be quite enjoyable. This was partly due to the prospect of leaving the dismal place behind and of returning to civilisation. However, the very manner of their departure had caused his spirits to improve considerably. The burning of Saint Andrews had been quite a spectacle to behold. The King had shown that he had a flair for the dramatic when he insisted that the town be put to the torch only after dusk had fallen. The flames of the conflagration had illuminated the countryside for miles around and, like a beacon, it signalled the price of disloyalty to the thousands of Scots who had witnessed it. As the flames of the inferno had been fanned by the wind, one minor noble had commented that it would be hard for the poor town's inhabitants when winter came. Edward had laughed with pure pleasure and told the man that he hoped that it would be so and that once the peasants were tired of their suffering, the Scots would have no armies with which to fight.

The burning of Perth was equally fine and, though not as bright, it burned on long into the dark night. The city garrison had been plagued with rebel attacks in the King's absence and they all revelled in the knowledge that the disloyal Scots must have been watching, powerless in the darkness. The blaze at Stirling was even more exhilarating to behold, the castle heights providing the perfect platform from which to view the whole city being consumed by the flames. Edward had enjoyed himself immensely and was most amused by the screams of the peasants who found themselves trapped in the cramped alleys just outside the castle's great walls. He just could not understand why they would stay to save such meagre possessions, when the air was already filled with choking, black smoke.

Their last planned port of call would not match the spectacle of the fiery destruction of the Scottish cities, but it was likely to be just as satisfying. The army was expected to arrive at Bruce's castle in Ayr in the middle of the afternoon and Langton was relishing the prospect of a final blaze before escaping back to England. He was already daydreaming about the comforts of his London home when the King's voice tore him from his reverie.

'What is this?' Edward demanded.

Langton followed the King's eyes to the horizon and saw the column of smoke rising high in the windless sky. He clenched his fists tight in frustration and cursed furiously to himself.

'De Bruce means to defy me by burning his own castle to deny me that pleasure. What kind of man does that? Destroys his own castle out of spite? I will burn all of his strongholds and turn his estates into ash!'

The King's fury carried him all the way to the border and continued as he wound his way back down through England. What was clear was that Scotland was unfinished business and that the King would be returning to finish it just as soon as he was able.

24

In his first weeks in command of the patriot
camp in the Forest of Perth, Eck the Black had
succeeded in further burnishing his reputation as
a fearless and skilled warrior. His leadership
credentials, however, were more open to
question, as many men found him to be a dark
and intimidating figure, who was prone to acts
of recklessness, which left them open to the risk
of suffering harm. Others found the opposite and
followed him loyally, knowing that if there was
glory to be found, Black Eck would lead them to
it.

This was true of the attacks he led on the
garrison at Perth. Before the King's departure
for Saint Andrews, there were many who
thought that it would be foolhardy to mount any
kind of attack and argued in favour of waiting
for Englishmen to venture out onto the road.
Eck, impatient with the waiting, led a small
group of men across the Tay. He ordered them
to crawl stealthily on their bellies until they
reached the outer sentry line. There they were to
slit the sentries' throats without giving their
presence away. The night had been long and
hard and it had taken hours to patiently crawl

across the moor in complete silence. Afterwards, they all agreed that it had been worth it and roared with laughter at the thought of the new sentries finding four of their fellows with their heads mounted on the points of their own spears.

Such attacks on the garrison were dangerous and were only attempted when no other target presented itself. Most of their time was devoted to tracking the carts which brought supplies to Perth. These carts were always moved in columns with escorts of foot and of horse. On rare occasions, a broken wheel would leave easy pickings, but mostly any victories were hard-won. When a full attack was assessed to be too risky, they resorted to opportunistic sabotage and became quite skilled in this craft. A thin ditch dug across the road near the foot of a slope would often result in a broken axle or wheel. If the site was well-chosen, this could prevent the whole column from progressing and the escort would have to choose between its abandonment or standing guard through the darkness of night. Those brave souls who elected to stand would find their numbers thinned by spears and arrows in the long hours between dusk and dawn and, when they were sufficiently diminished, would find Eck in their midst with both his blades flying and his men coming in at his back. As word spread about the persistence and ferocity of the patriots, the English soldiers grew reluctant to be part of the escorts and they deserted in greater numbers and set off on foot for the south. These men left alone or in small groups and proved to be the easiest of prey. As the weeks passed by, their mouldering bones could be found all through the Forest of Perth.

After Edward had burned the city and led his troops off to the south, the patriots found that they had little to do, as there were no English to be found. The few hardy souls who had remained behind to protect what their king had won, sensibly shut themselves away behind their walls and settled down to await relief when Edward returned again in the spring. Eck led his men to Stirling in search of work for his swords, but found the siege already in stalemate with the English huddling behind their fortifications. With nothing to do and supplies running low, the men of Perth tramped back to Scotstoun to see out the winter in the village.

When the struggle did not resume in the springtime, the men laid down their swords and set themselves to the planting of seeds. They worked on through the summer and then gathered the harvest with not a single invader in sight. By the time the leaves began to fall from the trees, Scotstoun was ready for winter, with the fruits of their labour stored away for the frigid and barren months ahead. The men were hard at work felling trees to improve their shelters, when they were told Malcolm Simpson had come.

Malcolm sat at the table in Andrew Edward's house and looked around at the assembled company with a broad smile on his face. 'My God! I have never seen you men so fat. I see that the peace has agreed with you and you have taken the opportunity to rest and feast while you can.'

'You're no' looking so skinny yourself Malcolm.' Scott shot back without hesitation. 'You must have been doing much feasting of your own.'

'Aye.' Malcolm laughed. ''Tis hard to stay lean when sitting about at a siege. The Wallace has forbidden us to go off in search of sport and that leaves us little to do but eat. Even he has put on a bit of the beef.'

'Have you any successes to report?' John suspected that he already knew the answer and asked the question more in hope than expectation.

'Naw!' Malcolm replied. 'The few English left are content to stay in their towers and wait us out. They are convinced that Edward will not abandon them and we can neither persuade them to leave nor force them out. Wallace says that it is enough to contain them, as they can do no mischief and inflict no misery if they cannot venture out.'

'So, why have you come?' Eck asked. 'I doubt that you have travelled all this way to tell us that nothing is happening and that we should settle in and make ourselves cosy for the winter.'

'You're right my friend, I do come with news, though I know not if you will take it for good or for ill. The Bruce tells us that he has it on good authority that Edward has called on his nobles to muster in York this very month.'

'And he intends to march in winter?' The Robertson asked incredulously.

'So it would seem.' Malcolm replied, shaking his head to show his disbelief. 'Sir William is delighted and says he would like nothing better than to see the English King waste his gold and have his army perish in the snows.'

Walter Langton was struggling to keep his temper as the King refused to listen to reason once again.

'Are you forgetting, my Lord, that I conquered Wales in winter when every voice counselled me against it and said that it could not be done. I proved them wrong then and will do so again.' Edward's face had reddened as the discussion went on. 'The magnates have frustrated me at every turn this spring and summer and now it is November and my garrisons still wait for me to relieve them. They will think that their King has forsaken them and I will not have that stain on my character. I am not weak like my father and will not have the veracity of my word questioned. If the King says something, people must know that he means it.'

Langton bit his lip to stop himself from responding. If Edward had been a man of his word, they would not be in this predicament. If he had awarded the magnates the Scottish lands he had promised them, not only would he have avoided alienating and infuriating them, he would also have them as staunch allies in this latest campaign, as they would have a vested interest in its success. If he had kept his promise to curtail his powers and reduce the size of his forest holdings, he would not have earned the enmity of the majority of the remaining nobles. Langton could scarcely believe that Edward still expected the nobles to answer his call to provide men and materiel for a hasty and risky winter campaign.

'My Lord, need I remind you that the Treasury is near empty? Even if we arrive at York in the morning to find that a huge host awaits us, we do not have sufficient silver to pay them with. If we cannot pay them, they will desert in droves as the winter closes in.' Langton succeeded in keeping his voice even and calm.

King Edward shook his head in slow disapproval. 'How can the coffers be empty, my Lord Bishop? I broke the siege of Saint Andrews and loaded your carts with chests heavy with gold. Where is that gold? You told me that it would be sufficient to fund this campaign as well as clearing our debts.'

Langton took a deep breath to calm himself and selected his words with care. 'You are, of course, correct my Lord. There was sufficient gold at the start of the year. Unfortunately, most of it was used up in your building projects and in the diplomacy relating to your lands in Gascony. Building and diplomacy are expensive, especially when pursued with such great passion.'

Edward's cold eyes locked onto Langton's. 'You might think me a fool, my Lord Bishop, but I am not half as much a fool as you. It is not my job to find the coin, that responsibility is yours.'

'And where should I find it, my Lord King? The nobles refuse us any more taxes, the church will pay us nothing on the orders of the Pope and we have squeezed the merchant classes until it is scarcely worth their while trading with us.'

'That is not my concern, Langton. When I arrive at York tomorrow I will have my army. I expect you to find the means to pay it and keep it supplied. I will not wait a moment longer to bring the rebellious Scots to heel.'

Langton barely slept that night as his mind raced with potential solutions to their financial predicament. As quickly as the ideas came, he rejected each one out of hand. If the King would not give ground to the nobles, the campaign could not be funded, it was as simple as that. He was miserable and his stomach clenched with anxiety as he mounted his horse and made his way to the King's side. It was a small mercy to find that the King would not ride this morning, but would instead recline in his litter.

Langton had always thought the walls of York to be amongst the most impressive in the land, but today he scarcely noticed them. What did capture his attention was the muster ground on the edge of the city. Edward had commanded his nobles to provide him with four thousand knights and had authorised his recruiting officers to offer higher rates of pay to secure the sixteen thousand foot soldiers required for the final conquest of the Scots. Langton did not consider himself to be an expert in military matters, but even he could see that less than five hundred knights and no more than two thousand foot were encamped below the walls of York.

He turned to Browby, who rode at his side, and whispered so that they would not be overheard. 'I am saved Browby. The nobles have unknowingly saved my skin. By defying the King, they deny him an army and thus I will have no campaign to finance.'

'Congratulations, my Lord.' Browby laughed. 'The King will not be happy.'

'Jesus Browby! He will be apoplectic with rage. Let us take ourselves off to the cathedral and leave others to face the storm. I have suffered my share of his bile and think it is time for others to take their turn.'

It was evening before Langton turned his feet towards the castle with a belly full of ale. The relief of being freed from the King's deranged commands to pluck the funds for a campaign from the air had raised his spirits no end. He had celebrated this release with Browby and now, light-headed with drink, was in need of his bed. Just when he was sure that the day could get no better, a familiar figure strode dejectedly out through the castle gates. John de Seagrave was the most senior knight in the household of the King's bête noire, Roger Bigod, the fifth Earl of Norfolk.

'Seagrave!' Langton shouted, concentrating to keep himself from slurring. 'How goes it?'

Seagrave groaned and rolled his eyes. 'Langton. Just when I thought my day could not become any worse.'

'What could possibly ail the Baron Seagrave?' You look most disheartened.'

'If you must know, I have spent the afternoon with the King. With the Earl absent owing to his poor health, I have been the recipient of his rancour and rage. I have been threatened, accused of treason and my face is coated in his spit. Tis not easy to be caught betwixt a King and an Earl.'

'Come Seagrave, let me buy you a drink. I know only too well how it is to feel the King's wrath. Come the morrow, I expect that I will feel it again now that his plans for invasion have come unstuck.'

'That's not what he thinks.' Seagrave responded, as Langton shepherded him towards the inn he had left only minutes before. 'He is determined and has now postponed the infantry muster by a week and has moved it to Berwick.'

'By God, he is determined. Do you think that it will make any difference?'

'Not a jot.' Seagrave replied with absolute certainty. 'The Earls are as determined as he and will provide no men until the King has made some concessions to them.'

'Good, good!' Langton responded, relieved to hear that there would still be no requirement for him to procure the funds for an invasion. 'Now tell me what you think would bring the magnates back to the King's side with men and materiel. I

319

have his ear and may be able to bring him to reason.'

The conversation with Seagrave proved to be quite productive. The man, being aware of the Earl's strong distrust of the Treasurer, was guarded at first, but warmed to him as the ale did its work. He gave away no secrets, but provided direction as to what the King might have to concede. Langton stored this away and set about enjoying himself.

'If you thought the King was harsh with you today, you should have seen him when your Earl refused to fight for him in France. His face was crimson with rage and he shouted at Bigod, 'By God, Earl, you shall either go or you shall hang!' The Earl stared back in defiance and shouted, 'By the same oath, o King, I will neither go nor hang.' The King raged about it for days and, at times, I feared that he would suffer a fit.'

Seagrave laughed at the tale and ordered the serving wench to fetch them more ale. 'You will pay for this in the morning, Langton. The King means to leave for Berwick at dawn.'

'It would be better that I stay drunk. The journey will be fruitless and I will count the days until I can return to London.'

In the end, the expedition was neither as painful nor as drawn out as Langton had feared. The King did rage for days about the nobles treating him like a child and a deceiver, but, by the time the stiff winds of Berwick were assailing their skins, he had accepted that there would be no invasion this year. Once this sorry admission was made, he was more open to Langton's plotting and scheming and they began to plan the destruction of Scotland anew.

Rank pushed his thumbs into the waistband of his trews and tried to stretch it out so that it did not dig into him so painfully. The material creaked as it strained, but did not stretch. He gave up and cursed, annoyed that he would have to have them let out yet again. Life at Dragan Hall was very much to his liking, but was not without its problems. He could eat and drink to his heart's content and his bulging belly was testament to his tendency to over-indulge his appetites. He had free rein with the serving girls and the daughters of the more minor tenants on the estate. He had also found great pleasure in the bed of the Lady Ingrede. He might have to sneak to her door in the dark, but that was a small price to pay for the delights that awaited him there. High-born she might be, but her desires were as low and as dark as his own. He had lost count of the dawns which had seen him crawl back to his chamber exhausted, spent and with weals, bruises and bite marks all over his skin. He was yet to find an act that was too depraved to excite her and he, for his part, never failed to be aroused by her filth.

Rank was unsure if Tarquil, his master and Lady Ingrede's husband, was unaware of their nocturnal adventures or if he genuinely did not care. He seemed happy to immerse himself in his painting and music and spent much of his time with the stable master's handsome, young

321

son. That was one scab Rank chose not to pick. In a life full of hardship and suffering, the months spent at Dragan Hall were easily the best of his life and he would do anything necessary to ensure that they did not come to an end. In return for his life of luxury, his only duties were to act as the weakling Tarquil's guard and to command the estate's militia.

He had found this to be in a woeful state, Tarquil's brother having marched the best fighting men and all their equipment off to Scotland, where he had promptly lost them all. Rank was left with little more than boys, old men and half-wits. At first, he had despaired of the task, but had grown to view it as a welcome distraction, as even he could not drink all day every day. He had begun by summoning all of the men on the estate and selecting the fifty best physical specimens. He had then drilled them on the green each Sunday and trained them in the use of the sword and the spear. Annoyingly, Tarquil had interfered and insisted that he design them a tabard to give them a uniform, martial appearance. Rank had tried vainly to dissuade him, but was unable to dampen his enthusiasm for the project. In the end, Tarquil commissioned both tabards and caps and, despite his initial reservations, Rank had been forced to reluctantly agree that the result was most splendid. With their new pikes and swords, the Trasque battalion was an impressive sight.

Today was set to be their finest hour as, at sunset, they would parade for none other than the Prince of Wales himself. Tarquil had worked

322

tirelessly for months to bring the Prince to Dragan Hall. He had hired painters and sculptors and brought them to work on the estate. He had written a hundred letters to ensure that the nobility were aware of the cradle of creativity he had constructed. He had engaged players and writers and invited any titled guest who would come. The arrival of the parchment with the royal seal had sent him into paroxysms of delight and he spent the following weeks in frenzied preparation for the coming visit. The Lady Ingrede was similarly excited, even although she did not share her husband's refined tastes. Rooted in practicality, she saw royal patronage as one more barrier to her family's attempts to divert the riches of Dragan Hall into their own pockets. Rank, for his part, cared little for the fuss, he would be content just as long as it did not impact on his easy life.

25

As Rank drilled his men for the Prince of Wales,
Scotstoun received an honoured guest all of their
own. Lamberton, now consecrated Bishop of
Saint Andrews by the Pope, arrived under
Wallace's protection, accompanied by a retinue
of tonsured monks. Before joining in the feast
laid on in welcome, the Bishop had, quite
rightly, insisted on celebrating mass in the
village kirk. With so many monks to assist him,
the congregation agreed that the Eucharistic
Celebration was much more impressive than
when conducted by their own, unassisted Father
MacGregor. He, to his great credit, showed no
resentment and seemed to enjoy the spectacle in
his kirk just as much as everyone else.

The Bishop's presence served to make the
feast a more sober occasion than was normally
the case in Scotstoun's square. Though bellies
were filled with meat and bread and these
washed down with generous quantities of good,
brown ale, the chanters remained tucked away
and no-one took to their feet to dance. When
Lamberton had eaten his fill, he stood to deliver
a blessing. He then endeared himself to one and
all as he excused himself from their company.

'I must speak with your leaders and so will leave you to your feast. I will be sorry to miss the drink and the dancing, but I hope you will make up for my absence by partaking enthusiastically in both.'

The people of the village needed no second invitation and the Bishop was swept to Andrew Edward's house on a wave of laughter, music and the thump of dancing feet.

The Bishop looked around the assembled company, his youthful features serious and determined. 'I have come here because we enter a new phase of the struggle and we require you to play your part. King Edward has abandoned his invasion as he did not have his nobles' support.'

Eck Edward banged the table with his fist. 'Then it is done! We have beaten him.'

'If only that were the case.' Lamberton replied wryly. 'He will not be beaten so easily and I fear that this is only a delay. At best, according to my informants, we have until the summer, but have no doubt that he will return.'

'So, Lord Bishop, what part can we play? With no invasion coming, we have precious few Englishmen to fight. Those who remain are already besieged and there is no need for more men to keep them trapped behind their walls.'

Wallace leaned forward and answered John's question. 'Everything you have said is true. But instead of waiting here for the English King to make his move, the Bishop is suggesting that we take the fight to him.'

'Sir William is correct.' Lamberton kept his eyes on John as he spoke. 'We cannot sit on our hands while King Edward gathers his forces. There is more than one way to win a kingdom and, having frustrated Edward's ambitions with our swords, it is now time to see if we can finish him with our words. I have asked Sir William to lead a delegation to the court of the French King and that of the Pope. If we can make friends and allies there, we might just put an end to the struggle without recourse to further bloodshed.'

'And what part can we play?' John asked.

'I need your men to stay fit and ready to harass the English when they come. We cannot afford to grow fat and complacent during this lull in hostilities.' More than one man at that table subconsciously sucked his belly in as the Bishop spoke. 'Sir William has asked that you John, your brother Scott and your cousin Alexander accompany him to France and then onto Rome. Our enemies will lurk in both those places and he will need good men to guard him and, if those men have mastered both French and Latin, then that is so much the better.'

John sat back in his surprise and saw that his brother and cousin were as wide-eyed as he.

'There will be others in the delegation, but I have chosen you three, Malcolm Simpson and Jack Short to accompany me. There will be dangers, that I cannot deny, but I hope that you will agree that it is worth taking the risk. I cannot order you to come, but ask that you do. I will understand if you need time to think it through.'

None of the three required any such time and agreed to come on the spot. The months of inactivity had left them in need of excitement and now they had it aplenty. John's mind reeled at the prospect of seeing such far flung places and his wife and six-month-old son did not enter his head until she struck it hard with the flat of her hand. Even that did not dent his enthusiasm and he comforted her with craven apologies and promises of presents from those far-off lands.

His joy did not last the first hours of the voyage. His experience of boats was limited to fishing on the smooth waters of the loch and one ferry trip over the Tay at Dunkeld, and that he could scarcely remember as he was deep in a fever at the time. The little merchant ship creaked and groaned as the huge, grey waves first tossed it high and then brought it crashing back down in troughs so deep they blocked any view of the sky. The sails were viciously buffeted by the winds and John expected that the masts must snap with each violent gust. He did not believe that it was possible to survive such a tempest and was mystified by the indifference shown by the crew. He clung desperately to the gunwale and, with his eyes tight shut, prayed for God to save him. If given the choice, he would have chosen to be back in the schiltrom at Falkirk, where at least the ground did not pitch and heave as if the end of the world had come. His brother and cousin made matters much worse by taking great amusement in his plight. Such was his fright, he had no words to throw back at them when they chastised him for being such a frightened, wee girl.

He would later remember those first hours at sea as being relatively pleasant, for the next few days were nothing short of a slow descent into the very depths of hell. Many times he prayed for his own death, just to escape the terrible sickness which afflicted him. The volume of vomit he produced was truly a wonder, for it far exceeded what a single human body could hold. He spewed until he was empty and then puked on dryly in spasms of sheer agony. His comrades revealed their true, callous natures by taking delight in his wretched state. When Scott called others over to witness just how wonderfully green his skin had become, he could have quite cheerfully killed him, if only he had been able to raise himself up from the deck.

When the ship docked briefly in Norway, he had stumbled quickly down the gangplank, only to find, to his great horror, that the solid ground now rose and fell as if it itself was afloat. The rest of the delegation had enjoyed the full hospitality offered by the dockside inn, but poor John retched at the mere sight of food and could sip only water, as just the slightest whiff of ale was enough to bring on the boke. When the time came to reboard the ship, John did so with great reluctance and only once the Wallace had finally convinced him that riding overland would take far too long.

After making landfall in Brittany, it had taken a full two days before John felt completely steady on his feet and his stomach stopped its churning and painful clenching. From this point on, he took great delight in the journey and marvelled at both the differences and similarities between this land and his home country. As was their habit, the Scots talked endlessly about the climate and marvelled at how warm it was for the time of year, especially when compared to what it must be like back home. The food they found in France was the other major topic of conversation. Hours in the saddle were spent discussing the bread which was available for a few coins in every village they passed through. Scott was able to consume whole loaves as he rode and would spend his evenings interrogating innkeepers about their recipes and how the loaves were baked. Garlic and its use in cooking was a topic which served to divide opinion and fuelled arguments over whether it improved or poisoned a dish.

The number in their happy party grew the further towards Paris they travelled. Most of those who joined them were priests and monks sent by Bishop Lamberton to school and advise Wallace on the task ahead. The French King had also sent six cavalry officers to offer some protection on the road. These men were surly and, for the most part, ignored any attempts to befriend them and stayed determinedly apart from the group. Wallace believed that they had been sent to monitor their activities, rather than to provide any safeguard. In the latter they proved to be useless and did nothing to stop the first attempt on Sir William's life.

They had stopped for the night at the most agreeable of inns and ordered their usual fayre. A Scots priest, who resided in France, had recommended that they must try the local wine. All had agreed that the tart, red liquid was as delicious as any they had tasted. Three flagons were brought to the table and the company set to draining them all. Relaxed and deep in wine-lubricated conversation, not one of them noticed the assassin's approach. The man was neither short nor tall and smiled as he came close to their table. The French escort paid him no mind as he passed them by, his smile sufficient to persuade them of his good intentions. It was when he stopped at Wallace's back that he reached into his sleeve, extracted a sharp dagger and pulled his arm back for the strike. The blow was aimed at Sir William's neck and he would have died in a pool of his own blood if it had landed. The blade's tip was already arcing downwards, when Eck's desperate, instinctive swing connected and reduced his nose to a mess of bloody gristle and splintered bone. The blade still found the Wallace's shoulder, but inflicted a small, deep puncture instead of the intended fatal blow.

The man was dragged to the back of the inn and interrogated in both English and French. Though he was tortured most thoroughly, he gave away no information about his masters and, while he screamed horribly when he was burned, he proved unfailingly loyal and steadfast to the end. The gold coins in his purse were embossed with the head of King Edward, which left little doubt as to who he had served.

The attempt on the life of their leader served to transform the atmosphere of the journey and the gaiety and light conversation of its first days were replaced with a seriousness of purpose and a heightened degree of caution.

'We were too lax.' Wallace concluded. 'The beauty of our surroundings and the weight of Bishop Lamberton's coin lulled us into a false sense of security. We must be on our guard as we have as many enemies here as we do at home. The good Bishop warned me that we are entering a den of vipers, so we must keep our wits about us.'

Under other circumstances John would have teased Wallace, for his face was as white as a sheet after his brush with death. The former Guardian had not spared his jibes when the sea had turned John's face as green as grass. He wisely decided that his planned retort should be kept for when the shock was less raw.

'Aye, Sir William.' He replied. 'We shall take greater care as we advance.'

The delegation could not be blamed for being distracted when they were greeted with their first sight of Paris. For most of their number, it was like nothing they had ever experienced before. On either side of the great river, the settlement stretched off into the distance in all directions. While much of the city was made up of familiar low, wooden and stone-built houses, its vista was studded with great limestone buildings, fortresses, a cathedral and more church spires than they would have believed it was possible to have in one place. Wallace, having visited the city before, took time to point out key points of interest, including the French King's palace on an island in the middle of the Seine and, to the great excitement of the younger men, the Templar fortress at Marais. The Edward lads had been brought up on tales of the Knights Templar, the Temple Mount, the Crusades and the siege of Acre and squirmed in their saddles with boyish delight to see solid evidence of the legends before their eyes. Wallace had to remind them of the serious business at hand, but relented and promised that they could visit the fortress if the time could be found.

Their jubilation was somewhat tempered when they entered Paris itself. The narrow streets made them feel claustrophobic and they gagged on the stench in the air. The muddy lanes were thick with human waste, animal droppings and the detritus of everyday life. Every road was cluttered with people, horses, carts and animals and there was scarcely a second which was free from their din. Their complaints and discomfort eased off when they finally reached the great wooden bridge over the Seine. They marvelled at the wooden houses which clung to its sides from end-to-end and wondered how a bridge could be strong enough to bear all that weight. They were stunned into silence when they emerged onto the island and caught sight of King Philip's great palace, which was so magnificent it was hard to believe that it had been built by mere men. Wallace told them that it was intended to inspire wonder and make any man entering feel small, that way, he explained, the King would have an advantage over anyone who came here for an audience, as they would quail in the face of his power.

John did indeed feel small as his party was waved into the great ante-chamber and he could not help but gaze up, open-mouthed at its high, vaulted ceiling. He thought that all of the houses of Scotstoun would fit within this one room. The feeling of awe was dissipated as the afternoon wore on with no sign that a royal audience was imminent. John took to pacing the stone floor as Wallace regularly approached the attendants to enquire as to how much longer they would have to wait. It was well into the evening by the time the large wooden doors were pulled open by the liveried guards. The man who swept into the ante-chamber was richly dressed, around forty years of age and his greying brown hair was neatly clipped at a level just above his shoulders. He strode confidently towards them, his right arm held out before him with his fingers together and his hand angled down at the wrist.

'Sir William!' He declared with a smile. 'Allow me the pleasure of welcoming you to our great city. I have been kept informed of the progress of your journey through our wonderful countryside. I hope that you have found much to admire along the way.'

Wallace stepped forward and held out his hand in greeting. The man stopped and retracted his hand in puzzlement, before allowing himself a snigger.

'I am Guillaume de Nogaret, Councillor and Keeper of the Seal to His Highness, Philip of France. You must kneel to kiss my hand, not shake it.' He delivered this advice in a good-humoured whisper, as if he intended to save Wallace from embarrassment at his faux-pas.

Wallace did as he was bid and thanked Nogaret for his welcome.

'You are fortunate indeed to meet me on your first day in the city. Most petitioners never have the pleasure or, if they are lucky, they only do so after waiting for many weeks. Now, I understand from our mutual friend that you seek an audience with His Majesty. I have made him aware of your arrival and I know that he is very keen to meet with you. He is particularly interested in hearing how you destroyed King Edward's army before the town of Stirling.'

'Please tell His Majesty that it would be my honour to share my experiences with him.' Wallace replied, inclining his head as he did so. 'I would also like to speak with him about the situation of King John Balliol who, after Edward released him from captivity in the Tower of London, now sits in Papal custody. I would also like to consult with him on how we might advance the alliance between our two countries.'

'Yes, yes, Sir William.' Nogaret waived his hand dismissively. 'There will be time for that anon. I will endeavour to grant your audience, but you should know that a thousand men crave an audience with the King. It may take days or weeks for us to find a time which would suit His Majesty.' Nogaret shook his head and touched Wallace on his upper arm. 'But I do not need to tell you this. As Scotland's Guardian, you must have had a taste of the burden which leadership brings. From urgent matters of state, to quarrels over the smallest parcel of land, all of these matters furiously compete for consideration. There is an art to dealing with the clamour. You have practised it yourself, have you not?'

Wallace glanced at Jack Short and nodded. He had himself used Jack as an intermediary to prevent him from being overwhelmed with every petty petition that landed at his door. He did not relish being on the receiving end of just such a rebuff, no matter how prettily it was delivered.

Nogaret smiled. 'Excellent. I think we understand one another and that is good. I will do my best for you, on that you have my word. Now, we must ensure that you have adequate accommodation for you and your men whilst you are in the city.'

'Bishop Lamberton has already made arrangements, we have quarters close to here, on the far bank of the Seine.

'No, Sir William, that will not do.' Nogaret shook his finger as if he admonished a naughty child. 'Your apartments were not appropriate for a guest of His Majesty, so I have had them cancelled and arranged something much more suitable. The house of the Comte de Bonnaire is at your disposal. I am sure that you will find it most comfortable. My man will take you there.'

'Please pass on our thanks to His Majesty. His hospitality does him great credit.'

Nogaret nodded to acknowledge Wallace's thanks and waved him closer as if he was about to share a confidence. 'Pardon me, Sir William. I hope that you will not think me rude. I cannot help but notice that your attendants are still dressed for the road. It is normally considered a courtesy for petitioners to don appropriate dress before entering the palace. Can I assume that they possess such suitable attire? It is stored in your baggage perhaps?'

Wallace turned to look at his men. Until this very moment, he had thought them to be as smart and as neat as he had ever seen them. Certainly, he had spent freely of Lamberton's coin in improving their wardrobe before they had boarded their ship. Now, in the presence of Nogaret and his fine garments, he found that they looked quite scruffy, like poor relations at a feast.

Nogaret read his thoughts and patted him reassuringly on the arm. 'No matter my friend, I will send my tailor to the house. He will know exactly what is required.'

With that, the Scots delegation was led out of the palace and into the streets of Paris, on their way to the House of Bonnaire.

26

Nogaret had not exaggerated when he praised the magnificence of the House of Bonnaire, but he had been wrong to predict that the Scots delegation would be comfortable there.

'How can they call this a house?' Jack Short asked. 'It is bigger and is of a more sturdy build than most of the castles I have seen.' He stared about himself as he spoke, his eyes wide at the scale of the place. 'It has more rooms than a manor and the walled garden is as big as a village field.'

'It is no castle.' Wallace replied. 'It's a prison. A richly appointed one, but a prison nonetheless.'

'A prison?' Scott asked, his head still swivelling as he tried to take it all in.

'Aye!' Sir William replied, dropping his voice to a whisper. 'Do you not notice that the guards from the road stand at the doors? I have no doubt that they are charged with keeping us here, rather than with keeping others out. Did you not notice the distance between here and the palace? They could hardly have put us further from its doors.'

'Are you sure?' John asked. 'We can hardly complain about our quarters and the servants buzz around us like flies.'

'Bishop Lamberton warned me about this. He said that they might keep us waiting until we grow bored or run out of coin and leave without asking the King for our favours. It is not the first time the tactic has been used.' Wallace lowered his voice further and pointed his finger towards the door. 'The servants scarce leave our presence, so that they miss nothing we say. I don't doubt that our every utterance will be reported back to Nogaret, so he can gauge whether our resolve is being tested.'

'But why would they do that?' Scott demanded. 'We are supposed to be on the same side.'

Wallace laughed without humour. 'Their only side is their own. They will entertain us only if it brings them some advantage. If they see none, they'll leave us to rot or find some way to stop us from pestering them. We must always be on our guard. There is no way to know what plotting and scheming goes on behind our backs.'

Wallace then marched over to the fireplace and pointed to the coat of arms carved into the stone above the mantle. 'That,' he said, 'tells me that something smells very bad here.'

John had noticed the carving when he entered the room, but it was only now that its significance hit him. He drew his sword and closely examined its hilt. There was no doubt, the coat of arms exactly matched that which was engraved into the gold on the pommel of his sword. The works of both the stonemason and the goldsmith depicted Le Lion Du Nord.

'Now do you see it John?' Wallace demanded. 'It is no accident that we have been placed here. We must tread very carefully.'

Under normal circumstances, the Scotstoun men would have very much enjoyed the luxuries offered by the House of Bonnaire. The interior was sumptuous, great fires burned at all hours in every room and the beds were big enough for a whole family and so soft a man could be lost in their depths. The servants were ever attentive, leaving no glass empty for more than a moment and constantly bringing plates of fruit, meat and bread and trays of delicious pastries, which melted as they entered the mouth. Boredom and paranoia conspired to diminish their joy.

After four days of sitting around and talking only in whispers, the arrival of the tailor provided some welcome relief. He set up shop in a room at the rear of the house and saw each of the party in turn. Once Wallace, Jack Short and Malcolm Simpson were done, John was called in to be measured and outfitted in more courtly attire. He was amazed to find the chamber transformed, with the floor covered with rolls of cloth of every shade and weave one could possibly imagine. The tailor grinned at his astonishment and waved him over to be measured for his garb. He had a kindly face and used a length of knotted string to record all of John's dimensions. John found the process to be quite uncomfortable, as the tailor did his work at close quarters and left not one body part untouched.

'I am told that you are to have cloak, tabard, shirt, trews, cap and underclothes. Now you must choose your cloth.'

John looked around at the bewildering range of choices before him and was uncertain how to proceed. The tailor smiled at his indecision and came to his aid.

'Alright, how about something like this?' He held up a bolt of light blue cloth for John's inspection.

'That's a bit, you know, like something a woman would wear.' John replied, unable to imagine himself in such a bright colour.

'You would be surprised.' The tailor laughed. 'The men at court often strut about like peacocks, their outfits outshining even the most glamorous of noble women. But that is not for you. How about this? The dark grey would make a fine cloak, but is nicely understated.'

Before too long, the tailor had helped John to arrive at an ensemble which would not attract the mockery of his fellows. He had overcome his early awkwardness and enjoyed the tailor's company.

'Pardon me for asking,' he said, 'but your accent sounds familiar. Where does it come from?'

The tailor stiffened slightly and answered the question with a vague flick of his hand. 'Oh, from somewhere to the east of here.'

'I have heard it before in Scotland, from a man who asked for my protection upon the road. His name, if I recall it correctly, was Malachi Crawcour.'

The tailor's eyes widened with surprise and he cast his eyes around the room to check that they were alone before he responded. 'I have a cousin of that name. I was told that he had gone into hiding when the English King banished our people.'

'That's right. I met him not long after he had crossed our border.' John nodded as he spoke. 'I left him safely in the company of our nobles.'

'Ah, that is good to hear.' The tailor sighed with relief. 'I thank you for any help you gave him.'

'You and he are both most welcome.' John hesitated before he continued. 'He looked quite different to you.' John used his index fingers to mime curls at his temples.

'Malachi has always worn his religion on his sleeves. Here in France, that is not so wise and so I keep it below the covers.'

John nodded and winked to indicate that he would keep his secret safe.

'Oh, I just had a thought!' John exclaimed. 'My wife was not happy when she heard that I planned to journey here. I seek a gift that I can present to her to soften her on my return. I would be grateful if you could suggest something suitable.'

It was the tailor's turn to wink. 'I know the very thing. I have at home a scarf of the finest silk, which was imported from the east. The colours are beautiful and bright and I guarantee that you will see none better on any Scottish lady's head.'

The price was steep, but John reckoned that it would be gold well-spent.

A further week passed without the arrival of an invitation to the palace. Wallace had initially insisted on making the journey there each day, but had relented when the attendants finally convinced him that days spent on the hard palace seats would do nothing to speed his audience with the King. The only distractions on those long days were the visits from the tailor. The men took great delight in mocking the sartorial choices made by their fellows. The Edwards were pilloried as dour and dull, as John and Scott had dared not stray from grey and Eck, predictably, had chosen the darkest shades of black. Malcom's bright red tabard had been met with gales of laughter and for days they had addressed him as Bishop. Jack Short had gone for the light blue cloth which John had so quickly rejected. Despite the jeers and insults, Jack had paraded unabashed with his nose held high in the air. By the way he pranced and preened, Scott reckoned he would fit right in at court. Wallace had initially joined in the merriment, but then reminded them of the cost of their new attire and bade them lay out their outfits in their chambers to keep them clean for when they were called to the palace.

The next week brought no word from the palace, but the servants informed them that the Comtesse de Bonnaire would be returning in two days from now. She sent her apologies for her absence and invited the whole delegation to join her at table on the night of her arrival, to toast to the success of their mission. Sir William informed the company that they should adorn themselves in their finery, but warned them that he would kick the arse of any man careless enough to despoil or stain their cloth.

Even for men as well fed as they, the feast was a sight to behold. The stout oak table groaned under the weight of silver plate and the mountains of delicacies they held. Six servants stood sentry with silver jugs full of fine wine and rushed to replenish their goblets the moment even one mouthful was quaffed. The Comtesse herself deserved praise for being the most attentive of hostesses. Scarcely a moment passed by when she was not urging her servants to bring more platters to table or encouraging her guests to sample a particular dish. Wallace, sat at the far end of the table, did not fail to observe that she was at great pains to see that her guests did not go thirsty, but that her own goblet was the only one that was never refilled.

The Comtesse raised many a toast, some to the brave Scots for their resistance to tyranny and just as many to their alliance with France. She spoke of her sadness at the death of Lord Andrew Murray and told fond tales of the time she had spent with him in Scotland as an emissary for King Philip. She drew all of her guests into the conversation and was most keen to hear their stories of their fight with the English King. When Wallace spoke of the Battle of Stirling, she hung on his every word and, when he described the part played by John Edward, she insisted that no detail be left out. John had blushed when she held him in her gaze, as she was undeniably a beautiful woman and she seemed only to have eyes for him.

When the feast had drawn to a close and the Comtesse had bade her guests good night, John rose and set off for his chamber. Wallace stopped him on the stairwell and put his mouth close to his ear.

'Take care, John. I sense that there is intrigue in the air. I do not know what specifically, but I am certain something is afoot.'

'I will, Sir William.' John replied, keeping his voice low. 'I have my wits about me and will be on my guard.'

'That woman is a snake, my every sense tells me so. She is uncommonly interested in you, John. Make sure she does not sink her fangs into your flesh.'

John assured Wallace that he would be careful and took himself off to bed.

He was laying his shirt and tabard carefully out on the floor, when a knock sounded at the door of his chamber. Thinking that it would be his brother or cousin, he invited them to enter without turning away from his folding. It was her scent that alerted him to his mistake. Its thick, musky sweetness reached his nostrils before the door had closed behind her. He spun round to find her with her hair down at her shoulders, dressed only in a long, white nightdress. Standing in only his trews, he felt strangely exposed in her presence. The fine lines around her eyes and the traces of grey at her temples seemed to enhance rather than detract from her beauty. Her nightdress was loose, but seemed to cling to her body and emphasise her generous curves.

'We should talk.' She purred.

'Not here.' John responded. 'There will be time aplenty to talk on the morrow.'

'I want to talk now.' She responded, with a sly smile on her face. She kept her eyes on his as she walked towards him, her hips swaying as she approached. 'I assume that you know who I am?'

'I have been told,' John replied, 'that you are my aunt. My mother's sister.'

'Ah, dear Isobelle. Does she speak fondly of me?'

'In truth, she has never spoken of you. I know that she was born in France, but neither she nor my father will speak of it. They say that the past is best left where it lies.'

She laughed as her eyes took in John's bare chest. 'They would say that, I suppose. That way the can stay hidden and safe from those who would harm them.'

John could feel her breath on his face and was enveloped in a cloud of her scent. 'Who would want to harm them?'

'There are many who would do your father harm, if they could but find him. He has done well to hide himself away for so long. I cannot believe that I now have his strong and brave, young son before me. Would you have me tell you the tale and learn your parents' true nature?'

John, still discomfited by her closeness, nodded, his curiosity overcoming his instinct to run from this encounter.

'Very well. I will keep it brief, as you need know only the essentials. My beloved sister Isobelle, your sweet mother, was betrothed to the Comte de Bonnaire. He was a beautiful man, rich and well-respected at court. This was a fine match for our family, one that my father had worked at for years. Then, only weeks before the wedding, she encountered a young, Scottish knight, whose Lord was sworn to the Comte. That was it. Without a thought for her family, she spread her legs wide and gave herself to the knight. The Comte caught them as they tried to elope and was forced to defend his honour. Your father bested him and left him to die in a ditch, taking that sword with him as he left.' She pointed to where John's sword was propped up against the head of the bed.

'With the Comte gone and Isobelle too, my father had to look elsewhere to ensure my family's fortune. That was when I, at only thirteen years old, was betrothed to the Comte's successor and only living relative, his old uncle. Now, he could not have been more different from his nephew. He was an ugly, mean-spirited, cruel, alcoholic gambler. Can you imagine how it felt to be forced into his bed at such a young age? To be dribbled on and

346

violated in whatever manner pleased him. I thought of my sister and her brave Scottish knight each and every time he climbed onto me. Ten years I suffered at his hands. Ten long years of such nights before he fell from his horse and suffered a fit which left him a drooling vegetable. Can you understand why I hate your mother so?'

'I would be more inclined to blame your father.' John replied. 'After all, it was he who arranged the match.'

'My father had little choice. Isobelle's departure left him with only one daughter to barter.' The Comtesse forced a smile onto her lips and ran her index finger slowly down John's bare chest and onto his belly. 'Enough of the ancient history. I have a half-naked, young man before me and a husband who is in no condition to protest.'

With these words, she pulled her nightdress down over her shoulders and revealed her large, pendulous breasts. John could not help but gape at her stiffening nipples and he felt himself become aroused in spite of himself.

The Comtesse licked her lips and placed her hand on John's crotch. 'This is why I prefer younger men. They are always quickly ready for battle.'

John teetered on the brink of giving in to his passion and it was only the thought of his Lorna that kept him from leaping into the abyss. He firmly grasped the Comtesse's wrist and gently pushed it away.

'I cannot!' He insisted. 'I am married and will not betray my wife.'

The smile on the Comtesse's lips twisted into a sneer. 'You Edward men are always so romantic. I don't doubt that your little country girl will weep when she hears how you hanged.'

'Hanged?' John asked in bewilderment.

'Yes. In a moment I will scream for my guards and they will come running to find me naked and at your mercy. In France they will hang any commoner who would dare to violate a woman of title. Imagine how your mother will grieve when she hears how you met your end. She will know that it was her selfish actions which led to your untimely death. I expect that her suffering might last for as long as ten years. I consider the repayment to be fair.'

John jerked in surprise as a voice interrupted her from the direction of the door.

'I cannot deny that your scheme is well-constructed, Comtesse, but it might have been better if it had not been witnessed by as many as this.' Wallace pushed the door fully open to reveal Malcolm Simpson and two of the French monks who had joined the Scottish delegation. 'We just happened to be passing and caught the last part of your speech. I doubt that the testimony of two such holy brothers would serve to strengthen your case.'

The Comtesse angrily pulled her nightdress up to cover her nakedness, but not before the good brothers had seen enough to add excitement to their dreams. Her face reddened and she seemed about to speak, but instead

348

pushed her way out of the chamber without meeting the Wallace's eye.

Wallace waved away John's attempts to thank him for coming to his rescue. 'Don't thank me John, for now you will have to share your bed.' He gestured to the brothers to enter the room. 'These two will now be your constant companions, to keep you safe and protect your virtue for as long as we are within these walls.'

27

Nogaret nibbled the last of the beef from the rib and snapped his fingers at the servant to indicate that he should remove the plate and the soiled napkin.

'Show her in,' he instructed his attendant, 'and after fifteen minutes, come back and announce that the King has commanded me to attend him at once. I have neither the time nor the inclination for one of her long conversations today.'

When the door was reopened, Nogaret rose quickly from his chair and went to greet his guest. 'Comtesse! How lovely to see you again. You grow more beautiful with each passing year.' He returned the bow of her head and took her hand to kiss it. 'You have no idea how much you have brightened my day. For one who is always surrounded by wizened old scribes and hard-faced petitioners, your elegance and handsomeness is like a shaft of pure sunlight to a prisoner in the darkest of dungeons.'

'You are always so charming, my Lord.' The Comtesse de Bonnaire replied coyly. 'I blush to be so complemented by a gentleman as handsome and as vigorous as you.'

Nogaret giggled with delight. 'Now I know that you are lying, but I will not ask you to stop. I would have you do it all day.'

He bowed at the waist and indicated that she should take a seat on a well-upholstered couch by the window. 'So, my Lady, how fair our honoured guests? You have made them comfortable no doubt.'

'There is nothing they can complain of. The servants pander to their every whim and they have already consumed a cellar full of wine. They do little but drink and complain about the length of time it is taking for their audience to be arranged.'

'Do you think that their patience wears thin? It would suit his Majesty's purpose if they were to give up and leave. The situation with England is delicate and this is not the moment to unsettle things by giving concessions to these Scots.'

'This man Wallace is not, in my judgement, one who will give up and walk away.' The Comtesse looked Nogaret directly in the eye and shook her head. 'I think that he will try your patience long before you test his.'

'That is good to know Comtesse.' Nogaret replied. 'It may be that we will have to help him on his way. What else have you learned about their intentions? I know that your servants have the keenest of ears.'

'I have to confess that I have less to report than I would like.' The Comtesse responded, again shaking her head. 'These Scots do indeed speak English, but they growl it like dogs and it is hard to make out a single word that they say.'

351

With no further meaningful intelligence to be had, Nogaret lost all interest in the conversation and merely nodded politely as the Comtesse spoke and awaited his attendant's interruption. When it came, he excused himself with the greatest of regret and thanked the Comtesse profusely for all of her invaluable assistance to the crown.

King Philip was not known as Philip the Fair for nothing. Nogaret genuinely believed that he was the most handsome king to have ever sat upon a European throne. He never failed to be amazed by the advantages his handsomeness brought. Nobles who were embittered by the quantities of gold he had extracted from them, were mollified and soothed by a mere hour of exposure to his beauty and charm. He was also known as le Roi de Fer, the Iron King, and Nogaret was convinced that this sobriquet was one that Philip would not have earned without him at his side. It was not that he lacked resolve, but that he required counsel and persuasion to ensure that his actions were properly directed to bring about the greatest advantage.

'Did I not promise the Bishop Lamberton that I would meet with his delegation?' Philip asked. 'Explain to me again why we keep them waiting. I am keen to hear how this Wallace fellow managed to defeat the English King. He may well be able to provide information on strategy which would be of benefit to our generals in the future.' The King laughed, 'In any case, I think I would enjoy hearing the tale for its own sake, even if it was to teach us

352

nothing. I would have loved to see King Edward's face when he heard the news of his army's annihilation.'

'Your Majesty, it is a question of maintaining a delicate balance. We continue to contest King Edward's claim on his lands in Gascony, but without pushing him so far that he mounts another campaign against us. These last years he has been no threat to us as he has concentrated on conquering the Scots and adding that crown to his own. Each unsuccessful campaign erodes his treasury and makes an attack on France less likely. Thus, it is very much in our interests to ensure that the Scots do not lose hope and continue to resist him. They will fight on if they believe that we will help them. We must give them enough to keep them fighting, but not so much that Edward is provoked into attacking France.' Nogaret paused for breath and waited to see the effect his words had on the King.

'What about the Pope?' Philip demanded. 'Where is he on this question? It is hard to keep up, his settled view seems more unsettled with each passing month.'

'Like us, he seeks to preserve a balance. He uses the Scottish question against Edward when it suits him and drops it when it brings him no advantage. I have heard that English emissaries have recently arrived in Rome. It would be well if we were to await the outcome of that mission before determining what crumbs to give the Scots.'

'My God Guillaume! I am glad that I am King and not Keeper of the Seal. The constant scheming and conniving would surely drive me mad. I do not know how you can stand it.'

'It is,' Nogaret replied with a smile, 'what I do best. I have a talent for it and I take great pleasure in advancing your interests, Majesty.'

'Very well. Let us await word of developments from Rome and, in the meantime, you must find the means to keep this Wallace and his delegation distracted.'

'I will your Majesty. I have a few tricks up my sleeves.' Nogaret replied with the slyest of grins.

The second attempt on Wallace's life was made within the walled garden at the rear of Bonnaire House. Sir William, John, Scott, Eck and Jack Short were seated at a marble table enjoying another fine, red wine, when a figure emerged from the shrubbery and ran straight towards them. The five men did not move until he was three paces away and the light flashed on the blade of the dagger grasped in his fist. Eck leapt onto the table and stopped the assassin in his tracks by smashing his boot heel hard into his face. Scott, who had been sitting opposite Eck, swivelled around and finished him off by striking him repeatedly with a heavy, clay flagon full of wine.

Just as Scott was landing his third blow, another five men burst out from the bushes and went straight into the attack. Eck jumped into their midst, drawing both swords as he went. He parried with his right hand and then viciously gutted an attacker with his left. John faced off against the biggest of the four and struggled to fend off his frenzied, downward blows. He shuddered under each hammering stroke and it was all he could do to stay on his feet. Then, as the man drew his sword back once again, John sent a crunching kick into his knee. He screamed out in pain at the sound of a terrible crack and then collapsed to the ground as the ruined leg gave way. It was to his great credit that, despite being so disabled, he continued to fight and caused John to have to leap back to avoid the swing of his sword. Eager to avoid another leg wound so soon after the last one, John finished him with three downward stabs to his heart.

The smallest of the group went straight at Wallace and slashed at him with his dagger. Sir William was unarmed and suffered serious cuts to his arms before he was able to grab the assassin's wrist and lift him from the ground by the throat. He continued to strike at the Wallace with his free hand and rained in kicks with his boots. Wallace squeezed his great fist with all of his might and stilled his resistance by breaking every bone in his neck. He then employed the jerking, twitching corpse as a shield and drove his full weight into another of their assailants, sending him crashing onto the ground with the combined weight of his body and that of the corpse smashing his skull wetly onto the hard, stone slabs.

The last of the six antagonists was faring no better than his fellows. Eck had backed him into the corner formed by the garden wall and that of the house and was toying with him as a cat does

355

with a mouse. He did not come close to laying his blade on Eck, but had suffered deep slashes to his arms, torso and legs. Though his clothes were soaked heavy and red with his blood, he refused to relinquish his sword and instead muttered darkly in French and motioned at Eck to engage. He made a final lunge forward and then opened his eyes wide in surprise at finding himself skewered on Eck's sword.

'I hope you didn't break that flagon Scott.' Wallace gasped as he fought to catch his breath and examined the deep, bloody cuts in his forearms. 'I find that I am sorely in need of a drink.'

'Jesus!' Jack Short exclaimed, his face pale with shock. He was still sat at the table and gazed with astonishment at the dead bodies that lay all around him. 'Where the hell did they come from?'

'I'm just glad that they did not disturb you and force you to your feet.' John smiled as he spoke, but took satisfaction from seeing Jack wince as he needled him.

'It was so fast, I had no opportunity to react.' Jack responded, the pitch of his voice rising in spite of his efforts to keep it even.

'By Christ, it was fast.' Wallace stated. 'Not two minutes ago we were drinking and chewing the cud and now it's a slaughter house.'

The sound of running feet from inside the house caused the men to raise their swords and prepare to defend themselves from another attack. Seconds later, Marsaud, the captain of their French guards, dashed out into the courtyard with five of his men at his back. He stopped in astonishment at the carnage before him.

'Mon Dieu!' He exclaimed, his eyes flicking back and forth between the bloody corpses and the dripping blades pointed at him and his men. He quickly read the situation and lowered his own sword. 'No, no! This is nothing to do with us, I promise you that.' He assured Sir William, his open palm held out towards the Scot as if to discourage an attack. 'We are here to protect you. I would not countenance such an outrage.'

'Pardon me if my faith in your protection is waning.' Wallace replied coldly. 'That is the second time my life has been endangered while your men have been on guard. That tells me that you are either incompetent fools or that you have been complicit in the attacks. Whichever of these it is, I would be stupid if I was to remain here. We will be finding our own quarters, you can communicate that to your masters.'

'No, Sir William.' Marsaud insisted. 'Let my men investigate and allow me to speak with my lord. Pray stay here tonight at least, and once we have all the facts, you can decide on what course to take.'

'I will reluctantly agree, but only due to the lateness of the hour. If there is nothing to change my mind in the morning, we shall take our leave of this place.'

Sir William set guards for the night so that no chamber could be approached without challenge. He also ordered the men to pack and insisted that they would be leaving at daybreak. Marsaud appeared just as the day began to dawn and informed Wallace that his presence was required at the palace and that he and his men would accompany him there. Wallace refused the offered protection and instead set off with his own men around him. Their numbers might offer less safety, but at least he knew that he could trust in their absolute loyalty.

At the entrance to the palace, they went through the usual process of giving up their arms before being allowed to enter the all-too-familiar antechamber. They had only waited moments when the doors were opened and Nogaret emerged with another well-dressed man at his side. The grim expression on the face of the Keeper of the Seal made Wallace uneasy, but it did not trouble him as much as the company of armed guards which followed on behind him. A quick glance to his rear told him that neither fight nor flight were viable options, as guards had appeared and now covered every door.

'What base trickery is this?' He demanded, as Nogaret approached.

'I am sorry, Sir William. I am afraid that I am powerless to intervene, no matter how much I would like to.' Nogaret shrugged slightly to communicate his lack of comfort with the situation. 'This is Enguerrand de Marigny, Grand Chamberlain of France and Minister to his Majesty King Philip. It is he who has summoned you here to answer the gravest of charges.'

Marigny fixed Wallace with a look of stern disapproval. 'Is it true that you murdered a man last night by crushing his throat?'

Wallace returned his gaze defiantly. 'It is true that I, an unarmed man, fought off an assassin who came at me with a dagger while I was enjoying the hospitality of your King.'

Marigny laughed mirthlessly. 'Then it is unfortunate that your attacker was of noble family and yet more unfortunate still that his cousin serves as a dresser to our Queen. It is on her orders that I am to detain you while the matter is investigated. You should know that penalties in France are most severe in instances where a commoner attacks a man of noble family.'

John stepped forward with his hands squeezed into tight fists at his sides. 'You know that you address Sir William Wallace, former Guardian of the Kingdom of Scotland?'

'In France,' Marigny replied dismissively, 'a commoner born remains so until he dies, regardless of what baubles are conferred upon him. Nobility here is about breeding and breeding cannot be bought or won through acts of courage. Your master will rightly be treated as a commoner before the law.'

Marigny then signalled to the guards and Wallace was secured and led away. 'Get word to Lamberton!' Wallace commanded over his shoulder. 'He will know what to do.'

Nogaret smiled ruefully at John and watched Marigny's back as he left. 'Alas, the good Bishop may be too far away to be of much help.

But you should not lose hope. I will do everything in my power to ensure that this unfortunate misunderstanding is cleared up without delay.'

'Nevertheless,' John replied, 'I will send word to Lamberton. I am sure you will understand my reluctance to place all of my faith in you.'

Nogaret nodded. 'I understand completely, my young friend. No-one regrets this regrettable turn of events more than I.'

The next four weeks were filled with boredom through inactivity, anxiety about the fate of Wallace and an increasing sense of paranoid uneasiness. The delegation moved in together in one wing of the house, so that guards could be posted night and day. One of the Scottish monks had been furnished with a heavy purse of Lamberton's gold and was despatched to Scotland to inform the Bishop of Wallace's arrest and to return with his advice on how best to proceed. This left the men to wait passively for events to unfold. As each day passed without news of their leader or the return of the monk, their spirits fell further. The sights and sounds of Paris might have offered some distraction, but they ventured out only on rare occasion when the claustrophobia threatened to drive them to madness. They were also reluctant to be seen to be enjoying themselves when Wallace's fate seemed to hang in the balance.

Much of their time was spent cursing the untrustworthy and treacherous French. It was disheartening that those they had been taught to view as allies had turned out to be as inconstant and as villainous as the English and their own turncoat nobles. They spent hours competing to come up with the most gruesome punishments for their enemies, but this served only to highlight their essential impotence. Some hours were wiled away bickering and bitching about each other's habits, as often happens when men are forced into close quarters for extended periods of time. Eck's custom of constantly sharpening his swords was perhaps the cause of most complaint, as the grate of stone on blade was almost impossible to shut out.

More than once, Scott was driven to distraction and shouted, 'For Christ's sake Eck, they must be fucking sharp by now! You'll wear them down to nothing if you continue to scrape at them!'

The focus of John's irritation was Jack Short. He tried to keep himself back from making petty complaints, but, no matter how hard he tried, he could not put Short's trickery out of his mind. It angered him that Short's lies had almost deprived him from having the honour of being present at Wallace's knighting. He was able to ration himself to the occasional jibe or snide comment, but this still had the effect of adding to the already sour atmosphere.

Marsaud blew all of this away like a morning mist when he popped his head around the door as the men took their breakfast and announced, 'I hear that your Sir William is to be released today.'

28

Nogaret smiled broadly as Wallace was admitted to his room. 'Sir William, it is such a pleasure to see you again. Now please come and sit. I will pour a goblet of wine for you.' The Keeper of the Seal busied himself with the silver pitcher and goblets, before turning back to the still standing Wallace. 'Oh, Sir William, you stare at me with such sternness. I almost think that you wish to leap on me and crush my throat, just as you did to your unfortunate visitor at Bonnaire House.'

'If you were to come at me with a dagger, then you would learn what it is like to suffer such a fate. You can be certain of that.' Wallace growled in response to Nogaret's teasing.

'Oh, come now Sir William.' Nogaret purred. 'I can understand your annoyance at being so detained, but did you suffer any hardship? No. I made sure that your conditions were most comfortable.'

Wallace's eyes smouldered and bored into those of the Frenchman. 'Like most of my countrymen, I am never comfortable when my liberty is taken away. If you understood that, then you would understand why the English

King has failed in all of his attempts to conquer us.'

'Oh, Sir William, you are so wonderfully dramatic! I love it so. King Philip will love it too.' Nogaret leaned towards him as though he was about to share a confidence. 'He so enjoys spending time with those with a flair for the theatrical. Your approach is very likely to win him over.'

'So, I am to have my audience with your King?' Wallace demanded.

'Yes, yes, Sir William. But first, I must ask that you indulge me. I am eager to make you aware of all of my efforts to have you freed. I went to a not inconsiderable amount of trouble on your behalf. I first had to uncover the truth of the matter and then I had to persuade Marigny of its veracity, which was not at all easy. Between us, he is the most cynical and mistrustful of men. With this done, all that remained was the gargantuan task of convincing the Queen to find in your favour in the face of the grief and outrage of her favourite dresser. Let me just say that it took an obscene amount of gold to ease the poor girl's bereavement. Luckily for us, her noble family have fallen upon the hardest of times.'

'So, my freedom was bought and my innocence was not proven?' Wallace asked, still refusing to sit.

'That is not true, Sir William!' Nogaret protested with a shake of his head. 'Your innocence in the matter is no longer in doubt and you have Captain Marsaud to thank for that. His investigation was most thorough and it was he who discovered the English gold secreted in the walls of the unfortunate young man's humble lodgings. It was clearly evident that his reduced circumstances unwisely led him to accept this murderous commission.'

'If that is the case, then why pay his family? It sounds like an admission of guilt.'

'Not at all, Sir William.' Nogaret replied. 'I would not dare to say that the Queen is an obstinate woman, but it is doubtful that any hard evidence would change her mind whilst her young lady remained deep in the throes of despair. The gold had the most wondrous effect and her sobbing and wailing stopped almost as soon as it was presented to her. Few other metals boast such properties of healing.'

'And now I will see King Philip?' Wallace asked without warmth.

'I think that the Queen is not the only stubborn person in the palace this day, Sir William. If my description of everything I have done on your behalf is not enough to raise a smile, then perhaps I can succeed in mollifying you by giving you the details of what I have arranged with His Majesty.' Nogaret raised his eyebrows and again indicated the place at his side on the couch. 'You are to be accorded a rare privilege in terms of both the length and the intimacy of your audience. I know of Dukes who have failed to gain such access in spite of their nobility and their willingness to spend years bowing and scraping in order to win favour.'

Nogaret did not succeed in winning a smile, but Wallace did sit and drink the Keeper's wine.

It would be an understatement to say that Tarquil de Trasque was beside himself with excitement. He had spent the morning in a fit of manic activity and had driven his lady wife and retainer Rank to distraction. He alternated between declarations of joy and despondent certainty that the day would be nothing short of a disaster.

'Tarquil!' Lady Ingrede admonished him. 'You will have a fit if you do not calm yourself. Leave the servants to their business. They organised many a tournament in your brother's time and will do better without you constantly pestering them.'

'They have,' Tarquil responded haughtily, 'never put on a tournament that their future king was to attend. The Prince will soon rise from his bed and all must be perfection by then.'

'At what hour did the Prince retire?' Ingrede enquired. 'My chambermaid said that his party were still drinking when the sky grew light with dawn.'

Tarquil grinned sheepishly. ''Tis true Lady, we drank right through the night and what a time we had.'

'Well, take care my husband, I do not want you dropping dead.' Lady Ingrede sighed, as Tarquil strode off to check on yet another detail of the events planned for the day.

'Has he hurt himself?' Rank asked. 'It seems that he can hardly walk straight.'

'He says that he twisted his leg during horseplay with the Prince.' Ingrede replied, with raised eyebrows.

'That,' Rank replied, 'I can well believe.'

The first nobles and local worthies began to arrive in the late morning and the stream of horses and carriages continued to make their way along the drive until well into the afternoon. By the time the Prince of Wales made his belated appearance, Dragan Hall's reception rooms and grounds were crowded with high-born men and women filling their bellies with their hosts' food and wine. They hurriedly followed the Prince and, with great anticipation, took their places in the stand. They cheered at the jousting and watched in admiration as young noblemen displayed their talents in single combat. All too soon, it was time for the final event.

'Sir Tarquil,' the Prince demanded, 'where is your armour? I had assumed that you would compete in the melee. I myself cannot, my shoulder is still stiff from when I fell from my horse in the hunt. Piers is to fight in my place.'

'My Lord Prince,' Tarquil responded. 'I only wish that I could. I damaged my back when fighting my way through the Scots at Stirling Bridge. These days I can scarcely wield a sword.'

'Then who will be your champion and fight for the honour of your house?' The Prince glugged down another goblet of wine, before rubbing the spillage from his neat beard. 'I take

366

it that it will be this fellow here.' The Prince used his thumb to indicate Rank, who stood, as always, at Tarquil's back. 'I can see that he is not in your service for his looks or quick wit. I only hope that he can fight.'

'I can fight well enough, my Lord.' Rank growled in response. 'Like Sir Tarquil, I too had to cut my way through the Scottish lines. I am no stranger to the sword.'

Tarquil grimaced internally as he knew that Rank would not be at all pleased to have been put into this position. His mention of Stirling was a clear jibe and a veiled reminder that Tarquil's lack of involvement in the battle could so easily be revealed.

'Of course, my Prince.' Tarquil announced. 'He will be my champion and will receive a purse of silver for standing in my stead.'

'Go on man!' The Prince commanded. 'Get into your armour! The melee is about to begin.'

'I won't need armour for these pampered, little bastards.' Rank growled, before striding onto the field.

The melee at Dragan Hall would not live long in the memory as a great demonstration of the chivalric fighting arts. However, as a pure spectacle, it would be undeniably hard to forget. Rank dispensed with the tradition of besting a man before demanding that he yield and instead set about knocking the young noblemen senseless with the mace he had selected for the task. His first five blows sent as many young knights crashing to the ground with dents in their fine, polished helmets. Shields were bludgeoned away and swords sent spinning from youthful grips. It was normally considered bad form to attack a man from the rear, but it was so entertaining to watch Rank tear through his opponents at speed, that only the relatives and sweethearts of those so dispatched were moved to make any complaint. In a mere matter of moments, Rank had clubbed all the good knights into submission, with the exception of the Prince's favourite and champion, the handsome and debonaire Piers Gaveston. Most onlookers, perhaps influenced by the Prince, would later recall that Piers had stood up to the beast and had only yielded after offering the stoutest of resistance. The truth of it was that it took only four strokes to relieve him of shield and sword and pitch him onto his back to cry his submission.

Much to Tarquil's delight and relief, the Prince declared the tournament to be a great success. As dusk drew in, they all retired to the hall for the feast. It was at the table that the inebriated Prince pulled Tarquil into his embrace.

'I have a secret for you.' He slurred.

'Oh, I adore secrets.' Tarquil responded excitedly.

'Shh!' The Prince hissed. 'No one must know. The King plans to campaign again in Scotland.' He nodded drunkenly and cast his eyes about to ensure that they were not overheard. 'But this time he will invade with two great armies. Can you guess who will command the second?'

Tarquil's eyes widened with astonishment. 'My Lord?'

'Exactly.' Edward responded, pointing his index finger towards his own face. 'I am to command it and you, my dear Tarquil, will be at my side. I will have need of men who know Scotland and the Scots. The King wants me to surround myself with capable men and you were the first man I thought of.'

If the Prince had been less drunk, he might have noticed that his companion's face turned pale at these words. He might even have intuited that Scotland was the last place on God's Earth that Tarquil wished to find himself in.

Wallace had to grudgingly agree that Nogaret had delivered well on his promises regarding the audience with King Philip. He was sure that Lamberton would have been content if he had secured just half an hour of Philip's time and would therefore be delighted when he heard that he and two of his party were to enjoy an intimate dinner with the most powerful ruler in Europe.

The venue for the dinner, a small dining room just off the King's own chambers, was more opulent than anything the party had ever experienced before. Even the more travelled Wallace could not help but stare about him at the frescoes and fine tapestries which adorned the room. The table itself was exquisitely carved, with place-settings of polished silver which glistened in the light of the many candles.

John Edward gazed around himself and felt as if he was in a dream. He had never expected

369

that Wallace would select him to be part of the audience with King Philip. The older Scottish monk, Montrose, had been equally surprised, but perhaps should not have been, as he was the only representative of Lamberton still with them in Paris. John had allowed himself a smile at Jack Short's sour face as he left Bonnaire House in all his finery. He felt that it was a victory of sorts to have been chosen above him. He did recognise that such pettiness was beneath him, but could not deny that it gave him a great sense of satisfaction.

Nogaret had instructed them to take their places at the table, but, having just taken their seats, he immediately indicated that they should rise to greet King Philip. Even as he bowed his head, John saw that he was a most impressive figure. Tall, blonde and fair of face, he looked every inch a king.

Once the introductions were done with, the King bade them sit.

'I hope that the food will be to your liking. I have ordered the plainest of fayre. My stomach gives me a great deal of trouble these days and reacts badly to anything that is too rich.'

'I am sure that we will enjoy it, your Majesty.' Wallace replied graciously. 'We have greatly appreciated your hospitality and have eaten very well these last weeks. It will do us good to consume good, wholesome food.'

'Sir William,' Philip replied. 'Before we move onto the business at hand, I would be very much indebted to you if you would tell me of your experiences of battling with the English

370

King. I have, of course, received reports on the battles, but there is no substitute for a first-hand account.'

Wallace agreed readily and started with his account of the battle at Stirling Bridge. King Philip nodded as he ate and interrupted often with questions and requests for more detail. There was no doubt that he enjoyed it immensely, particularly when Wallace talked of the numbers of English troops who had been slaughtered upon the field. John's cheeks had burned red with embarrassment when Wallace detailed his part in the battle and he had felt beads of sweat appear on his forehead when King Philip turned his gaze upon him and complimented him on his ingenuity and courage.

'Once the Scottish question is settled, there might well be a place for you in my army. We are always looking out for capable men.' Philip paused for a second before continuing. 'The fact that you have mastered the French tongue would be a great advantage, even although your accent is most strange.'

John thought that this would be a fine tale for a Scotstoun feast, but doubted that anyone would believe a word of it.

'Mon Dieu, Sir William!' King Philip declared. 'Can you imagine how humiliated King Edward of England must have felt when he learned of the destruction of his great army? You know that he was here in France when it happened? On his lands in Gascony? My spies tell me that he attacked the poor messenger who brought him the news. They say that he would

371

have killed him in his temper, if his attendants had not pulled him away.'

'I am glad, your Majesty,' Wallace replied. 'That our success on the field drew our common enemy away from his avaricious ambitions here in France.'

'Yes, Sir William. We were very glad to see the back of him and remain ever grateful to our fine Scottish allies. But let us not move onto matters of business just yet. I would hear more of your exploits. For instance, tell me of the fate of King Edward's confidante, Cressingham. I heard that you skinned him alive and made yourself a belt from his cured flesh.'

Wallace detected a hint of mockery in Philip's tone and sought to downplay the savagery of the Treasurer's death. 'I fear that accounts of Sir Hugh Cressingham's death have been somewhat exaggerated, your Majesty. Though, it is true that I executed him myself for the suffering he caused to my people, as well as for his many other crimes.'

'It is little wonder then, Sir William, that King Edward repeatedly crosses your border, returning to Scotland just as soon as he has enough gold to fund another campaign. The execution of a valued minister is something no king could ignore.'

'I believe, your Majesty,' Wallace replied, 'that he comes to win a second crown, one not being sufficient for his head.'

'You do not need to tell me of his greed, Sir William. He is my vassal on account of his lands in Gascony, but is reluctant to pay what is due to his King. Now tell me about his latest campaign. Nogaret tells me that he won a great victory at Falkirk, but still failed to complete the conquest due to the stubborn resistance of the Scots.'

'He was victorious at Falkirk,' Wallace conceded, 'but his army was grievously weakened, as he lost many horse and foot on the field. His progress north was then hampered by his inability to keep his men adequately supplied. This, combined with the constant harassment of his officials, sent him back over the border before winter closed in.'

Philip clapped his hands in delight. 'I do so enjoy hearing about Edward's difficulties and it gladdens my heart to know that he expends his men and his gold in Scotland, rather than here in my kingdom.'

Nogaret quickly intervened to cover the King's indiscretion. 'His Majesty has often declared his admiration for the brave Scots, for their willingness to stand against such a powerful and ruthless enemy.'

Wallace then told the King about the detail of the campaign, the slaughter at Falkirk and the attacks on the English garrisons. He also spoke of Edward's most recent, abortive invasion and the imminent threat of him returning yet again.

'I am eager to do what I can to help the noble Scots in their struggle.' Philip's expression was earnest as he addressed Wallace and his fellow delegates. 'I have discussed this at great length with Nogaret and my other ministers and there are actions we can take and others which are not possible at this time. I would very much like to send men to support my great ally, but this is out of the question at present, as I am forced to deal with other pressing threats to my territories. However, that does not prevent us from taking bold actions on the diplomatic front. I will propose three potential actions, all of which I hope will meet with your approval. Firstly, I will write to Pope Boniface and ask that he releases King John Balliol into my custody. I am sure that the release of your King will provide great encouragement to your people in the struggle ahead. Secondly, I will encourage the Pope to issue a Papal Bull condemning Edward's outrages against the people and sovereignty of Scotland. Thirdly, I will insist that Scotland's freedom is at the centre of the negotiations regarding Edward's lands in Gascony. That way, he will only be able to regain his lands once the Scottish question has been settled.'

Wallace bowed his head and thanked King Philip. 'I would not have asked for more, your Majesty. I know that Bishop Lamberton would want me to add his thanks to mine. We are most grateful.'

King Philip took his leave shortly thereafter and returned to his apartments. He was joined there moments later by Nogaret.

'They were satisfied?' Philip enquired.

'Quite satisfied, your Majesty.' Nogaret replied. 'I expect that they will quickly communicate the success of their mission to Bishop Lamberton.'

'They are easily pleased. I promised nothing except that I would write a few letters. If only all of our petitioners were so easily appeased.'

'They are simple, straightforward men, your Majesty.' Nogaret replied blithely. 'They take what we say at face value, which serves our purpose. They will leave Paris with a spring in their step and take to the struggle with Edward anew.'

'They are savages, Nogaret. Did you not hear him try to avoid admitting that he stripped the flesh from Cressingham while he still lived?' Philip shivered and rubbed his hands up and down his robe as if to clean them. 'They made my skin crawl.'

'Savages they may be, your Majesty,' Nogaret replied with a grin. 'But they are most effective when it comes to occupying our enemy and keeping him far from our door.'

Walter Langton, Lord High Treasurer and Bishop of Coventry and Lichfield, reined his horse in at the palace gates and watched the three men stride towards the bridge over the Seine. He pointed in their direction and addressed the liveried guard.

'I have seldom seen such rugged men within the palace precinct.'

'Yes, my Lord.' The guard replied. 'It is the Scottish delegation. They have been regular visitors in recent times and their speech is even rougher than their beards. I have never heard my mother tongue so tortured in its delivery.'

'And that man is their leader?' Langton pointed, indicating the largest man in the group.

'Yes, my Lord. That is William Wallace.'

'Tis a pity.' Langton responded. 'I did not think he could survive this long with so much gold paid to prevent it.'

'Pardon?' The guard asked in confusion.

'Tis nothing. I have an audience with the Keeper of the Seal. Now I must try my best to undo the Scotsman's work.'

29

Not one man in the delegation was sorry to leave
Paris behind. The weeks of waiting and intrigue
had been a time of frustration and were
characterised by a growing sense of
claustrophobia. The journey towards Rome saw
their spirits lightened, partly by the success of
their audience with King Philip and partly
through the sheer joy of escaping the walls of
the House of Bonnaire. They took great pleasure
from the warmth of the sun and from air that
was not polluted by the filth of the city. Their
guards accompanied them as far as the border
and it was there that they bade Marsaud and his
men a fond farewell. The departure of their
protectors felt more like a release than an
abandonment and they continued happily on
their way.

Given the attempts on Wallace's life, they
travelled quietly and incognito. Though they
never tarried anywhere for long, they did devote
some time to taking in the sights along their
route. Though not as impressive Paris, they had
admired the cathedral and Roman ruins in
Besancon and marvelled again at how mere men
could construct buildings of such magnificence.

Their conversations were fuelled by each city they passed and they were left with memories of Turin, Piacenza, Modena, Bologna and Florence. The journey was not without its difficulties, but, with gold enough to pay bribes, they were able to pass quietly and without recourse to the sword.

The architecture and wealth of these cities did nothing to prepare them for their first sight of Rome. The city walls stretched far into the distance and seemed to enclose an area which dwarfed that of Paris. Wallace, who had visited the city before, pointed out that the Romans had a liking for building walls and delighted his men by mentioning that at least two Roman emperors, Hadrian and Antoninus Pius, had been forced to build walls to protect themselves from the Scots. If the mighty Roman Empire could not conquer them, he argued, then Edward Plantagenet was unlikely to succeed.

Their delight and awe grew once they had paid to pass through the city gates. The scale of the city was even greater than the extent of its walls had suggested. They were amazed to find that large areas of the city were devoted to agriculture, with pasture for beasts and fields for the growing of crops. Rome had a feeling of space and was not as cramped or as crowded as Paris. Sir William took great pleasure in telling his followers that what they were seeing was the slow decay of a once great empire. He told them that when the Romans ruled the greater part of the world, the city had indeed been full to the brim and that now its walls protected a population that was greatly diminished. As they made their way towards their lodgings, he took great care to point out famous landmarks such as the Pantheon, the Colosseum and the Forum, as well as innumerable shrines, public baths, temples, arches and aqueducts. The young men marvelled that the ancient Romans could erect such structures, while their own generation was incapable of creating anything of equal splendour.

The elegance and beauty of Rome's imperial architecture contrasted sharply with that of their humble lodgings. The building was an old Roman stable that had been converted into living quarters for the monks who served in the Papal apartments. Though it was constructed solidly from great blocks of stone, the interior had been cheaply partitioned with rough, wooden walls to form small, monastic cells, each containing only a hard, wooden pallet in the place of a bed. Wallace was highly amused by his comrades' downcast and forlorn expressions.

'King Philip has spoiled you.' He chided them. 'Did you expect another palace with servants running to cater to your every desire? The Church will shower you with no such luxuries, but will give you the gift of humility instead.'

Jack Short's nose twisted with distaste. 'The stench of monks' shit is quite overpowering. If this is the smell of humility, then I have already had my fill.'

'I will pray that we will not have to wait as long in Rome as we did in Paris.' Malcolm Simpson added sourly. 'I do not think I can stand it here for too long.'

'Listen to yourselves!' Wallace declared, his hands on his hips in a stance of mock reprimand. 'Think of the homes you left behind in Scotland. Not one of them was as fine a building as this.'

'And was not our Lord Jesus born in a stable more humble than that which houses us now?' Scott tried valiantly to keep his face straight, but quickly dissolved into laughter and was soon joined there by his companions.

Once their baggage was stowed, Wallace led them to a nearby tavern, as they were all ravenous after their journey. They were soon ensconced at a corner table and served with generous bowls of stew, loaves of bread and goblets of sweet ale. As they chewed and drank noisily, Wallace leaned forward and spoke with quiet urgency.

'Though we be surrounded by good brothers and men of the cloth, we must still be alert. This place is, if anything, a pit of intrigue deeper and more perilous than the court in Paris. Pope Boniface is as ambitious as any king and seeks power in both the real and the spiritual worlds. This puts him in conflict with both Langshanks and Philip the Fair. We must tread carefully while we are here. It is our country's misfortune to be caught up in the power struggles of kings and popes, but, if we can step nimbly enough, we may turn their rivalry to our advantage.' Wallace paused and looked into the eyes of each man at the table. 'But make no mistake, the second they believe we can bring them no benefit, they will throw us to the wolves. If we serve to hinder their ambitions, cloth or no cloth, they will have our throats slit without the slightest of qualms. Be in no doubt that the good brother in the cell next to yours will have his ear pressed hard to the wall. Guard your words carefully, as not a single one will go unremarked or unreported.'

Malcolm Simpson articulated perfectly the thoughts of the whole group. 'As I said before, I will be praying that our stay here is of the shortest duration.'

The very next morning, an Italian Priest knocked gently on the door of Wallace's cell and informed him that he had been summoned to an audience with Cardinal Ranieri early that afternoon. This news sent the delegation into immediate and hurried preparations for the audience. Their fine clothes were unpacked, brushed off and smoothed and buckets of water were brought so that they could wash away the dust and dirt accumulated on the road. Wallace sat shirtless upon an upturned bucket while Jack Short saw to the trimming of his beard. As his unruly facial hair was tamed, the one remaining French priest in their party set about preparing him for the meeting ahead.

'Cardinal Teodorico Ranieri was appointed a Prince of the Church by Pope Boniface himself. He was further appointed as Camerlengo of the Holy Roman Church and, as such, is responsible for the administration of all properties and revenues of the Holy See.'

'So, a very powerful man.' Wallace stated, as Short pushed his head back to get at the straggly hairs under his chin.

'Second to only the Holy Father.' The priest agreed. 'You must address him as Illustrissimo.'

The opulence of the Cardinal's palace suggested that its master had dispensed with any pretensions to either humility or poverty. Any king would have been content with a residence of such ostentatious splendour. The great marble columns and the domed roof were undoubtedly Roman, but, unlike the majority of ancient buildings in the city, this one had been maintained to the highest of standards and showed no sign of ruin or decay. Wallace and his party had scarcely begun to study the elaborate mosaic floor before silent monks ushered them into the main reception chamber. Their footsteps echoed loudly as they crossed the marble floor towards the imposing, scarlet-robed figure, who sat upon a richly decorated, wooden throne at the far end of the hall. They all bowed as they approached the throne, just as they had been instructed, and then took turns to kneel and kiss the Cardinal's ecclesiastical ring. The Cardinal then gave a hurried blessing and seemed anxious to dispense with spiritual matters and move onto issues of a more temporal nature.

'Sir William, I hear that you have already met with our good friend King Philip.' The Cardinal's tone belied his words and indicated that Philip of France was not revered in Rome. 'His letters, it would seem, have travelled more quickly than you.' The Cardinal held out his left hand and an aged priest rushed to place three flattened parchments into his grasp. 'I assume that you are fully aware of their contents.'

'Yes, Illustrissimo.' Wallace replied with a bow of his head.

'Then you will know that you ask much of the Holy Father. You understand how difficult it will be to intervene in the business of kings?'

'Yes, Illustrissimo. I understand that the diplomatic situation is highly complicated and only ask that the Pope involves himself to aid the poor Scottish people, who have suffered great outrages at the hands of the English King and his henchmen.'

'If only it were that simple.' The Prince of the Church responded, steepling his fingers as he spoke. 'Both these kings threaten to cut off the life-blood of the Church. Philip has already prevented the transfer of clerical revenues to Rome and King Edward is of the belief that he has the right to tax that income in England. Making demands on behalf of your countrymen is likely to only inflame matters further. I cannot determine how such an action might benefit the Holy See.'

'The Holy Roman Church can only benefit from seeing that justice is done. Putting an end to Edward's incursions would send a message to the world about the power of the Pope and his ability to wield that power to spare good Christians from suffering. It should not be forgotten that the English King burns churches in Scotland and slaughters our priests.'

'Justice is a fine thing, Sir William, but can be costly to achieve. It must also be remembered that King Edward is not the only one to be accused of assaults on the clergy.' Cardinal Ranieri raised his eyebrows in disapproval to communicate that Wallace's own actions in the North of England had not gone unnoticed.

Wallace cast his eyes down upon the floor and hesitated before continuing. The audience was not going the way he had expected and he was surprised to realise that speaking with the Cardinal was as tricky as engaging in conversation with the wily Nogaret.

'Illustrissimo, would the Holy See not benefit from curbing the ambitions of King Edward? He must consider himself to be the Holy Father's superior if he feels that he can plunder church revenues with such impunity. It might be no bad thing to bring him down a peg or two and remind him of his proper place. Both Scotland and Rome would surely gain if he were less inclined to dip his fingers where they have no right to be.'

The Cardinal smiled broadly and nodded his head. 'There may be some truth in what you say. Let me raise this with the Holy Father and see if he can be persuaded of the wisdom of this course.'

The Scottish delegation was then ushered from the chamber and went to collect their weapons from the guards at the main entrance. Wallace exhaled sharply as he fastened his

384

sword belt and rubbed the beads of sweat from his forehead with the heel of his hand.

'Jesus! That was tougher than I expected.' He declared.

'You did well, Sir William.' John assured him. 'I was certain that he was set to refuse us.'

'I was certain that he was about to send for the guards to clap me in chains! Let's find a tavern. I am in sore need of a drink.'

The Scotsmen spent the next week as ordinary pilgrims and tramped the streets of Rome to gawk at vestiges of imperial grandeur and to pray for the success of their mission at a bewildering array of shrines and churches. The streets around these attractions were busy with visitors and peddlers eager to separate them from their silver. John was offered so many rusty, twisted nails and splinters of wood from the one true cross, if he had purchased them all, he would have been able to construct a whole cathedral from them. Scott was fascinated by the ancient Roman streets and spent hours examining the way rectangles of quarried and dressed stone had been embedded in the ground to form a surface which would not churn into mud with the slightest shower of rain. He was certain that he could replicate the technique and spoke at length about how it could transform the Scotstoun square. The others were content to leave him to his musings and set about emptying their purses in exchange for trinkets in the city's many markets. While they did marvel at all that Rome had to offer, they were never able to fully relax and were aware that they could be attacked at any moment. Several times they had reached for their swords, only to find that yet another quarrel had broken out between the excitable and voluble natives. They were only just beginning to tire of Rome, when Cardinal Ranieri's messenger arrived to inform them that the Holy Father would receive them the next morning.

The fevered preparations for their encounter with the Cardinal paled into insignificance when compared to the primping and preening which preceded their papal audience. No blushing maiden about to meet her beau would have expended so much time on combing, trimming, washing and general beautification. To have seen the Pope briefly and at a distance would have been honour enough. To meet the Bishop of Rome and Vicar of Christ face-to-face was beyond their wildest imaginings and would be a tale they told until they were old and toothless, if they were lucky enough to live that long.

Friends and family would scarcely have recognised the men as they approached the sacred Saint Peter's Basilica. Though the ancient building had plainly seen better days, it did not fail to inspire their awe. The church was enormous and could easily have accommodated several thousand faithful worshipers. The timbered roof soared above their heads as they crossed the mosaic floor and proceeded down the centremost of the five aisles. Though they might deny it later, every man in the party gaped at the magnificence of St. Peter's altar with its spiralling Solomonic columns. At its foot, they caught their first sight of His Holiness, Pope Boniface VIII upon an enormous, gilded throne. John thought that he looked every inch a king. Tall and a little fat around the jowls, he was dressed in robes of gold and scarlet, with a large, egg-shaped, golden crown upon his head and scarlet slippers on his feet. The elevation of his throne was such that the faces of petitioners were level with his knees, forcing them to gaze upwards at the Pope.

The unsmiling priest who had accompanied them from the atrium, indicated that they should wait. Though he whispered softly, a vague hiss echoed back from the walls and columns around them. He informed them that they would not have long to wait, as those in the line ahead had paid for blessings and would be dealt with quickly.

Just as the priest waved them forward, Cardinal Ranieri appeared on the platform at the side of the throne. He introduced them in turn and bade them kiss the Pope's ring. He then reminded the Pope of the delegation's purpose and of the support they had received from King Philip of France.

The Pope closed his eyes and waved Ranieri to silence. 'Yes, yes, I recall the matter most clearly. Bishop Lamberton begged the same favours of me following his consecration as Bishop of Saint Andrews.' He then fixed Wallace in his gaze, his cruel eyes reduced to slits by his frown. 'You ask a great deal, Sir William.'

'I do, your Holiness, but would ask for nothing if my people did not suffer so cruelly at the hands of the English King.'

Boniface again closed his eyes and waved his fingers as though he chased away a fly that dared to irritate him. 'I am aware of the sins of the House Plantagenet. The Bishops and nobles of Scotland, Wales and England write constantly to urge me to bring him to heel. Their missives arrive almost daily and urge me to take actions they dare not take themselves.'

'These men before you are cut from a different cloth.' Ranieri interrupted. 'For years they have resisted King Edward and taken up arms against his forces.'

Boniface nodded, his scowl softening slightly. 'I do have respect for those who are willing to risk their own lives in order to resolve their problems and are not content to merely ask others to act on their behalf. I am also eager to ensure that King Edward learns that the power of kings is subordinate to that of the Pontiff of Rome. Know that I am minded to support your cause and, though I can guarantee nothing, I will consider the most appropriate course.'

Ranieri indicated that the audience was at a close and, after a hurried papal blessing, the unsmiling priest ushered them from the presence of the Vicar of Christ.

'Time for a drink lads!' Wallace announced happily as they descended the Basilica's steps. 'It seems that this diplomacy is thirsty work. Let us toast our success and make ready for the journey home.

388

30

Though the months in Europe had been full of adventure and new and exciting experiences, every man in the party was now overcome with thoughts of home. Each of them yearned for the familiar faces of friends and family, for home-cooked and unspiced food and the refreshing chill of good Scots wind on their skin. Eck promised that his first act on entering Scotstoun would be to drain a barrel of its cool and bitter ale. Malcolm spoke of his family and John imagined aloud how his sweet Lorna would gasp when he showered her with gifts from these foreign lands. They all agreed enthusiastically with Sir William when he pointed out that they had a thousand stories to tell and that, with tales of kings, popes, assassins and high-born femmes fatales, it might be years before they would have to part with their own silver in exchange for a drink. Conversely, they had all groaned loudly and looked for items to throw when Scott tried to turn the conversation to stone paving and the benefits it could bring.

John's good humour and excitement at the prospect of returning home lasted less than twenty minutes aship on the first leg of their

389

journey back to Scotland. One moment he was enjoying the sunshine on deck with Eck and Scott, the next he was hunched over the side of the ship watching his half-digested breakfast fall into the sea. With each change of ship, he begged to be left behind to make his own way north overland. The seas seemed to become rougher with each passing day and, by the time they made port in Norway, he had lost so much weight and turned such an alarming shade of green, Sir William decided that they would have a few days in port to allow him some time to recover himself. After three days abed in the tavern, he seemed much better, was pale of face and had succeeded in keeping a few mouthfuls of broth in his stomach. Despite this, his companions were forced to seize hold of him and carry his struggling form onto the small, merchant ship.

After less than an hour of being heaved and pitched on the sea, John was back to his customary position clinging to the gunwale and puking dryly into the waves. He scarcely noticed as the skies turned from grey to black and seemed oblivious to the spray which soaked him to the skin and sent his fellows scurrying for cover. Neither was he aware of the commotion on the deck when passengers and crew alike crowded to the stern and gazed towards the coast, their eyes screwed up tight to bring the distant shapes into focus.

'How many did you count?' Wallace demanded urgently.

'Near twenty.' The ship's captain replied. 'All merchant ships waiting their turn to dock at Berwick.'

'How many would you expect to see there on a normal day?' Sir William enquired.

'The wizened captain rubbed his grizzled grey beard in contemplation before answering. 'I've seen as many as five there afore. Never near as many as this.'

'You think the Bastard King is on the march again?' Eck asked, his eyes still fixed on the merchantmen at anchor.

'Aye.' Wallace replied grimly. 'I am afraid that it looks that way.'

'Good!' Eck exclaimed emphatically, his face set hard in determination. 'My blades have been dry for too long.'

Wallace looked at him for a moment and shook his head. 'Sometimes you scare me Eck. I just hope that the English fear you as much.'

Wallace ordered the captain to take his ship further out to sea to avoid encountering any of the English vessels. He stayed on deck until well into the night and counted the lanterns shining in the darkness, knowing that each one illuminated the deck of an English ship as it made its way up the Scottish coast.

Walter Langton ducked down to avoid clattering his head on the inn's stone lintel. He could not fathom for the life of him why the Scots insisted on throwing up buildings which were scarcely big enough to accommodate a dwarf. It took a few seconds for his eyes to become accustomed

391

to the gloomy interior and he smiled when he saw that Sir John de Seagrave had arrived before him and had secured a table by the fire. He would not describe the man as a friend, the fact that his master was Roger Bigod, the Earl of Norfolk and a thorn in King Edward's side, precluded that, but he had found him to be a pleasant drinking companion and a source of useful intelligence. He signalled to the innkeeper that he should bring a flagon of ale and the man growled something unintelligible in response in an impenetrable accent. Langton was unperturbed by this. Since the King's army had arrived in Glasgow, he had not encountered a single native capable of communicating with a civilised Englishman.

'My Lord Bishop!' Seagrave called in greeting as he spotted Langton's approach and rose to meet him.

'Sir John.' Langton responded warmly, shaking the proffered hand. 'I think that, given our humble surroundings and our presence in enemy territory, we can dispense with the formalities. Please call me Walter.'

'As you wish, Walter.' Seagrave replied. 'Now please sit and tell me how goes the campaign. I hear nothing but positive reports.'

'When compared to last year's debacle, I doubt if I could be any happier. Back then, I spent two excruciating weeks encamped with the King at Sweetheart Abbey, just south of Dumfries, and was subjected to his endless, furious rants. To be fair, I had some sympathy with him after expending so much gold to gather less than two thousand horse and only nine thousand foot. If they had not started to desert in their droves as soon as the campaign began, we might have achieved more than the relief of Caerlaverock Castle.'

'My Lord Norfolk said that it was an ill-conceived campaign.'

'Tis regrettably true. I advised the King that it would be foolhardy to embark upon the venture without sufficient funds in the exchequer.' Langton shrugged his shoulders and held his palms upwards. 'But, you know how determined he can be and he is impatient to finish the Scots.'

'But this year's endeavour fairs well?' Seagrave enquired.

'The successes come thick and fast. The King's willingness to finally make concessions to the magnates has filled our coffers to the brim. Recruitment surpassed even Edward's expectations, with two thousand cavalry and seven and a half thousand foot for the King's army here in the east and one thousand seven hundred knights and fifteen thousand foot marching beneath the banners of the Prince of Wales in the west. The Justiciar of Ireland has joined up with the Prince, bringing another six hundred and fifty cavalry and sixteen hundred foot.'

'Surely enough to force the stubborn Scots to their knees.' Seagrave stated, as he poured himself another goblet of ale.

'King Edward likes to describe it as all the nations of Britain coming together to subdue the last remaining rebel province. When the two armies converge on Stirling, we will be able to raid north and south as we please and bring the lands of both Comyn and Bruce under our control.' Langton took a long drink of his ale before wiping his mouth with the back of his hand. 'It is difficult to see how the Scots can continue to resist once those two nobles are done with.'

'How fares the Prince?' Seagrave asked with a smile. 'The Earl of Norfolk has not a good word to say about the boy.'

'Not without reason.' Langton responded with a sigh. 'Even his father despairs of his many distractions. However, I cannot find fault with his conduct so far. He has forced the surrender of the Bruce's castles at Turnberry and Ayr. The King has gone to Glasgow Cathedral to give thanks for his progeny's victories. With his army not thirty miles from this spot, I expect that the trap will be sprung within a matter of days and Stirling will also be in our hands. Then we will be well placed to attack the Comyn strongholds in the north.'

'Turning to matters more personal, I was told that you suffered an attack of your own.'

Langton appeared momentarily confused before smiling in recognition as he realised what his companion was referring to. 'Ah, I take it you mean the parliament at Lincoln?'

'What else? Everyone I have met since has mentioned it. How the nobles attacked you and demanded that King Edward dismiss you immediately from his service.'

'I cannot say that it was one of my better days.'

'Come sir, it is not everyone who would prompt such a spirited defence from the King. I would wager that you were secretly bursting with pride.'

Langton nodded reluctantly. 'I admit to taking some small satisfaction from the exchange. I particularly enjoyed the part where he suggested that perhaps all of the nobles should have a crown and make decisions for the King. I could see that it stung them badly to be scolded so publicly. Anyway, enough about me. I will order more ale and you can tell me all that is happening with you.'

'Well,' Seagrave began coyly, 'I am not sure that I should.'

'Oh, come now Sir John. I can tell that you are bursting to share. Out with it! I won't let you budge from this spot until you have spilled every word.' Langton leaned towards his companion, his eyes wide with anticipation. His instincts told him that there was a secret to be learned and secrets could be more valuable than gold.

Seagrave slowly stroked his chin with the fingers of his right hand, as if he could not decide if it would be wise to confide in the Bishop. Langton kept silent and watched as the younger man's cheeks reddened with embarrassment. His internal conflict could be plainly read in his changing facial expressions and Langton's instinct and long experience in the extraction of information told him that he should patiently wait for Seagrave's need to share to overcome any vestiges of shyness or reserve.

The younger man leaned across the table and spoke in a whisper. 'Do you remember the feast the King held at Auchterarder Castle?'

Langton searched his memory but could not recall the occasion to which Seagrave referred. He now stroked his own beard in contemplation and slowly shook his head, his expression blank.

'You must remember.' Seagrave insisted. 'It was in the days after the victory at Falkirk.'

The Bishop's face brightened in recognition. The days spent in the castle had allowed the apothecary to do his work and fill the King's belly with enough of his foul concoctions to bring him back to his full strength. Before advancing on Perth, Edward had held a banquet for the loyal Scots nobles.

'It was a fine feast, Seagrave. But what of it? I doubt that your current excitement relates to the fayre served on that night.'

'Do you not remember who was there?'

'The hall was filled to bursting with a motley collection of minor Scottish nobles who were falling over each other as they fought to ingratiate themselves with the King. Most of them had been content to stay away until news of the slaughter of Wallace's army sent them scampering to declare their loyalty and to grovel in the hope that their lands and titles would not be taken from them.'

'But amongst their number was a girl, a young woman of great beauty.'

Langton strained his memory. He had found the feast to be a dismal and tedious affair and the guests to be the most mediocre and grasping wretches he had ever had the misfortune to encounter. He had brought the King to laughter by commenting that the pitiful Scottish nobles achieved the impossible feat of making their English counterparts look halfway decent in comparison. He also remembered making the King grin by pointing out the attractive, young woman who sat upon the third table at the feast. He smiled as he recalled her pretty face, her full lips, her beautiful, golden hair and the large bosoms that accentuated her slim waist. He had surreptitiously kept her within his sight throughout the evening as an antidote to the tiresome and obsequious conversation of the guests seated next to him.

Seagrave caught his smile and wagged his finger at him. 'See! You do remember her! I can tell it just from your expression. Lady Margaret Ramsey. Is she not magnificent?'

'My God Seagrave! Tell me that you have not fallen for her.'

Seagrave's cheeks reddened further, but he could not keep the wide grin from his face. 'She has bewitched me Langton. I find that I seldom think of anything else. I mean to marry her.'

Langton shook his head in disbelief. 'But there are many matches that would bring you much more in land and fortune. I doubt that Lady Margaret, captivating though she is, will bring anything better than a patch of bog or barren, rain-soaked hillside.'

'I care not for land. If I can possess her, then that will be dowry enough.'

'My God Seagrave, I can see that you have it bad. It is one thing to lose your head over a woman, but quite another to act upon the impulse. I would counsel you against any hasty actions. Take some time to see if you can work it out of your system. Shut yourself away for a few days with a barrel of ale and six lithe, young whores. I guarantee that the experience will leave you thinking more clearly.'

'I have no more interest in whores. She has captured my heart and I mean to make her my wife once this campaign has been concluded. My mind is made up.'

Langton raised his goblet in smiling resignation and toasted Sir John. 'I never thought I would see the day when the fearsome warrior Sir John de Seagrave was tamed by a beautiful woman. I drink to you sir and to the successful conquest of the fair Lady Margaret.'

They drank many toasts and consumed a huge quantity of ale as the night progressed and, through it all, Walter Langton could not help but shake his head at this turn of events. Sir John was, at his best, a hard and mercenary individual and it beggared belief to find him ruled by sentiment rather than cold, hard pragmatism. He just hoped that the Lady Margaret proved to be as satisfying in the bedchamber as her alluring looks suggested she would be.

It had taken Rank several weeks to overcome the urge to snap Tarquil's delicate neck. During the long ride to the border, he had occupied himself with thoughts of how he would torture him when the opportunity presented itself. Life at Dragan Hall had been idyllic, with cosy apartments, an unending supply of food and drink, copious amounts of silver, unfettered access to any peasant girl unfortunate enough to take his fancy and the nightly, dark delights of Lady Ingrede's bed. All of this had been wrenched away by Tarquil's social climbing and his fawning desperation to ingratiate himself with the Prince of Wales. Rank had scarcely been able to hide his fury when he was informed that the Prince had commanded Tarquil to accompany him on the latest Scottish campaign. However, he had soon discovered that a successful summer invasion was immeasurably more enjoyable than the miserable experience of occupying a land with limited manpower and being constantly besieged and attacked by its embittered, duplicitous people.

The Prince might be a fool who rouged his cheeks and spent his days roistering with the prettiest of the young knights, but he could not be faulted for his generosity. When the garrison of Ayr Castle had finally realised the hopelessness of their situation and surrendered, the heir to the throne had ensured that the spoils taken from the castle were shared out amongst his commanders. Rank was, presumably because of his relationship with Tarquil, included in this and, in the course of a morning, accumulated more wealth than he had in the whole of his previous life. The fall of Turnberry Castle several weeks later brought him a similar share of the loot and he had been forced to buy four horses to carry it for him and to order five of his men from the Dragan Estate to guard it. There had been some grumbling from the younger knights who were aggrieved that a commoner had been so rewarded, but, with his reputation newly burnished from his demolition of the melee at Dragan Hall, a couple of scowls and a baring of teeth had been sufficient to still their noble tongues. Rank had the sacks of gold and silver brought to his tent each night, so that he could touch it and reassure himself that he had not merely imagined or dreamed it. He could hardly believe that he had been so rewarded for doing nothing more than standing in sight of the castle garrison, when he had previously been forced to risk death or serious injury for a pittance which was frequently not even paid to him.

With his own force of men and the Prince's order that every town, village, hamlet and farmstead was to be razed to the ground, there was ample opportunity to grow his fortune still further. The Prince himself had publicly praised him several times for his dogged determination to lay waste to the rebellious province. As his own men had seen their purses swell with Scottish silver, they had developed a fierce loyalty to him and, such was his reputation, he was able to attract recruits from other parts of the army and now commanded close to one hundred men. He took great care to ensure that the loot from each ravaged village was split into four equal parts. One quarter went to the Prince of Wales, one quarter was earmarked for Tarquil, one quarter was split between the men and the final share he kept for himself. If truth be told, he also retained Tarquil's share, as his master was too engrossed in competing for the Prince's affections to concern himself with such trivial, financial matters.

His position also provided benefits other than gold and silver. He had lost count of the number of scrawny, pale-skinned and dirty Scottish girls he had brutally raped since crossing the border. He still tortured and mutilated them while he rode them to increase his pleasure, but lately he had refrained from slitting their throats once he was done with them. Instead, he let them live, as it amused him to think of them bearing his children and populating the country with little versions of himself. His men had followed his lead and reckoned that half of the inhabitants of Scotland would have English fathers if the campaign lasted for a few months longer. It was certain that there would be far fewer Scottish fathers in the future, as Rank had been both meticulous and tenacious in ensuring that no man was left alive after a village had been razed to the ground. He had tried to keep a mental tally of those he had sliced, stabbed, bludgeoned, hung, burned and tortured to death, but he had lost count several weeks before. Only yesterday, in a bid to be inventive, he had tried crucifying a grey-haired farmer on a tree, but he had eventually resorted to disembowelling him out of impatience, as his dying had been

401

tediously slow. He hoped that the Prince would move north soon, as the pickings in this part of the country were growing too thin to satisfy his appetites for silver and stimulation.

31

The return to Scotstoun had been of short duration, but had been a time of great joy. John Edward, already happy just to have his feet back upon solid ground, was thrilled to be reunited with his wife and son and delighted to see that his wife's belly was already swollen with another child. He also took great pleasure from Al's excited announcement that Mary, his wife, was also heavy with child. Pregnancy seemed to agree with both women and they glowed with good health. The feast of welcome had gone on long into the night, but there still had not been sufficient time to tell all of their tales of Norway and France and Rome. The whole village were transfixed to hear of the Edward boys' adventures and their meetings with the Pope and the King of France and none were prouder than their parents, Andrew and Isobelle and Angus and Mary, all of whom basked in their sons' achievements. The celebrations were over much too soon and the ashes in the fire pits in the square were still smoking when they left to keep their appointment at Scone Abbey.

Though not as impressive as many of the buildings they had seen in Paris and Rome, the

Abbey was still a remarkable structure. What its stone columns lacked in scale and decoration was more than compensated for by its history as one of the chief residences of the Scottish kings, the crowning place of those kings and, for many years, the resting place of the Stone of Destiny. The Scotstoun men looked in awe at the space before the high altar where the stone had sat before being looted by the English King. The stone, reputed to have been used as a pillow by Jacob, was said to have magical powers and they all wondered if some vestiges of that magic had been left behind. Wallace broke away from the group of men to the left of the altar and welcomed them with a smile.

'You look better than you did when I left you at Saint Andrews.'

'It was two full days before the ground seemed to stop swaying beneath my feet, Sir William.' John replied sheepishly.

'Aye.' Scott added with a mischievous glint in his eyes. 'And it was four days before his skin lost its horrible greenish hue.'

Wallace laughed and clapped John on the back with good humour. 'Come and join the discussion. It seems that we have work to do while we wait to see if our efforts abroad will bear any fruit. You know Bishop Lamberton and Edward de Bruce, but you have not yet had the pleasure of meeting our good friend, Bishop Wishart of Glasgow.'

Wishart turned to the newcomers and extended his hand so that they could each bow and kiss his ring. 'I have heard much about you

404

and would thank you for all that you do in support of our cause. These are dark times and, without men of good heart like yourselves, all would be lost and the English King would possess our country, just as he now possesses our sacred stone.' Wishart nodded his head to indicate the empty place before the altar. 'He thought that taking the Crowning Stone and placing it beneath his own throne would break our spirit and bring us to submission. Thanks to the resistance of patriots like yourselves, he is slowly beginning to learn that the stone, important though it may be, is merely a symbol and not the heart of the country itself.'

'The good Bishop knows King Edward well and has spent many a month in his custody for challenging his claim to the Scottish crown.' Lamberton nodded at Wishart and encouraged him to continue.

'There are some who argue that our fight has gone on for too long and caused too much suffering and that it would be better for the people if we were to bend the knee to Edward in return for peace.' Wishart's expression was grave as he continued. 'Those who make this argument do not understand the nature of the man and the pain and anguish he would bring. The lies leap from his lips faster than fleas jump from the carcass of a dying dog. Even now, he lies to his nobles to gain their support for his campaigns and risks plunging his kingdom into bloody civil war. He empties England's prisons to man his armies and, with his nobles away in Scotland, leaves his own citizens drowning in lawless disorder and chaos. He borrowed heavily from the Jews to fund his earlier campaigns and then turned to persecute them in order to avoid the repayment of his debts.' Wishart shook his head in sorrow as much as in anger. 'Even as a young man, he turned traitor in the hope of unseating his own father. Such a man cannot be trusted with our country. The moment his conquest is complete, he will turn his greedy eyes to France and drive our people into the ground in order to extract enough silver to fund his ambitions there.'

'You will find Bishop Wishart as constant as any other man here.' Wallace gave each of the Scotstoun men an earnest look to emphasise his point. 'As long as you resist the English King, you will find a friend in him. In the struggle to come, there will be times when you are in need of help and I have never known him to turn a patriot away, heedless of the danger or cost to himself.'

Lamberton nodded his agreement. 'But, for now, it is us who must ask you for assistance.' He waved the whole party across to a large wooden table set against the abbey wall. A map of Scotland had been unrolled upon the tabletop, with a heavy, gold candlestick placed at each corner to keep it flat. He jabbed his finger at the map. 'Edward's army is encamped here in the east, while his son and heir has concentrated his forces, and those of the Irish, in the Bruce's lands in the west. Our spies tell us that they will soon move north and join forces at Stirling.'

'That is something we cannot allow to happen.' Wishart interjected forcefully. 'If they take the Castle of Stirling, they will have a safe and secure base from which to launch attacks on both Bruce in the south and Comyn in the north. By concentrating their forces, they will simplify their lines of supply and make it very difficult for us to starve them into defeat, as we have done with Edward's previous campaigns.'

'So, we are to block their route to Stirling?' Edward de Bruce asked, his voice betraying his scepticism. 'And risk repeating the slaughter suffered at Falkirk?'

Lamberton shook his head emphatically. 'No. We must continue to avoid meeting the English in battle. What we propose is sending an army between the two English forces and deep into Bruce territory to their south. The English will not advance when their rear is threatened and will be forced to turn and deal with it.'

'At which point our army will melt away, having succeeded in delaying the English so that their supplies diminish further without securing a stronghold in Stirling.' Wallace nodded in approval of the strategy.

Lamberton shrugged his shoulders. 'If our prayers for an early winter are answered, this should be sufficient to doom this invasion to the same failure suffered by all of Edward's previous attempts at conquest.'

'And if our prayers are not answered?' John enquired.

'Then,' Wishart laughed, 'Lamberton will have to unfurl his map and place his candlesticks again, so that we can plan a new approach.'

Lamberton then ushered John aside and spoke with him quietly. 'Before you join Sir William and Edward de Bruce's forces, I need you to undertake a clandestine task, one which you must complete without being observed. It is of the utmost importance to our stratagem.'

'My Lord Bishop, you know that I will do my best to do as you command.' John replied earnestly.

Lamberton smiled kindly in response. 'That is why I have asked you, John. I have no doubts about your abilities or your sincerity. I need you and your men to escort a good friend of ours to the border. He must arrive there safely and unnoticed.'

'Am I permitted to know his identity?' John asked hesitantly.

'He is an old acquaintance of yours.' Lamberton responded. 'He goes by the name of Malachi Crawcour.'

Tom Figgins lay back on the grassy hillside and luxuriated in the warmth of the evening's summer sun. He could not recall a time when he had been happier. He had returned from his hunt with three rabbits, two of which he had given to his men, with the third now filling his belly after an hour of roasting on a spit. He had once heard John Edward say that rabbits were not a native species, but that they had been introduced to Britain by the Romans to provide an easy source of food. He did not know if they were native or not, but he did know that they were absolutely delicious and he patted his bulging belly with satisfaction. Life had been good since his return from dealing with his family affairs in northern England. With the Edward men away in Europe, he had been left in the Scotstoun camp with the task of equipping and training men with the bow and arrow. The defeat at Falkirk had resulted in the loss of almost every Scots archer with any degree of skill and John Edward had been keen to ensure that he had some small capability in this area. After months of hard work and daily sessions with targets set up in the woods, Tom had command of almost fifty men who could at least come close to hitting the side of a house at fifty paces.

His position as leader of the bowmen had given him some status in the village and he greatly valued the friendliness of the people and the respect they gave him. He had even contrived to reduce the frustration he felt at being unable to speak, lest his strong English accent gave him away. He had found that, if he growled a few words hoarsely, he could make himself understood and even contribute to conversations without giving away his enemy origins. His Scots comrades accepted his recovered voice without question, as they assumed that the injuries he suffered whilst being repeatedly hanged were partially healed. He had even managed to catch the attention of one of the village women, the widow Cumming, and had spent several cosy evenings at her fireside. So far, he had stolen only a handful of kisses, felt her large breasts against his chest and pushed his hardness against her wonderful, round belly, but he was optimistic that things would progress further. He supposed that he would have to marry her first, but, as she was a kindly woman, he felt that it would be a price worth paying.

His reverie was broken by the neighing of a horse to his rear. He leapt to his feet and ran for the cover of the tree-line. John Edward and all of their horsemen had set out for the border only that morning and they were not expected back for at least three days. The presence of horsemen in the area was therefore unlikely to be a good thing. He quickly climbed to the top of the hill and, lying flat on the ground, peered into the valley below. His eyes opened wide in astonishment as he caught sight of the group of men on the slope below him. Three were still ahorse, while two had dismounted and stood over a deer, which lay still with a spear protruding from its body. It was the horseman furthest away from him that he recognised first. The wavy, white hair and spindly figure could only belong to Sir Tarquil de Trasque. The horseman next to him was extremely tall and, even at this distance, his fine clothes marked him out as a nobleman of some wealth. The third figure was the one that sent Tom's heart racing. The unruly, greasy hair, the broad shoulders and pock-marked face were unmistakable. Tom emitted a snarl and kept his eyes fixed on Rank as he pulled an arrow from his quiver. He was oblivious to the danger of his situation and could focus only on the figure of his tormentor, the man who had tortured him, broken his face and body and left his neck deeply scarred from the noose. His actions were fluid and were driven by instinct and endless practice, rather than by any conscious thought. The arrow flew straight and true and rocked Rank almost out of his saddle as it thudded into his shoulder. The second arrow was already in the air by the time the five men turned their eyes towards the slope, their mouths wide open with the shock of the attack. Tom expected them to spur their horses up towards him and was surprised when they closed ranks around the tall man at their centre and hustled him away at the gallop. The final two arrows fell short of the horsemen and Tom cursed as he watched them disappear into the distance

Sir Andrew Legg had every reason to feel cheerful as he sat down to his breakfast. The plate laid before him might have been of common clay and badly chipped along its edge, but its contents would not have been out of place on King Edward's own table. The five eggs were newly laid with healthy yellow yolks, the bread had been dipped in pork fat and roasted until it was crispy and the slab of beef had been cooked so that it was scorched on the outside, but still pink at its centre. Sir Andrew rubbed his palms together in anticipation and set about devouring his feast. Lochmaben Castle might have been a hastily built, wooden fortification, which did not compare with his own hall of

411

dressed stone, but it was far superior to the leaky, mildewed tent he had inhabited throughout the last invasion of Scotland. When the Prince had commanded him to garrison the castle, he could scarcely believe his luck. With the armies of both the King and the Prince to his north and the English border at his back, he might well sit out the campaign in both safety and comfort and work at recouping his outlay on men and arms by stripping the surrounding countryside of anything of value. Even the weather seemed to favour him, as the heat of the sun was already driving away the chill of the night. The only cloud on his horizon was the captain of his guard pacing outside the door, his footsteps reverberating through the wooden floor.

'What is it now?' He snapped irritably, irked that he was to be interrupted in his breakfast when he had given strict orders that this should never occur.

'There is a problem with the sentries, my Lord, and with the scouts.' The captain, wary of his master's wrath, did not enter the room, but instead clung to the door so that only his head was visible.

'Jesus!' Sir Andrew cursed, wiping runny yolk from his mouth with his sleeve. 'I have already told them that they will be paid just as soon as the Prince's ship arrives with his silver. What in Christ's name do they think they will spend it on here in any case? There is not an inn for miles and I doubt that the local goats will charge them for their favours.'

'It's not the silver, my Lord. They've gone.'

'What?' Sir Andrew spluttered. 'All of them?'

'I am afraid so, my Lord. When we went to relieve them this morning, their positions were abandoned and not one of the scouts has returned.'

'Did they take their pikes and helmets too?'

'Yes, my Lord. They left nothing behind.'

Sir Andrew banged the table with his fist, causing the flesh to redden and bruise and his captain to jump in fright. 'Do you know how much silver I paid for those arms? I did not conjure them up from thin air.' The commander of Lochmaben Castle screwed his face up in repressed anger and jabbed his finger at the red-faced captain. 'I blame you for this. If you had better control of your men, none of this would have happened. If you were man enough to whip the first ten men to complain about the delay in their payment, this whole business would have been nipped in the bud.'

'Yes, my Lord.' The captain replied miserably, his eyes fixed upon the floor. 'I am sorry, my Lord.'

'If you were not my wife's cousin, I would have you whipped for this. I knew that I should not have brought you. There has always been a weakness to that side of the family, but I let her persuade me against my better judgement. Now, take twenty men and horses and pursue the deserters. Bring them all back here alive and then you will hang them in the courtyard. Understood?'

'Yes, my Lord.'

Sir Andrew dismissed him with an abrupt flick of his hand and returned his attention to his breakfast. He stared forlornly at the cold, congealed mess before him and pushed it away with a curse.

Although his supper, unlike his breakfast, did not suffer from any tiresome interruptions, Sir Andrew found that he was unable to enjoy his repast. His captain had not yet returned and he had been forced to send out the remainder of his scouts to locate him and order him back to the castle.

'The useless bastard has probably lost his way.' He grumbled to himself as he stood on the battlements and scanned the darkening landscape in the hope of catching sight of returning horsemen. If anything had happened to the young fool, he knew that his wife would never tire of chewing his ear about it. When all light had faded, he took himself off to bed, but found that sleep eluded him and he tossed and turned until the first light of dawn crept onto the horizon. He was just about to throw back the covers, when men on the walls began to cry out the alarm. He leapt up and strode out onto the battlements in his nightshirt, but not one man turned to stare at the sight of their commander's dishevelled appearance. Every eye was fixed upon the castle grounds and the ranks of spearmen who now encircled them.

Sir Andrew would have cursed if he had been able to catch his breath and still his racing heart. He leaned heavily upon the wooden battlement

414

and tried to take in the surreal vision before him. Just hours earlier, he had looked out upon these empty, rolling fields and it did not seem possible that they were now filled with spearmen and mounted men-at-arms. He groaned as he realised that his missing men had not deserted, as he had feared, but had undoubtedly fallen at the hands of the savage Scots. Lochmaben Castle no longer felt like a safe haven within which the war could be seen out in safety and comfort. Its walls now appeared quite fragile and, while the Scots were incapable of fielding any siege engines worthy of the name, they would have no need of them when fire would be sufficient to destroy the stronghold. Sir Andrew's stomach churned with fear and he was conscious that his trembling knees would be visible to any man who chose to look in his direction. It was to his great credit that he was able to swallow his dread and mask his trepidation, so that his panic would not spread to his men.

'Saddle my horse!' He barked, as he turned back to his chamber. 'I will ride out and tell these dogs that they have chosen the wrong fortress to besiege.'

When he emerged from his chamber and pulled himself into his saddle, the frightened, pot-bellied, old man in his stained nightshirt had been replaced by an English knight resplendent in polished maille and plate. His men cheered him on as he rode out from the castle gates and spurred his horse towards the savage horde. Five horseman immediately broke ranks and came out to meet him.

415

The largest of the four, a broad-shouldered man with a wild mane of hair and piercing blue eyes, smiled and hailed him with great cheer.

'Good morning to you, Sir Andrew! So kind of you to come out from behind your walls to greet us this fine morning.'

'I did not come to greet you.' Sir Andrew responded without returning Sir William's smile. 'I came to inform you that you are wasting your time here. I have one hundred men to man the battlements and fifty crossbowmen to rain bolts down upon your men, should they be unwise enough to assault my walls. We have stocks enough of food and water to last a year or more, though you can be sure that King Edward and the Prince of Wales will come to our relief long before our supplies are exhausted. I have already dispatched messengers to their camps to alert them to your presence. The prudent course would be to march away from here, while you still are able.'

'You have no need to worry about your messengers.' Eck interjected dryly. 'Or your scouts, sentries and horsemen. We have taken good care of them all.'

'What Eck says is true.' Edward de Bruce added, as he nodded his head in agreement. 'Given the men you have lost already, I doubt that there are more than forty men now behind the walls of my brother's castle. As for crossbowmen, we have seen not a single one in the three days we have been watching you. I suspect that the Prince of Wales has taken them all north with him. I also doubt that he was

416

generous enough to leave you as well-provisioned as you claim. Our spies tell us that he has scarcely enough to feed his own men and those of the Irish. I would suggest that the most prudent course for you would be to do as we ask.'

'I will not give up the castle that my Prince has ordered me to hold. Come at us if you must, but you will find that any assault will cost you dearly.'

Edward de Bruce smiled and shook his head. 'We do not ask that you meekly surrender, Sir Andrew. I would not insult your honour by demanding such a course. All we ask is that you keep your men safe behind their palisades and send word to your masters that you are under siege.'

The English knight looked at each of the Scottish leaders in turn, 'I will have no part in your foul strategy and will not betray my King. I see now that you mean to lure our armies south and so frustrate the conquest of this province. I will send no messengers. You must do your worst and know that I will resist you so long as a single man remains alive upon my walls.'

Edward de Bruce nodded at Sir Andrew's words. 'We thought that you might say that. Young Eck here has something that might change your mind.'

Eck turned in his saddle and signalled to the ranks. Scott Edward and Strathbogie came forward dragging a bloodied and tattered figure between them.

'This boy says that he's your nephew.'

417

Sir Andrew's eyes widened in horror. Though his face was bloody, bruised and horribly swollen, he recognised his hapless captain at once. He quickly recovered himself and stared back at Eck impassively. 'He's no nephew of mine.'

'I do not doubt his word.' Eck replied coldly. 'I had to take off two of his fingers before he revealed the information. Most men cough the truth before even a single finger is taken. Your kin did well and only revealed himself once the second was cut away. Look! I took one more for luck, but left him with two. Enough to pick his nose and scratch his arse, whilst leaving him unable to ever again wield a sword against my countrymen.'

Sir Andrew struggled to keep himself from retching at the sight of his captain's mutilation.

John Edward spurred his horse forward so that he could address the Englishman from close quarters. 'I would do as we ask, if you do not want his screams to disturb your sleep for many nights to come. No finger of blame will be pointed in your direction, as they will see that it was your duty to alert your masters to our presence outside your walls.'

Sir Andrew hesitated as he considered what John proposed. He gazed at his battered captain and shivered at the thought of informing his wife of his demise. If he sent no messenger, the pall of smoke rising from the burning castle would bring the King and Prince south in any case and the loss of his and his men's lives would have been in vain. He met Wallace's eyes and nodded reluctantly. 'I will take him with me now.'

Wallace signalled to Scott and Strathbogie to release the wretch into Sir Andrew's custody. 'You will send the messenger to me. I will read the missive before I send him on his way.'

32

Malachi had been anxious and unable to relax
from the moment John Edward and his men left
him and young Allard at the border. Their
progress south had been slow, steady and
entirely without incident, but the old man still
found himself jumping at shadows and he could
not sleep for fear of being discovered. His young
companion was faring much better, largely
because he had little understanding of the extent
of King Edward's network of spies and
informants and had no appreciation of just how
far he would go to take revenge on his enemies.
Even arriving at their objective had done little to
settle his nerves. Hull had been transformed
since his last visit and the King's hand could be
detected in all of the changes. The town and port
had been enlarged to better enable him to supply
his armies in Scotland, a mint had been
established and an exchange built so that
merchants could buy and sell their goods.
Edward had even seen fit to rename the town
Kingston on Hull, so that no-one could doubt its
ownership. Malachi felt that he had entered the
lion's den and was determined to complete his
business and be gone as soon as possible.

With two markets each week, the town was always full of merchants buying and selling wool, wine, grain and military supplies. Malachi and Allard had therefore attracted little attention when they secured a room on the top floor of the inn. The older man had not left the building since they arrived and was reliant on Allard to carry his messages and gold and issue his instructions. With most of these tasks now completed, there was little to do except await the arrival of the ship from France. Each day was an agony of boredom and tension and Malachi could not help but jump at every creaking floorboard and every set of footsteps upon the stairs. The boy, for his part, sat nonchalantly behind the door to their chamber with his sword across his knees. He had received some training from the guards at Robert de Bruce's castle, but Malachi prayed that his skills would not be put to the test. The knocking on the door was gentle, but caused them both to rise quickly to their feet.

Allard hefted his sword and called out. 'Who is there and what is your business?'

'My business is with my brother.' A voice replied.

Malachi waved his hand and instructed Allard to remove the bar from the door. The sight of his brother brought a smile to his face and he rushed to embrace him and kiss him on the cheek.

'Cael! It is good to see you. I cannot tell you how much it cheers me.'

'Malachi! It feels like an age since we parted. Let me look at you! You look older, my brother.

There are new furrows in your brow and your beard is fully grey.'

'That is because I am older.' Malachi laughed and waved his brother to a chair. 'Now tell me how fares my family?'

'All are well, brother, though we miss you terribly and say prayers for you each day.'

'Good, good! That is well. I hope that my work here will soon be done and we can be together again.'

'I fear that I may have to move the family again before too much longer. I hear whispers that the French King means to emulate his English cousin and expel our kind now that he has built up such debt to fund his military campaigns.'

Malachi nodded sadly. 'I hear those self-same whispers Cael. It seems that kingship comes with duplicity just as it comes with crown and sceptre. You should take them to safety now, before the trap is sprung. We were fortunate to escape London when we did, I would not risk such a close-run race again.'

'To Tuscany?' Cael asked with a shrug of his shoulders.'

Malachi nodded his agreement. 'And warn our friends, but only those you trust. They should sell their debts before they go, so they may reduce their losses.'

'But who would buy Malachi, when it is known that King Philip and Nogaret plot this course?'

'The Templars, Cael. They are the only ones King Philip will dare not touch, though they will

422

likely pay no more than one tenth of what they buy.'

'And what of this business? Have you done your work?'

'Aye, I have done what I can. My gold has bought me the services of twenty ships, but I had to pay dearly to persuade their captains to take the risk of incurring Edward Plantagenet's wrath. I doubt that I would have paid much more if I had purchased the ships themselves. It will be worth it if the captains keep their word and leave his armies without their grain. How have you fared?'

Cael smiled broadly and reached into his cloak to extract a sheaf of carefully folded documents with a flourish. 'I have brought thirty-eight contracts for the transport of wine from every French and Flemish port.'

'And the terms are generous?' Malachi enquired with a raised eyebrow.

'The terms will be difficult for any ship's captain to refuse. I am confident that the Scottish ports will be much quieter in the weeks to come. The number of vessels arriving there will be unlikely to meet with royal expectations.'

'You must take care in this, Cael. Word of these commissions will travel quickly and Hull is infested with Edward's spies.'

'Do not worry, dear brother, I have no intention of hawking these around myself. I have engaged an English agent to work on my behalf. He will bear the risk in return for gold and I will be far out to sea before he even makes a start. I would advise you to be similarly on your way before the break of day on the morrow.'

Malachi grinned and reached out to pat his brother's knee. 'I will start to pack now.'

John lay in the thick layer of damp leaves at the forest's edge and watched with rapt attention as the top of Bothwell Castle's circular keep tower emerged from the swirling autumn mists and seemed to float there above the earth. It was mid-morning before the feeble sun succeeded in burning through the fog to reveal the full extent of the siege. The castle sat in a bend in the river and the land around it was filled with tents, cook-fires, horses and men readying themselves for the day ahead. Though they had been ordered to count men and horses and assess the condition of King Edward's army, John, Eck, Scott and Al had eyes only for the five siege engines arrayed on one side of the castle. The trebuchets were huge contraptions constructed from thick oak beams, which had been transported from England in fifty ships before being assembled in sight of the castle walls. Large rocks were piled beside each of the engines and men struggled to load them as they prepared to fire.

'Right lads!' John instructed. 'Let's count the men and horses and then be on our way. I am to meet with Wallace at Stirling the morn and I want to get there before it gets dark.'

'I would put it at no more than five thousand men and seven hundred horses.'

John nodded in response to Al's tally. If he said that there were five thousand men arrayed before the stronghold, then John knew that he could be confident in that number. 'That would mean that he's lost near half of his men already.'

'Aye.' Eck replied. 'That feels about right, given the number of deserters we caught on our way up from Lochmaben.'

John dug his elbow into Al's ribs and pointed towards the castle. 'What are those piles of earth there, to the right of the gate?'

Al screwed his eyes up as tight as he was able and peered in the direction John had indicated. 'Looks like they're digging tunnels to undermine the walls. From the amount of earth they have dug out, they must be near half-way to the walls by now.'

'I doubt that they'll be able to hold out for much longer.' Eck declared with a sigh. 'One way or another, the bastards will bring that wall down.'

'The longer they hold out, the less time Edward has to take Stirling Castle before winter sets in.' John shivered and pulled his cloak around him. 'There's already a wee chill in the air, so let's pray that they can keep him here for a few weeks more.'

'Amen to that!' Eck replied. 'Though I wouldn't want to be trapped inside those walls.'

'Right, we've seen what we came to see and I'm getting soaked here. Let's head off and get on the road for Stirling.'

'Come on to Christ John!' Scott moaned. 'Let's just wait until they crank those things up.

Don't tell me that you don't want to see them working.'

In truth, John was in two minds. He desperately wanted to witness at least one of the trebuchets in action, but, at the same time, he was loath to find entertainment in the spectacle when the assault was directed at his own countrymen. As is often the case, curiosity won the day and they remained prone in the sodden leaves for another hour and watched three of the trebuchets launch great chunks of rock at the castle walls. The first projectile crashed into the earth just short of the castle wall, the second bounced off with a resounding crack, but seemed to do no more than chips the stones, and the third also hit its target and succeeded in leaving a barely visible indentation in the stonework. The remaining two siege engines did not appear to be working and it was assumed that the men swarming over them were attempting to repair them.

'You happy now?' John asked acidly.

'Aye, I suppose.' Scott replied unenthusiastically, his demeanour revealing that he had not been overly impressed with the English display. 'At this rate, it looks like it's going to take them a while to get into the castle.'

The Scotstoun men then crawled away from their vantage point, retrieved their horses and set off for Stirling. By the time they arrived at the castle gates, they found that they had already been secured for the night and they were forced to go off into the town in search of accommodation. John's already foul mood soured still further when they were only able to procure the meanest of lodgings in the attic space above a decrepit inn. Eck and Al were lulled into sleep by the familiar sound of the Edward brothers bickering and carping at each other. The bitching was resumed the following morning when John discovered that the inn could not provide them with their breakfast and they only desisted from nipping at one another when they were ushered into the presence of Wallace and the Bishop of Glasgow. John immediately observed that the two men seemed to be in the best of spirits and that even the normally stern Wishart was unable to completely banish the smile from his face.

'So, how fares the English King?' Wallace demanded. 'Not well, I hope.'

John delivered his report and was gratified to see that his intelligence served to further improve the mood of his superiors.

Wishart clapped his hands in delight. 'Edward has always had a passion for building and for the construction and employment of the apparatus of war. While he plays with his catapults like a boy with his wooden soldiers, his campaign loses momentum and will soon, praise God, come grinding to a halt.'

'We have already intercepted his messengers with communiques berating his exchequer for their failure to keep him adequately supplied with silver and others that threaten ship masters and merchants with dire consequences should deliveries of grain and barley not be made with the utmost speed.' Wallace's eyes sparkled with

427

satisfaction as he continued. 'We are also told that the Prince's army is now much diminished, as the Irish boarded their ships for home soon after they broke our siege at Lochmaben. The young Plantagenet has lingered in the south for much longer than we expected and, with his infantry reportedly deserting in their droves, may not now advance to join forces with his father.'

'But that is not the best of it.' Bishop Wishart interrupted and then exchanged meaningful looks with Wallace. 'You should have the honour of telling them, Sir William, given that it was you that they joined in the enterprise.'

Wallace's grin stretched from one ear to the other as he paused deliberately to heighten their anticipation of the news he had to impart. 'It would seem that our travails have not been in vain, as our embassies in Paris and Rome have borne the sweetest fruit. The Holy Father has released our own King John into the custody of our good friend Philip of France. Even as we speak, the King is at large on his estates in northern France.'

'Tidings of the King's release will rekindle the fire in every patriot's belly and spur them on to even greater deeds to send King Edward home.' Wishart turned and indicated a table piled high with parchments. 'We will send messengers to every corner of the kingdom to spread word of this joyous news.'

'But that is not the best of it. The good Bishop has a use for you, John Edward.' Though still smiling at the morning's revelations, something in Sir William's manner and expression caused John to feel uneasy. He could not quite put his finger on what was amiss, but he felt his shoulders tighten with tension.

The Bishop stepped to John's side and slipped his arm around his shoulders. 'Now that the King is free once more, we must quickly learn of his intentions. If he wishes to reclaim his crown, we will move quickly to facilitate his return to Scotland. If, as is possible, he is reluctant to return and lead our struggle, we must counsel him to silence on the matter so that he does not harm our cause. Our enemies will seek to prevent us from corresponding with the King and so we are in need of an emissary who is not known to them.'

A feeling of dread flared in John's chest. 'You mean?'

'Aye John!' Wallace boomed with great delight. 'A ship has already been secured for your passage. You will set sail in two days from now.'

Even Bishop Wishart seemed to take an unchristian pleasure in John's discomfort. 'Sir William has told me that you are no lover of the sea, but has assured me that you would not refuse a task of such great importance.'

John realised that he was the only man in the chamber who did not have a grin spread wide across his face. 'I don't know why you bastards are grinning.' He snapped at his brother, cousin and friend. 'I'll no' be travelling on my own.'

Poor weather delayed their departure by almost a week and the seas were still heavy when the merchant ship cast off with John, Scott, Eck, Al and Strathbogie upon its deck. Lorna had provided John with a bag of herbs which, when chewed, were supposed to keep the nausea at bay. Though John furiously ground the herbs between his teeth and sucked their juices down, the Scottish coast was still in sight through the misty morn when his spewing and puking began.

Walter Langton glared at the French Ambassador with cold and ill-concealed fury. He gripped the arms of his chair tightly, as though he was restraining himself from leaping across the table and punching the old man's face into a bloody pulp. Philip de Marigny, for his part, seemed oblivious to the threat of imminent violence and continued to sip at Langton's wine with an expression of mild amusement on his face.

'When I met with your brother at King Philip's court, he led me to believe that this matter would be resolved quite differently.' Langton normally made a virtue of his self-control, but his frustration was so great, his anger was evident in every word.

Marigny treated Langton to an elaborate shrug. 'My brother is not the only man to counsel the King. Nogaret seems to have won the day in this matter, my Lord.' The old man chuckled and bowed his head. 'I apologise if I do not address you properly, sir. You seem to have so many titles, I do not know which one to use. Treasurer, Lord High Treasurer, Lord

Bishop, Counsellor, Chief Minister. I do not know which one takes precedence.'

'It would seem,' Langton spat in response, 'that I have as many titles as your King has faces.'

Marigny chuckled in response, his shoulders moving up and down in mirth. 'His Majesty will enjoy that quip immensely, my Lord Bishop. Such wit is sorely lacking in matters of diplomacy.'

'King Edward will be far from amused to hear that Philip refuses to restore his lands in Gascony unless the Scots are left alone.'

Marigny shrugged again. 'It should be of no surprise to him that we stand beside our allies. The Pope readily agreed to this condition in the negotiations over King Edward's claim. The Scottish delegation seem to have gained as much favour in Rome as they did in Paris.'

'Ah, Pope Boniface,' Langton retorted. 'Another man who seems to have many faces to choose from.'

Marigny's expression was filled with mischief. 'Am I to assume that you have already received his Papal Bull, Scimus Fili? I doubt that King Edward was happy to be so admonished by the Holy Father himself. He was clear in his determination that your King has no claim to the kingdom of Scotland and was explicit in his instruction that all English officials should be immediately recalled from the realm. Tell me, how did he react?'

'The King is occupied with the reduction of the fortress at Bothwell. He has commanded that

431

he not be distracted until its destruction is complete.'

'What I would give to be present when you tell him.' Marigny teased. 'I do not envy you the task.'

Though his stomach churned and gurgled horribly in nervousness, Langton went straight to the King when he arrived at his encampment at Dunipace. He did not relish the prospect of the King's fury, but had steeled himself for the onslaught and persuaded himself that he should get it over with as soon as possible.

'Langton!' Edward declared, as his Treasurer was ushered into his pavilion. 'You look as bereft as I feel. Come sit! Let us drown our sorrows together.'

'I doubt that we have enough wine left to complete that task, my Lord.' Langton replied miserably. 'The bad tidings arrive at our door with unrelenting frequency. I do not know which one we should immerse first.'

Edward filled a goblet to its brim and passed it to his Treasurer. 'If we are to compete with tales of woe, then let me make a start. The whining Scots have succeeded in their whispering to our false friend, Pope Boniface. He has released that fool Balliol and he now walks free in France. No doubt he plots to reclaim his crown and all else I stripped from him.'

Langton was both surprised and relieved to find Edward in such an even temper and decided to seize the opportunity to deal with all his bad news before his mood declined. The King nodded glumly at the duplicity of the French and clenched his fists in frustration when told of the Pope's condemnation and his support for the Scottish cause. When Langton had finished, he drained the wine from his goblet and immediately lifted the jug to fill it once again.

'I am sorry to say that I can better you on this occasion, as I have yet more gloom and adversity to impart. I fear that the campaign is all but over and that, once again, our supply lines are to blame. Stirling Castle is but a short ride from here, but we will take not a single step further towards our objective. Our men desert in their hundreds, as we have no silver left with which to pay them. Two-thirds of my infantry were lost before we were finished at Bothwell and I have just been told that the archers and crossbowmen at Berwick have mutinied for the self-same reason.'

Langton cast his eyes upon the floor and made no response. He had advised the King that they should not delay at Bothwell, but he had insisted on trying out his trebuchets, as he thought it would be a shame to miss the opportunity when so much gold had been spent on their manufacture and transport. He suspected that the King's lack of fury came from the realisation that he himself was to blame for their inability to advance on Stirling.

'And what of the Prince?' Langton enquired, when the silence began to grow oppressive. 'Can he not bring his forces here?'

'My gentle son?' Edward responded sadly. 'His early successes persuaded me that he might amount to something. I now suspect that the successes were won by his commanders. The Irish have abandoned him and he cannot join with us here, as he has taken himself off on a pilgrimage to St Ninian in Whithorn. I am told that the Scottish climate has caused him problems with his skin and, in his wisdom, he has decided that seeking a cure at Saint Ninian's shrine is more important than the furtherance of our campaign.'

Langton had heard the same thing, but had decided to leave it to others to bring word of it to Edward's ears.

'I marvel at your fortitude, my Lord.' The Bishop said with genuine admiration. 'I would not have blamed you if you had become disheartened by the failure of yet another campaign to subjugate the Scots.'

'Fortune has worked against us this time Walter, but I know that it will turn in our favour if we have the strength and faith to persevere. My determination has not been diminished, if anything, it has been hardened. I will bring the Scots to heel, even if it takes me until my last breath to achieve it.'

Langton nodded to show his understanding. 'So, I assume that we now strike out for home to lick our wounds and make our plans anew.'

Edward sat back in astonishment, spilling some of his wine as he did so. 'No Walter, there will be no home and no licking of wounds. I will not show my enemies that they have defeated

434

me. I will defy them by wintering in their midst. I will command the army to move to Linlithgow and prepare to celebrate Christmas there. Then, in January, I will hold a tournament on the field at Falkirk.'

Langton threw his head back and laughed. 'You really mean to rub their noses in it.'

'Aye!' Edward roared in delight. 'We will make them witness the prowess of our English knights upon a field of Scottish bones.' He paused to drain his goblet, before thumping it back onto the table. 'But you, Langton, will see none of it, for you will travel to Paris and Rome while I remain here to plan our next campaign. If we are to prevail here, the war must be fought with vigour on every front.'

33

The fishing boat had taken them in as close to shore as its keel would allow, leaving them to wade through the frigid, chest-deep water to the beach. Scott had suggested that they build a fire to warm and dry themselves, but John had insisted that they set off for King John's chateau immediately.

John was still nauseous and was not in the best of moods. 'Remember what the Bishop said.' He snapped. 'We are to proceed with the utmost stealth, so that our presence is not noted. Be sure that the English will have spies lying in wait for anyone who attempts to meet with King John.'

'My boots are still filled with water.' Strathbogie moaned, squelching loudly as he walked.

'My breeks are chafing me.' Scott chipped in. 'My crack will be red raw by the time we get there.'

'Quit yer moaning.' John spat back. 'We'll be there by noon if we step to it.'

Al had gone forward to reconnoitre the road ahead and he now reappeared in the weak, morning light with his finger pressed urgently to his lips. 'Horsemen ahead.' He warned in a whisper. 'They block our way.'

Strathbogie hefted his great axe, but John stayed him with his hand. 'I will go ahead to see if anything is amiss. I doubt that they will have any interest in us.'

John strode along the curve in the road and soon caught sight of the mounted men straddling the track. He counted them as he advanced and reckoned that there were ten men still mounted and five horses with empty saddles. He relaxed a little, as it seemed that the men must have stopped so that a number of their comrades could dismount to empty their bladders. He stopped dead in his tracks when a voice called out to him.

'It is good to see you again, John Edward. You arrived a little later than I expected.'

John's mind raced. The voice was familiar to him, but the identity of its owner momentarily eluded him.

'John, you do not remember me? I am a little offended by that, as I thought you had so enjoyed our time together.'

John peered into the rising sun and finally made out the features of the man who addressed him. 'Captain Marsaud! What the hell are you doing here?'

'I missed you so much, I just had to come and see you.' The Frenchman laughed and turned to share his amusement with his fellows. 'I make a little joke for you. To be serious, Keeper of the Seal Nogaret has ordered me to come and escort you to the Chateau de Helicourt. We cannot have our good friends wandering around the countryside without protection. Come! I have brought horses for you and your four fine friends. It is not good for you to be walking in boots that are so wet.'

John was stunned and could think of no response.

Marsaud stood up in his stirrups and shouted down the track. 'Eck! Scott! It is Marsaud from the House of Bonnaire in Paris. Come! I have horses for you. We will arrive at King John's estate in time for breakfast.'

As they trotted along with Marsaud's men to their front and rear, Eck leaned towards John and demanded in a whisper, 'How the fuck did they know we were coming?'

John had no answer to give and merely shook his head and stayed silent until King John's estate came into view.

The Chateau de Helicourt must have been impressive in its day, perhaps even as fine as Bonnaire House. Its two levels were built solidly from stone and some kind of plaster had been smoothed over the blocks to give a finish devoid of imperfections. John reckoned that it would have been stunningly white when it was fresh, but it had now deteriorated to a dark, cream colour with darker patches caused by water damage. Every entrance to the house was covered by guards wearing the same uniform as Marsaud and his men.

'Do you think that they are here for the King's protection or to act as his jailers?' Eck whispered to John from the side of his mouth.

'That, I do not know.' John replied. 'But I can think of worse places to be imprisoned. I suppose we will learn more when we meet with King John.'

They were to wait a while for their audience, as Marsaud informed them that the King was still abed and was unlikely to rise for several hours. 'Like all you Scots, he likes to drink late into the night and then sleep it off until the sun is high in the sky.' He leaned in close to John and tapped the side of his nose as if he was about to share a confidence. 'I think that the Pope was not generous with his wine and your King is making up for lost time now that he has the freedom to drink from his own cellars.' He raised his eyebrows in a comical expression. 'I think he means to drain them dry all by himself.'

Marsaud then ushered the Scots into a light and airy room and invited them to break their fast. The table was already laid with fruit and bread and servants soon appeared with trays of pastries and a steaming pot of porridge. The party found that they were famished and quickly set about filling their bellies. Even John found that his queasiness had receded sufficiently to tempt him into cutting himself several slices of the freshly baked bread. The hours passed quite pleasantly as the Edward men talked with Al while Strathbogie snuffled and snored quietly in his chair with his chin upon his chest. Their thoughts had just begun to turn to their stomachs once again, when they were summoned to join King John for lunch.

439

They found their sovereign already at the table, with a napkin tucked into his collar as he attacked a plate of eggs. He remained seated and gazed in astonishment as the Scotsmen dropped to their knees and addressed him as their King. His face, which was already red when they entered the room, now reddened to a dark crimson and he waved them irritably to their feet.

'I am no king and you should not address me so.' He snapped angrily. 'Now come and join me at table and tell me what business you would have with me.'

'My Lord,' John began, 'we are sent by the Bishop of Glasgow and Sir William Wallace.'

King John held his hand out to silence John and shot glances over both his shoulders. 'You must not utter that man's name here. My wife would have you thrown out on your ears for the mere mention of it in her presence.'

John stared back at the King, his blank expression indicating that he did not understand why this would cause such grave offence.

Balliol held his hands up in exasperation and looked around the company for support. 'The outrage at Stirling Bridge!' Being met with nothing but more blank faces, Balliol turned back to John. 'The army Wallace slaughtered at Stirling was commanded by De Warenne, the Earl of Surrey, my dear wife's brother. The humiliation stung him badly and he has shared his pain with his sister through his letters. For months she spoke of little else.'

John nodded his understanding and decided that it would be wise not to mention his own involvement in that great battle. 'The Bishop of Glasgow has sent us to find out what your intentions are. If you mean to return to Scotland and reclaim your throne, arrangements will be made to ensure your safe passage.' John leaned towards Balliol and lowered his voice. 'I can see that King Philip means to keep you here. Please know that we are ready to aid you in your escape should you so wish it.'

Balliol pushed his plate of eggs away from him and reached for his goblet. 'My God man! Why would I wish to escape from here? Those men at my door are the only thing that prevents King Edward's agents and the Bruce's assassins from rushing in to cut my throat. I would not last a day outside these walls. And why would I wish to have that crown of thorns forced back onto my head? I rue the day that I ever sat upon the Crowning Stone. My arse was scarcely off it before the nobles began to plot and scheme and chip away at my authority. Not one of them raised so much as a single finger as Edward heaped humiliation after humiliation upon me. Christ! Each time one of them raised a grievance against me, he could not rule in their favour quickly enough. Not a voice was raised in my defence when he uncrowned me at Stracathro and ripped the royal badges from my jerkin. And how am I remembered in my homeland? Not as Good King John or John the Bold, as once I might have dreamed, but as Toom Tabard, the empty jacket! I have no desire to repeat the

441

experience and you should have no doubt about the certainty of its occurrence. I might have been incarcerated in Edward's tower or exiled in Rome, but I still heard of every invasion when Edward crossed the border with impunity. If I was to return, he would not rest until my head was rotting on a spike and there would be no Scottish army capable of preventing him from doing as he wished. I will be staying here where I may find some peace, you should tell your Bishop that.'

John blinked in astonishment at this tirade and took a moment to gather his thoughts. 'But what of your loyal subjects who, like us, resist the English King and risk their lives in your name?'

Balliol snorted in derision. 'An army of commoners cannot stand against the ranks of English knights. Stirling was an aberration and will not happen again. If you wish to see the future of your resistance, you need look no further than the bloodied field at Falkirk.'

'That army was no force of peasants. There were nobles upon the field as well as pikemen and your own kinsman, John Comyn, stood with us that day.'

'And much good that did you. He was a fool to make common cause with Wallace and I have written to tell him as much. He cannot prevail when the forces of King Edward and half the nobles of Scotland have ranged themselves against him. If he was wise, he would make his peace with Edward and, if he is lucky, retain his title and estates. Only a fool would wager all on a cause that is already lost.'

'Then I must be a fool.' John retorted, as he felt his temper fray.

Balliol locked eyes with John and scowled fiercely. 'I cannot deny that I admire your loyalty and courage and that of your fellows, but my experience tells me that both are misplaced. I would counsel you that to place your faith in any of the Scottish nobles would be a grave mistake. I guarantee that they will sicken you, if you are fortunate enough to live long enough, and will leave you as wretched and hollow as I. They will use you when it brings them some advantage and then turn from you the instant it does not. If you are wise, you will leave them to their games.'

John returned Balliol's gaze and decided that he did not like what he saw. The man's eyes were watery with fear and his fingers trembled uncontrollably. 'I can see that your mind is made up. Bishop Wishart suspected that you might choose this course and has instructed me to ask that you keep your intentions strictly to yourself.'

'Ha!' Balliol exploded. 'The Good Bishop never fails to disappoint. No doubt he intends to spread word that King John builds an army and will soon return to free his country and will use this myth to exhort anyone foolish enough to believe him to fight harder against King Edward. That man whispered constantly in my ear just so long as the crown was perched upon my head. As soon as it was removed, I heard his whispers

443

no more. Into whose ears do his words now drip? Wallace? Bruce? Comyn? I have no doubt that he tells them all that they could be king, if only they heed his counsel. Every king or pretender to a throne finds himself surrounded by those who whisper and scheme, but who lack the courage to take the crown for themselves. Tell the Bishop that I will stay silent, but that I will hear no more from him. Tell him that I am finished and will no longer suffer him disturbing my peace.'

Balliol declared himself too agitated to eat and left the delegation at table.

'I am sorely disappointed.' John stated, with sadness in his voice. 'He is not the man I believed him to be.'

'I don't think he's right in the head.' Scott added sagely.

'How could a weakling like that end up being the King of Scotland?' Eck wondered aloud with evident disgust. 'I doubt that he is capable of anything more than leading himself to his next drink.'

'I think that you are too harsh.' Strathbogie interrupted, as he chewed a mouthful of bread. 'You forget that, unlike many others, he had courage enough to defy King Edward and all his might. It was just unfortunate that he suffered such a devastating defeat at the Battle of Dunbar. Only a few of us were able to escape into the Forest of Ettrick and half the lords of Scotland ended up in Edward's dungeons. With half of the nobles in chains and the other half hungry for his crown, it is little wonder that

444

King John was crushed by the English King.' He paused briefly to swallow. 'What we have seen here this morning, is a good and decent man who has been broken by the power and avarice of powerful and greedy men.'

John was still contemplating Strathbogie's words when Captain Marsaud strode into the room with a smile upon his face.

'I am told that you will be leaving now. It would seem that you have already tested your own King's hospitality to its limits.' The Frenchman paused to look around the company with some amusement. 'But do not be disheartened my friends, for I come with an offer of hospitality from a King who has both a crown and a realm to rule.'

'I am afraid that we must return home to report on our audience with King John Balliol.' John responded curtly. 'It would not do for us to tarry here.'

Marsaud winked and tapped the side of his nose with his index finger. 'Come now John. We both know that your ship will not return for you for another week at least. That leaves you more than ample time to indulge King Philip's wishes. It seems that you have impressed him, for he has commanded me to escort you to witness a real battle. It seems that he is keen to persuade you and your comrades to join his army. For some strange reason, he believes that your experiences at the Bridge of Stirling would be of benefit to his commanders.'

John hesitated, again surprised that the French seemed to know more of their planned movements than they did themselves.

'You will enjoy it, John Edward. The Castle of Courtrai in Flanders is besieged by a Flemish force of rebellious peasants. King Philip has commanded Count Robert of Artois to destroy it. He marches there now and, if we move quickly enough, we will arrive in time to see all the knights of France ride into battle. Do not tell me that you are not tempted. Such a sight will make anything you have seen before appear as nothing more than a drunken brawl in comparison.'

Despite the Frenchman's arrogance, John was indeed tempted and, with nothing to occupy them before their ship returned, he nodded his agreement.

Langton gazed around himself and had to reluctantly admit that England had few cathedrals which could be compared favourably to the splendours of Rome. The palace of Cardinal Teodorico Ranieri, Prince of the Church and Camerlengo of the Holy Roman Church, stood as testament to the man's power and wealth. The Bishop of Coventry and Lichfield had only just begun calculating how much gold it must have taken to erect the palace's great columns and domed roof, when he was interrupted by footsteps approaching him on the exquisite mosaic floor.

He dropped to one knee and took the Cardinal's outstretched hand before bowing his

head to kiss the proffered ring. 'Illustrissimo.'
He declared warmly. 'How pleasant it is to see
you once again.'

'The pleasure is all mine, Lord Bishop,' the
Camerlengo replied, 'unexpected though it is. I
am sure that you are aware that the Holy Father
has left the city for his winter palace. You will
have a lengthy wait if you seek the honour of an
audience.'

Langton smiled in response and rose to his
feet. 'An audience with the Holy Father will
give me only half a chance of persuading him of
the virtue of my proposal. If I am able to
convince his most trusted counsellor of the
wisdom of my proposition, then I believe that
the odds of a successful outcome will lean more
heavily in my favour.'

'You flatter me, Lord Bishop. I am little more
than a humble priest.'

'In my experience, Illustrissimo, it is the
humble man who sits at the right hand of the
powerful leader who most often directs events.'

Ranieri raised his hand in objection. 'I cannot
claim to control the Holy Father's actions,
though it is true that he listens to me most
carefully.'

'You are too modest, Illustrissimo.' Langton
replied with a smile. 'Let us just agree that we
both have influence with our respective
superiors and cut straight to the heart of our
business.'

'I too consider brevity to be a virtue. Let me
pour you some wine while you summarise your
thoughts. I assume that it concerns King

Edward's ambitions in Scotland. If so, I must warn you that the Holy Father's decision to free John Balliol is irreversible, as is his command that your King must remove all his officials from that benighted realm and desist from doing harm to its clergy, nobles and common people.'

'My proposal is not entirely unrelated to Scotland, but it comes from a perspective which should bring great advantage to both our masters, should they be willing to proceed with sufficient pragmatism.'

The Cardinal savoured his wine and invited the Bishop to continue.

'It seems to me that the Holy Father and King Edward are faced with the self-same problem and that the adoption of a single course could bring both to a satisfactory conclusion. Just as His Majesty seeks to tame a rebel province in the north, the Holy Father struggles to impose his authority on the rebellious Sicilians.'

'The tumult in that kingdom does greatly trouble the Holy Father. They are a stubborn and ungrateful people who defy his rightful authority.'

'King Edward says the same of the Scots. If only they both had sufficient silver to raise the armies necessary to restore order and rightful authority.'

'And so, we come to the nub of the matter. Spit it out, good Bishop, you have piqued my curiosity.'

'The English Church presently pays no taxes. The Holy Father issued a Bull exempting the clergy from any tax imposed by King Edward

448

and he, in his turn, forbade the export of any monies to Rome. If Rome and England were to reach an understanding, those taxes could be collected and divided between us to provide us with the means to subjugate our troublesome provinces.' Langton retained his passive expression, but his excitement was rising as he could sense the Cardinal's growing enthusiasm.

Ranieri licked his lips subconsciously. 'And this money would be divided how? I recall previous discussions with Edward's emissaries where only one fifth was to come to the Holy Father.'

'That was a long time ago, Illustrissimo.' Langton replied evenly. 'The situation is very different now and we must cooperate closely to protect the interests of our friends. King Edward could be persuaded to take only half of the silver raised.' Langton allowed himself a smile. His every instinct told him that the deal was already done. The Cardinal would undoubtedly hint at difficulties and protest that he could only put the proposal before Pope Boniface, but Langton knew that his scheme had been successful.

Cardinal Ranieri let out a long sigh. 'You ask a great deal of the Holy Father, Lord Bishop. He issued the Bull on Scotland only because of his great concern for the suffering of the people there. He will also be reluctant to retract his judgement lest he be thought to be somehow indecisive or weak.'

'I doubt that any man of note will think him weak once he has shown his strength by crushing the Sicilians beneath his heel.'

'You are most persuasive Bishop Langton. I will bring the matter to the Holy Father's attention as soon as he returns to the city. Now that your business here is done, will you return immediately to England or will you dally here a while? I am told that you take much pleasure from the whores here in Rome.'

Langton smiled in amusement at the barb. 'I like them well enough, Illustrissimo. Their golden skin and fiery natures make for a pleasant change from the pale and submissive English whores. I assume that you too have a liking for their delights, they seemed to know you well in the establishment I have been frequenting.'

Ranieri smiled at Langton's response. 'You should buy a couple and take them home to warm you on those long and rainy English nights.'

'There are whores enough for me in London, Illustrissimo. Though I will take your advice and stay a few days longer to indulge myself.'

Cardinal Ranieri watched Langton walk the full length of the palace and out into the street. Only when the door had closed upon his back did he gesture to a young priest and bade him approach. 'Fetch me parchment and ink! I would have you take a message to the Holy Father at once.'

34

Captain Marsaud spurred his horse up the small
hillock and led the Scotsmen into the presence
of the French Commander, Count Robert of
Artois.

'The Count would like to speak with you.'
Marsaud informed John loudly. 'King Philip has
told him of your involvement in the battles of
Stirling and Falkirk and he is eager to hear your
thoughts on his strategy.'

The Count turned his head at this and waved
John to his side. John felt quite shabby in
comparison to the French commander. He was
tall, broad-shouldered and slim, even although
his silver hair and beard suggested that he must
be near to fifty years of age. He was clad in
polished plate from head to foot and John
wondered if it was silver, for he could see no
sign of rust or tarnish. A great, silver cavalry
sword hung at his waist and a highly polished
shield decorated in purple with yellow fleurs-de-
lis was strapped to his left arm. John doubted
that any king had ever been so well turned-out
for battle.

'Greetings Sir John!' The Count announced
happily. John returned his greeting and

451

pointedly ignored his comrades as they rolled their eyes in response to the Count mistaking John for a knight. 'You almost arrived too late. I mean to attack just as soon as the morning mist has cleared. His Majesty King Philip tells me that you have been forged in battle and may be able to teach us a trick or two. I doubt that I have much to learn from one so young as you, but, as we have some time, please give us the benefit of your great wisdom.'

John ignored the acid in Count Robert's tone and surveyed the field before him. 'The Flemish forces are well-arrayed. Their infantry are formed into a square of packed ranks, so that any attack will be met by the point of a wedge. Their rear is protected by the river and they have dug trenches to their front to disrupt any cavalry charge. They outnumber your foot by two to one and have prepared their ground well to negate any advantage you might gain from your superiority in heavy horse.'

The Count shrugged his shoulders. 'I will give you credit for having a good eye, but there are several crucial points which have eluded you. Firstly, their infantry do outnumber ours, but there is a great difference in quality. The Flemish force is made up almost entirely of peasants and militia armed with pikes. The men I command are predominantly noble men-at-arms and are more experienced and are well-drilled. Each of our men is worth at least three of theirs. Secondly, I have command of almost three thousand knights, each one of whom wears heavy armour and is mounted upon a heavy

452

horse. Such a force would slice through peasant ranks without breaking sweat.'

'Your force of knights is indeed impressive, my Lord.' John replied. 'If they can be brought to bear, I have no doubt that they will inflict heavy casualties.'

The Count ignored John's interruption and continued stiffly. 'And thirdly, almost all of the Flemish nobles have wisely chosen to defect to King Philip and have therefore left this rabble with scarcely a single competent officer to lead them. I will send my infantry in to soften their ranks and our servants will follow them and fill their trenches with wood, so that they will not disrupt our cavalry charge. Once this is done, I will signal for the infantry to withdraw and send my noble knights to finish them. I intend to take my lunch in the castle before the sun reaches its highest point.'

'I have seen a peasant force armed only with pikes turn a cavalry charge to bloody ruin, my Lord. I would counsel you to greater caution. I see that you have near a thousand crossbowmen upon the field. It might be prudent to send them forward with your infantry, so that they can punch holes in the Flemish lines and make them more vulnerable to your attack.'

'The King would string me up by the balls if I was to resort to such low tricks to defeat a bunch of miserable, murderous peasants. They have offended His Majesty by slaughtering his officials and it is only right that they are put to the sword by his noblemen. I could not hold my head up at court if the victory was won by such mercenaries, while I kept half the lords of France from the fray.'

'But surely any victory is better than even noble defeat?'

The Count shook his head impatiently. 'It may be different in your country, but we set great store in honour here. Anyway, where was it that you saw peasants destroy noble cavalry? Not Falkirk surely? I had heard that it was the peasants who were slaughtered there.'

John could not deny this fact and turned his eyes back to the field.

Count Robert laughed heartily. 'I thought as much, Sir John. Now you must leave me to my work, it is almost time. I will dine with you in the castle once the siege is lifted and you can impart more of your martial wisdom while I eat my fill.'

As Count Robert moved away, John turned to find Captain Marsaud staring at him with his mouth wide open.

'What?' John snapped irritably.

'Jesus Christ John! You were expected to exchange a few polite words with the man, compliment the positioning of his troops, tell him that his knights have the shiniest armour you have ever seen and marvel at how colourful his banners are. I did not expect you to critique his battle plan minutes before he engages with the enemy.'

Behind Captain Marsaud, Scott beamed cheerfully. 'I doubt King Philip will be hiring now, Sir John. I suspect you'll just have to rough it wi' us common folk.'

John's curses just seemed to increase his comrades' hilarity, so he turned his head away and waited for the battle to unfold.

The advance of the infantry and the pikemen was indeed impressive. The men marched in time with the booming rhythm of the drummers and, in their bright, crisp uniforms, the ranks provided a greater spectacle than anything John had seen in Scotland. But, as they receded into the distance, the disparity in numbers became more apparent and it was evident that the much smaller French force would not be adequate to break down the tight-packed Flemish ranks. The shouts and screams of men were carried back to them on the breeze, as servants scurried forward with sacks of wood upon their backs. Even at this distance, the Scots could see that their loads would not come close to filling the defensive ditches. Messengers rode frantically between the infantry and Count Robert's command post, but John did not need to hear their reports to know that the French attack had failed to break the Flemish lines and that it was now stalled in a bloody stalemate, which could only serve to further whittle away at the French ranks.

Sharp horn blasts signalled that the attack was at an end and the remainder of the French infantry immediately turned and ran though the ditches and towards the safety of their own cavalry. A few Flemish pikemen rashly pursued their fleeing opponents in their enthusiasm for blood, but discipline was soon restored and their lines remained unbroken. The advance of the cavalry was heralded by more horn blasts and the air was instantly filled with the din of horses' hooves and the clank of metal on metal as armour plate, maille, axes and swords rattled against each other with each equine stride. From the perspective of the hillock, it was difficult to disagree with Count Robert's opinion. It seemed impossible to believe that mere men with pikes could stand against the massive weight of horse-flesh and armour, when its passing was enough to shake the very ground as it closed upon the Flemish square. Three thousand knights, with their lances pointed skywards and their pennants fluttering in the breeze, would normally be sufficient to send any force of infantry fleeing for their lives. Whether it was their courage or the river to their back that kept the Flemish rooted to the spot, John could not say. What he did know was that their lines stayed unbroken while the ranks of French knights fell into disarray from the moment they reached the first ditches. He could not know who had determined the placement of the ditches, but it was plain to see that he was a very clever man. By positioning them irregularly and at a variety of angles, he had ensured that the French knights had no opportunity to realign themselves before they hit the square. For long moments, it seemed that they might prevail, as the line of defence curved back horribly under the weight of the attack. Though it bent, it did not break and it was the screams from injured horses which signalled that the peasants were not being swept away by all the lords of France.

Marsaud had turned quite pale and rivulets of sweat were running down his face from under his helmet, although there was still a chill in the air. 'Mon Dieu!' He exclaimed in horror. 'Do you see them fall?'

No-one answered his question, for they could all see for themselves that the ranks of knights were being quickly thinned as the pikes did their bloody work. They watched on as the heavy horse were forced gradually backwards and more of the beasts crashed to the ground in bloody, thrashing heaps. John sensed movement to his right and turned in time to see the crossbowmen turn tail and run, many of them dropping their weapons as they went, so that their weight would not slow their escape. Those of the French infantry who had sought shelter in the ditches and trenches to allow the cavalry to pass, now sensed that defeat was inevitable and joined the exodus from the field. It was now that the screams of men and horses reached its crescendo, as the rows of pikemen moved forward and tirelessly plunged their weapons down into the flesh of both men and beasts.

Captain Marsaud stared across the field in horror. 'Why do they not show mercy to those who yield? The ransoms for those men still standing would bankrupt the kingdom for a generation. It is madness to put them to slaughter, when just one prisoner would bring his captor a fortune.'

'They do not fight according to your rules of chivalry.' John responded. 'They fight for their freedom and do not mean to leave a single man alive who might come back and steal it away from them.'

'They are animals!' Marsaud spat in disgust.

'That may be true, but they are animals who have defeated the cream of French society.'

Marsaud put his hand to his head in despair. 'Half the men on this field were favourites at King Philip's court and through them he was able to rule his realm with a fist of iron. Now he will be left with old men, hairless boys and those lords who have shown themselves reluctant to honour their sovereign with military service. This is a disaster which will leave the King in a much-weakened condition. All of France will weep at news of this debacle.'

'Not all of France, Captain.' Count Robert interrupted, as he approached from their rear. 'There will be no tears from those who have fallen on the field. No sobbing from their torn and shattered corpses.'

John bowed his head and cast his eyes upon the ground rather than meet the Count's haunted, desolate gaze.

'No words could shame me more than your inability to meet my eye.' The Count declared miserably, his voice wavering with distress. 'In my arrogance, I dismissed your counsel and am wretched now that the day has unfolded exactly as you had predicted. I apologise for my rudeness and hope that you will forgive me.'

John forced himself to face Count Robert, though he found it hard to see him so broken and diminished. The proud and noble knight of just two hours past was gone and in his place stood a stooped and hollowed shell, still shaking from the shock of the speed and manner of his defeat. 'I take no pleasure from this turn of events, my Lord. It pains me deeply to see our ally brought so low. Now, you must come with us. The Flemish foot still advance towards us and they seem set on slaughter rather than on forcing your surrender.'

The Count shook his head wearily. 'It will be some time before they reach us. Look! See how they halt to strip our nobles of everything of value. There will be far more wealthy men among the Flemish before this day is done. Captain Marsaud! You must take our friends and escort them away so that they are not overrun by our savage enemies. King Philip would not like to hear that they were lost.'

'You must accompany us, my Lord. They will hack you down if you do not flee.'

'I am already dead, Marsaud.' The Count replied tiredly. 'My daughter Mahaut is my only heir and my death may serve to spare her from the worst of the stench of my defeat. Please tell her that I died well with her sweet name upon my lips.' He smiled weakly when Marsaud nodded his agreement. 'The Flemish horde moves once again. I mean to deny some of their number the joy of their victory.'

With that, the proud Count kicked his golden spurs and sent his mount towards the ragged Flemish lines at the gallop. They watched as he slashed down hard with his sword and sent several pikemen falling to the earth, their spurting blood crimson against the sky. Then he

459

was encircled and his horse's legs were cut out from underneath him and both man and beast disappeared beneath the stabbing pikes and were lost from sight.

'Time to go mes amis!' Marsaud announced urgently, and led them away from the slaughter.

Langton's ship had already cast off and was easing away from the dock when the messenger galloped up and tersely ordered the captain to throw his ropes ashore so that the dockhands could pull the vessel back.

'This had better be good!' Langton growled menacingly, as he snatched the parchment from the messenger's hand and broke the seal with his fingernails. He was keen to make land in England as soon as possible, as he had made it his policy to be in close proximity to King Edward when there was good news to impart. He would strangle the messenger if this delay allowed another to beat him to Edward's side with the happy tidings of his successful diplomacy in Rome. He quickly scanned the parchment and then read it again to make doubly sure that he had not misunderstood it. His smile transformed his face and the messenger exhaled sharply in relief.

'You,' Langton announced, as he jabbed his finger into the messenger's chest, 'will eat and drink your fill in Paris tonight and I will give you the pick of the finest whores that city has to offer.' He then turned to his attendants still aboard the ship and gestured that they should hurry. 'Unload it all and find us horses. We must make haste to King Philip's side before he has the chance to recover himself.'

By the time Langton met with Nogaret at dawn the following day, he had good reason to regret that night's premature celebrations. His head thumped painfully, his mouth was dry and the stench of the sour wine on his breath made him want to retch anew. Despite his delicate condition, he was determined to enjoy this encounter to its fullest extent and forced a smile onto his lips as Nogaret approached.

The Keeper of the Seal's expression was thunderous and his tone sour and petulant. 'It seems that bad news travels fast, my Lord Bishop.'

'That rather depends on the efficiency of one's informants.' Langton retorted, happy to let his feelings of smug satisfaction display themselves openly on his face. 'In truth, I just happened to be close by when word reached me and I just had to hasten here to offer my support.'

'I can imagine what form that support will take.'

'My dear Keeper, you do me a disservice. While it is true that our masters have had their disagreements in the past, you cannot believe that we would seek to turn your misfortune to our advantage.'

'My dear Bishop, that is exactly what I expect you to do.'

Langton nodded and leaned closer to Nogaret. 'If we are to speak plainly, I will detail what I require of King Philip. King Edward's lands in Gascony are to be returned to him in their entirety, immediately and with no conditions attached. In addition, His Majesty will also publicly rescind his alliance with the Scots and give an undertaking that he will play no further part in any diplomatic machinations on the Scots' behalf.'

'You are free with your demands, my Lord, but make no mention of what His Majesty is to receive in return.'

'Well, that is the beauty of my proposition, Keeper Nogaret. King Philip will receive nothing in return, except the knowledge that he has, at a single stroke, removed any possible motivation for King Edward to land an army here in France, whilst simultaneously giving him complete freedom of action in his northern province. Given his current weakened position, I am sure that King Philip will prefer to see his counterpart fully engaged elsewhere. As we speak, King Edward builds a great army, where he deploys it remains to be seen.'

Nogaret stared at Langton with barely concealed dislike. 'Very well! I will speak with His Majesty and write to you with his response. My messengers will find you in London?'

Langton slowly shook his head. 'I'm afraid not. I must insist on having the documents in my possession by the time I leave Paris this evening. I will see King Philip's letters to the Pope and the Scottish nobles before they are sealed. I must also insist that I take them with me and use my own messengers to convey them to their recipients. We would not want any misunderstandings to arise as a result of any communique being lost en route.'

'You ask too much, Lord Bishop.' Nogaret hissed between tightly clenched teeth.

'I think not, Lord Keeper.' Langton replied nonchalantly. I will return here in the evening to collect the documents in person. Please tell His Majesty just how much I am looking forward to seeing him. If I am needed, you will find me at my usual apartments. I have a thumping headache and plan to return to my bed while you busy yourself.'

The Lord High Treasurer found that he was feeling much better as he left the palace and stepped out into the morning sunshine.

35

William de Lamberton, the Bishop of Saint
Andrews, was ashen-faced as he listened to John
Edward's report. As he neared the conclusion of
his account of the disaster at Courtrai, the
Bishop winced as though he was in pain and
massaged his temples firmly with his long
fingers. John could not tell if it was his words
which caused the Bishop to tremble or if he
shivered due the frigid air in his wind-lashed,
coastal castle.

John stepped back in fright when the
normally poised and restrained churchman leapt
to his feet and swept his hand across his desk,
sending goblets, jug and candlesticks crashing
onto the floor. 'Jesus Christ!' He hissed, his face
twisted in fury and frustration. 'All of our work
is undone. Every advance has been reversed and
each day our position worsens.'

Wallace raised his hand to placate the
Bishop. 'Calm yourself, Lord Bishop. We have
suffered reverses before and will surely suffer
them again before this war is done.'

'I fear that the tide has turned against us and
that all our efforts will not turn it back, Sir
William. These last few days have seen such a

deluge of developments which harm our cause, I fear that they will surely drown us. We have lost our strongest friends and those that remain are more set on fighting amongst themselves than they are on keeping Edward and his horde of rats from swarming over our borders.'

'I cannot deny that Balliol's refusal to return and the loss of King Philip's support are heavy blows to bear, but they are not mortal wounds and we must not let them drive us to despair. Today we have no king, but neither did we yesterday and, though King Philip was a friend to us, not a single soldier did he send to aid our cause. In truth and in practicality, I do not see that we are worse off than before.'

'Your optimism and determination are to your credit, Sir William, but you do not know it all. We have lost more than Balliol and Philip, for just this morning I have received word from the Holy Father. He has withdrawn his condemnation of Edward's actions and now admonishes his Scottish Bishops for resisting their rightful king. We are now abandoned and are truly alone in this struggle.'

Wallace paused in astonishment and blinked his eyes in disbelief. 'But how can this be so? The ink is barely dry on his Bull commanding Edward to withdraw from our lands.'

'It would seem, Sir William, that we are not the only ones who can send delegations to Paris and Rome. It also seems apparent that the English emissaries possess greater skills than our own. But that is not the half of it. While Edward rallies his great army, our magnates can scarcely be restrained from baring their fangs and flying at one another's throats. The Bruce is on the verge of striking out, as he fears that King John is about to return and Comyn, for his part, is impatient to land the first blow to ease his kinsman's way home. If only those two could be persuaded to join their forces, we could strike at King Edward's encampment at Linlithgow and end this at one fell swoop. With them so divided, the English King is able to defy us and to winter in our midst and, come the spring, there will be nothing to stop him from marching back in to complete his conquest.'

'So, we will have to do what we have done successfully in the past.' Wallace replied evenly. 'Harry and harass his officers, disrupt his lines of supply, limit English rule to the confines of their castle walls and then starve them back across the border as winter begins to bite.'

Lamberton shook his head. 'We cannot rely on that tactic to last forever, not when we have lost so many friends and those that remain to us cannot be stopped from destroying one another.'

Wallace smiled and put his arm around the Bishop's shoulders. 'Then we shall find new friends and fight on. Whatever the bastard Edward throws at us and so long as one of us remains standing, we fight on.'

Walter Langton wrapped his furs tightly around his body and made his way towards the King's pavilion. There was no part of Scotland which could be inhabited by civilised men in winter, but the area around Falkirk was particularly desolate and the wind seemed to whip down directly from the snow-capped hills and slice through to his bones, no matter how many layers of clothing he piled upon himself. Though he yearned for his house in London, he did not regret his decision to make his way to Edward's side from Paris just as fast as his ship could carry him. His reception at Linlithgow would live with him for the rest of his days and the memory of Edward's joy at hearing of his achievements at the courts of Philip and Pope Boniface still warmed him in spite of the frigid climate. He did not expect today's audience to be straightforward, but was confident that the successes he had won so recently would ensure that the King would not treat him harshly.

'Ah, Langton!' Edward declared happily. 'I was expecting you. Now come and warm yourself at the fire and tell me what is of such urgency that it could not wait until after the tournament.'

Langton basked in Edward's approval and could not keep the smile from his face. 'I come to speak with you of love unrequited.'

King Edward returned his Treasurer's grin before his face transformed into an exaggerated expression of mock offense. 'I hope that you do not insinuate that your love for me is not returned, for you will offend me if you do. You are well aware that I love you better than a king should love his counsellor.'

Langton laughed and took the proffered goblet from the King's own hand. 'I am secure in your love, My Lord, and give daily thanks to

God for it. I come to speak of another and not of myself, though it is not the romance of it which will appeal, but rather the advantage it may bring to our cause.'

'Well, spit it out, Lord Bishop, you have succeeded in intriguing me.'

Langton then told the tale of how the bold Sir John de Seagrave had lost his heart and his head to the beautiful Scots noblewoman, the Lady Margaret Ramsey. He then explained that the renowned beauty had spurned his advances and refused his suit and had instead announced her betrothal to Sir Henry St Clair of Rosslyn, a minor adherent of John Balliol who had fought at Dunbar and had been captured and briefly imprisoned thereafter.

Edward shook his head in annoyance. 'You do not think to ask me to intervene in such a matter? I have neither the time nor the patience to involve myself in something so inconsequential when I am busy with my preparations for this summer's campaign.'

'Of course not, my Lord. I was just getting to the point which will be of great interest to you. Amazing though it seems, Sir John has raised near twenty thousand men at his own expense and seeks your permission to immediately lead them across the border to punish his rival and take his lady's hand.'

'My God Langton!' Edward exclaimed in amused astonishment. 'That is a substantial number of men. Not much less than the army I commanded here at Falkirk. Can he not delay the muster and come north with my army in the summer?'

'I fear not, my Lord. He has already gathered his army and has not the means to keep them in the field for so long. I would humbly submit that you should approve his enterprise. It will keep the Scots from their rest and may even soften them in preparation for your own advance.'

Edward again shook his head in disbelief. 'Very well, Walter. Tell him that he has my leave to proceed. This Lady Margaret must be quite a woman. If I had not so recently remarried, I would be half tempted to look at her for myself.'

'She is very beautiful, my Lord, and would be welcome in any man's bed. Whether she is worth the fortune required to raise twenty thousand men, I could not say.'

'That is the trouble with you Langton. It is always about the coin, the coin and nothing but the coin. The world would be a very dull place if all men thought as you do.'

'On the subject of coin, my Lord. I did want to raise one particular item of expenditure with you. I ask only because it seems to have been commissioned during my absence and is consuming gold at an astonishing rate.'

Edward's expression hardened somewhat, but the Treasurer was relieved to see that his smile did not disappear altogether. 'Am I to assume that you are referring to the construction of the pontoon bridges at King's Lynn?'

'That is correct, my Lord. It would seem that every carpenter in southern England has been

469

dragooned into service and that they consume whole forests of oak in building not one, but three pontoon bridges, each equipped with its own drawbridges and giant crossbows. The exchequer tells me that a fleet of thirty ships has been engaged to transport the pontoons north. I just wanted to ensure that you were aware of the costs being incurred in your name. By the time they are completed and transported, they will have consumed more gold than it would have taken us to enlist ten thousand foot.'

'The pontoon bridges are central to my strategy, Lord Bishop. They will allow my army to bypass Stirling Castle and move on to burn John Comyn's lands in the north. His estates have been left untouched by my previous campaigns and this, I now believe, explains our failure to bring the rebellious dogs to heel. You will see that this gold is not unwisely spent.'

'I can see the wisdom of the pontoons, my Lord, it is just the scale of the expenditure which gives me pause.'

Edward silenced him with a small gesture of his hand. 'I think you mean to chastise me for wasting hard-won silver on the construction of my devices.' He waved away Langton's attempt at protest before continuing. 'I have learned my lesson from Bothwell and can assure you that my interest in those pontoons is driven not by passion, but by hard pragmatism. I will now convince you of the merits of my decision and demonstrate why we will not suffer from marching with ten thousand men less than we might have mustered.' King Edward now turned to his attendant and commanded him. 'You may now bring our visitor into our presence.'

Langton looked on in puzzlement as the attendant rushed from the pavilion and Edward reclined in his chair with an expression of smug satisfaction on his face. 'You are about to see that I have not been idle in your absence and that you are not the only one who can achieve great things through negotiation rather than through the force of arms.'

A few moments later, the attendant pulled back the canvas flap and a tall, dark and familiar figure stepped into the pavilion.

'Robert Bruce, Earl of Carrick, I bid you welcome!' Edward boomed with great relish. 'I have asked the good Bishop to join us so that he can witness the moment you kneel before me and beg me to welcome you back into my peace. Then you will join me at the tournament, so that all will see that we are reconciled.'

De Bruce nodded curtly in Langton's direction and then fell to his knees and asked King Edward to forgive him his crimes against the crown. King Edward limited himself to inflicting only small humiliations upon the magnate and reassured him that his enemy Balliol would not be restored to his throne and that the Bruce and his kinsmen would have to swear fealty only to Edward and to no other.

Later, in the midst of the jousting, the King leaned close to Langton and whispered in his ear. 'See! We had little need of popes and kings when the Scots nobles can be manipulated into defeating themselves. Now, only the River Forth and the Comyns stand between us and our objective. The first we will bridge with good English oak and the second we will burn and harry into submission. The job's as good as done.'

Langton had never seen the King in spirits quite as high as this and his mood matched that of his sovereign so much that he did not even blink at Edward's generosity when he rewarded the winner of each bout with purses heavy with gold. He found that the cold air and biting wind no longer troubled him and he was able to sit back and enjoy the tournament. The finale of the melee on the field of bones was the cause of much excitement, as the flower of English knighthood was battered into submission by a tall and pock-marked commoner who stood as champion for a young friend of the Prince of Wales. His victory was all the more notable because he wore no armour, bore no shield and had his left shoulder bound up from an arrow wound suffered whilst defending the Prince from the Scots. The whole audience held their breath when King Edward called the lowly beast forward and announced that he could not tolerate seeing men of such high birth being laid low by such a mean and humble peasant. All men there had feared the worst when the King commanded the wretch to kneel and called for his sword to be brought to him. They cheered uproariously when the grinning Edward knighted him upon the field and then led him off to join the feast and celebrate his unexpected elevation.

Sir John de Seagrave leaned closer to the fire and drummed his feet against the hard ground in a bid to restore the circulation to his aching toes. His face was so close to the flames his skin was near roasted and his beard singed, but yet his back was frozen. His men still struggled to erect his tent as the frost-hardened earth defeated all their attempts to hammer in the stakes which would hold the guy ropes tight. Despite his current discomfort, he could not help but wonder at the speed of his progress. It had been mere weeks since he had begun to recruit men for this expedition. He could still scarcely believe that his master, Roger Bigod, Earl of Norfolk, had readily agreed to his request for funds and that he had provided almost two thirds of the twenty-four thousand men who now accompanied him, with another four thousand generously provided by the King. He had been both humbled and touched when the childless Earl told him that he saw him as his own son and would do all he could to help him win Lady Margaret for his wife. The memory of his kindness served to warm him, but not as much as the recollection of sweet Margaret's full, red lips. He had sworn to himself that he would hack his way through any Scot who blocked his way to Lady Margaret's side, but his advance to Linlithgow had been swift and unimpeded, with not a single Scot brave enough to make even a token challenge.

As soon as his tent was up and a brazier fired to warm it, he would call a council of war with his commanders and detail their plan of attack.

With little danger of the Scots fielding a force to confront him in open battle, he had decided to divide his army into three so that his objectives could be achieved with the utmost speed. While he himself would proceed to Rosslyn to capture Sir Henry St Clair, his rival for Lady Margaret's hand, the second force, under Sir Ralph Confrey, would march on Dalhousie Castle, Lady Margaret's home, to secure her, and the third, under the command of Sir Robert Neville, would attack nearby Borthwick Castle and so ensure that its garrison would be unable to come to the aid of either Lady Margaret or Sir Henry. With so little opposition in sight, he dared to hope that he would be able to whisk Lady Margaret back across the border in a mere matter of days.

Sir John cursed silently to himself as he realised that the icy wind had chilled his bladder so that it now ached to be emptied. He strode to the edge of the circle of light thrown out by the flickering flames and began to unfasten his trews. With the temperature dropping fast, he did not tarry and emptied his bladder as quickly as he could and hurried to lace his breeches as his pish formed crystals of ice at his feet. If he had lifted his eyes from his fumblings and cast his gaze towards the bushes to his left, he might have seen the two pairs of eyes which observed him and seen the flames of the fire reflected there. If he had glanced in their direction, it is likely that he would have noticed that one set of the eyes appeared to be human, whilst the other most likely belonged to a wolf or an uncommonly large dog.

36

Prior Abernethy became aware of the watchers less than an hour after he, and the four brothers who accompanied him, had set out from the Cistercian Priory of Mount Lothian to distribute bags of meal amongst the poor of the surrounding villages and hamlets. There had been two at first, but he could now see that another four had joined them and that they matched the pace of the walking monks. When he saw that they spurred their horses on, he had no doubt that they had gone to block the road ahead. Two of the monks had accompanied the Prior on his return to Scotland from France and, unlike the two novices recruited from the local villages, they both had some martial training and, like the Prior, carried plain, stout staffs. He addressed them tersely in French so that they would be prepared if the situation was to turn nasty. When they reached the apex of the lazy curve in the road, it was no surprise to find that the horsemen now blocked their way.

The Prior smiled his most benevolent smile as he came to a halt before the rough and well-armed horsemen. 'Peace be on you, my sons and may the good Lord shower his blessings down upon you.'

The leader of the horsemen glared back without responding and dug his thumb deep into his nostril in pursuit of some elusive but tantalising nugget. Only when he had secured his prize and taken the time to thoroughly inspect it, did he address the good brothers.

'What's in the bags?' He demanded.

'Tis nothing more than common meal intended for the sick and needy.' The Prior replied pleasantly. 'We try to do the Lord's work as best we can and minister to those who suffer.' The sound of the man's accent made the Prior tense imperceptibly and adjust his footing to be ready to strike if it should prove to be necessary. For English scouts to be abroad so far to the north did not auger well.

'Just drop the sacks and the silver cross that hangs from your neck and then fuck off back the way you came.' The scout replied with menace.

'That, we cannot do, my son.' The Prior responded with forced lightness in his voice. 'This meal is, as I have already told you, intended for those who have been brought to starvation by the long war and the harsh winter which has followed it. You and your men look as if you have been well fed and have less need than they.'

The scout's smile was not a happy sight, as his face was cruel rather than kind and the teeth he bared were more black and brown than they were white. 'You mistake me Priest! I was not asking and I will not tell you a second time.' He

476

drew his sword and indicated that his fellows should do the same. 'Begone or be dead. The choice is yours.'

Abernethy knew that the men before him were not trained fighters, but it was evident that they were practiced with their swords and would make easy work of five monks armed only with wooden staffs. He was confident that he could lay out two or three, but was equally sure that he and his brothers would then be hacked down and left to bleed their last upon the road. From the very corner of his eye, he detected some slight movement in the forest to the side of the track, but kept his eyes locked on those of the ugly scout.

'I beseech you, my son, let us pass and be about our works. This thin meal is not fit to fill the stomach of warriors such as you. In God's name, I ask you to let us walk on unmolested.'

The scout found these words to be most amusing and his smile widened to show that the rot was not confined to his teeth, but had progressed to infect his gums, leaving them black and rotten. 'You, I will kill last.' He announced, pointing his sword at Abernethy's face. 'We will see if pretty words still spill from your mouth when your guts are puddled on the earth.'

It was then that the armed men emerged from the trees and surrounded the English scouting party on all sides. 'I wouldn't do that, if I was you.' Announced the newcomer closest to Abernethy, as he drew his two swords and held them out at an angle at his sides. 'At least not if you want a quick and easy death. Drop your weapons and you have my word that you will all die cleanly. Hold fast to them and I guarantee that your end will be more painful than you can imagine.'

There was a momentary pause during which no man moved and no man spoke and then, suddenly, all was chaos and blood. Three scouts jerked back in their saddles as arrows thumped into them and pierced their flesh. Eck the Black flashed his swords and took the black-toothed scout's arm off at the elbow and slashed his thigh down to the bone. John Edward unsaddled another with one upwards thrust of his blade and Strathbogie's axe parted another from his left leg while Scott Edward cracked his lower spine with a single swing of his blade. The struggle lasted less than a minute and finished with six Englishmen lying and dying on the frozen ground.

John Edward approached the Prior and bowed his head. 'You may want to lead your men off now, Father. We must now torture these men for information and it will be bloody, dirty work.'

'I have no doubt that I have seen worse.' The Prior responded with a nonchalance which surprised the younger man. 'Their presence here tells me that an English army must follow close behind them. I would learn more of their intentions so as to be better prepared to spare my flock from harm.'

John could think of no reason to object and merely shrugged his shoulders in reply. The younger, Scottish novices turned white and averted their eyes as limbs were removed, eyes pierced and knuckles crushed under heels, but the Prior and his two French monks looked on without wincing and took in each word the scouts uttered and screamed in response to their questioning. When the last of them had been separated from his soul, John turned back to Abernethy.

'We must be away now, Father. My lords must hear of what we have learned this morning.'

'You should take us with you.' The Prior responded. 'The brothers and I have tramped these roads for many years as we seek salvation in our work.'

'We have no need of salvation.' Eck Edward interrupted. 'You heard these men speak of three English armies who now come this way. We must be on our way with haste to prepare for their arrival.'

'The good monks of Mount Lothian can aid you in those very preparations.' Abernethy responded. 'They know this area better than any man and their knowledge could make the difference between victory and disaster. Can you afford to spurn my offer when you a face a force greater than any that has hitherto marched this far north and when you still do not know how many good Scots will stand against them?'

'He speaks true.' Strathbogie interjected with reluctance, as he too was eager to rendezvous with whatever patriot forces had been brought together.

'How far?' John demanded.

'Now that we have horses, we can be there and back in less than an hour.' The Prior responded, already gathering up his robes so he could mount the horse so recently in the possession of the rotten-mouthed scout.

Mount Lothian Priory was much less impressive than its name suggested and John stayed impatiently in his saddle as the Prior disappeared through its crooked, wooden doors. He counted ten robed monks as they ran barefoot from the Priory and mounted the English horses, two to each saddle. He was on the verge of calling on Abernethy to hurry, when the older man strode through the doors and caused John's jaw to drop in astonishment. Gone were the worn and threadbare robes of rough, brown cloth and, in their place, the Prior was dressed in plate and maille, a heavy broadsword hung at his hip and a faded white surcoat adorned with a crimson cross was secured at his waist with a thick, leather belt adorned with a cross of silver.

Abernethy ignored John's gaping mouth until he was settled in his saddle. 'I was not always a humble priest.' He said with a smile, as he kicked his horse on.

'So, you were…?' John began to ask.

Abernethy nodded and replied in Latin. 'Non nobis, Domine, non nobis sed Nomini tuo da glorium.'

'Not unto us, O Lord, not unto us, but to thy Name give glory.' John translated. 'You were of the Knights Templar?'

480

'Aye!' Abernethy responded. 'Until I put down my sword to dedicate myself to praising God. I feel that He now calls on me to wield it once again in the face of tyranny and evil men.'

John fell in beside the Prior as he was keen to engage him in further conversation.

'Your comrade there, him who slew the mouthy Englishman. He seems an interesting fellow.' The Prior nodded in the direction of John's cousin as he spoke.

'He is my cousin, Eck. He delights in swordplay and finds that one blade is not enough to satisfy his lust for English blood.'

The Prior turned his head and looked John directly in the eye. 'I sense a darkness in him. It hangs about him like a thunder cloud.'

John nodded and watched Eck ride ahead. 'He was once the most light-hearted of men, but he near died from an injury suffered at Stirling Bridge and came back from it much changed. Whatever darkness afflicted him as he hung over the abyss has stayed with him and is only lifted when the arrows fly and men charge at him with blades raised in their hands.'

'Does he dream of it?' Abernethy enquired, his eyes also fixed on Eck's back.

'Aye!' John replied with some surprise. 'Almost every night.'

'I only ask because I once knew a knight who suffered the same fate. If God grants me the opportunity, I think that I could help him. Such a man, whilst an asset in times of war, will be a liability when the fighting's done.'

481

John nodded, heartened by the Prior's confidence that he could aid his cousin. 'If we live through the coming fight, I would be grateful if you could try.'

John's spirits were raised on approaching the forest to the east of Roslin Glen, when the presence of sentries told him that the patriot army was already gathered there. He was directed to a clearing where the leaders stood in a circle with Al at its centre. Wallace turned and came to greet him, the mud which spattered him from head to foot testament to how far and fast he had ridden to be there.

'You arrive just in time. Young Al was about to make his report.' Wallace's eyes now travelled past John's head and alighted on his companion. 'Prior Abernethy!' He declared happily. 'I had not thought to see you here.'

'William! It is good to see you. I thought that you might make some use of the good brothers' knowledge of the terrain. John here and his companions did a grand job of interrogating some captured English scouts and it seems that we will be up against it.'

Wallace roared with laughter. 'There is no denying that we will need all the help we can get. We face near twenty-five thousand men and, although John Comyn, Lord of Badenoch and Sir Simon Fraser of Neidpath have joined their forces with mine, we have scarcely eight thousand men with which to oppose them. Come and join us. We are about to make our plans.'

The circle was widened to admit the new arrivals and John glanced around and exchanged greetings with those he knew. He was surprised to realise that he had fought alongside almost every man there. He had stood with the Red Comyn and his man Peter Davidson at Falkirk, with Sir Henry St Clair and others at Stirling and had joined Sir Simon Fraser and his men in harrying the English during their last campaign. Al stood at their centre and scratched at the earth with his dagger to show where each of the three English armies were positioned. Prior Abernethy asked questions, made suggestions and confirmed that Al's observations of the lay of the land were accurate.

'Now that we know what we face, we must determine our course.' John Comyn declared. 'I would know your thoughts.'

Sir Simon was the first to speak and voice the opinion held by most of the men. 'We are far outnumbered and will be slaughtered if we face them in the open. The most prudent course would be to deny them battle and harass them as they move.'

'That is easy for you to say.' Retorted Sir Henry St Clair. 'It is not your lands and family who are threatened.'

John Comyn stepped forward and raised his hand in a placatory gesture. 'You speak true, Sir Henry, but leading our men to their deaths would be of no benefit to either your lands or to your kin. Caution must be our watchword. Intemperate action will likely be our downfall.'

'And bold action our salvation.' Wallace interjected thoughtfully. 'A prize has been laid out before us. Let us ensure that our caution does not prevent us from grasping it. Sir John Seagrave has unwisely divided his army in three and so we do not have to face twenty-five thousand men with our own eight thousand. We can meet one part of it on equal terms. The loss of one third of his army would undoubtedly be sufficient to send Sir John back south in disgrace.'

Prior Abernethy took a pace forward and pointed down at the scratchings in the earth. 'And Al here has identified the army that is most vulnerable to attack. Sir John himself has encamped in Roslin Glen with an embankment of the River Esk at his back. If we were to approach through the forest, we could take them by surprise and drive them to their deaths over that steep drop. There would be no room for him to deploy his cavalry and so it would be an equal fight.'

John Comyn rubbed at his beard and peered intently at Al's scratchings. 'But surely such a march would take near a full day.'

'Aye, it would at that.' The Prior responded. 'But if we set off now, we could be in place to attack when Seagrave and all his men are fast asleep. The good brothers of Mount Lothian can lead us stealthily right up to their sentry line. A third of their number would be cut down before they could gather their wits.'

'The prospect of snatching such an unexpected victory would give strength to our legs for the long march ahead.' Wallace added with rising enthusiasm. 'I'll wager that we'll have no better chance.'

John Comyn nodded. 'Then let us be bold. Sir William will take the left wing, Sir Simon the right and I shall lead the centre. Sir John Seagrave is to be taken alive. To have King Edward's favourite in our hands will make the victory that much sweeter.

Sir John de Seagrave sat with his blankets wrapped around his shoulders and a goblet of wine clasped in his hand and stared up at the stars sparkling in the dark, winter sky. Thoughts of Lady Margaret lying under that self-same sky had kept him from his slumber and sent him in search of wine to both warm and numb him. He paid no mind to a squawking from the forest and dismissed it as nothing more than a bird disturbed by his sentries. The few hours left before dawn seemed to be an eternity, as he was impatient to have Sir Henry in chains at his feet and the fair Margaret on his arm. He sighed deeply and tore his gaze from the twinkling host above, as he felt that its magnificence served only to make him more melancholy and his yearning greater for that which was so nearly in his grasp. He idly wondered why the trees did move when there was not a breath of wind and then realised with growing horror that men rushed out quietly from the woods and advanced from every direction. In the seconds that it took him to shake off his disbelief, the alarm was cried out across the camp and the enemy roared and increased the pace of their attack.

Not a single Englishman had the time to don his armour. Rudely ripped from their slumber, they had to hastily snatch up their swords and turn to face their assailants at close quarters. They were forced back by the speed of the Scots' advance and soon found themselves herded close together with the rocky cliff at their back. With only their foremost ranks able to wield their swords, the Scots were able to hack them down in greater numbers and soak the earth with English blood. The onslaught pushed them gradually backwards, until those at the rear began to lose their balance and screamed as they fell to their deaths on the jagged rocks below.

Sir John fought most bravely until his surcoat was soaked with his sweat and with the gore of Scot and Englishman alike. He did not so much as see the blow which laid him out and so was spared from the sight of his army being destroyed. The axeman who had gently tapped Sir John's skull, leaned down and grasped his silky locks to pull him from the slaughter. He dragged the unconscious knight to his master's feet.

'There you go, John. The Comyn will thank you for this captive and may even share his ransom.'

John Edward grinned at Strathbogie through a mask of blood and sweat. 'Come and slake your thirst. This English wine is the sweetest I have tasted since we sailed from France.'

Strathbogie first drank from thirst, but, before long, it was in celebration, as the English threw down their swords and surrendered before they were all put to slaughter. The patriots cheered and set about binding English hands. A long and arduous march had been rewarded with a victory which would shock the English King and, if God was good, persuade him that Scotland was not his to conquer.

John Edward laughed to see that his brother had crawled into an English bed still warm from its previous occupant. Many Scots soon followed his example and collapsed from exhaustion, leaving their weary fellows to guard the three hundred defenders who had survived the swift and surprise attack.

37

Wallace sat with a beaming smile and ate heartily of the breakfast intended for the English. The surrounding camp was in disarray, with corpses lying all around. English prisoners sat shivering on the ground, having lost their cloaks and boots to the victorious Scots, and tired and footsore patriots slumbered wherever a space could be found.

'You know,' Wallace said as he chewed, 'after Falkirk, I never thought that I would see such a victory again.' He nodded his head in contemplation. 'It feels good, John. It feels really good.'

John smiled in response and stretched his foot out to tap Sir John Seagrave's head with the toe of his boot. Sir John moaned gently, but did not stir.

'I hope Strathbogie has not broken his skull. Comyn will not be happy if he is left with nothing but a drooling imbecile to ransom.'

'I would not concern yourself, John.' Wallace replied. 'With such a vicious fight in the near darkness, he will count himself lucky that he has more than a corpse to barter with.'

Prior Abernethy joined them at the fire. His surcoat was now more red than white and the offal dripping from his blade indicated that he had done far more than observe the battle.

'Why so grave, good Prior?' Wallace enquired, as he invited Abernethy to eat. 'A hundred years from now, they will sing of this famous battle and celebrate the part which you played in the victory.'

'I fear that it may not be remembered as a victory, Sir William.' Abernethy replied bleakly. 'The good brothers tell me that not every Englishman fell or was taken prisoner. A few have made good their escape and may already have reached Sir Ralph Confrey's force at Dalhousie Castle.'

Wallace shook his head. 'I think you concern yourself too much. I doubt that they would march here.'

The Prior arched his brow in challenge. 'And what would you do, Sir William? You know that your enemy has marched through the night and then fought a bloody battle. Would you stay your hand and wait for those men to recover from their exhaustion?'

Wallace closed his eyes and cursed. 'Where's Al?' He demanded.

'He took his scouts out before dawn, Sir William. We will soon know what, if anything, comes our way.' The Prior then turned to John. 'You have a good man there. I have met few who have his instincts and his ability to track and scout. I hope that you treat him well.'

489

'He is my friend.' John replied. 'I treat him as well as he will allow me to.'

'And how do you treat your prisoner?' Prior Abernethy enquired. 'He still seems quite groggy.'

'I think that he begins to stir. I will keep him alive until I can offload him onto John Comyn's men.'

Sir Ralph de Confrey had been incredulous when the first red-faced soldier was brought to him to tell of the disaster that had fallen Sir John and his men. By the time a third man had been brought in to tell the same tale, he had been forced to abandon his disbelief. It seemed that Seagrave had allowed himself to be taken by surprise and that his force had been destroyed by the ragged Scots militia. He immediately ordered that the siege of Dalhousie Castle be lifted and that his near nine thousand men march for Roslin Glen to bring retribution to the impudent and exhausted Scots. He could not help himself from imagining how King Edward would react when he was told of Sir John's failure and of his own subsequent victory. He had already decided that he would slaughter every last common Scot, as he was sure that this would win his sovereign's approval.

He was somewhat surprised when his scouts rode in to report that the Scots had marched from Roslin Glen and had arrayed themselves along a ridge only a short ride ahead.

'If they marched through the night before attacking Seagrave's camp, I can scarce believe

490

that they have now advanced to face us. Their foolish leaders will have driven them to exhaustion.'

'Tis obvious, Sir Ralph.' His captain replied. 'They think that if they occupy the higher ground, then we will hesitate to risk an attack up such a long and steep slope.'

'The slope may slow our charge, but, in their weakened state, they will break even if we fall upon them at the walk. No man can march and fight without sleep and then do the same again. Order the men into ranks and we will advance up the hill and finish them.'

As his captain issued his commands, Sir Ralph examined the terrain before him. The incline was steep, but, with only a sparse covering of trees and bushes, there was little to impede their progress. He climbed down from his saddle and drew his sword, determined to lead the charge himself. He called a halt three quarters of the way up to let his men catch their breath and rest their weary legs. Above him, he could make out the figures of the enemy through the trees and the air was filled with taunts and insults as the wretches dared the English to make their attack. It did not escape Sir Ralph's notice that the Scots' numbers were more sparse than he had expected. It seemed that Seagrave had put up a stiffer resistance than had been reported. His confidence only grew as he looked along his own ranks and saw that they had superiority in both numbers and quality. He roared his men into the attack and onto glory.

He realised his mistake only when he burst through the treeline and saw that the slope did not rise evenly to the position taken by the Scots, but was broken by a rocky crag which left his troops facing a sheer cliff of a height of three men or more. It was then that he saw that the men perched on the rocky outcrop were not men-at-arms or common foot, but were ranks of Scottish archers. Though their bows were small and did not match their English counterparts, they were deadly at close quarters and more so when fired down onto a mass of men. As volley after volley of shafts were loosed with devastating effect, Sir Ralph screamed at his men to withdraw outside the archers' range. It was only when they turned that they saw the Scots foot charge out from the crag's sides and encircle their entire force.

The Scots archers fired until their quivers were emptied and their arms burned from repeatedly drawing back their bowstrings. The ground beneath them lay thick with jerking, spasming corpses and with the wounded, who screamed and moaned as their punctured flesh leaked blood and entrails onto the cold and rocky ground. Tom Figgins reckoned that he had brought down a man with each arrow he had put to flight. With fifty arrows in his possession and one hundred men at his side, he believed that more than half the English force had already fallen beneath the crag.

The remaining half had fallen into ragged disorder as they tried to escape the death which flew in from above. Although he screamed at the top of his lungs, Sir Ralph was unable to bring them back to discipline and the holes in their lines were filled with whirling, slashing Scots, who ripped the breaches still wider. When, at last, the English broke, only Sir Ralph and a few other brave souls held their ground and attempted to halt the charge. In mere moments, they were cut down and the Scots moved on to slaughter those now trapped beneath the crag. This only stopped when the last two hundred Englishmen threw down their swords, fell to their knees and begged for mercy.

John Edward dropped his sword and collapsed onto the ground. When he had caught his breath, he wiped the congealing gore from his face. Eck grinned at him, his teeth gleaming white in a face darkened by filth and blood.

'Christ John! You look like a devil! There is scarcely a patch of white left on you.'

John spat as he tasted something unspeakable on his lips. 'You can talk. You have some fucker's ear caught in your hair.'

Eck scrambled his fingers through his matted hair until they closed upon a lump of bloody gristle. He examined it briefly before shivering and throwing it away in disgust. His face then took on a look of sheer panic. 'Shit! Was it my own ear?' John roared with laughter as Eck grabbed at his ears to check that both were still attached to his skull. 'Jesus John!' He exclaimed. 'That's no' funny. I thought it was one of mine.'

Strathbogie then appeared, dragging his axe behind him. 'I can hardly lift the bloody thing.' He explained, as he too sat down upon the ground. 'I don't even have the strength left to loot the bastards.'

The Wallace seemed to have fared better than them, as he strode towards them with his great broadsword across his shoulder, blood still dripping from its tip.

'Two English armies in one day!' He declared cheerfully. 'If we finish the last one before dinner, then we can all go home to our beds.'

'Be careful what you wish for, Sir William.' Prior Abernethy interjected from their rear. 'The good brothers have just informed me that Sir Richard Neville has lifted the siege at Borthwick Castle and marches here with all haste.'

Wallace groaned and his chin dropped onto his chest. 'That'll teach me to hold my tongue. I have no fight left in me.'

The council of war held on the slope of the Langhill was the oddest that John had ever attended. The Scots leaders sat or lay on the earth, their faces, hands and clothes soaked with blood and gore. As the Red Comyn spoke, John could not help but notice that a piece of ragged guts or flesh was stuck upon his cheek.

'The men are dead on their feet and are in no condition to stand again. To attempt it would be madness.'

'I am in agreement with Lord John.' Sir Simon Fraser declared loudly. 'The Neville's

494

men are rested and would cut through ours with ease. We must disperse and make our way from here. We have won two victories here today. Such a great achievement must not be lost. If we engage this third time, then it is only that final defeat that will be remembered.'

'I seem to recall,' Wallace replied, 'the same argument being made only yesterday and then again this morning. If we had heeded those calls, then we would have already been away without a single victory to boast of. Caution may well be the right path to take, but we should not rush into its embrace.'

Sir Henry St Clair cleared his throat and spoke hoarsely, for he had screamed his way into both the day's engagements. 'We must also question the wisdom of flight. Our men are exhausted, as Lord John has said. If we are to disperse, they will be easy prey for the English horsemen, who will be keen to run us down.'

'My men cannot run and can scarcely lift their swords.' John stated plainly. 'If they cannot run, then they must stand and let God decide their fate. I will not order them to hobble away like scalded dogs. They have lifted themselves to greater deeds this day than any one of us could have imagined. They deserve better than to be ordered to flee and die like cowards. The men of Perth will stand here and take whatever is thrown at us.'

'There is another way.' Prior Abernethy was the only man in the company still upon his feet, though he too must have been exhausted, as he had been at the centre of both battles and had marched as far as any man. He was also alone in having taken the trouble to walk to the stream and wash away the worst of the blood and gore from his face and hands. 'Our friend Al tells me that Sir Robert Neville's army marches not here to aid Sir Ralph, but to Roslin Glen where Sir John de Seagrave was encamped. It is likely that they will use the narrow cart track on the other side of this hill. The good brothers tell me that, not half an hour's march from here, that track is bordered on one side by a precipice and on the other by a slope even steeper than this.'

'And if we attack them sideways on down that slope, then they will be trapped against the precipice.' Sir William finished the Prior's argument for him.

'It would seem to be the least of the three evils before us.' John Comyn responded with some reluctance. 'It still remains to be seen if we can rouse our tired and weary men from where they now lie, spent and devoid of all energy.'

John Edward stood with Sir William and watched in admiration as Prior Abernethy addressed the troops and attempted to rouse them to even greater deeds than the miracles already achieved that day. Though they were in desperate need of rest, the men gathered and did the Prior the courtesy of listening to his words. They could hardly have stayed away, as they were well aware of the debt they owed to him and his good brothers and none who had seen him swing his great sword and hack down their enemies would show him anything less than the greatest of respect.

John leaned close to Wallace so he would not be overheard. 'At least he does not claim that God has spoken to him as you did to fire up the men before Stirling.'

'Mock me all you like young Edward, but did the men not sprint across that field and fly at our enemy with furious anger? That is how I recall it.'

'The Prior faces a stiffer test today. I am surprised that so many have even risen to their feet.'

Aye.' Wallace replied. 'Let us hope that he preaches at least half as well as he fights.'

No man could deny that the Prior spoke well. He started both quietly and slowly and then gradually increased his pitch until he roared and raged at the injustices rained down upon the kingdom of Scotland by the unholy, merciless and vicious English King. He did not restrain himself in condemning Edward for the bloody sack of Berwick, when he had ordered the murder of every last man, woman, child and beast in retribution for the resistance they had shown him. He spoke with fury of the desecration of Scone Abbey and of how the Lord of Hosts would hurl vengeance down upon the Plantagenet line for the vile theft of the Stone of Destiny, an outrage which no Christian man could leave unpunished. He brought murmurs of agreement when he talked of Scotland's proud history and elicited cries of anger when he skilfully appealed to each man there by speaking of all that they had suffered under the rule of Edward and his cruel and grasping English officials. Not a man present could fail to be roused by these accusations, as not a single one of them had been untouched by the theft, vandalism, murder, rape and brutality visited upon the population by that ungodly, damnable race.

John, not for the first time, found himself impressed by the Prior. He had roused the men to anger when it had seemed unlikely that he could succeed in rousing them from their rest. Whether it would be sufficient to give them the strength to march over the hill and face a professional and rested English army, which far outnumbered them, remained to be seen.

Abernethy then switched from his vilification of the English King and instead called upon examples from antiquity to inspire the men. He spoke of how King Angus had despaired when faced with a superior English army at Athelstanford and of how God had favoured him with a sign in the form of a cross of white clouds against the blue of the Scottish sky. The appearance of the cross of Saint Andrew had so strengthened King Angus, that he had abandoned his plans to run away and had instead attacked with full vigour and left the corpses of the English scattered across the land.

Abernethy then pointed to the Pentland Hills to the west and cried. 'See! The Lord of Hosts so favours us this day! He has sent us a sign so we will know that we are his sword and his shield and that he commands us to strike down every Englishman who now threatens this blessed land.'

John, along with every man there, turned to the west and gasped at the sight of a great saltire of silver and blue aglow in the setting sun. Swords were drawn and pointed to the sky and the men roared in exultation.

'Will we suffer these sinners to live?' Prior Abernethy roared, his own sword unsheathed and held high above his head.

'No!' The patriots screamed in response.

'Will we charge over that hill and slaughter them all!'

'Yes!' Came the response with great enthusiasm and no little hysteria.

'Will you follow me now!'

'Yes!'

'Kill the prisoners!' Abernethy roared and the men rushed to cut down those Englishman lucky enough to have survived the engagements of that afternoon and morning.

John had to move quickly to reach Sir John de Seagrave and drew his sword to protect him from having his throat cut by those who already approached him with murderous eyes and daggers drawn. Both men watched grimly as hundreds of Englishmen, most with their hands bound behind their backs, were stabbed, slashed and stamped to death. It did not make sense to leave so many able men at their backs when faced with a superior force, but John still winced as the work was done.

'I owe you my life, sir.' Seagrave stammered, his face pale and drawn. 'It is to your credit that you would step in to save an English knight from such savagery.'

'You owe me nothing!' John spat in response. 'I prefer to leave my English knights dead on the field.'

'Jesus!' Wallace exclaimed, as he came to John's side. 'He fair took us by surprise there. Comyn will have only a few prisoners to ransom now.'

'You must give the Prior credit, Sir William. The men's' tempers are up. I see not one man still lying upon the ground.'

'I would never underestimate that man. He told me that he instructed his monks to go and erect a canvas saltire where it would best capture the sunset. He did it while we rested after the struggle in Roslin Glen this morning. He always intended that we would engage all three English forces and thought that it might provide inspiration.'

'He is both wise and courageous.' John responded in awe.

'He's a cunning, old bastard.' Wallace responded wryly. 'But I thank the Lord that he is with us.' Sir William then turned to Jack Short. 'Jack! You are to guard Sir John here till the fighting is done. If he tries to escape, put the point of your sword through his knee. If it is the English who come back over that hill, cut his throat and make off before they catch you.'

Jack Short took no trouble to hide his displeasure. 'He is John Edward's prisoner and so, it is he who should guard him. My place is at your side.'

'Christ Jack!' Wallace snapped back. 'I have not the time for this. I need my best men with me, so you must stay here and guard our prize.'

With that, Wallace and John Edward set off after Prior Abernethy with haste, lest he lead their army into the fight and leave them behind.

Sir John Seagrave let out a low chuckle. 'That must have hurt Jack. I would have been cut to the quick if my master spoke to me the way Wallace just spoke to you.'

'Still your mouth!' Short spat back venomously. 'Or you can be sure that I will still it for you.'

Though the light was fading fast, John Edward crouched in the bushes close enough to make out the features of the English horsemen as the column advanced along the narrow track. When he estimated that approximately four thousand men had passed his position, he signalled to Tom Figgins that his archers should begin their work. Though many of their shafts had been damaged on entering or being retrieved from the bodies of Sir Ralph de Confrey's men, the proximity of the enemy and the downwards trajectory of their fire meant that the Scots archers dropped their opponents with great ease. The English column was so shocked by the silent and unexpected onslaught, that they did not react until after the third or fourth volley had withered their ranks. Unable to see their assailants in the gloom and trapped between the incline and the rock precipice, they fell immediately into indiscipline and barged into

501

their fellows in their haste to find shelter from the shafts that hissed down into them.

Sir Robert Neville and his retinue had trotted on, unaware of the tragedy unfolding to their rear. Only the agonised cries of the fallen brought them to a halt and made them turn to see what was amiss. Sir Robert narrowed his eyes and peered into the gathering twilight in a bid to ascertain why his men had so suddenly fallen into disarray. At first, it seemed that men were randomly falling to the ground and it was only when a great rush of roaring Scotsmen surged down the slope, that Sir Robert realised that he had been taken unawares. He did not hesitate, but drew his sword and spurred his horse on into the fray. He slashed down hard at Scottish skulls and added their corpses and anguished cries to those of his fellow Englishmen. Three times Sir Robert was pushed back by the weight of attacking Scots and three times he immediately turned his horse and forced his way back into the throng. There can be no doubt that he would have been brought down and ripped open by Scottish blades if his attendants had not grabbed his reins and led him away, despite his protests.

Some of those fortunate enough to find themselves at the front or the rear of the column were able to creep off and lose themselves in the darkened forest. Though few of their number would succeed in completing the long and perilous trek to the border when pursued with dogged enthusiasm by Scots with a thirst for English blood, at least they escaped the carnage beneath the escarpment on Glen Roslin's bloody track.

Eck Edward took little joy from his work, as he swung his blades, not like a swordsman or a warrior, but like a butcher attacking unarmed beasts. The panic had swept through the English ranks like a wave and men ran around in search of escape and either threw themselves against the rock face, or onto the waiting Scottish blades. Eck's arm muscles were stretched to the point of snapping and he scythed down with each arm in turn, the horrific rhythm allowing each limb a brief respite before it had to slash down once again. The corpses at his feet were piled so high, he found that he had not the strength to lift his knees over them and so he stayed rooted to the spot and killed all that came within his reach.

Strathbogie and the good Prior Abernethy stood and fought side by side. They gasped to take in great ragged breaths, but took no respite from the struggle. A brave Englishman had chopped his sword down into the Prior's shoulder and, while he tried to pull it from the bone, Strathbogie's axe reduced his skull to pulp, splattering his brains wetly across the faces of the fellows to his rear. The Prior did no more than nod his thanks before he resumed his hacking, the pain of his wound reigniting his fury and causing him to forget the heaviness in his arms.

Scott Edward feared that he had breathed his last when his standing foot landed in a heap of steaming, bloody guts, causing him to slip and

503

crash hard onto the ground. Dazed and without his sword, he looked up to see a snarling, pock-faced Englishman lunge forwards with a wicked, pointed blade aimed at his throat. Scott froze in fright and could only raise his hands in a futile, silent plea. He gazed on in astonishment as that murderous snarl was transformed in an instant into a bloody, torn cavity, by a rock that was propelled viciously into his face. He turned his head to see that Tom Figgins had ordered his archers to pelt the English with stones, now that their quivers had been emptied. He nodded his thanks and received a grim smile in response, before Tom snatched up another heavy stone and pitched it over the Scottish line to come crashing down on English heads.

Sir Simon Fraser knew that the day was won when he saw Englishmen throw down their swords and raise their arms above their heads. The corpses of the English were piled far along the track and Sir Simon could see, in spite of the fast-encroaching darkness, that the greater part of the English force now lay dead, dying or grievously wounded. He ran along the line and commanded that quarter be given and that any man who gave up his sword was to be spared. It is testament to the power of the Prior's words that the patriots did not immediately take this opportunity to spare their already weary limbs from further toil. He had so inspired and enraged them that they stayed hard at the slaughter, their enthusiasm hardly dimmed, even now that their victory was clear. Those Englishmen foolish enough to disarm themselves were immediately cut down, their warm blood melting the ground-frost and turning the track's surface to thick, gory mud. Even when his voice was joined by those of Comyn, Wallace and St Clair, they struggled to divert the patriots from their business and had to resort to pulling men bodily away. The last to be halted in the killing was the good Prior Abernethy. Only when Sir William's hand closed tight around his wrist, did the humble priest lower his sword and bring the battle to its close.

38

As soon as the near five hundred prisoners had been bound and herded beneath the precipice, the patriot men began to lower themselves to the ground to rest, in spite of their closeness to the gore and stench of the slaughter. Sir Henry, greatly relieved that his life, estate and Lady Margaret had been spared from the English attack, ordered men to ride to his home and empty his larders and stores into carts and command his servants to accompany them here with all haste. Within two hours, his servants busied themselves with the lighting of fires, the preparation of food and the distribution of Sir Henry's ale and wine.

Sir John de Seagrave's stomach growled as the aroma of roasting meat reached his nostrils. He doubted that he would be fed and tried to distract himself from his hunger by engaging Jack Short in conversation.

'John Edward seems to be a rough and lowly fellow. How is it that Sir William favours him so?'

Jack did not reply immediately, but his sour expression confirmed that he had taken the dangled bait. 'He has the luck of the devil and just seems to have the knack of being in the right place at the right time.'

'If you were my man, I would not treat you so badly. I think that Wallace takes your service for granted and treats you with contempt.'

'He shows little gratitude, that I cannot deny. I work tirelessly by his side, but it is John Edward he favours, though he is often away on his own business and only returns when it suits his purpose.'

'If Wallace does not look after your best interests, then you must look to them yourself.'

Short stared back at him with distrust in his eyes. The bait was taken and Sir John now jerked at the hook. 'If you knew of the preparations King Edward makes for his invasion, you might well conclude that Wallace's cause is all but lost. With Earl Robert on his side, he cannot fail to prevail. What will happen to you once the kingdom falls and Wallace is cast out? Will he hold you close or abandon you in favour of John Edward?'

Again, Short did not reply, but Seagrave sensed the battle that raged behind his eyes.

'I know a man who would not hesitate to shower you in gold if you were to hold Wallace in contempt and help to bring him low. With a single stroke, he would make you richer than any man here. He is Walter Langton, the High Treasurer of England.'

Jack Short's eyes grew wide with astonishment and beads of sweat formed on his upper lip.

'My God!' Seagrave exclaimed. 'You know him already. I can see it written in your eyes.' He threw his head back and laughed heartily. 'The good Lord sees fit to ensure that my expedition is not entirely fruitless.'

Though drained and weary almost to the point of collapse, it was unthinkable that the patriots would not celebrate their great victory. No army in all of history had fought three battles in a single day and emerged victorious with so few casualties. Sir Henry's servants toiled diligently at their fires and thrust hunks of bread and still sizzling beef into the hands of hungry warriors. With their bellies filled, the patriots were renewed and chattered excitedly amongst themselves, eager to share tales of their own courage and of the great deeds that they had done. As barrel after barrel of Sir Henry's ale were drained empty, there came a great clamour for song. A band of rough-voiced Bordermen sang of Stirling Bridge and of how the brave Sir William had cut the English down. Most men there knew the song and lustily joined in with the chorus, which told of the hated Cressingham and how he had screamed when his flesh was torn away in strips.

The cheers had scarcely died away when Comyn's man, Peter Davidson, was forced up onto his feet. Though his cheeks burned red from so many eyes being set upon him, he took a breath and launched into 'The Tale of Eck the Black'. It mattered not that his voice was hoarse and could scarcely carry the tune, for he had only reached the second line when a thousand voices roared along with his. The glen fair echoed in celebration of Black Eck's deeds upon the field of Falkirk and of how he had defied the hated Edward with a sword in baith his hands.

No gathering involving Scottish warriors and a generous supply of ale would be complete without a touch of melancholy to make salt tears run down men's cheeks. It was Strathbogie who dragged the Cumming boy to the centre and prodded him to sing. The poor lad looked terrified and could not bring himself to raise his head. Men began to lose interest and turned away to converse with their fellows, doubting that such a hairless boy could give them entertainment. Strathbogie gripped his shoulders and whispered sharply in his ear. Young Cumming nodded miserably and took a nervous breath. Though they could scarcely hear him at the start, the sweetness of his voice caused every warrior to turn his head and the chatter fell to silence and they listened, entranced and rapt. The lad sang of a poor, young girl, the most beautiful in the land, she fell in love with a farmer boy, who asked her for her hand. Before they could elope to exchange their vows, her furious father killed the lad, and soon she followed him to heaven, as she could not stand to be so sad. Some men were embarrassed as the tears rolled down their cheeks, others were unabashed and did not wipe their eyes and still others struggled manfully to keep themselves in check. But when the Cumming boy left the last sweet note hanging in the air, there was but a

moment of silence before they roared and
thundered their approval. They snatched him up
onto their shoulders and ran him around the
encampment to take his applause. The poor boy
must have sung the song a dozen times and had
a full barrel of ale poured down his throat before
he was allowed to sleep.

It was later said that the length of the
celebrations, more than the duration of the
fighting, was the real testament to the stamina of
the Scots gathered in Roslin Glen. As the weak,
dawn light filtered through the trees, the scale of
the carnage was fully revealed for the first time.
The English dead lay in piles where they had
fallen and, despite the chill of the winter
morning, the stench of decay filled the air and
clouds of flies rose from the corpses when any
man walked by. The prisoners sat shivering on
the ground alongside the carcasses of their
comrades and watched fearfully as the patriots
began to stir and pull their stiff and sore bodies
up, while groaning and clasping their throbbing
heads in their hands.

John Comyn drank deeply from a skin of
wine and groaned deeply. 'I have such a thirst
and my head fair pounds. As soon as this wine
works its magic, I will be away.'

Sir Simon Fraser looked no better than Lord
John, but could not stomach so much as a whiff
of wine. 'Shall we set the prisoners to burying
the English dead, my Lord?'

'Let them rot!' Comyn declared sourly. 'If
we bury them, some priest will see fit to say

prayers over their graves and they deserve no such blessing. Leave them for the wolves and rats.'

'What of the prisoners?' Wallace enquired. 'I think it best that we put them to the sword.'

Comyn shook his head and grimaced at the thought. 'I doubt that any man here will have the stomach for it this morning. Make them swear never to set foot in Scotland again and set them free.'

'Shall we stripe their cheeks?' Sir Henry enquired, annoyingly bright for one who had drunk as much of his own ale as anyone else. 'That way we will know them again if they do not keep their word.'

John Comyn did not seem to have much enthusiasm for scarring the faces of the prisoners. 'Do it if you must. I doubt that many of them will make it as far as the border without boots or cloaks to keep them warm. Those that are not frozen to death, will likely be killed by any of our countrymen they encounter on their way back south.'

Sir Henry bowed his head in response and strode off to see to the bloody business. The screams of the prisoners as they were cut already filled the air when Comyn mounted his saddle and turned to say his farewells to Wallace and Fraser.

'Go home and see out the winter there. With Bruce in King Edward's pocket, this summer will be harder than any we have yet faced. We will need all of our strength if we are to prevail once again.' Comyn paused and nodded at his allies. 'My spies tell me that the English King spends gold like water in the recruitment of men and the purchase of ships. When he hears of our great victory here, I have no doubt that he will dig even deeper into his pockets.'

39

Sibilla Douthwaite had seldom taken the trouble to climb the hill outside the village to see her son as he tended to his goats. It was not as though she would be rewarded with any conversation. Though the warmth of the summer sun had tempted her out into the open, it was the radiance of her mood which had prompted her to favour her son with her presence and a heel of bread for his lunch. The heavy purse hidden in her petticoats chinked with every step she took. Though not yet across the border, the soldiers in King Edward's army were ravenous and thirsty and had paid good silver for every goat's cheese she had made and every skin of ale she had brewed. Even when she had cut the cheeses in half and added water to the ale, she had discovered that she could still command the same price. Her only regret was that she had no more to sell, but with sufficient coin to see them comfortably through the winter, she found that she could not complain.

She paused for a moment to catch her breath and wipe the sheen of sweat from her brow. She could already see that her son sat in his customary spot. From here he could be mistaken for a hale and handsome lad. It was only when one drew closer, that his vacant eyes and drooling mouth revealed the accident of his birth. Sibilla let out a long sigh and was surprised that the sight of him still raised the sickly pressure of sadness in her breast. She tried to reason that he had been blessed with his skill with the herd, but, despite her many prayers, she still yearned for what might have been if the chord had not tightened around the infant's throat. She climbed on and smiled to see that the old and battered donkey lay in the sunshine at her poor son's side. She often wondered where it had come from and how it was that it had appeared and befriended him when he was abandoned while the accursed Scots had raided and burned the land. Her daughter, whose head was filled with silly thoughts, had suggested that the Good Lord had sent the donkey, so that her brother would not be alone. Sibilla had long ago abandoned her faith in God's capacity for kindness, but found that she smiled whenever this thought crossed her mind. It seemed right that someone above would look out for a poor imbecile.

She eased herself stiffly down onto the grass at her son's side and unwrapped the cloth tied around the loaf. She then tore off a goodly chunk and pushed it into his hand.

'Ba!' Ba droned in response to his mother's presence.

They sat back and watched the column of troops ride and march through the valley below. The sound of their advance crashed up the valley and echoed off its sides like thunder. Sibilla thought that she had never before seen such a wondrous sight. The sun glinted off polished armour and picked out the vivid colours of pennants, surcoats and shields. The column's head had already left the valley and the rear had not yet come into view. Sibilla could claim no expertise, but knew that this army was greater than any that had passed through their valley before.

Overcome by her enthusiasm, she cupped her hands to her mouth and cried, 'Go on now! Give the wicked Scots all that they deserve!' She fell back onto the warm grass in laughter, as her high-pitched call echoed back to her.

The sudden noise disturbed the old donkey and she flicked her mangy ears in fright and brayed in disapproval.

Ba slowly tilted his head towards the beast and responded in kind. 'Hee-haw!'

Sibilla froze in momentary astonishment and then rocked with laughter. It might have taken him more than twenty years, but the doubling of Ba's vocabulary brought his mother immeasurable delight.

Sir John de Seagrave had promised himself that he would not return here, but something had drawn him inextricably back to the scene of his disgrace. The site of his encampment would have been completely unremarkable if it had not been for the sea of bones scattered upon its surface. The Scots had stripped most of the clothes from the corpses, leaving them with only

515

their soiled and bloody undergarments. The elements had withered these away so that only small scraps of greying, ragged cloth still clung to whatever bones the dogs and rats had not carried away to gnaw. Seagrave had to stop himself from counting the skulls, as it only increased his misery.

He had left King Edward's army encamped at Montrose, where they awaited ships carrying the siege engines required to reduce Brechin Castle. With thirty of his own men, he rode, not in the expectation that he could regain the favour of the King, but in the hope that he could avenge himself on those he held responsible for his heavy fall from grace.

'Sir John!' One of his captains called. 'The guide asks if you wish to visit the site of Sir Ralph de Confrey's battle.'

Seagrave glared absently at the ragged, half-starved peasant and found that his gaunt countenance served to irritate him.

'And what, pray tell, would I see there?' He demanded menacingly.

The guide read Sir John's temper accurately, bowed his head submissively and mumbled a quiet and lengthy response.

'What the fuck did he say?' Seagrave demanded impatiently. 'I could not understand a single syllable.'

His captain laughed at the man's discomfort. 'I think he said that the site is worth visiting and that many Scots have already travelled there. He says that the locals call it Shinbanes Field on account of the number of English bones that are scattered there. He says that there are few skulls left, as those not crushed under the wheels of the carts passing through the valley have been carried off by Scots as trophies from the battlefield.'

'By Christ! These people are worse than savages.' Sir John's face turned red with anger as he spoke. 'There were monks amongst the Scots that day, but not one of them has seen fit to give our men a decent, Christian burial. Monk or no monk, I will see every last one of them strung up by the neck.' He turned back to the cowering guide. 'Now lead us to Roslin. I am owed a bloody debt by Sir Henry St Clair and I would see him repay it before the day is out.'

His blood boiled more furiously when he discovered that Sir Henry had already taken his bride and chattels and retreated north, away from the advancing English army. Not a single stick of furniture remained within his house and its very emptiness seemed to mock Sir John. He set his men to burning it, but the gesture was as empty as its chambers. The building still smouldered when he and his men set off in the direction of Abernethy's Priory, with Sir John set on punishing both the Prior and his good brothers for their crimes.

Although a great pot of oats still bubbled and spat upon the fire, Sir John and his men found the Priory completely abandoned, with not a Prior or monk in sight. Abernethy sat high up in the forest and tried to catch his breath. The warning had almost come too late and the last brother was scarcely in the trees when the thundering of hooves sounded down the track. The destruction of the Priory did cause Abernethy some pain, but he found that he was still able to laugh as he watched Sir John roar in frustration and lay furiously into some poor peasant with his heavy boots.

Rank sat on his black charger and looked out at the grey sea off the coast of Aberdeen. 'Why the fuck does he even want to conquer this miserable place?' He asked aloud. 'Tis high summer and the wind still chills me to the bone. It must be a frozen hell come winter.'

Aymer de Valence laughed cheerfully in response. 'You are the last man who should complain about this place. If it were not for the King's ambitions here, you would have not been knighted on the field at Falkirk and the Prince would not have rewarded you with a prime estate in the south. In truth, you should leap down from your horse and kiss the arse of every Scotsman who passes you. If they had not put up such stubborn resistance all these years, you would still be putting a pretty shine on Sir Tarquil's boots.'

Rank could not deny it, he now had lands adjacent to those of Sir Tarquil and led two hundred men of his own. The King had left a trail of devastation and ashes in his wake as he marched his army north and Rank had worked diligently to do as his sovereign commanded and had gathered great riches as he did so. However, he prayed that King Edward was right to describe this as the final Scottish campaign, as he now had riches enough to live out his life in comfort and would be content to enjoy his possessions without ever setting foot in Scotland gain.

De Valence interrupted his train of thought. 'You will soon have to endure this hellish climate without me. As soon as King Edward's ships arrive with silver to pay his foot, I will be free of the responsibility of keeping them from deserting and will march south with Robert Bruce to deal with the forces of Comyn and Wallace and keep them from harrying our men in the borderlands and from raiding into England's northern provinces.'

'I had hoped that the King would turn south and bring them to battle.'

'He is adamant that he will not leave the north until John Comyn's lands have been burned and his holdfasts reduced to rubble. In any casc, he expects the Bruce to show his loyalty by crushing any resistance in the south.'

'Watch your back with that one.' Rank hissed between his teeth. 'He changes sides so often, you cannot be sure whether he is friend or foe.'

Valence laughed heartily. 'Tis true and I will be ever watchful, though I doubt that he will turn on the King while he lays siege to John Comyn's possessions. The only thing he desires more than his crown is to see his rival harmed.'

'How do you fare Sir William?' Comyn boomed with a twinkle in his eye. 'You look thinner about the face and have more grey in your beard than you did when last I saw you.'

'And you, my Lord,' Wallace replied with a grin, 'seem to be having less trouble squeezing into your armour these days.'

Comyn laughed and patted at his stomach with both hands. 'I cannot deny that the English have kept me on my toes. It is hard to pile on the beef when you are harried from your breakfast and denied a moment of peace to have your supper.'

John was glad to see Sir William and the Earl, but their good humour could not make their meeting less grim. With his five hundred men and the thousand with both Wallace and Comyn, their joint forces would do nothing to scare the English and would be even less intimidating if their enemy could see how thin and emaciated they all were. With Aymer de Valence and Robert Bruce chasing them in the south while King Edward raped the north, they had not enjoyed a moment's rest through the long summer and deep into the autumn. They did what they could to harass the English, but the truth of it was that they spent more time running than they did attacking.

'It has been a sare fecht.' Comyn declared, as he sat to warm himself by the fire. 'Edward has reduced all of my strongholds to rubble, thrown hundreds of my men into his dungeons, burned every church, farm and building from Montrose to Kinloss, carried away every valuable and emptied every store of its grain and barley.'

'Aye.' Wallace responded, rubbing his hands together to warm them. 'But the English suffer too. With their lines of supply stretched so far north, their deserters tell us that their men have gone unpaid for months and are constantly on the very edge of starvation. I doubt that he has a quarter of his army left.'

'Tis true, Sir William. That is the fight now. The side that can suffer the longest will be the one that prevails. My people already starve and will know real famine come the winter. The question is, who will starve the quicker? Them or us?'

'Now that the King and his son are encamped with their armies at Linlithgow, it may be that we can increase their suffering and hasten their flight south. My scouts are due here soon and will help us choose our course.'

Al was waved into the presence of the patriot leaders the moment he heaved himself stiffly from his saddle. As ever, he was the scruffiest and most unkempt man in the company. The knees of his trews were caked with earth and leaves and twigs clung stubbornly to his cloak and jerkin. His appearance was not improved by the mud that had been rubbed into his face and his inability to maintain eye contact gave him a shifty countenance. At first glance, no man would consider him to be fit for such exalted company, but all there knew of his skills and that if there was anything to be seen at the Linlithgow encampment, then Al was the only man you could be sure had seen it all.

'They are all there.' Al said with a finality that brooked no argument. 'I saw King Edward's Dragon Banner, the Prince's standard, the

521

pennants of the Earls of Carrick, Pembroke, Ulster and Norfolk and that of Sir John de Seagrave.'

Comyn did not miss the look that John shot in his direction. 'Do not chide me, John Edward. We nobles exchange prisoners for ransom. It is the way of things.'

'How many men and in what condition?' Wallace demanded urgently, eager to get at the heart of the matter.

Al nodded as he attempted to rub some of the crusted earth from his knees. 'I counted less than ten thousand men, including the Irish. Their condition was poor. They stand in rags and I saw that some boiled grass to eat. I lay in hiding for close to two days and saw not a single cart arrive from either the Firth of Tay or from the east. They are close to starving.'

John Comyn clapped his hands to his knees in delight. 'Thank Christ for that! If you had told me that they were fat and rosy cheeked while we starve, I would have mounted my horse and ridden immediately to Linlithgow to make my surrender.'

'You think that we should gather our men for the attack?' It was a measure of Wallace's respect for Al that he would seek his opinion in such an important matter.

Al shook his head and met Wallace's flinty gaze. 'Why would we risk the lives of our men when the English teeter on the very brink of failure? Let us leave their hunger to defeat them. Their men desert nightly, even although sentries are set to keep them imprisoned in the encampment. Our men would be better employed in ensuring that no supply cart reaches them with sustenance.'

'Agreed!' Earl John snapped. 'I will take the road to the east and Sir William will cover the road to the west. Let the winter drive them home!'

Walter Langton kept his eyes fixed firmly on the veins at King Edward's temples. They bulged fatter than ever before and pulsed horribly as he built his rage. He would not have been surprised if one was to pop and send royal blood squirting across the pavilion's floor. He smiled inwardly at this wicked thought, but was careful to keep his face perfectly straight. He was content for the King to be directing his bile in the direction of Aymer de Valence, the young Earl of Pembroke, and dared not risk bringing himself to King Edward's attention when his blood was so high.

'You think to command your King?' Edward demanded, with acid dripping from every word. 'Perhaps I should place this crown upon your head and bow down to take your orders.'

'No, my Lord.' Aymer stuttered. 'I just thought…'

'Ah!' Edward roared, sending a shower of spit into the air. 'You just thought! You just thought that I should lift my robes and run for the border. No matter that I have beggared my kingdom, driven half of my nobles to rebellion and allowed the nation to fall into lawlessness and disorder. You just thought that these things are of no consequence and that I should so easily turn to cowardice and abandon all of our hard-won advantage. Christ! I hang on here by my very fingernails and you would seek to prise them off.'

'My Lord, I must protest.'

'You must protest?' Edward thundered. 'It is I who should protest. I should protest at the weakness of my commanders. It is I who has brought us to this point and forced Scotland to its knees. And now, at the first sight of adversity, you would have me run off and let John Comyn repair what we have so recently destroyed. Perhaps you think that I enjoy constantly returning here to see my ambition thwarted. Perhaps you think I have nothing better to do than follow one failed campaign with another.'

'No, my Lord.' Aymer spluttered, visibly quailing in the face of Edward's scolding. 'It is just that we have neither then men nor the resources to continue.'

Langton had now started to enjoy the spectacle. The young Earl had not the sense to hold his tongue and realise that his position as favourite would ever be a precarious one. Edward only wanted your opinion when it reinforced his own or when he was desperate, needed rescuing and had no ideas of his own.

'It is you who lacks resources, not I.' Edward spat venomously, as he shook his clenched fists in frustration. 'It seems that I have misjudged you. I thought that you had courage and tenacity, but I now see that I was mistaken. I am ever cursed with weak and incompetent commanders, but I will tolerate it no longer. I swore that I would complete my conquest before the year is out and I will keep my vow. I will not let you turn my words to lies. The winning of a crown requires a king's strength and courage and you will see that these will not be diluted by your spineless snivelling. We will winter here in the midst of our enemies, so they will see that they cannot defeat me. My army will encamp on the banks of the Forth at Dunfermline Abbey. Let the miserable Scots see that I defy them by occupying the sacred burial grounds of their kings. The Prince of Wales will similarly flaunt himself on the banks of the Tay and display our power by occupying their crowning place at Scone. The symbolism of their impotence will not be missed.'

'Very well, my Lord.' Aymer de Valence responded, in a tone heavy with resignation.

Edward glared at him with cold, cruel eyes. 'You must stiffen your resolve, my Lord. Hang every deserter to deter their comrades from running. Press every Scots noble to add to our forces. Send south for help. Do all in your power to keep us from defeat. The crown of Scotland is so nearly in our grasp. Do not let it slip away. A fallen crown would be a shameful addition to your family crest.'

Valence turned pale at this suggestion and forced himself to greater enthusiasm. 'I will not fail you, my Lord. Not while blood still runs in my veins. I swear it.'

Langton felt his bowels loosen as King Edward turned his fearsome gaze upon him. 'And you, Langton, must raise yourself to greater efforts. Squeeze every purse and then squeeze them once again. My coffers will be in need of silver if I am to keep an army through the winter. Leave no stone unturned in your search for gold. Send your agents south to arrest merchants and ship owners. Tell their families that they will only be released when the warehouses in the south are emptied and their grain and barley delivered to the Forth and Tay. Spare no cruelty in this task or I will see to it that a fallen crown shall also be you mark. Be not mistaken, I will have my crown or I will perish here. I doubt that history or God above will look kindly upon those responsible for such a failing.'

Langton nodded his agreement in spite of his conviction that the King's demands could not possibly be met. Every line of credit had long since been exhausted, every form of taxation already exploited to its fullest extent and every corner of Scotland looted and left stripped bare. The sale of the ruinously expensive and unused pontoon bridges at Stirling might raise enough coin to last a month, but only if a buyer could be found. Blackmail and extortion might squeeze a further month's funding from the nobles, but at the cost of further antagonising them and leaving him open to their vengeance when King Edward died or abandoned him. In the face of his ruler's unshakeable determination, he set himself to overcoming the insurmountable obstacles in his path.

40

The winter months had been grim for the men of Perth, not merely because of the presence of the Prince of Wales' army on the Tay, but also because the poorness of the harvest had been exacerbated by the early frosts and heavy snowfalls through December and January. John Edward's men had worked tirelessly to harry the English forces, but found that hunger and the elements conspired against them. The English seemed content to spend the winter huddling beneath their walls and only ventured out to provide escorts for their supply wagons. There rare forays were undertaken in strength and so denied the patriots any tempting opportunities for attack. They had to satisfy themselves with capturing messengers or chasing down the ragged English deserters, who now ran in much smaller numbers. A few English ships carried modest numbers of fresh troops, along with the barley and the grain, and, though their numbers were inconsequential, John's heart had sunk to see them even slightly reinforced.

The arrival of the priest with a parchment from Bishop Lamberton had served to raise the men's spirits and they had crowded around in the snow to hear John tell them what it said.

'The Bishop respectfully requests our presence at Saint Andrews in four days from now.' John declared with a smile. 'We are to proceed there in secrecy, on a matter of great import.'

'I'd wager that his spies have told him that King Edward is soon to withdraw.' Scott's grin split his face in two as he shivered from the cold.

'It's about bloody time!' Strathbogie snarled, though he too smiled broadly in expectation of good news. 'I was beginning to think that they would never go.'

They left for Saint Andrews the very next morning, as they expected that the journey through the snow and ice would be long and arduous. It was well that they left early, for they were overtaken by a blizzard that first day and were forced to take shelter in Coupar Angus and wait until the gales abated. They arrived at the castle shortly before the appointed time and hurried inside in the hope of finding a fire to warm their frozen fingers. The scene which greeted them in the hall caused John to shiver from a chill unrelated to the freezing temperatures.

Wallace sat slumped in a chair at one side of the great fire, his shoulders bowed and his head resting in his hands. John Comyn stood at the other side of the grate, his face red and his expression sour. A little way back from the flames stood Robert de Bruce and the Bishops

Lamberton and Wishart. To their rear, Sir Simon Fraser, Malcolm Simpson, Sir Henry Saint Clair and Jack Short stood and curtly nodded their heads in greeting.

Bishop Lamberton waved the Perth men towards the fire. 'Come gentlemen, you must warm yourselves. I am afraid that we started without you, as we thought you were delayed by the snow.'

The atmosphere in the hall was so heavy, it seemed to weigh down upon the men gathered there. John stepped tentatively forward and enquired. 'What has happened? It's like a wake in here.'

Wallace remained in his seat, but turned towards John with a snarl. 'These men invite us to join with them in bowing at King Edward's feet and begging for his mercy. Bruce is here on the King's behalf and comes to offer us terms.'

Comyn rounded on Wallace. 'Our people starve, Sir William, and still King Edward sits with impunity in our midst. Only a fool would fail to recognise that we have lost. We must have the wisdom and the strength to know when we are beaten and bring the nation's unnecessary suffering to an end.'

Wallace shook his head and stared into the fire. 'I cannot bear to look at you when you speak of wisdom and strength. You are neither wise nor strong, but betray your friends and kinsmen just so that you can cling onto your lands and titles. I should fly at you with my dagger drawn, but I am overcome with sorrow at your weakness and your betrayal of our cause.'

530

John found that his legs were trembling and that he could scarcely find his voice. 'Is it true, Lord? Do you abandon us and make common cause with our bitter enemy when we have bled so much and lost so much fighting side by side?'

Comyn shrugged his shoulders violently. 'And what should I do? My people starve, I cannot ask them to suffer more for a cause that is already lost. My God Man! Look at your own men. They are reduced to walking bags of bones.'

John did not need to look. He had seen his men grow thin and gaunt and their cheekbones jut sharply from their greying flesh. He was met with the self-same sight in Scotstoun and every village he rode through on his horse.

Wallace turned and looked directly at him, a thin and hopeless smile on his face. 'But you are yet to hear the worst of it. Earl John will not scamper at Edward's feet alone. Our good Bishops are both determined to do the same. After all their years of whispering and persuading others to risk all and resist, they now wish to spare themselves from discomfort by swearing loyalty to the English King. They invite us here to persuade us to surrender, as that is the price they must pay to enter Edward's peace.'

John turned to the Bishops and saw Sir William's words confirmed in their expressions. Lamberton could not meet his gaze and dropped his eyes to the floor in shame. Robert Bruce then stepped forward and cleared his throat.

531

'Wallace speaks true. King Edward will generously accept an oath of fealty and guarantee no loss of liberty, lands or titles, but only if the rebellion is brought fully to a close.'

Wallace pushed himself to his feet and crossed the floor to face the Bruce. 'I will not betray my country, I will not kneel to your bastard king and will resist him just as long as there is breath in my body. A tyrant can only rule if men like us are weak enough to let him.'

Sir William was standing so close to him that Robert Bruce had to look up to meet the taller man's gaze. 'That is just as well, Sir William, for you are excluded from the offer. It seems that, while Edward is content to forgive the outrages at Falkirk and Roslin, his magnanimity does not extend to the slaughter at Stirling Bridge. He cannot forget that you humiliated him before his enemies in France, brought shame upon the house of his great friend the Earl of Surrey and tore the flesh from the bones of his favourite Cressingham. You are to be outlawed and will be hunted wherever you may hide.' The Bruce then turned towards the others gathered there. 'That is the choice left to all here. Agree to swear loyalty to Edward as your sovereign, or be cast out and hunted down.'

'And be not mistaken, my friends.' Wallace said with scorn. 'It will not be Englishmen who snap at your heels. It will be Scots under the command of the traitors standing here who will seek to bring you to the noose. Each of them will fall over themselves in their haste to capture you and so prove their loyalty and gain King

Edward's favour. Think carefully before you decide, for you may end up fugitive in your own land.'

Robert Bruce's cheeks reddened at these words and told John that Wallace had spoken true.

'I will not turn traitor.' John announced defiantly. 'I have seen too many fall at English hands to bring myself to betray their souls.' Strathbogie, Eck, Al, Malcolm Simpson and Sir Simon Fraser joined their voices with his.

'Be not hasty.' Lamberton implored, having finally found the strength to overcome his shame and pull his eyes up from the floor.

'It is you who is too hasty in abandoning your countrymen. I do not know how you can stand the shame. It sickens me just to share your company and I find I must take myself away.' Wallace then spun on his heel and marched out of the hall without looking back.

John caught up with him as he made ready to mount his horse.

'You cannot go home now, John. They will hunt us just as soon as they have knelt at Edward's feet. I will make for the forest at Selkirk and would urge you to melt into the forest at Perth. Make your camp at the place where we first met and I will find you there when the snows have gone.' Wallace then embraced him and pulled himself into his saddle. 'Do not lose heart, John Edward. We are without friends now, but we will find others where we can. You must keep faith and fight on.'

John watched him ride off with Malcolm
Simpson and Jack Short at his side. The ice in
his heart was matched by that in the wind and it
was all he could do to keep himself from
weeping.

The return to Scotstoun was the bleakest any of
them could remember. The feasts and
celebrations held in the square after Stirling, the
rape of Northern England, the knighting of Sir
William, the diplomatic missions to Paris and
Rome and the great victories at Roslin were
mere ghosts of memories. John had to force
himself to hold his head up, as his news weighed
heavily upon the shoulders of people already
deep in their suffering. Neither the villagers nor
the fighting men objected to his decisions, as the
seriousness of his expression told them that
there was no other choice if they were to
survive. He ordered fifty of the fighting men to
accompany him and told the rest to bury their
weapons and play the part of simple peasants
when either English patrols or treacherous Scots
found their way to the village. Such was the
threat, they did not even stay the night. They
said their goodbyes and, once their horses were
loaded with provisions, they immediately rode
out into the snow and set about hiding
themselves away.

The old camp seemed much smaller than
when they had left it all those years ago. John
smiled when they entered it through the ravine
and saw that the stream bed was still strewn with
the bones and skulls of the Englishmen who had

attacked them there. The bones lay thicker at the ravine's end and Strathbogie pointed out that it was he who had led the desperate defence at its edge. He also pointed out that the bones there were more splintered from his axe and those of his men.

The first nights were miserable, as the embankments did little to soften the bitter winds and life only became bearable when they had chopped enough wood and gathered enough thick moss to throw up shelters which gave them some little warmth. Tom Figgins and his small band of archers soon proved their value by bringing in sufficient game to supplement the oats and grains carried off from the village. Al kept the men busy by posting sentries and sending out scouts to give them warning of any impending attack. It cannot be said that the men were entirely without their comforts. Each week, a few men were given leave to travel secretly back to Scotstoun under the cover of darkness. That way, John saw his Lorna, Al saw enough of his Mary to leave her belly swollen with child and a happy Tom Figgins saw all that the widow Cumming had. By the time the snows melted and buds began to appear on the trees, the camp had settled into a comfortable routine and no Englishman or Scots traitor had seen fit to disturb their peace.

With no other visitors for months, the arrival of Sir William Wallace was the cause of no small excitement. As John went to embrace him, he could not help but notice the change in him. He was even thinner than before and his eyes were haunted and constantly flicked around him, as though he feared an imminent attack.

'Come sit at the fire!' John said as he waved at Wallace and Malcolm Simpson to sit. 'Tom here brought down a stag just yesterday, so you must eat your fill of meat, Sir William.'

Wallace emitted a hollow laugh. 'You should not call me that. You well know that it was the Bruce who bestowed the title upon me. I have no doubt that the honour has long since been rescinded.'

The two men attacked their meat like ravenous wolves and seemed not to notice as the juices ran down their chins and darkened their beards. When their frantic chewing finally slowed, John asked them how the winter had been.

Wallace shook his head and sucked the meat juices from his moustache. 'Bad! The longest we stayed in one place was a week. The whole forest is infested with hunters after the bounty on our heads. Christ! You would not believe it. Not three weeks ago, our pursuers were not English or Scots, but French! They were good. They used hounds and came close to capturing us. We were lucky to catch them in an ambush and, when we tortured the survivors, they told us that King Edward has offered so much gold, people will cross seas to try and claim it.'

'Their hounds were absolutely delicious.' Malcolm Simpson declared with relish. 'We were so hungry we could scarcely wait for them to roast right through. The first we ate was still pink, but it was tasty all the same.'

'Aye!' Wallace agreed. 'These bastards turn us into animals, but each day that we survive makes a mockery of them.'

'Have you been raiding and attacking the English?' John enquired, a little sheepishly, as he and his men had not done so for months.

Wallace again shook his head. 'There are hardly any English here. It seems that King Edward is happy to let Comyn and Bruce do his work for him. I had heard tell that Lamberton has been made third Guardian and is charged to keep the peace between our two treacherous magnates. The appointment will bring him no end of torment and grief, but it is no less than he deserves.'

They talked long into the night and, fuelled by a bitter, cloudy ale brewed by Scott Edward, they relived past glories and commiserated over their defeats. Wallace seemed to regain his old spark and brought cheers from the men with the tale of how he had slain the cruel Sheriff Heselrig at Lanark. He spoke of that vile man's penchant for cruelty and his desire to stretch the necks and chop off the heads of as many Scots as he could manage. He told of how that villainous and arrogant man had wept and cried for mercy as Wallace dismembered him. They dissolved into howls of laughter when Wallace declared that he fondly remembered the day that Heselrig was dismembered. John thought that the rhyme was not so witty, as he had heard it from Wallace before, but the camp was not awash with entertainment and he laughed as heartily as his comrades.

Wallace resisted all entreaties to tarry longer in the camp and saddled his horse at the break of dawn the very next day.

'Come John!' He instructed. 'Walk with me a little, I would speak with you before I take my leave.' When they were out of the hearing of their fellows, Wallace stopped and turned to John and held him in his flinty gaze. 'I would not have blamed you if you had taken the Bruce's offer at Saint Andrews. The path we have taken is full of peril and darkness and may well lead to only pain and death.'

'I would take pain and death before I would betray my people.'

Wallace nodded slowly. 'You do not need to tell me that. It seems that there are precious few who share our strength or are as true of heart. I want you to know that, though I have valued your loyalty, I have treasured your friendship more. The knowledge that I do not fight alone has kept me going through the hard winter months when all else was despair. I want you to have this, as a token of my esteem.'

John watched in astonishment as Wallace extracted the gold cross from his jerkin and pulled the thick, gold chain over his head. He held up his hand in puzzled protest.

'What are you saying, Sir William? It sounds as if you are saying goodbye.'

Wallace laughed sadly and closed John's fist around the cross and chain. 'In my youth, I was an inveterate and irredeemable gambler. I would wager on fights, tests of strength, horses, archery and anything else I could entice another man to

538

risk his silver on. As well as impoverishing myself, I learned about the odds of winning and those of losing. I know that the odds are now stacked so heavily against me, my luck will not last much longer. I have separated myself from my men so that I do not bring them down with me. Now I am left with only those so loyal I cannot shake them off.' John interrupted him to protest but Wallace waved him to silence. 'I do not give up, John Edward. I will fight until my dying breath, but it would be madness to think I can evade my legion of enemies forever.'

John blinked back the tears that forced themselves into his eyes. 'It has been an honour to stand with you, Sir William.'

'No, John.' Wallace replied. 'The honour has been all mine. In everything I have achieved, you have never been far from my side. If you wish to honour me, then do as you do now. Keep faith with the cause and ever fight on, fight on. As long as men such as you refuse to bend, the light of freedom will be undimmed.'

John nodded and rubbed at his eyes. 'Know that I will fight on, Sir William. Your example will ever light my path, the more so when the world is dark.'

'Why so grim, Lord Bishop?' Sir John de Seagrave enquired cheerfully. 'People flock from miles around to see the King's siege engines in all their glory, but I see no wonder in your expression, only darkness and despair.'

'It is six long years since we defeated the Scots at Falkirk, yet I find myself still trapped in this damnable country. The King refuses to cross the border until every last stronghold is in English hands and he insists that I must stay at his side until the job is done.' Langton turned and spat to show his disapproval.

'Do not despair, Lord Bishop. You will see your London whores before much longer. The thirty men behind the walls of Stirling Castle cannot endure for long. With twelve trebuchets working from dawn till dusk, it can be only a matter of days before they offer their surrender.'

'You have been saying that for almost four months now.' Langton replied bitterly. 'The ground was still white with frost when the first stones crashed into the castle walls. Now we suffer through what passes for summer here and still the walls remain stubbornly upright. I seem to remember that it was a full month ago when you promised that the Greek Fire would cause Sir William Oliphant and his garrison to throw down their arms in fright. Despite the great cost of that attempt, Sir William and his walls still defy us and block my path home.'

'But, what a spectacle, Lord Bishop! The explosions lit up the night and boomed so loud they were heard ten miles away. Surely a worthy testament to the power and majesty of our King.'

Langton shook his head. 'All light and sound without any consequence. The walls were blackened here and there, but did the garrison rush out and offer us the castle keys? No! They remain within and we remain without.'

'Put a smile upon your lips, Lord Bishop. When Master James of St George has finished his construction, we will see the greatest trebuchet in the world turn those walls to rubble.'

'The Warwulf?' Langton spat in derision. 'You are as bad as the King with his obsession for these contraptions. Master James burns through gold faster than a Cardinal burns through candles. If it were up to me, I would save the gold and leave the bastards to starve. It's not as if they are any threat to us.'

Sir John turned his head at the sound of approaching hoofbeats. 'Sir Aymer!' He cried. 'What brings you here with such urgency?'

Sir Aymer de Valance beamed with delight. 'I have glad tidings for the King. Sir William Oliphant is to surrender. Even as we speak, the men of the garrison rub ashes into their scalps and cast off their shoes in readiness for throwing themselves at their sovereign's feet and begging for his mercy. The conquest of Scotland is now complete.'

Langton and Seagrave looked at one another in disbelief and then followed the young knight, as they were eager to be present at such a historic moment. They arrived in time to hear King Edward's response.

'Tell the garrison to wash the ashes from their heads and put their shoes back upon their feet.' Edward commanded sourly.

'But, they surrender, my Lord.' Valence replied in confusion. 'The war is won!'

541

Edward put his arm around Valence's shoulders and turned him towards the site of the Warwulf's construction. 'Do you see that fifty men work day and night upon enough oak to build a ship?'

'Yes, my Lord.' Valence replied.

'Do you imagine that they give their labour to their King without taking coin in return?'

'No, my Lord.'

'Do you think that the oak was felled, dressed, cut, shaped and transported here for nothing more than the King's approval?'

'No, my Lord.'

'Do you believe that the men who have stripped the lead from the roof of every church and cathedral from Berwick to Aberdeen to make the counterweights did so for the love of their King alone?'

'No, my Lord.'

'Do you imagine that I would spend such vast quantities of gold and then walk away with the great weapon untested?'

'No, my Lord.' Valence replied miserably.

'No, my Lord!' King Edward replied. 'Now get back on your horse and tell Sir William that his surrender is premature. The Scots nobles will think twice about rebelling once they have seen the Warwulf reduce their greatest stronghold to a miserable pile of stones.'

Langton groaned inwardly as he realised that his departure was to be delayed further while the King amused himself with his toys.

41

Jack Short knocked on the heavy wooden door
three times, paused, and then knocked a further
three times. He glanced quickly up and down the
Glasgow street as the door was unbarred and
opened to admit him.

'You were gone a while Jack.' Wallace said
as he barred the door behind him. 'I was starting
to wonder if you had been captured.'

'No, nothing like that.' Short replied as he
started to empty his sack onto the rough,
wooden table. 'I got mutton, bread, apples and a
flagon of wine.'

Wallace's face lit up and he reached out for
the bread and the wine. 'I have scarcely moved a
muscle these past few days, but I find that I have
a terrible thirst and my stomach growls from
hunger.'

'Drink, Sir William, and I shall make a stew
from the mutton and the apples.'

Wallace tore off half the loaf and filled his
goblet with the wine. 'I think I have hidden here
for long enough. At dusk tomorrow, I mean to
set off north and go to see John Edward and his
men in the forest at Perth.'

Short sliced at the fatty mutton and threw chunks of it into the pot already heating on the fire. 'I'll go out tomorrow and purchase the horses for our journey.'

'No need Jack.' Wallace responded, his mouth already filled with bread. 'Malcolm Simpson will accompany me there. You should head home to your family and I will send word should I have need of you.'

Jack scowled as he hacked at the last of the raw meat. 'I will await your call with baited breath.' He then reached into his jerkin and pulled out a carefully folded square of parchment, which he unfolded to reveal a small pile of red powder. He hesitated for a moment, took a long breath and then tipped the powder into the stew. He then stirred at the pot to stop its contents from burning and sticking to the bottom.

'That smells good Jack!' Wallace exclaimed, as he wiped the crumbs from his beard. 'I'm famished.'

'I do hope that it will be to your taste, Sir William.' Short replied with a sickening grin on his face. 'You deserve a feast such as this.'

'What? Are you not joining me?' Wallace asked, as Jack placed the heaped, wooden platter before him.

'No, Sir William. You will need your strength for the journey ahead. I will deny you not a single bite of this.'

Wallace nodded and began to spoon the steaming stew into his mouth. 'It has a peculiar taste. Are you sure that the mutton was not on the turn?'

'It is not the mutton that turns, Sir William.' Jack replied sourly.

Wallace's eyelids began to droop and he rubbed furiously at his face in an attempt to revive himself. 'Jack! I am not well. I am sickening.'

'You are sickening, Sir William, and it's no-one's fault but your own. You have treated your most loyal servant with contempt and must now pay the price for your scorn.'

Wallace sagged forwards at the table until his face was almost in his stew. Jack reached forward and slapped him hard across the cheek, bringing him woozily back to consciousness. 'I would have you know that you are betrayed, Sir William, just as I have been so cruelly betrayed by you. It need not have turned out this way and you only have yourself to blame. If my master does not look after my best interests, then I can only see to them myself.'

Jack let Wallace's head fall back onto the table and went to unbar and open the door. The three men who entered the house each took a moment to gaze upon Wallace's inert and stupefied figure. 'You two, go and fetch the cart!' Jack ordered briskly, before turning to the third man. 'And you must ride now and take word to your master. Do not halt or be diverted from your purpose. We will have need of his protection before this business is done.'

The dark sky was already edged with the light of dawn, when the outline of Dumbarton Castle came into view. Jack Short exhaled sharply in relief, as he had been rigid with tension throughout the cart's rumbling, rattling journey west. The fear of being stopped on the road, with Wallace bound and covered in the bed of the cart, had caused his guts to twist painfully as they made their way through the darkness. He told himself that the worst was over as he approached the castle gates and called out to the sentries to go and wake their master.

Sir John Menteith, Sheriff of Dumbarton, strode into the courtyard half-dressed and still trying to wipe the sleep from his eyes. 'This had better be good!' He snapped with irritation. 'I was not long in my bed and your disturbance is not welcome.'

'It may be even less welcome when you see what I have brought for you.' Jack replied, as he pulled the filthy blanket from the figure lying at his feet.

Menteith peered at the shape in the half-light and then stepped back in fright. 'No! You will not bring this to my door! Take him away before I have my men cut your throat. I will be hated by every common man in the kingdom if I accept this prisoner. Go! Take him to some other fool. I will have no part in this.'

Jack Short smiled and shook his head slowly. 'My master told me that you were weak and craven and that you would react this way. Tis for that very reason that I despatched a rider to carry news to him of your capture of Sir William Wallace.'

'You are a fool to tell me of this. I will have the messenger ridden down and your corpse thrown into the sea. I will not be so entrapped.'

'You are already too late, Sir John.' Short replied. 'The messenger left from Glasgow many hours ago. He will already be across the border and the Lord High Treasurer will have word of your prisoner before many more hours have passed. You can murder me and release Sir William from your custody, but your treason will be known and you will hang for it.'

Menteith looked around himself in panic, as though he expected the courtyard stones to provide a solution to his predicament. 'Langton!' He hissed between clenched teeth. 'But why pick me? If Wallace was taken in Glasgow, why not imprison him there?'

Jack laughed at Menteith's discomfort. 'It seems that the Treasurer did not trust the Bishop of Glasgow to be loyal to his King. On the other hand, he was certain that you would be too spineless to do anything other than comply. Your present agitation tells me that his judgement was most accurate.'

'You will not find me spineless when I split you with my sword.' Menteith hissed in fury. 'I may have no choice in this, but Langton will not blink to hear that you are murdered.'

'The Lord High Treasurer has given me his protection. I am to tell you that he will seek retribution if a single hand is put upon my person.'

547

'You unnatural bastard! This night's work will put a stain on my family's name that may never be washed away.'

'Langton also told me to tell you that you will be richly rewarded for your part in this. He said that he would shower you with gold.'

'Leave my castle!' Menteith barked. 'I swear that I will cut you down if I ever lay eyes upon you again. You betray your master and destroy my reputation with your betrayal. Go now! Before I have you thrown from my walls!'

Jack turned and aimed a kick at Wallace's back. 'My master is now in Newcastle and I will ride there directly to tell him of your cooperation.'

Menteith watched as Jack Short rode out through his gates and onto the road south. He then had his men carry Wallace into a cell and chain him to the wall. 'Ready my escort!' He ordered tersely. 'We will take the prisoner south before anyone learns of his presence here.' He looked down at Wallace before adding, 'Keep him hooded! I do not think I could stand to look him in the eye when he awakens. It would have been better if he had fallen in battle and not be brought low in this foul manner.'

The Lord High Treasurer's boots were still thick with mud when he was ushered into the King's presence. Edward was not to be disturbed as he toured the northern shrines to give thanks for his conquest of Scotland, but Langton had decided to ignore protocol so that he would be the first to deliver the news.

'Walter!' The King cried in greeting. 'It is so good to see you. I will enjoy an audience with one who does not come to me with open hands in search of repayment for men or grain sent north to Scotland. The nobles are like little birds in the nest, who never cease in their squawking and whose beaks are ever open.'

Langton hesitated for a second, as he had intended to ask the King for lands in Northern England. His expression must have given him away, as the King's eyes narrowed in suspicion.

'Not you as well, Walter? I thought that you at least would come with your beak firmly closed.'

'No, my Lord.' Langton responded with a bow of his head. 'I come to give, not to take.'

'Ah! That is just as well, for I have grown tired of men's greed and will enjoy taking for a change. What gift do you have for your King?'

Langton smiled and paused for effect. 'I have more than one, my Lord. I think both will bring you pleasure.'

'Out with it then, Lord Bishop. You know that I cannot stand to be kept in suspense.'

'My first gift to you, my King, is news from Scotland. As we two stand here, the outlaw William Wallace is in chains. I have him within my control and will have him transported to London for execution in a matter of days.'

'Alive? You have taken him alive?'

'Yes, my Lord. You said that you would see him in chains and I have worked tirelessly to make it so. The messenger arrived with news of my success while I was at my lunch. I left my meat upon the table and rode here without delay.'

It was often difficult to tell the difference between the King's brown-toothed grin and his snarl, but on this occasion Langton had no doubt.

'You can now have this traitor crawling at your feet, with all the people of London watching on as he grovels on the ground.'

Edward shook his head. 'I cannot soil my own hands with this. It would not be seemly for a great King to be involved with the execution of a common outlaw. I must be kept apart from this and have no involvement whatsoever.'

'As you wish, my Lord.'

'Though there are certain requirements which must be met.'

'Of course, my Lord.'

'There must be a public trial so that justice is seen to be done. There must be evidence of his many crimes, including those against the church. His reputation must be so diminished that even the most rebellious Scot will despise him and hold him in contempt. Most importantly of all, he must be publicly broken and made to beg for mercy. A man cannot be a martyr if he dies a snivelling, broken mess. You must see to this Walter. I will hold you responsible for it.'

These words caused Langton's enthusiasm for Wallace's execution to evaporate. It was, in his experience, best to avoid being held directly responsible for anything where success and failure could be easily discerned. 'It might, my Lord, be unseemly for a man so closely connected with the King to be so directly involved in this matter. Some might take it that I represent you in the business.'

Edward tapped his index finger on his chin in contemplation. 'You are right, of course. I must maintain a respectable distance. Still, I must have someone reliable to oversee the trial. Who would you suggest?'

'What about John de Seagrave? He is keen to regain your favour.'

Edward arched his eyebrows as he weighed the suggestion. 'I suppose we might trust him with this. It is not as if he could lose a whole army in overseeing a simple trial and execution.'

'Precisely, my Lord.' Langton replied. 'I will set the wheels in motion.'

'Very good Walter. Now, what is this second gift? I doubt that it could match the first.'

Langton clapped his hands together and four servants came into the room and laid a great, folded cloth upon the chamber's stone floor. Langton ordered them to unfold it and spread it out flat before the King. 'I had this made for you, my Lord. Twenty craftsmen have toiled at it for five long months. I thought that you might hang it upon the palace walls.'

Edward stood and drew himself to his full, impressive height and watched as the tapestry was unfolded. The quality of the piece was immediately evident, the colours were vibrant and the figure at its centre was unmistakably that of the King himself. Edward took his time in examining it and Langton had to restrain himself from asking for his verdict.

'It is beautiful Walter. I can see that this panel represents my victory at Falkirk. The embroidery is so fine I can make out a hundred individual arrows as they fill the sky above the Scots. This one here is Stirling castle, with the Warwulf sending Greek Fire streaming into the sky. But the motto, Walter, Edwardus Primus Scottorum Malleus, where does that come from?'

'It is what the nobles are calling you, my Lord. The Hammer of the Scots.' It was true that some nobles were indeed using the name, but there were few of them and their number included only those beholden to Langton or those willing to be cringingly obsequious in order to win his favour.

'The Hammer of the Scots.' Edward repeated as he stroked his beard. 'Tis not as impressive as Alfred the Great or Richard the Lionheart, but I like it better than William the Bastard or Ethelred the Unready. Not a bad legacy I suppose.'

'Not at all bad, my Lord.' Langton replied. 'Not for a conquering king who brought all of Britain under his rule.'

'You have ever been loyal and true to me, Walter. You must name your reward.'

'There is a vacant estate just north of Newcastle, my Lord.'

'Say no more, Walter. Have the papers made up and I will sign them in your favour.'

Malcolm Simpson found John Edward in Scotstoun and brought him the news of

552

Wallace's capture. Andrew Edward summoned a meeting of the village in the square, so that a course of action could be decided upon. A few voices were raised against anything which risked bringing any trouble to the village. A few others shouted for arms to be snatched up and horses saddled to free Sir William from his captors. Most stayed silent and waited to see which way the wind would blow.

'It would be madness to ride into England to attempt to free Wallace.' Andrew Edward argued. 'I like this no better than you, John, but you would be hopelessly outnumbered and in a land that is not your own. As soon as you open your mouth, they will know that you are Scottish and you will join Sir William in an English prison, or worse.'

'Aye.' Angus Edward agreed. 'It would be suicide. You could not hope to succeed. If challenged, you would have to respond and your voice would give you away in an instant. I cannot see how you can get around that.'

'Perhaps I can help.' A voice piped up from amongst the crowd of villagers. Sir Nigel Thwaite pushed his way through to the front and stood before the Edwards. 'I believe that I could lead a small party across the border and, if challenged, pass myself off as a knight with lands in Scotland leading his retinue south. My family name carries some weight and should be sufficient for our purpose.'

Angus Edward had never been completely comfortable with the Englishman living in their midst and his eyes narrowed with suspicion.

'And how can we know that you are to be trusted? Anyway, I doubt if Esmy will let you out of her sight.'

Sir Nigel was ever cheerful and Angus Edward's words diminished this not one bit. 'I do not see that you have much choice and, for your information, it was Esmy who suggested it to me.'

John Edward leapt to his feet. 'It is decided then. I will take ten men and Sir Nigel can lead us south. Go and ready our horses, we leave immediately.'

Eck Edward clapped Sir Nigel upon the shoulder. 'Thank you, Sir Nigel. Though I am surprised that you are willing to risk all your comforts here on a fight that is not your own.'

Sir Nigel smiled and gave Eck a conspiratorial wink. 'I confess that it is the fear of having my comforts withdrawn that has driven me to this action. In any case, there is no risk for me.'

'How do you mean?' Eck responded in confusion.

'My Esmy, as you well know, has the gift of second sight. If she saw that any harm was to come to me, she would not let me go.'

Within the hour, John led seven Scotstoun fighting men, Malcolm Simpson and Sir Nigel out of the square and on towards the road to Perth.

Lorna Edward slipped her arm around her mother's waist and pulled her close. 'Why do you look so afraid? I know that you would not have allowed Nigel to go if there was any

554

danger to his life. You must know that he will return safe.'

Esmy turned to her daughter and tears welled in her eyes. 'I do not know that he will come back safely to me.' She paused to gather herself and rubbed her hand across Lorna's swollen belly. 'But I know that if he does not go, John Edward will not return and your babies will have no father.'

Lorna gazed at her mother in astonishment and fat tears spilled onto her cheeks. 'Oh, Maw!' She cried and pulled her into a tight embrace.

Sir John de Seagrave leaned against the damp cellar wall and watched impassively as three of his men rained blows onto the body of the manacled Wallace.

'Not his face!' He ordered tersely. 'I do not want it known that he was beaten before his trial. Just do enough to sap his strength and leave him too pained and weary to show defiance. No matter if he cannot stand, we can hold him up, but make sure that he is conscious.'

He let his men continue for a few moments more and then ordered them from the cellar. He looked down at the filthy, gasping creature and felt nothing but contempt.

'You can expect no mercy here.' He stated flatly. 'Just as you offered none to the men you slaughtered at Roslin, though you will not die as well as they. You would be well advised to remain silent during your trial and to beg for mercy before the executioner. If you do not, I will see that your death will be long and your suffering excruciating.'

Wallace's breathing was ragged and it took some effort for him to raise his head and fix his piercing, blue eyes on those of Seagrave. 'You can torture me all you like, but none of it will change the fact it is because of me that the bones of fifty thousand Englishmen now lay scattered across good Scots earth. My life seems but a small price to pay for all of theirs.'

Wallace's stubborn bravado caused Seagrave to exhale sharply with annoyance. Langton's instructions had been clear. The wretched outlaw was to be humiliated, his reputation was to be destroyed and his body was to be mutilated. There could be no defiant martyrdom. He called for his men and commanded them to return to their task with greater vigour.

By the time Wallace was dragged into Westminster Hall, he could barely stand and the guards on either side of him held his arms to keep him upright. A crown of laurel had been pushed onto his head to mock him as the king of outlaws. Seagrave noted his condition with satisfaction and made his way to the bench to take his place alongside his fellow judges, Peter Mallore, Justiciar of England, Ralph de Sandwych, Constable of the Tower of London, John le Blunt, the Mayor of London and Judge John de Bacwell. Mallore, a small, grim and shrivelled man in the habit of wearing a black, felt cap, was to lead proceedings.

Seagrave leaned towards him and whispered in his ear so that the gathered nobles would not overhear and repeat his words to King Edward. 'Let us get this over quickly before he gathers himself. You read the indictment and then I shall pronounce the sentence.'

Mallore nodded and hammered his thin hands upon the table to bring the nobles to silence. He then read from the parchment before him and detailed the many charges levelled against the outlaw Wallace. Seagrave fought to conceal his irritation and impatience. Mallore's scratchy and reedy voice vexed him at the best of times and he could only will him on to increase the pace of his delivery. It was, he would concede, necessary that there was a thorough examination of all the traitor's crimes, but it was more important that the wretch did not have time to recover his wits before the sentence was passed.

Mallore droned on and on as he recited the long list of outrages committed against the authority of King Edward. The list included the vile murder of Sheriff Heselrig, the sack of Scone, the siege of Dundee Castle, the slaughter before Stirling, the pillage of Northern England, the bloody murder and mutilation of Cressingham, the Battle at Falkirk, the siege of Lochmaben Castle and the Battle of Roslin. It was just as Mallore spoke the name of Roslin that Seagrave became aware that Wallace, although his head was still bowed and his body still sagged in the grip of his guards, was staring at him across the hall, with just the hint of a smile upon his lips. He felt his stomach lurch as he realised that the prisoner had regained his

557

senses. He tapped the table with his fingertip to urge Mallore to recite more quickly.

Mallore continued on and detailed Wallace's sins against civilians and both God and church, when he had led his army across England's northern border and spared neither age nor sex, monk or nun. Seagrave felt some measure of relief when he saw that the Justiciar's finger had almost reached the bottom of the parchment, as he read out the most heinous charge of all, that of treason against the King. Mallore's quiet monotone had almost lulled the watching nobles into sleep and many of them were startled when a strong, clear voice sounded out and echoed around the hall's walls and vaulted ceiling.

Wallace's eyes bored into Seagrave's as he spoke. 'I cannot be a traitor, for I owe Edward no allegiance. He is not my Sovereign. He never received my homage and, whilst there is still life in this persecuted body, he will never receive it. To the other points whereof I am accused, I freely confess them all. As Governor of my country I have been an enemy to its enemies. I have slain the English. I have mortally opposed the English King. I have stormed and taken the towns and castles which he unjustly claimed as his own. If I or my soldiers have plundered or done injury to the houses or ministers of religion, I repent me of my sins, but is not of Edward of England that I shall ask pardon, but of God and God alone.'

Mallore had tried manfully to silence the prisoner, but found that his thin voice was drowned out by the strength of Wallace's.

Seagrave cursed at the sight of the nobles' open-mouthed astonishment and signalled to the guards to shut him up. A hard jab into his shattered ribs caused him to gasp and his eyelids to flutter as he edged into unconsciousness.

Seagrave moved quickly to deliver the sentence. 'William Wallace, you have been found to be a traitor and will suffer a traitor's death. You will be stripped and taken from this place to be dragged by horses to the Elms at Smithfield. There you will be hanged and released on point of death to be emasculated and to have your bowels drawn from your body and burned before your face. Once you have suffered these agonies, you will be beheaded and your body will be cut into four parts. As a warning to others, your head will be displayed on a spike on London Bridge and your limbs will be so displayed in Newcastle, Berwick, Stirling and Perth.'

Seagrave gave a curt nod and two of his men drew their daggers and cut Wallace's clothes from him. The gathered nobles gasped in shock, not at his bruised and broken body, but at his public nakedness. Seagrave marvelled at how a man could be so humiliated and brought so low, just by having his naked body exposed to the eyes of others. He followed on as the traitor was dragged outside and tied to the wooden hurdle. He mounted his horse and watched on as Wallace was dragged through the streets filled with baying Londoners, who crowded round and fought with one another in their desperation to aim kicks, stones and vegetables at the prisoner as he passed. The route taken to Smithfield was circuitous and chosen deliberately to expose the traitor to as many of London's inhabitants as possible. By the time the horses were reined in at the place of execution, Wallace was battered and bleeding, his limbs badly skinned and he was barely conscious. The crowd roared in a state of near frenzy when the traitor was suspended from the gallows, his legs kicking wildly as his face turned bright crimson for the want of air. Their shouts increased in volume when he was dropped hard onto the wooden platform and the executioner approached him with a long, sharp knife. They shrieked and thundered their approval when his manhood was cut away and the bloody flesh held aloft for their inspection. They fell to silence when the hooded executioner sliced into Wallace's stomach and howled in nasty and perverse delight when he reached in and pulled the steaming intestines from their cavity.

Seagrave was standing close by when the entrails were dropped into the brazier to steam and sizzle on the glowing embers. Wallace gasped and shuddered in his agony, but Seagrave thought that he spoke and leaned in closer to try and hear him over the howling mob. The words were faint but clear. 'Fight on! Fight on!'

Seagrave followed the line of Wallace's desperate gaze and opened his eyes wide in astonishment. Standing not ten paces from him was the Scots rebel who had saved him from slaughter at Roslin. Their eyes locked for a

second and then his face was lost in the churning
crowd.

42

The men were wary of Sir John de Seagrave's temper and left him alone to seethe beside his campfire. He stared down at the small purse in his fist and relived the conversation with Langton.

'The King has asked me to give you this.' The Treasurer said as he proffered the purse.

'What is it?' Seagrave had responded as he attempted to read the Treasurer's grave expression.

'Twenty-five shillings in payment for you transporting the traitor Wallace's quarters north.'

Seagrave had bowed his head in disappointment. 'So, all my efforts have not regained me the King's favour?'

'No.' Langton had responded with genuine regret. 'He was not pleased to hear that Wallace had the opportunity to refute the charges set against him. He fears that just those few words will give heart to our enemies and make him a martyr to their cause.' He had hesitated for a second before continuing. 'I did tell you to brutalise him and leave him in no condition to offer you defiance.'

Seagrave had snarled back at Langton in fury. 'Who was it that went running to the King with their tales?'

The Treasurer shook his head. 'You should not trouble yourself with thoughts of vengeance. Near every man at the trial hurried to the King's side to inform him of what transpired. Go north and lose yourself for a while. This will all blow over soon enough and I will judge when the King's temper has cooled.'

Seagrave cursed at the memory and cursed Langton harder for winning him the commission of the traitor's trial. He now suspected that Langton had recommended him for the task to escape carrying the responsibility himself. He turned the purse over in his hand and tried to think of what he would do once the traitor's quarters had been delivered to Newcastle, Berwick, Stirling and Perth. He would not stay in Scotland, for the mere thought of the place served to bring his spirits low. His estates in the south were the most comfortable, though those in the north were the most in need of his attentions. He was ripped from his thoughts by a cry of alarm from one of his men. He leapt to his feet and ran towards the tents. An arrow flew past him close enough to make him drop to the ground in fright. A second later, the largest of his men fell to the ground with an arrow jutting from his bloody face. He screamed at his men to take shelter behind the trees.

'One archer!' His captain shouted from up ahead. 'I count another five men crouching in the trees.'

Seagrave strained his eyes in the fading light and made out several shadowy figures lurking in the gloom.

'Hell's teeth! Who would attack us here? It would be a foolish brigand who would dare to attack soldiers on the King's business.'

'We should rush them and flush them out!' His captain replied. 'I do not doubt that they will take to their heels and leave us to our supper in peace.'

'Let's cut them down. I find that I am in the mood for blood!' Seagrave then commanded his men to charge and rushed into the forest with his blade ready to strike at those who would assault them.

The brigands indeed took to their heels and retreated into the forest, but they stayed within their pursuers' sight and led them on further into the growing night. Seagrave thought that they had advanced nearly a mile, when their quarry melted away and sight and sound of them was lost. He then clapped his hand to his head in exasperation.

'The bastards have lured us away deliberately. As we stumble through the trees, their comrades will have fallen upon our camp and spirited away our horses and our possessions.'

Seagrave led his men back at the run and they burst out into the clearing with their swords held high. They found that the camp was just as they had left it. The fires were burned down to glowing ashes, but their horses were still tethered to the trees and their packs were yet safely stowed under canvas. Seagrave shook his head in relieved confusion and called for a flagon of wine to quench his thirst. He drank deeply, threw wood onto the fire and retook his seat. He glanced down between his feet and saw that something had been roughly scratched into the earth. The first part was unmistakable, a letter 'W', and beside it, a symbol in the shape of an eye. He puzzled over them for a second before a sickening realisation came over him. He rushed over to the pack horse and cursed when he saw that the oxhide containing the traitor's quarters was gone.

He stumbled about in panic until his captain grasped his shoulder.

'We are damned!' He cried in desperation. 'We shall be hanged for this incompetence!'

'We shall not.' His captain replied calmly, pointing in the direction of their fallen comrade. 'We must deliver quarters as the King has commanded and poor Thomas there has no more need of his limbs.'

Seagrave nodded and instantly recovered his nerves. 'Fetch the axe. I am certain that Thomas would not wish us to suffer when he can save us from our fate.'

John Edward stood at the Crag's edge and looked down across the plain to the winding Forth and Stirling Castle beyond it. The last time he had gazed out from this spot, an English army had been encamped on the other side of the river. Now the castle was garrisoned by Scots loyal to the English King. It seemed impossible that everything the patriots had so dearly won was now lost. He turned his head as Prior Abernethy approached him.

'Thank you for conducting the burial service, Prior. Sir William will have been glad that the words were spoken by a loyal patriot and not those turncoats who now stand around his grave in pretended grief.'

Abernethy glanced at the men who now conversed beside the fresh mound of earth. He knew that John did not refer to Strathbogie, Laird Robertson, Andrew Edward, Angus Edward, Al, Eck, Scott or Malcolm Simpson, but to the Bishops Lamberton and Wishart, Comyn's man Davidson and Edward de Bruce. The Prior opened his mouth to counsel John against judging them too harshly, but then closed it again as he realised that such words on his lips would be false.

'You did a brave thing, John. I know of no other man who would have ridden into our enemy's midst to attempt his rescue. I can still scarce believe that you attacked the escort and carried away his mortal remains. You could not have honoured him more.'

Tears sprang into John's eyes and he made no effort to wipe them away as they rolled down his cheeks. 'Even as his guts burned in the flames, he locked eyes with me and urged me to fight on. Even in his agony, I know that he saw me nod my agreement. But now that I am home, I cannot see how I can keep my vow. There are no English to fight against, only Scots who do the

Bastard King's bidding. I cannot fight my own countrymen.'

'He would not have wanted that.' Abernethy agreed. 'But I have seen enough of kings to know that things will not remain as they are now. My counsel would be to bide your time, lick your wounds and raise your family. This land has not seen the last of English soldiers and your sword will be needed when they return. Keep it hidden, but keep it sharp. The fight is not yet over.'

'Thank you, good Prior. Now we should be away before our presence here is noticed.' John wiped his eyes and turned to make the climb back down the Abbey Craig, only to find his way barred by Bishop Lamberton.

'John, I can see that the anger still burns in your eyes, but would urge you to not condemn us. We are patriots still and only do as we must in these dire circumstanccs.'

John nodded slowly. 'Tell me, Lord Bishop, did King Edward smile down upon you as you knelt at his feet? Did he reach down and pat your head as he would pat a faithful dog?'

Lamberton's cheeks burned red at John's words and he seemed to struggle to keep his annoyance in check. 'You may come to forgive me in time and I will pray for you until then. In the meantime, I offer you a token to show that I am not the cold-hearted turncoat you think me to be. My love for Wallace was no less than yours and I grieve for his loss as hard as you.'

John took the square of parchment without replying and called on his comrades to leave with him. Only once he was in his saddle at the foot of the Craig, did he unfold the parchment and read the location written there in the Bishop's own hand. It appeared that there was work to be done before his sword was to be hidden away.

Jack Short pulled on the reins and brought his horse to a halt on the summit of the hill. He breathed deeply of the northern English air and surveyed his domain, while the village elder gasped and puffed and stumbled as he tried to catch him up. The manor house Langton had gifted him stood atop the hill opposite and all the land between them was now Jack's, to do with as he wished.

The elder fought to control his wheezing and pointed down the slope. 'The old Master cultivated all this land here. He had us sow barley, wheat, rye, peas and oats. When the harvest was good, he earned enough silver to build his house in London.'

'Really?' Jack responded, his mind reeling at the thought. The manor was run-down and the fields overgrown after years of neglect. The old Master had fled and abandoned the place when the Scots came over the border and had later surrendered it to the Treasury in lieu of unpaid taxes. 'I will want to do the same and so generate an income beyond that paid by my tenants.'

The old man croaked with laughter and shook his head. 'That much land cannot be dug over by your tenants and their serfs. The old Master had

568

an iron plough made for him. It took four heavy horses to pull it, six if the earth was dry. It turned the earth over so that the seeds grew thick and strong. But after the thieving Scots, begging your pardon sir, took it away, most of the fields were left fallow. It would be impossible to turn so much earth by hand.'

'Then I shall have an iron plough made for me. I have more than enough gold to pay for it. Now tell me about the river. How much fish can I expect each year?'

Jack questioned the old man until the sun began to set. He did not think that the old bastard would last the winter and was keen to gain his knowledge before the frosts carried him off. He dismissed him and cantered down the hill. His spirits were high as he could picture a long, happy and prosperous life here. With a little work, he could build a fortune from these lands and he was keen to get started.

His mood soured as he neared the manor house and saw that no lights had been set and that no smoke rose from the chimney. He cursed Magge Hadley under his breath. She had been the old Master's housekeeper and he had inherited her along with the house. She was in her late thirties, fat, lazy and overly familiar. Jack cringed at the thought of the coy, coquettish glances she gave him and of how she would flutter her eyelashes flirtatiously and hint at her intentions by mentioning that his bed must be near as cold as hers. He shuddered at the thought of lying with her and being smothered by her huge, sagging bosoms. Irritated by the prospect of entering a cold, dark house, he decided that he would dismiss her from his service that very night. He already had designs on a young girl he had glimpsed in the village and, as he knew that her father was behind in his rents, he was certain that there was a bargain to be made. He smiled at the thought of having her lithe and supple body to warm him while he searched for a suitable wife.

After stabling his horse, he strode through his door and marched into the kitchen to chastise Magge for failing in her duties. With no fire in the grate and no candles lit, the room was as dark as pitch, but he could still make out her rotund figure laid back in her usual chair.

'I thought I told you to light a fire for my return.' He snapped angrily.

He froze in his tracks at the sound of a growling voice, deeper, rougher and less enticing than Magge's. 'You will have a fire, Jack. Don't you fret about that.'

Jack spun around on his heel and drew his sword from its scabbard. Even in the kitchen's gloomy interior, he could discern the grim expression on John Edward's face.

'You!' He spat. 'What business have you here?'

'We're here to give you what you deserve!' The words came from his left and he flicked his head around to see Eck Edward step towards him.

Another voice came from his rear and he turned towards it whilst keeping his sword pointed at John Edward. 'Did you think that we would not hunt you down, Jack?' Scott Edward snarled at him.

Jack took a step back towards the door. 'You dare not lay a hand upon me. I am under the Lord High Treasurer's protection. He will have your heads if you do me any harm.'

'He will have to catch us first.' Malcolm Simpson growled from his rear.

'I have gold!' Jack spluttered, his voice made high by fear. 'I will give it all to you.'

'Not one man here will touch your traitor's gold.' Strathbogie stated menacingly, as he stepped forward with his axe dangling from his hand.

'Please! There is enough to make you all rich. Take it and leave. I will tell no-one that you were here.'

'Where is your gold, Jack? Where have you hidden it?' John asked. 'I would see how much it took for you to betray a man worth a thousand of you.'

'I have hidden it under the floorboards in my chamber at the top of the stairs. Please take it.'

'Tom!' John commanded. 'Go and bring it here to me. Scott, spark life into these candles and light the fire. We must see as we do our work. Eck! Take the traitor's sword. He will not be needing it again.'

Eck flicked his blade and took Jack's right hand clean off at the wrist. The hand thudded to the floor and his sword clattered to the boards.

'Bind his stump!' John ordered. 'I will not have him cheat us by squirting his life's blood away.'

Strathbogie turned his axe over and scythed at Jack's legs with its flat side. His left leg splintered with a sickening crack and he fell hard and screamed his agony.

'Strip him and bind him!' John ordered.

Once his arms and legs were secured, Malcolm Simpson crouched down beside him and pierced his left eye with the point of his dagger. He said nothing but spat into the bloody mess and punched Jack's mouth viciously, breaking half of his teeth.

'Leave the other eye, Malcolm. I would have him see his fate, just as we suffered the sight of Wallace's torture.' John's face was impassive as he stared down at Jack's sobbing, bloody body.

Tom Figgins dragged two heavy sacks into the now bright kitchen and dropped them at John's feet. John hacked at the sacking and a river of shiny gold coins spilled out across the rough, wooden boards.

'Eat them!' John demanded. 'If you can swallow them all, I will kill you quickly.'

Jack shook his head as tears poured from his remaining eye. He sobbed some plea, but his swollen and broken mouth slurred it so much, it was impossible to tell which words he had intended. John nodded at his comrades and they seized poor Jack, forced him into a sitting position and began jamming the gold coins into his mouth. Despite Jack's retching, and with much encouragement in the form of kicks, punches and slaps, he must have swallowed near three pounds of gold before the drool from his mouth became thick with blood.

'Quick now!' John ordered tersely. 'We must do this while he is still conscious.'

Malcolm Simpson drew his dagger, reached down between Jack's legs and hacked his manhood and sack from his body. He then forced the bloody flesh into Jack's mouth and clamped his jaws shut around it. Jack bucked and kicked out, but there were hands enough to restrain him. John sliced deep into his belly and strained his arm so that the blade cut through flesh, muscle and gristle, until his puddings began to slither out into his lap.

Strathbogie stepped to the fire and drew a poker from the flames. The tip glowed red from the heat and it sizzled and sent a great cloud of steam into the air as it was thrust deep into Jack's guts. Eck marvelled that the man could take such agony and still be living and awake. He smiled down at Jack's eye and gave him a cheery wave.

Scott Edward kneeled at the traitor's head and worked away with his knife. 'Christ! Hold the bastard still. I can hardly see what I'm doing with all the blood. Give me his shirt to wipe it away!' Scott sat back on his heels and assessed the quality of the job. 'That's no' bad, eh John?'

John nodded his approval. The 'W' carved into Jack's forehead would send a clear message to his masters. 'Right! Quarter the fucker!'

Strathbogie raised his axe above his head and sent his comrades scurrying away from the traitor's side. Jack's arms and legs pushed weakly against the floor and his eye widened in panic as the blade fell and took his left arm off

573

at the shoulder. He arched his back and cried out in agony, but the flesh lodged between his jaws reduced his screams to a horrific, muffled gurgling. Strathbogie moved quickly so that Jack would live to see all of his limbs removed and his torso hacked in two, but it is doubtful that he even saw both his arms cut away, as his blood flowed from him like water.

John stood in the spreading pool of filth and gazed down at Jack's mutilation. 'We are done here!' He intoned flatly. 'Cut out his tongue and bring it with us. I have a use for it.'

Magge Hadley had struggled against her bonds for most of the night and was only able to free herself once the sun began to rise and the murderous Scots were long away. She sobbed and gazed down upon her master's broken body in its pool of congealing gore. She wept for Jack and from the fright caused by his grisly end, but most of all, she cried for herself and her uncertain future. Life would be hard for a spinster with no means to support herself. Her sobbing was halted abruptly when she caught sight of something amidst the guts and carnage. She stepped daintily through the blood and, leaning down, poked around with her finger. Though the cold and sticky guts disgusted her, she persevered and unearthed one gold coin after another. Even the shit from Jack's punctured bowel did not divert her from her task and a mere hour of fishing around was rewarded with sufficient gold to keep her comfortably for years to come. She cleaned her haul, packed up her few possession and set her feet upon the path to a new life free from want and surly masters in nearby Newcastle.

43

Sir John Menteith sat at his breakfast and
smacked his lips with satisfaction. The trout had
been cooked to perfection and, though he had
only recently risen from his bed, his belly was so
full he thought that he might doze awhile upon
his couch. Though he had not sought it, King
Edward's gold had been well spent and he took
pleasure from all that it had bought. The castle
was now fully staffed with servants, who ran
around to make sure that his every wish was
fulfilled. The gold had even brightened his
wife's sour face, as she took undue delight in
summoning tailors to make her new dresses.
There was even hope that his wealth would soon
increase, as he had heard whispers that the King
was of a mind to grant him lands on both sides
of the border.

The patronage and protection of Robert
Bruce made him feel secure within his walls and
his part in the betrayal of William Wallace had
faded from his memory and, from what he could
tell, from the memories of his countrymen. In
the days after he had handed the patriot leader
into John Seagrave's custody, he had huddled
behind his walls and found himself jumping at

shadows. He had seldom dared to venture out and when he did, he was ever vigilant and could not lower his guard until his gate was once again closed at his back.

Menteith yawned, waved the hovering servant in and sank his arse into the fine cushions on his couch. Without a word of thanks, he snatched the parcel from the servant's hands and waved him from his presence. A small shiver of anticipation ran up his spine as he unwrapped the cloth from the unexpected gift. The wooden box was finely carved and its weight told him that some delight was hidden beneath its lid. He pulled it open impatiently and his brow furrowed at the rough carving on the inside of the lid. 'A traitor's tongue?' He asked himself in puzzlement, as he pulled the cloth from the box. He dropped the box in fright as a chunk of rotting flesh fell into his lap. The delicious trout vomited out onto his fine, new couch, as he realised that a decaying human tongue had been sent to him. Even although his servants came running and whisked the obscenity immediately away, Sir John Menteith found it harder to banish it from his memory and suffered as its foul and threatening message kept him from his sleep and it seemed that no amount of gold could keep his fear at bay.

Walter Langton could not recall a more enjoyable meeting with Simonetti of the Riccardi Bank of Lucca. Though as cold, calculating and as greedy as it was possible for a man to be, the stylish, well-groomed and richly dressed Tuscan was unfailingly polite and was always pleasant company.

'I do hope that the dates are to your liking, Lord Bishop.' Simonetti intoned smoothly. 'I had heard that you have a taste for them and thought that I should have a box brought over for you.'

Langton chewed at his date and savoured its sweetness. 'Thank you for your kind thought. They are most delicious. However, I fear that you may want to rethink your gift. I have asked you here to inform you that we wish to increase our repayments.'

Simonetti smiled and flashed his straight, white teeth against his golden skin. 'There is no need, Lord Bishop. The Riccardi Bank is most happy with your current rate.'

Langton laughed with the pleasure of the game. 'You should be happy. The interest you charge will keep the kingdom indebted to you for a hundred years at least. We mean to reduce that term by a quarter, if not more.'

'Why fret about the duration of the loan? Half the kingdoms in Europe will be in our debt after both you and I have long since departed from this life. It is not worth the worry.'

'But I do worry, my dear Simonetti. The conquest of Scotland near bankrupted us. Now that the King busies himself with giving thanks to God at every shrine to every saint in England, I find that our expenditure is much reduced. I can think of no better way to employ the funds than freeing the kingdom from your exorbitant charges.'

'So, the Scots have been brought to heel? Tis a pity. The last ten years have been most lucrative for us. I feel as if I have spent half my life pouring gold into the treasury, just so King Edward could mount his many campaigns.'

Langton laughed at the Tuscan's good-natured teasing. 'I will not deny that it has taken much longer than any of us had feared. A lesser sovereign would have given up and admitted defeat long ago, but King Edward is made of sterner stuff. With their resistance broken beyond redemption, the Scots magnates now rule the realm in Edward's stead and their animosity towards each other guarantees that his authority will not be challenged.'

'So, the flames of rebellion have been extinguished?'

'The flames have been extinguished, the embers crushed beneath our heels and the ashes thrown into the wind. You will find no further profit in rebellious Scots.'

Simonetti smiled, but Langton did not miss the slyness in his eyes. 'And now King Edward is happy to devote himself to prayer?'

Langton paused before he answered, but could not grasp precisely what the Tuscan was hinting at. 'Now that his kingdom is complete and at peace, he naturally seeks to secure his rightful place in Heaven.'

'I think you underestimate your King's level of ambition, Lord Bishop. I am thinking that he will not be satisfied with a place in Heaven. It strikes me that he wishes to take his place at God's right hand.'

'I do not know what you mean.' Langton replied, his brow furrowed in consternation.

Simonetti leaned forward conspiratorially. 'I hear it whispered that King Edward engages in correspondence with the new Pope and tries to persuade him to support a Crusade to the Holy Land.'

Langton shook his head. 'The King is too old to return to the Holy Land.'

'Maybe so, Lord Bishop. But he would not be the first King to believe that a special place in Heaven would be the reward for falling in the service of the Lord. I am told that Pope Clement has already reached agreement with King Edward on what share of the expense will be borne by Rome and what will come from your own Treasury. Perhaps we should leave the repayments at their current level until you have spoken with the King. It would be unwise to renegotiate our agreement, if you are about to increase your debt.'

Langton tried to mask his shock at this unwelcome revelation and waved at the priest loitering by the door and bade him approach with the parchment in his hand. He paled visibly as he read of Jack Short's fate.

'Perhaps we should leave things as they are for now, Simonetti. It seems that the embers of rebellion in Scotland may not have been extinguished quite as thoroughly as we had thought.'

Made in the USA
Las Vegas, NV
04 October 2021

31704382R00340